Please return or renew this item
by the last date shown. You may
return items to any East Sussex
Library. You may renew books
by telephone or the internet.

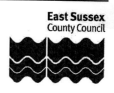

East Sussex
County Council

0345 60 80 195 for renewals
0345 60 80 196 for enquiries

Library and Information Services
eastsussex.gov.uk/libraries

THE KARMA FARMERS

THE KARMA FARMERS

PIERRE HOLLINS

This edition first published in 2017

Unbound

6th Floor Mutual House, 70 Conduit Street, London W1S 2GF

www.unbound.com

All rights reserved

© Pierre Hollins, 2017

ISBN (eBook): 978-1911586302
ISBN (Paperback): 978-1911586050

Design by Mecob

Cover image:
© Shutterstock.com

To my parents; and to my beautiful children.

Dear Reader,

The book you are holding came about in a rather different way to most others. It was funded directly by readers through a new website: Unbound.

Unbound is the creation of three writers. We started the company because we believed there had to be a better deal for both writers and readers. On the Unbound website, authors share the ideas for the books they want to write directly with readers. If enough of you support the book by pledging for it in advance, we produce a beautifully bound special subscribers' edition and distribute a regular edition and e-book wherever books are sold, in shops and online.

This new way of publishing is actually a very old idea (Samuel Johnson funded his dictionary this way). We're just using the internet to build each writer a network of patrons. Here, at the back of this book, you'll find the names of all the people who made it happen.

Publishing in this way means readers are no longer just passive consumers of the books they buy, and authors are free to write the books they really want. They get a much fairer return too – half the profits their books generate, rather than a tiny percentage of the cover price.

If you're not yet a subscriber, we hope that you'll want to join our publishing revolution and have your name listed in one of our books in the future. To get you started, here is a £5 discount on your first pledge. Just visit unbound.com, make your pledge and type BIGKARMA in the promo code box when you check out.

Thank you for your support,

Dan, Justin and John
Founders, Unbound

Super Patrons

James Bearcat
Mark Billingham
Marcus Brigstocke
Jen Brister
Jim Burton
Jarred Christmas
Sean Collins
Caroline Cooke
ian Coppinger
David Cox
Derek Cuff
Jane Douglas
Pip Evans
Dan Evans
David Fulton
Chris Gurney-Champion
Hattie H
Daniella Hadingham
Mike Haith
Neil Ham
Dom Holland
Phoebe Hollins
Rollo Hollins
Sue Hollins
Pam Hollins
Pierre Hollins
Tony Hollins
Megan House
Steve Jameson
Milton Jones
Nobby Kash
Dan Kieran
Richard Lett
Rudi Lickwood

Carey Marx
Neil Masters
Kevin McCarthy
Caimh McDonnell
Ray McGuire
Philip Middleton
Amanda Miles
John Mitchinson
Lucy Moffatt
John Moloney
Ali Moosavi
Pierre Novellie
Mark O'Neill
Janice Phayre
Justin Pollard
Rob Riley
Loz Sawbridge-Praties
Julie Shackson
Malcolm Sherman
Andy Smart
Will Smith
scott stanawich
Nadene Stapleton
Ian Stone
Paul Thorne
Paul Tonkinson
Henning Wehn
Chris Whippy
Sophie Whippy
Annie

With grateful thanks to Hattie H and Tony Hollins who helped make this book happen.

Deep down the consciousness of mankind is one. This is a virtual certainty because even in the vacuum matter is one; and if we don't see this, it's because we are blinding ourselves to it.

David Bohm

We have drunk the soma, and have become immortal;
We have gone to the light, and have found the gods.
What can the hatred and malice of a mortal do to us now,
Oh Immortal One?

Anon, Rig Veda, c.1200 BC

Contents

Several Weeks Ago...

She's dressed like an anarchist from the pages of *Vogue*. A tall fashionista ninja, slinking down Queens Road from the station towards the Brighton seafront. At a glance you might be persuaded she had nefarious intent, but up close you'll notice the black hoodie is a mohair number (by Alexander McQueen), the black rucksack is deerskin leather (from Mulholland); monkey boots and black skinny jeans (Prada).

She's dressed like a terrorist with ruination on her mind. Today's assignment: the liberation of the proletariat. But secretly, and almost beyond logical definition, her true mission is to destroy the walls surrounding some poor chump's heart, and lay waste the bastions of his commitment phobia.

The man is blithely unaware of these deeper intentions. He walks proudly by her side, sporting an original 1970s US Army jacket. He wears it with moody disregard, like a film buff attending a director's cut of *The Deer Hunter*. There's an anarchy logo in black felt tip on the sleeve, representing defiance and opposition to surrender. Yet in spite of this improvised revolutionary uniform, he's a mild white hipster dude, with demob quiff and a seafarer's beard. Over his shoulder he too carries a rucksack.

They stop by the clock tower, an island in this sea of human traffic, and silently contemplate their target. Looking serious. Exchanging glances. She adjusts her hair, tucking the stray coppery strands back under her beanie. He rolls a cigarette, more out of habit than need. Takes a couple of drags, throws it into the road. It's time to move. No hesitation. Get the job done. He nudges her with his elbow. She breathes out hard, psyching herself up, eyes wide open; he notices how they sparkle, made moist by the sharp air blowing in from the sea.

'Okay...?' he asks.

She nods, hopping from foot to foot, trying to shake the fear from her limbs. They walk over the road towards the Waterstones bookshop. He takes a determined lead while she follows close behind, tripping over her toes as she looks back across her shoulder.

Inside the shop they separate, according to plan. He heads into Fiction on the ground floor, while she races up the stairs towards Politics and Philosophy on the third.

In Fiction there's a corner out of sight from the cash desk. There are cameras of course, but the man pulled on a baseball cap as they entered the shop. His collar is turned up. He doesn't even acknowledge the camera angles in the high corners of the room. He's just another customer; a customer who is now taking out a small handful of books from his rucksack and forcing them into spaces on the Fiction shelves, more or less at random. Wherever there is a space, he attends to it. Altogether, he leaves about 30 copies in less than 20 seconds. He meanders back into the body of the shop, before drifting up towards True Crime on the first floor.

There are no obvious hiding places in the True Crime section. He's in full view of other customers and the enquiry desk. He stays calm, picks out another handful of books from his rucksack and holds them by his side. After a crafty glance around, he applies himself to the task; locates some space and arranges his copies among the other publications on the shelves.

He turns, looking around for Cult Fiction, because if his book was designed to be left anywhere... He scans the room and catches the eye of the fellow on the enquiry desk, holding his gaze before making a subliminal empty-hand gesture, then turns away to amble along the shelves. He doesn't look up again, acting natural, thinking of the great titles his book might be sitting with if he could locate Cult Fiction: André Gide's *The Immoralist*; Mailer's *Tough Guys Don't Dance*; anything by Bukowski...

The section he's looking for must be on another floor. He turns to the stairs, but before he moves forward she springs back into view, grinning with success. It's a sign to forget the Cult Fiction drop and head out. They fall into step down the double stairs, holding hands over the banister and hit the ground floor at a fair pace. Through the main doors, out into the street, chuckling, losing all sense of the discreet cool their mission started with.

Brad and Jane have spent most of the afternoon distributing seditious home-published literature in all the quality bookshops in the Brighton area. Their task is complete and the relief palpable. They run most of the way down North Street, lurch round the corner into Bond Street, and end up hovering outside the Costa Coffee shop, where she throws her bag onto an empty table to catch her breath. They're grinning at each other, still half expecting to get caught.

He says, 'Thanks, partner. That was really cool. *You* were cool.'

She looks surprised. 'Didn't I look scared?'

He doesn't want to disappoint her. He says, 'Babes, you looked fabulous.'

She laughs. It sounds like silver.

He takes a bottle of water from his rucksack and glugs at it. Wipes his mouth with the back of his hand. Passes the bottle to her. She takes a couple of sips. Then they're looking at each other again, wondering what happens next.

He says, 'Hey. What would you have said? If you were caught?'

'I don't think I ever imagined being caught.'

'Really? I was so prepared for being caught.'

'I mean, I thought we might be confronted by someone—'

'Yeah?'

'Like maybe another customer, wondering what we were doing?'

'Of course!'

'And my escape plan was to shimmy past them, throw a little side step, run to the stairs – maybe slide down the banisters – and straight out the door.'

'Leaving speechless confusion in your wake!'

'Ta-dah!'

Jane strikes a brief pose like Catwoman, or some such action hero of her imagination.

Everything she does wins Brad's admiration, over and over again. So he plays pretend-antagonistic.

'But really? That was your *plan*?'

'Why not? I didn't have to use it.'

Again, she floors him with perfect logic.

They sit for a while, enjoying the fresh air, letting their buzz settle. Relaxing into the anonymity of people-watching.

He says, 'You know… I almost wanted to get caught just to see what would happen.'

'Yeah…? But when you think about it, we weren't really doing anything wrong.'

'We were distributing revolutionary literature, to facilitate the downfall of The Capitalist State.'

She laughs. 'You make it sound so righteous!'

He says, 'I know! What's it feel like being married to a radical?' As the words leave his mouth, he acknowledges the confusion. Of course, he presumes *married* to mean *associated with* – as in, *What's it like being associated with such a radical boyfriend?*

But Jane entertains the blunder as a Freudian proposal of fidelity; and before Brad can backtrack and explain, she allows herself a glimpse into this possible future.

He apologises by blaming the English language, with its devilish double meanings, and half way through distancing himself from her, he says, 'Here's the thing though, and I'm sorry about this… I know it's unprofessional when we're planning a revolution and everything, but I've been wanting to say this for days. I think I might be in love with you.'

Jane half shrugs, half smiles, and says, 'Yeah? You're okay too.'

'You think? Okay then,' he says, thrown by the coolness of her response, and slightly embarrassed by his admission.

He walks to the kerb. She studies him as he stares into the middle distance. Then she joins him on the pavement, hooks her arm around his neck, pulls his head down to hers and they kiss, oblivious to the pedestrians, the traffic and the cold. And before letting him go she whispers, 'You know… I think I love you too.'

It's the first time they have admitted to the love thing. There's a slight awkwardness, so she leans back and gives him a playful punch on the bicep. He reacts with a slow-motion stagger backward, falling into the road, arms flailing. Then he's up on his toes, and bouncing right back to the clinch. They play-wrestle for a few seconds.

You know what it's like: that first admission of love, that nervous rush as intimacy becomes the sparkling focus of existence. And the whole world shakes its head at this shameless display of affection; not because it disapproves, but because the bond is so exclusive – it leaves room for nothing else.

'Wow, I feel like I'm drunk,' announces Brad finally. 'I need to calm down. Let's drink coffee. Macchiato?'

'Yes please, daddio.'

He turns to go inside, and once hidden from his sight she puts a hand over her mouth and breaks into a silent scream of delight. The entire day has been beyond logic and common sense; but this single moment is the reason the world continues to turn. It is the entire story.

They sip coffee, hunched over the little cardboard cups. Sitting with chairs very close, leaning in towards each other.

'Seriously, though,' he says. 'What would you have said if you were caught? If they caught you hiding copies of my book on their shelves, and they wanted to know what it was all about?'

'I would have said, I'm sorry I'm doing this, but my boyfriend couldn't find a publisher.'

She starts to laugh, and it makes him laugh too, but in reality he's a little hurt by the joke. This bandit distribution of over 300 copies was a coherent plan, not a default decision. In the book he contends that all events are linked by intention, therefore the book itself will gravitate towards the attention it needs, its very distribution being the validation of the content. So her comment makes him introspective and vulnerable. She puts an arm around his shoulder, rests her head next to his in apology.

If she's completely honest, Jane doesn't follow Brad's ideas to the letter. When listening to his theories, to their detail and the proof that he insists is real and cutting-edge, she lets them wash over her, because theoretical science so often sounds like personal opinion. There are enough mathematical theories to support any flavour of human optimism. But she loves his unlikely fascination with metaphysics, and his commitment to the cause. She plucks a random line from memory, and whispers, '*We are all one consciousness experiencing itself subjectively.*'

He looks up, genuinely impressed by her quotation; but it reminds him that his book now exists in the public arena, where he'll be judged; and he's embarrassed by the sweeping grandeur of the words.

'So what next?' she says. 'Now the book's out there, what do you expect to happen?'

She's trying to be pragmatic, wanting him to acknowledge the difficulties of making an impact in the publishing world. But also she's curious to know where he thinks this adventure might go, because as of today she's an accessory to the crime.

Brad shakes his head. He sighs.

Revolutionary action is always preceded by philosophical innovation, which in turn is inspired by scientific advancement. The human race has just lived through an entire century of radical science, and he's certain there exists a middle path between the secular and the sacred; a desire line between science and religion. But honestly, in the dull light of the everyday, will anyone actually care?

It's difficult to maintain revolutionary zeal at all times. Today's book-drop is simply an invitation to the debate; and yet it feels like he's nailed a proclamation to the church door, a rallying cry for reformation. He feels like a man in space, light-headed and miles from home. His subversive ideas finally inhabit the real world.

He says, 'Maybe I'm just trying to cure myself. This book – it's like an affliction. I want done with it. But then I think how important it is to me and I realise I'm looking for validation.'

As a mission statement, it sounds woefully thin. Jane remains positive, but she hopes today's exercise will lead Brad towards more traditional ambitions.

He looks worried now, shivering as the excitement wears off.

'… And thanks for helping me out today, Jane. Really – for taking a day off work and everything. Really cool of you.'

She gives him a friendly salute. 'My pleasure, Captain.'

'And what I said earlier, about the love thing? I mean it. It's not the endorphins talking, it's an objective truth.'

She pecks him on the cheek.

'I know. It is for me too. And as we're having a day of revelation and honesty...'

'Yes...?'

'Would you mind having a shave?'

Brad looks genuinely perplexed. 'Really? I didn't see that coming.'

She nods apologetically.

'You don't think I look like a salty seadog? All rugged and dreamy?'

'I think it's more Homeless than Hipster, if that's what you mean.'

'Well, if it's a deal-breaker, I'll shave right now.'

He stands up, as if to look for beard-cutting scissors and a mirror. In spite of his bravado, Jane can see he's struggling to process this request. He believes he stands at the vanguard of a revolution, and *all* revolutionaries have beards. He'd be happier sitting still and worrying, but instead he's attempting to be the man she wants him to be: proactive regarding matters of comportment.

She picks up their rucksacks, walks over to him and quite firmly rubs her hands over his beardy face.

'Come on, you. Let's get in the shower and shave this mess off.'

And so The Revolutionaries walk back to Brad's flat, arm in arm. The future is a white screen of unwritten possibility. They are as happy as a burst of oxytocin; their thoughts entangled like electric smoke in a spotless sky. The only rain cloud is of Jane's own making, as she worries about the potential hordes of crazies who will now come seeking him out because of the book-drop. It doesn't bear considering, and as they walk away, she holds him close to protect his beautiful brain from the dark vultures of her paranoia.

Thursday...

The Cadillac Coupe De Ville Hearse

All the best stories begin with a detective: it's a sentiment Walsh often returns to when drinking with colleagues after work. Some of them argue for a missing person or a dead body, but Walsh knows he will always find brutality lurking in the hearts of men. For him, the most illustrious stories start with the arrival of the detective, to confront this iniquity and return the status quo. It's an argument he usually wins… *because, gentlemen, we are the cavalry and the justice.*

The memory of work banter keeps him amused. It's been a long drive. He gives the hip flask a shake, and hearing the last splash of Hennessy, unscrews the cap and tilts the flask to his mouth. Drains it. His laugh is a mixture of resignation and relief, for the conceit that he lived his life by has become void. As of this week, Walsh is an ex-detective.

He is driving along an unremarkable stretch of motorway. It's almost dawn. The air is luminous, and the future curls away in a slow, winding, downhill drizzle. The car responds effortlessly; man and machine, bonding as one. He has often fantasised about this moment, during those dread-long years that led towards his retirement, and now it's here: he is finally living the dream.

The early-morning traffic is building, forcing him to slow down to just below a ton. He doesn't mind. Even at this reduced speed he still weaves past inferior drivers in their mundane cars, all of them travelling to work. He feels compassionate towards them; a deposed king among peasants. And into this reverie, in a blind spot of early-morning light, a monstrous black shape appears ahead of him, can-celling his line of vision: an impenetrable weight of black steel and burning oil.

It's a random event. There is no warning. No lightning flash, no dark-ening of the clouds or vapour trails. The truth is, it just appears, inches away on the road in front of him: an ungainly humpback whale of a vehicle, rear door the size of a morgue fridge, tall glowing brake lights embedded within pounds of chrome; fishtailing on the greasy tarmac ahead, its tyres spinning, fighting for traction. Then it roars away, leaving Walsh with images of black lace curtains and voodoo grave soil.

Walsh hears himself shout as he jumps on the brakes, pulling the wheel to avoid collision. He's still a stranger to the car's temperament and he oversteers, sliding across the outside lane into the central barrier. He ricochets back into the road, and wrestling for control, spins across the width of the motorway in a perfect one-eighty. He somehow avoids impact with a Transit van of builders, and a family of Sikhs in a yellow saloon before slamming into the massive wall rising up from the hard shoulder, coming to a scraping, juddering, nut-wrenching halt facing the oncoming flow of traffic.

Less than 12 hours ago, ex-Detective Inspector Graham Walsh spent a vast amount of his retirement pay on the most perfect man-made object his imagination and libido could afford, namely this midnight-blue, two-year-old Jaguar XK8. A 4.2-litre V8. Cream leather interior with obligatory walnut trim. It's not the supercharged XKR, but he's had the speed limiter disabled and on this maiden journey from Birmingham to Brighton managed to exceed the normal factory setting of 155mph.

Every time he pictures the car in his mind it feels like the underside of his balls are being scratched by Diana Ross's perfectly manicured fingernails. And right now, this mechanical wet dream has surrendered to a mountainous resolve of concrete and brick embankment. His lip is bleeding where he bit down in reflex action. He can taste the blood. He knows he's still alive, but this fact does nothing to console him. His heart bangs about, trying to force blood, oxygen, and cortisol through his scarred arteries. He struggles for breath. A ripping muscular pain begins in his chest, shooting across his neck and arms. He's covered with hundreds & thousands of broken-glass diamonds, twinkling in the motorway lights. A yellow talcum powder settles on everything as the expelled airbag deflates.

Nausea.

Everything seems quiet and slow, like shouting in a vacuum.

The hearse has long gone, and part of his mind races after it, searching for a reason. He knows he should follow procedure, because there's always procedure. He followed procedure for 40-odd years. He should be making notes while the vision is fresh in his mind, before the imagination constructs alternative versions. He must hold onto reality. But he does nothing.

Walsh knows the vehicle didn't descend from an empty sky. He assumes he fell asleep for the briefest moment, during which time the vehicle overtook him, creating the illusion of it falling; but he seems to remember how the rear lights trailed as the car dropped into the traffic ahead of him. He remembers the tyres burning on impact with the road. Surely someone else saw this? He desperately looks for clues, but the motorway, the traffic, the dawn, tell him nothing. His chest is throbbing to the rhythm of white noise. The scene replays itself in his mind, and he shrinks away from it, spasming with aftershock.

From perfect moment to hopeless travesty took less than seven seconds.

Pain and remorse attack from all directions. Gravity pulls at his internal organs and fluids. Invisible hands squeeze the life from his grasp. The last thing he remembers is how angry his wife was when he spent his entire retirement nest egg on a car. Now she'll never understand. Chasms of lost opportunity will remain between them forever. He wonders if this event has anything to do with her. He wonders if the hearse was a construct of his subconscious mind, warning him of life's natural conclusion.

There are so many things he planned to do during his retirement, but he can't remember any of them. There just remains a bitter, choking need to punish those responsible. He can't accept this was his fault. He needs someone to blame. He needs someone to punish. What kind of twisted story begins with the death of the *detective*? This can't be happening! He needs to act – but he does nothing. He barely has time to ride out the violent coronary that is now threatening to steal his last breath.

Frank and Norman

The hearse continues to massacre the speed limit on its journey east.

'See that?' Frank nods to the scene of carnage that has just played out in the rear-view mirror.

'Behind us! Dude collides with the barrier and spins off the road.'

Norman, riding shotgun, looks up from his notebook. Peers behind him to witness the aftermath.

'No. Missed it.'

'I overtake, he panics, hits the central barrier, and bounces back across all three lanes.'

'That'll be the conservation of momentum, the reason he kept moving after collision with the barrier.'

Frank raises his eyebrows.

'Say that again?'

'The conservation of momentum!'

'Yes...?'

'Which is mass multiplied by velocity... And velocity, which is distance multiplied by time. Mathematically speaking, momentum is a reluctance to change.'

'And that's how you react to human tragedy?'

Norman shrugs. 'Just saying...'

Frank is enjoying Norman's current fixation with science. That last phrase, for example: *momentum is a reluctance to change*. It sounds like poetry. It's a revelation to Frank that simple, cold-hearted physics can reveal so much about the human condition. They have been discussing such things all week.

Norman returns his attention to the notebook – a black A5 Moleskine, full of handwritten notes regarding Newtonian Mechanics, molecular structure, chemical bonding etc. And Frank tries to focus on the task of driving. He silently admits that being overtaken by a hearse could give any driver reason to lose concentration. But he doesn't cite himself as the cause for the accident. *Too much momentum*, he thinks to himself; the driver had *too much momentum* and *a reluctance to change*.

He continues at Daytona speed, gripping the wheel so hard his knuckles go white, and the faded blue tattoo ink shows a pattern of esoteric symbols on the back of his hands. Two miles later he takes the exit and heads south for Brighton. Norman looks up at the change of direction.

'What time is it, anyway?'

'Seven.'

'At night?'

Frank turns away from the road to look at Norman.

He says, 'In the morning! Seven in the morning!'

Norman peers through the windscreen. 'Well, it seems a little dark.'

'You're wearing dark glasses.'

Norman takes his sunglasses off and squints through the rain, pulling a disconsolate face.

'Still looks bleak. We're going to Brighton. I expected sunshine.'

Frank remains incredulous. 'You really didn't know if it was morning or night?'

'Don't make a thing of it. I've been preoccupied.'

Norman puts his shades back on – classic Ray-Ban Aviators, like a 1960s throwback.

Given the nature of their work, Frank and Norman look deep into the face of death, in a most literal sense, most days of the week. Business is good. People will keep dying.

Within the intimacy of their daily grind, they've developed a particular way of talking to each other, almost thinking their thoughts out aloud; acting like two halves of the same working objective. Like a binary hive mind. Sometimes it's difficult to tell which one of them is talking.

Frank says, 'Wait until the sun rises. It'll burn the cloud off.'

At the thought of the imminent sunrise he slows the beast down, sliding into the left-hand lane, rolling his head from side to side with an audible click of released tension, allowing the traffic to overtake.

'When the sun *rises*?' asks Norman.

Franks sighs; a reaction to pedantry.

'Sun rise, sun set… We know the sun is actually stationary.'

Norman looks up and studies the sky, then goes back to his book, flicking through the pages to find a diagram showing the relative orbits of the planets. Frank stretches back in the driving seat, enjoying the chaos of rainwater and the vehicles hurtling past; the fragility of these thin steel boxes with their soft warm cargo; all this life thriving among an outrageous potential for destruction.

Frank says, 'All this rain. Could make you believe the planet was predominantly water.'

'It is.'

'That's my point.'

Norman stares through the dawn's gloom looking for evidence of planetary movement. One half of the sky is lighter than the other, an insipid chicken soup slowly expanding as the darkness recedes. They drive on.

Frank says, 'What's his name again? The writer?'

Norman rummages about in his messenger bag, finds a slim volume, protected in a clear plastic Ziploc.

'Holmeson,' he says. 'Bradley Holmeson.'

Norman holds the book up for Frank to see. It's a self-published, serious-looking piece of agitprop, the cover printed in black and red, with the title *Death and Physics*.

Frank says, 'So, let's be clear… This Holmeson character won't be testing our knowledge of secondary-school science: that book is based on *theoretical* physics; he's into *concepts*. If we want to prepare for this meeting, we need to come up with abstract notions.'

'I'm just getting an overview of the basics. If you don't have that, how can you conceptualise?'

'Point taken.'

'Example: everything you see outside' – Norman gestures at the world racing past them – 'is normally described by its physical form, by what it looks like. But it might be more accurately described as a series of interconnecting forces, whose behaviour is governed by mathematics and geometrical diagrams.'

Frank laughs in agreement. 'That's it! That's conceptual. That's the shit we need to talk about.'

Norman shakes his head. The more he studies these basic rules of physics, the more unapproachable the subject becomes. And yet Frank is happy to treat it like a joke. Norman can't understand where the man gets his confidence.

They drive in silence as the three-lane motorway becomes a two-lane A-road, and Frank looks for somewhere to park up. His loose driving riles the other road users, but he doesn't care. One thing he knows about driving a hearse is that it protects him from any real confrontation. No one argues with the chauffeur of death, not even when he drives like a boy racer.

Ten minutes later, he bullies the giant car into a lay-by, leaving it at a weird angle, right up on the kerb and thrust into the foliage growing rampant beyond the tarmac, obstructing any further access to the layby.

'Get out the car, Norman.'

Norman obeys, clambering onto the verge, muddy and soft under his boots, aware he's stepping on a living thing. Not just this roadside vegetation, but the entire planet covered with vital organic matter; how it spreads away from his feet, and will keep going until it circumnavigates and comes back to find him.

He's learned a lot about science theory in the past few days, and gems of mind-blowing information keep returning to him. Like right now, standing on this rough carpet of grass at the side of the road: he remembers how everything, every living thing, this whole vast ecosystem of organic complexity, originated from a single common ancestor. His mind reels from the evolutionary timescale involved. He remembers it took more than twice as long for the early primates to evolve into modern man than it did for the Indian subcontinent to collide with Eurasia and form the Himalayas.

Frank swings around the tombstone bonnet of their car and joins him. It has almost stopped raining. They stand side by side, looking back at the road. Both men are in their late forties, but that's where the physical similarities end. Frank is the taller, with long, thin limbs and an angular face. Nose like a broken bird of prey. Deathly pale Nordic skin offset by black facial hair. Yet he displays a British belligerence, which is often playful in design but always construed as vexation. Norman is second-generation Black British, his Afro-Caribbean ethnicity tempered with Caucasian blood. He has a squat, muscular build, slightly losing itself to middle-aged puffiness. They both sport shaven heads; both dressed in black suits and white shirts, but you wouldn't rate them as regular undertakers, in spite of the obvious function of their vehicle.

Frank folds his arms against the bitter fresh chill of the morning. Watching his breath as he exhales. Shivering slightly. Norman rubs his head with fat, energetic fingers, encouraging his thoughts to speed up. They study the dark form of the South Downs, rising in the near distance. The dark-green richness of vegetation looks almost black in the early light. And over to the east the sky is warming up, as promised, showing tangerine and turquoise through the gloom.

Frank has left the engine turning over. It's an affectation he has, petrol being so expensive. He enjoys seeing random strangers try to calculate how many pounds-per-hour he's wasting by leaving the engine running when the car's stationary, when he's not even sitting behind the wheel. And it's a thirsty beast: a 5-litre V8 that idles with a throaty mechanical rumbling, beneath which you can hear the manifold sucking in air through the chromium grille.

'What's happening, Norman? Talk to me.'

'Nothing's happening,' he replies, digging his heels in.

Frank sighs. Lights a cigarette. Throws the pack to Norman. The situation has to be resolved, because Frank won't take silence as an answer. Norman just doesn't know where to begin.

Then he says, 'You know how I sometimes say, when you leave the engine turning over, that it sounds like the car's breathing?'

Frank nods. He's heard this before.

'And the car *could* be breathing, because it's drawing in oxygen for combustion, and it exhales carbon gasses?'

'We've been through this.'

'So you might say the car is *respiring* like a living thing, but it's actually an example of mechanical combustion.'

'What's your point?'

'My point is that life is full of ambiguities, but scientific truth is exact, and I find it consoling.'

'So... Where's the problem?'

Norman shakes his head and says, 'In spite of my enthusiasm and all the study I've put in, I don't think I can bluff my way with a real Theoretical Physicist.'

It is quite clear to Frank that the author of this seditious booklet, this Bradley Holmeson, isn't a real Theoretical Physicist. It is clear to Frank there are other issues here. He knows from their long association that whenever Norman is having problems he will seek solace in bookish facts and random information. He's been doing it for days now, under the guise of wising up for this meeting. But it isn't about the meeting...

Frank waits. Watching the cars race past. It's just after 7.00 in the morning. The rain has stopped but the traffic continues in a streaming torrent; the sound of tyres on the wet tarmac is faintly mesmeric.

Norman says, 'Are we on the right road?'

'You mean geographically, or as a statement of intent?'

Frank is trying to keep things buoyant, but Norman ignores his attempt at levity.

'We're book dealers.'

'Yes.'

'Rare book dealers.'

'Correct.'

'So why are we planning to arrive at Holmeson's house this early, like a dawn raid?'

'To catch him in?'

'Why didn't we just phone?'

'Because we're keen! We love his book! We want to help him take this project further.'

'But why don't we just phone?'

'Because we're in the area on other business, and we want to impress him with our sincerity, our enthusiasm – whatever. I don't know. We can wing it.'

Norman clearly isn't happy about winging it, leading him to the heart of his worry.

'I'm not even sure why we're involving him. We don't even know him. How do we know we can trust him?'

'We don't need to trust him. We're just involving him.'

'Meaning what? That we have a witness?'

'Not to the killing! He won't be a witness to the killing; just the consequences.'

'And you think that's wise? That means he can still connect us to—'

'To what? To the body? Have a look…'

Frank gestures to the hearse.

'What's anyone going to say? That two undertakers were seen with a dead man?'

The way Frank says this makes everything normal again. For the first time in several days, Norman's mood begins to lift.

'Sorry, Frank. I'm not usually this uptight. But I can't stop thinking how it's going to work out.'

'No one knows. That's the adventure.'

'I suppose…' says Norman, but he's not convinced.

'You know Jim White?' asks Frank.

'The music fella…'

'That's him. Had a conversation with him once about his song *Handcuffed to a Fence in Mississippi*. I love that song, and he explained to me why I loved it. He said it was due to the song's subtext of pessimistic optimism. Example: you wake in the morning and believe your life is fucked, but by the end of the day, if you don't have a hatchet protruding from your skull, well that's a victory, and you begin to feel pretty great about things.'

It's strange to realise that Frank is the more optimistic of the pair, being such a severe-looking dude.

Norman smiles. 'So if I'm not dead before night-time, things will look better?'

Frank shrugs. 'Things are always better than they seem, Norman. Always better than they seem.'

Some few minutes later, the hearse is again burning its way south. Frank fixes his thoughts on the road ahead, forming an idea of it in his imagination and steering according to the shape he sees. Norman is quietly reading passages from *Death and Physics*. His previous foreboding has abated somewhat, but he's aware that memorising phrases from Holmeson's book is a diversionary tactic.

As they approach the City by the Sea, momentum slows to an urban crawl. Frank winds his window down to be blasted by early-morning air as it rushes into the car, stirring up a whirlwind of excitement; the Mexican lace curtains in the rear windows flap like bats' wings.

'Feel that,' Frank shouts. 'Feel that air. Can you smell the ocean?'

Norman knows it's not an ocean but the English Channel, although it would be churlish to mention this.

Instead, he flips through the notebook and reads aloud: 'Seventy-eight percent nitrogen, twenty-one percent oxygen, with carbon dioxide less than one percent and traces of inert gasses, etc.'

Frank says, 'For me, the chemical composition of the air is not a need-to-know.'

'Just getting into character.'

'If you say so.'

Norman winds down the window on his side, letting the air blind him to the task ahead.

The Nepalese Temple Ball

It's 7.45 in the morning. Almost time for Brad to haul arse out of bed and get ready for work, but he doesn't move. He can't move. He's drained. Shattered. Trashed. He's been stuck in the purgatory of half-sleep for hours, and now waits for the new day to vanquish his mind-spiders and offer some clarity. But the clarity doesn't arrive; and the promise of rest & relief becomes another topic in the tape-loop of anxiety he's creating for himself.

Things happen for a reason: it's one of the things people say as consolation when horrible things happen. But if you know anything about science, then you'll know of course things happen for a reason, due to the cause-and-effect world of Newtonian Mechanics, which is purely mechanical and shouldn't suggest any moral judgement regarding the thing that happened.

People also say, *that was so random*, implying there was absolutely no reason for that thing to happen at all, as if the world fell in on some poor, innocent bystander completely accidentally and without warning. Although 'randomness' is often shorthand for *we don't have enough information to discover the actual cause of this event*. So when an innocent bystander *is* caught out by an apparently random event, they *are* often blamelessly complicit.

And then some people are accused of *being lucky* – as in the case of various famous sportsmen, to which the classic reply is, *Yes, I'm lucky, and the more I train the luckier I become*.

So: if things *are* causal, and good & bad luck is randomness which *can* be prepared for or protected against to some degree, then there *must* be an inherent pattern to our lives, which means *there will be signs*. And if we can read the signs then somehow the quality of our life will improve. And the more actively we look for these signs, the more they will manifest, leading to a greater knowledge of purpose.

Brad believes this.

And Jane, his girlfriend, also believes this, up to a point.

Where they differ is that Brad assumes the signs will become more obvious and potent if he continues his shaky habit of smoking hash. This is what their recent argument was about, causing him to say something ill-advised. Causing her to throw his stash out the window into the evening traffic. Causing him to shout. Causing her to storm out.

He hasn't seen her for three days. He has hardly slept for three days, and is currently lying in his lonely bed in a torment of idiot culpability, praying for resolution. Every time he replays their argument in his mind, it makes him short of breath. He thinks about people who die from sudden accidents and how lucky they are. They get it all over in an instant. No recriminations, just people crying at their funeral. The lucky, lucky bastards.

He has worked and reworked the incident over in his mind to try to make sense of it. He came home late, having randomly met a bloke recently returned from Nepal. In itself this was worthy of mention, but to discover he was carrying the sacred Temple Ball was surely a sign of crucial significance.

Nepalese Temple Ball is a very rare, almost mythical, brand of hashish. Brad remembers the first time he heard its name, when his friend Andy introduced it to him many years ago: 'This, Bradley, is what they call Temple Ball, because it is rolled into a ball and smoked in temples by Nepalese monks, and as such it remains the most sacred of all the sacred resins. That is why I will have to charge you double. But after you have smoked it you will not stress over the extortionate price, having reached a plateau of understanding where financial transactions are of secondary importance. Money will reveal itself as an artificial construct, and will cease to be a significant factor in your life. So before you light that joint, do remember you owe me 60 quid.'

Brad has never questioned the received legend that Nepalese monks smoke grade A hashish. He always accepted it as fact. And more than a decade later, the effect of this majestic Temple Ball must still be working for Brad has remained a man of modest financial ambition. Yet three nights ago he decided he could afford £120 for a quarter-ounce of this very same, insanely rare temple hashish; the very same nugget of hallucination that Jane hurled out the window.

She should have known!

And he should have stepped back from his emotional, kneejerk reaction and calmly explained. But how could he? Jane doesn't even smoke cigarettes. She has never taken acid, or mushrooms, or any chemical stimulant. She doesn't even like paracetamol. So banging on about the mystical-medicinal properties of this rare hashish would never persuade her to understand his enthusiasm. It would be like explaining the joys of a bespoke racing frame to a non-cyclist, or explaining Dee-lite's *Groove is in the Heart* to a man with two left feet.

Anyway, he wasn't in the mood for explaining. He was affronted that Jane didn't trust him. She seemed to be chastising him for his stoner habits, and Brad doesn't consider himself a typical stoner. For him, quality psychotropic drugs are an almost religious issue. Typical *non*-stoners will assume that hash and weed are all the same; that the purpose is to get wasted, reduce perceptions, and shield the user from daily realities. Maybe that's true. It's certainly true of the ubiquitous skunk that bulldozes its way into a dope-smoker's brain. But in any field of artistry there are certain achievements that redefine the genre and elevate the participant to a new level of appreciation. Nepalese Temple Ball is not about getting wasted. It is a doorway to divine inspiration; a portal, a key to Huxley's *Doors of Perception*, an invitation to Castaneda's shamanic visions, a direct line to the gods. Etc.

He didn't use this argument with Jane.

Instead he tried to be funny. He tried to be clever. He misread the mood and they argued. In reality the argument was about nothing, but neither of them could find an exit route.

And here's the difficulty with using semiotics as a life guide: Jane believes their argument points to Brad's drug problem; however, he thinks the signs point to a girlfriend problem.

Back in the present, Brad hears the doorbell. It wakes him up. Wakes him up to the misery of being alone. It's only been three days, but he so enjoyed her being here. Way more than he dared to admit. Everything about it was fun, sharing his life was fun, like a stay-at-home honeymoon.

He always thought of himself as a lone wolf, but having let his guard down to allow Jane in, having overcome his need for solitude, he can't live without her. It's tragic. He's been listening to Captain Beefheart's *Her Eyes are a Blue Million Miles* on repeat. He knows Jane's eyes are actually green, but that's not the point. It's the raw honesty of the voice that he finds so compelling; and the unrequited emotion in the lyrics has become an anthem to his melancholy.

A mantra of hopelessness.

Sung in desperation.

Because he misses her.

He also misses the hash she threw out the window; but he has sworn to the gods he'd give up drugs if she came back, or keep his usage more discreet.

The doorbell sounds again, and he pulls the duvet over his head. And now he hears knocking. The bell is accompanied by knocking on the door! It's a fucking liberty! Don't they understand he has no intention of answering? Who is it, anyway?

Then he realises it can only be one person at the door. No one else in the world would care to visit him this early. And for the first time in three days he exhales. The smile on his face is automatic and irrepressible. It's the beginning of a bright new day.

He gets up, wrapping the duvet round him, and pads over to the front door to let Jane into the flat. He doesn't rush. He's showing a cool self-restraint. He doesn't pause to consider why she isn't using her own key. He doesn't wonder why she hasn't phoned first. He assumes this is all part of her apology, her embarrassment and guilt following their argument.

He opens the door wide and sees two middle-aged men in black suits. Smiling at him. Smiling like they're sharing some brilliant secret. What the fuck are they smiling at, and where's Jane? What have they done with Jane?

Jane is less than a mile away, walking from her flat to the train station on her way to work. She passes The Brighton Book Cellar, the little independent bookshop where Brad works part-time. It gives her a pang of unsettled emotion; this is where they first met. She thought it was kismet, unpredictable fate, and it left her defenceless.

She's told the story umpteen times to her girlfriends: how she just popped into the shop on a whim, found a beautiful little book of Indian love poetry (purely by chance), which had absolutely no paper trail. A tiny volume, green hardback cover, pink pages, that somehow seemed to smell of incense. A singular book with no ISBN – that unique book code by which all volumes are identified and catalogued. So when she took it to the studious-looking hipster dude at the sales counter, they were forced to enter into a negotiation regarding the price.

There was something beguiling about him; the way he tried to persuade her to steal the book, tuck it into her pocket and walk out. Like it was a gift from the gods. That's how he described it. Of course, she couldn't just walk out with it, but at the same time they found it impossible to decide a fair price.

In reality, they didn't *want* to decide a fair price because that would put an end to this impromptu flirtation, so finally he takes a fiver from his wallet, puts it into a charity box on the sales desk, and says, 'Okay! That's done! Looks like you'll have to meet me after work for a drink as a return favour.'

Kismet!

Less than a month later, she's dressing like a terrorist and distributing his rebellious invective all over Brighton!

When they met up that same evening, he told her he'd written a book. That he'd been thinking about self-publication; and the incident with their sales negotiation had inspired him to distribute his book in the same fashion – he wanted other people to experience the same sales-desk encounter and thus regard his book as slightly magical.

And this is Jane's quandary: on balance she would prefer it if he wasn't quite so obsessed with this search for the Mystic Scientific Holy Grail, as outlined in his radical, drug-induced book; but without his passion for pondering the mysteries of existence, would she have fallen in love with him?

She can't quite believe their experimental let's-move-in-together phase ended so abruptly (and thank God she hadn't sub-let her own place in the meantime). She really thought he was The One. Fate had drawn them together. It was beyond logic. She was so certain.

She tries not to think about it; but every waking moment seems to suggest the flight to happiness might have taken off without her.

Back outside Brad's front door, on the fourth floor of Montpelier Mansions apartment block, stand Frank and Norman. The door is wide open, but it isn't the reception they expected. The man, Bradley Holmeson, is completely naked and swathed in a duvet. They judge him to be mid-thirties; three days of stubble, hair cut in that retro short-back-and-sides style; probably athletic when he was younger considering his height and build. It appears he was expecting a different visitor. No one acknowledges this awkwardness.

He stands there, holding the duvet tight to his chest. At least he retains the dignity of standing in a clean duvet cover. Like putting on a fresh shirt before you get run over. But this isn't his immediate problem. In the blind confusion of Brad swinging the door wide open, the two strange men have sauntered into his hallway. And having gained the advantage of easy entry, they watch impassively as Brad panics and spontaneously slams the door behind them. A pointless and involuntary gesture that now denies any of them an exit strategy.

Frank says, 'Sorry – were you expecting someone else?'

Brad doesn't respond, but the clues are obvious.

Frank continues, 'Maybe you thought it was your girlfriend?'

It's a technique known as cold reading. You pitch an opening gambit in response to initial signals, watch for a reaction and build a dialogue from the emerging story.

'Could be you had an argument with her, and you were hoping she was making an early-morning visit to put things right...?'

Brad knows about cold calling and assumes he can tell when he's being played, but he falls for Frank's line because it's true. He pulls a rueful face: the wayward boyfriend.

To capitalise on this small victory over Brad's suspicions, Norman takes the copy of Brad's book from his jacket pocket and holds it up in front of him.

He says, 'We've read your book. We love it. We were in the area. We hope you don't mind.'

All this information in such a short space of time is disarming. Brad staggers back a few steps and says, 'Yeah, that is my book, but...?'

'We love your book...'

'We wanted to meet the author.'

'Sorry if this is a bad time...'

It's rare that anyone describes Brad as 'the author', and it feels as though warm honey is being poured onto his ego. He begins to believe this meeting might be less sinister than it first appeared.

Norman launches into a description of how he came across Brad's book. It's an anecdote he can sell with good authority, because it happens to be true.

'I'm a dealer in rare books. We both are. Rare books and occult ephemera. We were down here in Brighton a few weeks ago and – I'll be honest with you, Bradley. Your approach to publishing and self-publicity...? Well, it made us sit up and take notice. Am I right, Frank?'

Frank nods his approval.

Brad mutters a gracious acknowledgement.

Norman continues, 'I mean, you left copies in several bookshops in the area, yes? I know this because I hunted down as many as I could find. Any numbered, limited edition is going to make good money on the market. But the genius of it...'

Norman makes a humble bow in Brad's direction.

'No ISBN number... Like modern-day *samizdat*. Am I right?'

Brad pretends to understand.

Norman says, '*Samizdat*. It's a Russian word, literally translates as *self-publishing house* – refers to the revolutionary literature produced by dissidents in the Soviet bloc. As Vladimir Bukovsky, the notorious activist, once explained...'

Norman clears his throat before paraphrasing the quote: '*We create it, publish it, distribute it, and get thrown in jail for it.*'

Norman laughs to himself, pleased with his impromptu explanation. But the mention of dissidents and prison startle the semi-naked Brad.

He says, 'Who did you say you were?'

Frank steps up to field this, seamlessly playing their good cop, good cop routine. 'I'm Frank. This is Norman. And like Norman was saying, among other things we deal in rare books and esoteric ephemera. And that moment of intrigue at the sales desk, forcing reader and bookseller into a dialogue about the value of the book...?'

Both Frank and Norman gesture their appreciation of Brad's bandit distribution policy.

Brad takes the copy of his book from Norman and turns to the inside cover. 'Did you read the dedication?'

They all lean in together and peruse the inside cover:

> *This book doesn't have an ISBN number. It won't appear on the bookshop's computer. If you want this book you will have to steal it, or argue with the bookseller over the price. I could have battled to have this work published under accepted conditions. Instead, I've taken this route as a random adventure. If you have any positive comments to make regarding the content of this material, please contact me by email. Don't find out where I live and visit me. Contact details printed inside.*

Brad reiterates the penultimate line out loud.

Frank shrugs (not apologetically, but to emphasise the moral intention of their actions).

'We are contrarians by nature, Bradley, as I'm sure you are too. And being completely candid, your address was easy to find. Electoral register. You're on the list.'

'Who did you say you were, again?' asks Brad.

'I'm Frank. He's Norman.'

Frank hands Brad a business card.

It reads, *Rare Books and Occult Ephemera,* followed by phone number and email address.

Brad looks back at them and suddenly flashes onto an image of Gilbert and George, the creepy gentlemen of Brit Art fame. He says, 'That's what you look like – like an occult Gilbert and George.'

They smile, nodding in agreement.

Frank says, 'That's a good call.'

Brad says, 'So what do you do, exactly?'

'We're like an occult Gilbert and George.'

Norman smiles. Frank smiles. In fact, they haven't stopped smiling, although now the introductions have been made, the situation doesn't seem quite as unnerving as before.

Brad decides he's on the threshold of a new discovery; something dark and intriguing. He's not sure if it's altogether innocent. They look decidedly cultish with their suits and Mormonic smiles, but as a writer and collector of bizarre stories, he'd be a coward to ignore this opportunity.

He says, 'This is highly irregular, but you're here. Give me a chance to find some clothes. Go to the kitchen and put the kettle on. And we'll talk, yeah? Give me a couple of minutes.'

And this is how easily Frank and Norman gain access to Bradley Holmeson's confidence, and attempt to involve him in Phase One of their ambitious, arcane experiment with death and necromancy.

Death and Physics

Never invite a vampire into your house. The thought flickers in Brad's mind as he walks into his kitchen. Frank and Norman are sitting at the table, completely at ease, but there's something otherworldly about them. Are they too relaxed? Concentrating too hard on appearing harmless? Because they look as disparate as hacksaw blades in a toy box.

Brad sees three fresh mugs of tea on the table. He didn't see the tea being made, and becomes irrationally paranoid about Rohypnol poisoning. He tries to disguise his foreboding by lighting a cigarette. He walks over to the window, opens it wide and smokes in the open air. It gives him an excuse to ignore his visitors while reconsidering his situation. But there's little he can do now. He invited them in. He no longer remembers why. So he concentrates on the cigarette, a brief delay before confronting this potentially awkward unknown.

His apartment block is 200 metres from the Brighton seafront, and from the window he has a view all the way down Montpelier Road to the promenade. And there, beyond the traffic and the turquoise Victorian railings, he can see the grey winter waves breaking on the pebble beach. If he concentrates, he can detect the faint smell of brine above the exhaust of humanity.

He turns to face his visitors, striking a pose with the half-smoked cigarette. He reminds himself that in spite of being outnumbered, this is *his* kitchen, and they're here to discuss *his* book. He tries to focus on the prospect of entertaining some new adventure, whatever strange flavour of activity the two men are peddling. 'So...' he says, looking again at their business card. '*Rare Books and Occult Ephemera...*?'

The men nod.

'Occult ephemera...? As in *the* occult?'

They nod again, not feeling the need to explain further.

Brad doesn't reckon much to occultism, associating it with council-estate witches and feckless Goths. He would normally dismiss the subject with prejudice; but confronted by these middle-aged men in suits he's forced to maintain an open mind. They exude the confidence of money and propriety; and there's a subtext of violence, which he finds oddly compelling.He says, 'I've never had much truck with the occult. Always thought of it as a fashion statement rather than a practice, you know?'

The two men say nothing.

Brad puts their card down on the table.

'Okay. That explains who you are. But it doesn't explain what you want.'

He takes a last couple of drags on the cigarette, throws it out the window into the busy street below. He's not quite relaxed enough to sit down, so he leans with his back on the kitchen counter, attempting to style it out.

Frank looks at Norman, and says, 'Bradley wants to know what we want.'

He's passing the buck, causing an unseen moment of humour to switch between them.

Norman turns to Brad and says, 'You could describe us as facilitators.'

'I'm not sure what that means.'

'We help people.'

'In what sense?'

'By putting them in touch with other interested parties.'

'You're still being vague.'

Norman is momentarily lost for words. Frank seems to be enjoying his discomfort but he's also aware this could undermine Brad's trust, so he picks up the baton.

'It's difficult *not* being vague, Bradley, because each situation we cultivate is different. We're benefactors. Sometimes we're paid handsomely for our services and this allows us to sponsor other projects.'

This answer is *still* incredibly vague, and Brad wonders if this meeting is a test of some sort, like making a pitch for artistic funding, because it's possible Frank and Norman *are* patrons of some description. They're certainly eccentric enough. He allows himself to be drawn in by the idea that they *are* benefactors seeking a new project. Which makes him wonder if the visit is entirely benevolent: if he accepts their help, would it leave him with an obligation?

Norman leans forward. 'What are you hoping to achieve with this book of yours?'

Brad wants to make the right answer. Assuming they *can* help in some way, what answer do they need for this to happen? He's not sure where to begin. The bandit distribution of his self-published book is just the tip of the iceberg – there's all manner of darkness and mystery lurking within the book's content. And the heart of the crisis is this: he can't imagine that one day his mind will cease to exist. It's a simple question: why would evolution take 4 billion years to create a sentience as brilliant and sophisticated as the individual human mind, and then snuff it out *for all eternity*?

He can't accept it, but neither can he accept the existence of God. The solution to this problem has to be resolved by science. So his chosen mission was to discover what thoughts and memories were actually made from, and would they survive physical death? Because that's the issue, right there…

Eighteen months of interminable reading, research and cross-reference; of mind-bending information and madness. All with the spectre of confirmation bias hovering at his side; the knowledge he might never find an objective truth, but only untruths that he wants to believe in.

Throughout his research, one name kept appearing: the late David Bohm. A Theoretical Physicist, colleague of Oppenheimer and Einstein, a Marxist in 1950s America; one of the most influential physicists of his generation, whose work was marginalised due to his political affiliations; a man who ended his days as a patient of Maudsley psychiatric hospital, south London.

David Bohm laid the foundation for a new theory of consciousness: a credible scientific paradigm that suggests consciousness will survive the death of the physical vehicle. Brad would love to prove this idea beyond doubt, but scientific method is beyond his remit; which leads to the real irony: he has rejected God due to a lack of scientific proof; and yet he has accepted an unproven scientific theory. Bohm's vision is based upon mathematics and conjecture, forcing Brad to employ a certain measure of faith to accept it. And his book, *Death and Physics,* boils down to one basic suggestion: that consciousness exists as a more fundamental force than the physical body.

Brad considers his book to be evolutionary science, but he's fully aware it sounds like mysticism, because it draws connections between the secular and the sacred, removes the fear of death, and has the power to transform the human condition. Which labels him a New Age flake, because he doesn't have the depth of knowledge to fully support his scientific ideas. Which is why it's difficult to pursue a traditional publishing route. Which is why he has two occultists sitting in his kitchen, waiting for an answer to their simple question.

'So what *are* you hoping to achieve with this book of yours, Bradley?'

Frank's voice brings Brad back into the room. He was lost in thought. And as he brings his attention back to the kitchen and the tepid mug of tea he's holding, he has the bizarre sensation that Frank and Norman have been listening to his internal monologue; as if he was thinking in their direction. He wants to mention this. They're now looking at him benignly and quietly, and he wants to ask if they can hear his mind turning over. But he doesn't ask. He's scared he already knows the answer.

They're looking at him from all angles at once. It's trippy. There's a word he hasn't heard in a long time, but he has a feeling of coming down from mushrooms: that otherness; when everything appears faintly luminous, creating a suspicion that the everyday world is a thin disguise covering a deeper level of reality.

In answer to their question he says, 'Maybe I'm looking for some kind of adventure.'

He means it.

Frank says, 'Then whatever happens next, you have to accept a level of responsibility.'

Brad laughs. 'Why would you say that? What do you think is going to happen?'

His question hangs in the air.

Frank turns to Norman and says (bantering, like they're part of a comedy double-act), 'How would this stand in a court of law?'

'In a court of law, it would be noted that Bradley invited us into his house, having initially attracted us here with his illegally distributed literature, then admitted he was looking for some sort of adventure. He would naturally be responsible for the fall-out.'

Brad appreciates their melodrama.

'Yeah, that's funny. You're winding me up. I get it. But I didn't invite you here. Remember? This meeting is completely random.'

'You don't believe in synchronicity?'

Brad makes a noise like a chess player who's been punched in the head. He tries to disguise this intellectual checkmate by clearing his throat. Who *are* these people? What do they *want*? He doesn't get their angle. What are they trying to prove? And how does it involve *him*?

His thoughts beat this circular path. He doesn't know how to respond. Of course he believes in synchronicity! Meaningful coincidence is something he guides his life by. He lives for it. It allows him to presume that things are moving in the right direction, as if he's glimpsed patterns of significance that connect our lives. Not that he'd admit to it in public; that would undermine his rationality. But even Carl Jung endorsed synchronicity as evidence of the collective unconscious. So Brad is always on the lookout for signs, for events that seem unconnected by any apparent cause yet reveal a governing dynamic. And now the subject has been raised, it validates the connection between himself and the occultists, making it impossible to deny them. They've played their trump card, but to what end? What do they want?

Brad sips his tea. He's forgotten the earlier worries of Rohypnol poisoning.

Frank says, 'How useful would it be if we could introduce you to someone who knew David Bohm? Someone who used to work with him?'

Brad chokes on his drink in disbelief; droplets of tea spray the table. He can't find the words to accommodate his astonishment. He waves his hands in apology at the messy reaction, wipes his mouth with his sleeve and fetches a tea towel to dry the table.

'Seriously? You know someone who used to work with Bohm? How?'

'One of our clients…'

'And he actually worked with David Bohm?'

'Yes…'

The possibilities are lighting new synaptic pathways in his brain. This could be the break he's looking for. This justifies everything.

'He's called Eugene Polonski. A Lithuanian American currently resident in England…'

'And you reckon he'd talk to me?'

'We'll suggest it to him…'

Frank looks at Norman as he says this.

Norman says, 'I don't suppose you'll be giving a book reading any time soon?'

Brad looks at him like, *How could you possibly know that?*

Norman laughs, apologetically, and explains. 'I noticed the flyers in the hallway as we came in. And it seems to me that a public reading of your work might be the perfect opportunity for our client to meet you.'

'Why are you doing this?'

'It's what we do. We make connections to everyone's mutual advantage.'

Brad holds his hands up in sustained surrender.

'I am in your debt. This is exactly what I was hoping for… Making connections, you know? This is ideal! Let me get those flyers. I've got the first one in a couple of days…'

Brad walks into the hallway, and they follow him. It seems their business is more or less concluded.

Brad gives Norman a handful of the flyers, pointing out the dates.

As far as Frank is concerned, everything is falling into place. He reaches into his jacket pocket and takes out another business card.

Brad says, 'It's okay. You've already given me a business card.'

Frank says, 'That was Norman's card. That was the number of his bookshop. This is our office number. If you need it.'

Brad says, 'Okay, sure… Thanks.'

He casually glances at the card, then looks again, reading it properly.

'*The Coupe de Ville Funeral Home*? You're… undertakers? I thought you were book dealers. You said you were book dealers!'

'That's mostly Norman's business, the bookshop. A little sideline. This is our nine-to-five, as it were.'

Brad is unable to process this information. It radically changes the atmosphere. It cuts into his elation. He has unbidden images of Frank and Norman in contact with dead people, and he doesn't like it. By three degrees of separation, that means dead people have been in contact with him. Not in a ouija board way, but in a real-life, dead-people-touching-things-in-his-kitchen way. He's sure there are certain standards of hygiene, but that's not the point. It's creepy. He wanted a *literary* adventure, and now he has undertakers in his flat. And all this before breakfast. This undermines *everything*, and he starts to hyperventilate.

Frank reads the signals, disengages, and walks down the hallway to the door. Norman pauses, looking for some means of diffusing the tension. And out of nowhere he says, 'Hey… What was the argument about? With your girlfriend.'

This is such a non sequitur it diverts Brad from further psychosis. It brings him back to his more pressing problem.

'The argument?'

'Yes. You had an argument with your girlfriend…?'

Brad shakes his head. He's forgotten the dead bodies paranoia; straight back to his girlfriend problems.

'I don't know what happened. Everything was perfect. I mean… we had no expectations when we first met, but it all fell into place. Like… like Tetris. Every new discovery about each other… We trusted each other, you know?'

'So what happened?'

'It was just the other night. Three nights ago, actually. I got tickets to a band, Chuck Prophet and the Mission Express, a very cool kind of guitar-driven Americana... I thought she'd love it; it was a surprise. But she works with bands all the time – she looks after the music talent for a radio station – and anyway she'd secretly planned a cosy night in for us both...'

Frank and Norman are giving his story their attention, and at this point they shrug, like *What can you do?* Brad acknowledges this and continues.

'So we both had our own plans, and being who we are, neither of us backed down. And I got home late sort of on purpose, but she was waiting up for me, which I didn't expect. She just wanted me to say something nice...'

'What did you say?'

Brad pauses, shaking his head. He can't believe this is the cause of his problems.

'I told her she looked like one of the inert gasses.'

Brad looks so forlorn when he says this that Frank bursts out laughing. It's rare for Frank to lose his composure – he's normally the granite face of solemnity – but this is causing an avalanche.

Norman, meanwhile, remains concerned and quietly pensive, before saying, 'I get it... the inert gasses! Like argon, radon, and... and neon! You were trying to say she looked like neon!'

Brad looks at Norman like he could hug him. Of course that's what he was trying to say! At last! Someone understands. Someone *genuinely* understands. Maybe things aren't completely lost.

She'd crashed out on the sofa, under that Peruvian blanket they'd bought together at Camden Market. He woke her up with his ineffective tiptoe entrance. He watched her rub her eyes and push the mess of ginger hair out of her face. She smiled with sleepy vulnerability, and all he wanted was to curl up next to her and hold her. He didn't want to talk. He knew not to trust his words. He was way beyond conversation, being high on the majestic Temple Ball; wildly overstimulated but fundamentally brimful with love.

He stood looking at her, and the distance between was them was pure electricity. Given time he could explain, because he understands the connectivity of all things: how there is no delineation between objects at an atomic level, and light is the transference of photons from object to the eye so, in that sense, part of everything we see becomes a small part of us.

His mood was way beyond the verbal, needing to feel her physical presence to calm him down because this hashish-brain has tipped him beyond the veil. He's seeing everything as atoms of energy bursting in and out of existence, and the shape they express is the two of them interconnected; nothing else exists but their togetherness. He sees her as a sparkling blue electric light...

But not everyone is conversant with the noble gasses and their complete complement of floating electrons that make them resistant to change; not everyone understands their inner strength. Not everyone can visualise the atomic structure of neon, how it can sparkle when turned on. That's what he meant. But as the words leave his mouth, he knows their meaning is lost.He tries to explain. 'I mean you sparkle when you're turned on.'

'I know about the periodic table, Brad. I know neon is an inert gas. I know you're trying to be clever, but for once... just say something simple and nice and normal.'

She didn't shout.

It was one of those things. She'd stayed in, hoping he might stay in too. He'd gone out, assuming she'd join him. Both of them obstinate as only childless adults can be; self-centred to a point of fanaticism.

He should have laughed, and hugged her and apologised. Instead he felt slighted, and started to roll a joint. He understands her aversion to narcotics, but he wanted to demonstrate how this was different. His previous high had been shot down, his illumination lost, and so he began a more unseemly riff about a highly unlikely method of marijuana harvesting – one in which naked women run through the flowering plants so that the pollen and resin sticks to their skin, which is then scraped off and gathered up, mixed with their perspiration. He assumes he's being somehow charming, and sometimes this brand of brash indelicacy can win the day; but Jane doesn't buy it. She knows he's trying to undermine her abstinence. So she snatches the precious lump of resin from his hands, walks calmly to the window and hurls it into the street below. Which was when he started shouting.

Norman is genuinely moved by Brad's plight. He slaps him on the shoulder like a kindly uncle. Frank is more philosophical. He says, 'This is your dark night of the soul, Bradley.'

He's serious.

Brad doesn't answer.

On balance it looks like Norman agrees.

Two against one.

Brad laughs in a resigned sort of fashion.

'Dark night of the soul, eh? Good phrasing. What's that from?'

Frank explains, 'It's the most brutal stage on the path to illumination.'

He's still being serious.

'Don't sweat it, Bradley. The adventure has started. You'll notice. You'll get moments of clarity, like divine inspiration, only to be punched back to earth. And it won't stop. You need some help? You call us.'

Frank turns away from the conversation and heads for the door. He knows Brad is hooked.

Norman takes a more conventional exit. He shakes Brad's hand, thanks him for the flyers, for the tea, and for his time.

And they're gone.

Brad can't explain what's happened. But he feels this might be what he signed up for. His ambition overrides any suspicion of being drawn into an occult experiment with strangers.

Coffee and Cigarettes

Frank and Norman descend the stairs of Brad's building to the ground floor, and step from the hallway into the direct glare of winter sun. Any perceived dourness of the English character is cast aside on mornings like this; less governed by a genetic code than by the vagaries of the weather, expectations normally battened down against pervading grey skies and impending doom. But, today, this morning brilliance carries a scent of optimism. Even here on Western Road, the central route through Brighton's main shopping area, where human activity is so relentlessly work-a-day, even here everyone seems invigorated by the promise of a new season, temporarily freed from their lurking existential dread.

Frank turns his collar up to shield himself from this blind contentment, and walks round the block to retrieve the parked hearse. He leaves Norman rooted to the spot; mesmerised by the smells of the sea, the screams of the seagulls, the warm breeze. It all reaches him. He senses everything is on the move, from the yellow-grey lichen clinging to the cracks of buildings, to the clouds in the sky, to the microbes under his fingernails. All of life is moving endlessly forward. And their current intrigue, in spite of its fiendish overtones, is just another footnote in the scheme of history.He joins Frank on the side street where they've parked, and finds him arguing with a traffic warden.

'You're actually writing a ticket? For a hearse?'

'You're lucky it's not been towed away.'

In the traffic warden's defence, the car has been parked ostentatiously on the pavement, barely allowing room for pedestrians to squeeze past.

Frank says, 'It is a shame people can't limit their demise to rural areas, where parking isn't a problem.'

'Say that again?'

'The fact of the matter, sir: we are currently working…'

'What do you mean, working?'

Norman joins in. 'Have a guess.'

The incident is gathering a small crowd. It's clear the traffic warden doesn't mind being judged harshly. It happens every day. But someone has started to film the incident on their phone, and he doesn't want his belligerence to go viral. He delays writing the ticket, gives Frank 20 minutes' grace and moves on, flinching from the sun and the glare of the crowd. Frank and Norman leave the scene, and head across the road towards the likelihood of coffee.

'Good work back there, Norman.'

'What's that?'

'With Bradley. Your mention of the inert gasses. Put the conversation back on a steady keel.'

Norman takes out his notebook, taps it on the side of his head: a reminder that his homework wasn't wasted.

Frank acknowledges the gesture and says, 'See his face when I let him know we were undertakers?'

They both remember Brad's reaction. It's one they're used to. Part fascination, part revulsion.

Norman says, 'Are we decided then?'

Frank stops walking.

'Shall I imply from your question that you're *not* decided?'

Norman says nothing. There are too many factors for him to consider. In answer to Frank's question, he remains silent. They continue walking to let their differences settle. On a side road off the main drag they find a small independent coffee shop with outdoor tables, half hidden behind a low perimeter wall. It's a tempting oasis of calm, inviting them to regroup and refuel. They wait outside. And in view of Norman's indecision, Frank answers for both of them. 'I think he's a good candidate. I think he's perfect for the job, and I think we're lucky to have found him.'

'You still believe we need a witness?'

'Yes. We need our actions to be judged. That's the whole point.'

They remain standing outside the café. There are a few customers seated in the open air, braving the morning's freshness, but none of them are close enough to overhear their conversation.

Frank continues. 'Do you want out? Forget the whole thing?'

'That's not what I'm saying.'

'All you have to do is say the word, and we're out.'

Frank announces this magnanimously, but he doesn't mean it. Things would become very difficult if Norman chose to bail. So he reiterates his position.

'We want our story to become legend, and for that to happen we need an observer. A witness.'

'But why involve outsiders?'

Frank turns to face his friend. 'We need others to talk about the Illumination of All Things Hidden; to translate the Light of Knowledge into everyday language that it might Dispel The Darkness and set the Golden Throne of Tetragrammaton ablaze with its power…'

As Frank begins this improvised call-to-arms, he grabs Norman by the lapels and starts shaking him, whispering intently into his ear.

'We need witnesses to write songs about us… As we descend from the hills in the name of Gog and Magog to lay waste the herd mentality. Our righteousness will burn like Himalayan snow, dazzling those who cast their dark shadows across the planet…'

Frank is well into it now, laughing as he intones his words through gritted teeth: 'From the bright hearts of those long dead, with bows of burning gold and arrows of desire, we are the Guardians and the Vanguard, and our ancestors will remind you once again that the whole wide world will be watching…'

Frank's spontaneous battle cry falters as he becomes aware of his own pomposity. He lets go of Norman's lapels, pats his jacket straight. It might look like Norman is being coerced, but he's in this of his own volition and nods in apology for his previous moment of doubt.

'Okay then…'

They slap each other on the shoulder. Frank lights a cigarette. They still haven't made a decision whether to have their coffee inside or out on the street.

Then Norman says, 'You know what bothers me though, in a general sort of way, is why we can't just talk to people *directly*? Why do we have to use all this subterfuge? Why don't they *trust* us?'

It's an old joke. It started years ago after a serious discussion about how to spread the news of their particular brand of occult practice: *Why don't we just tell people?* Norman had asked. *Because nobody wants to be told!* Frank replied.

It's true. No one wants to be told. No one wants to be preached at. Everyone wants to discover things in their own time and on their own terms. Discovery gives ownership to new ideas. It seems obvious in retrospect, but at the time Norman believed they could just start talking to random people and inspire them. So he occasionally drops back into this routine for Frank's amusement. It's like a party piece, and already Frank is anticipating some erratic entertainment at the expense of strangers. The road they're standing on is busy with pedestrian activity. Norman waves his arm in the direction of two young men walking towards them, skinny jeans and bedroom hair. He shouts to them, 'Hey! Hey, you! I want to talk to you. I want to talk to you about the esoteric mysteries…'

The two young men look at him, not sure if they heard right. But they maintain eye contact, because Frank and Norman are cutting a vision of sartorial pizazz. 'Hey,' continues Norman. 'I'm from the future, and—'

'Why don't you fuck off back there then?' one of them replies, without dropping a beat.

Franks roars at that; then chokes it dead. It's the third time he's laughed out loud today; he doesn't want it to become a habit.

Meanwhile, Norman salutes the young man's impeccable timing and watches as they stride away without a single thought for ancient wisdom.

He turns to Frank, and says, 'They didn't give me a chance to get started!'

He says this like he's surprised, but it's all part of the joke, his incredulity that no one will listen.

'They knew you weren't from the future.'

'I know. I thought it sounded like a good opening line.'

'It's a great opening line. I, for one, would enjoy meeting someone from the future. I'd have questions. Foremost would be *when do we get the jet packs and hover boards?* I know it's a question everyone asks, and there's clearly more practical information you might glean from such a person, like investment advice, where to live when global warming properly kicks in, is Keith Richards really still alive, and so on, but...'Frank stops talking, realising he's beginning to ramble. He shakes his head. It must be low blood sugar. It's ruining his cool. He throws his cigarette away and strides into the coffee shop to order breakfast.

Norman takes up residence at one of the outside tables. In spite of Frank's pep talk he still has trouble in mind. He pulls the notebook from his pocket and turns it over in his hands. He loves the information, the fact that such a small collection of mathematical rules can govern all the mechanical activity in the world. All the clamour and bustle, set out in a few pages of equations. The simplicity of it begins to calm him down.

He closes his eyes and tries to focus on the concept of mathematical precision. He wants to identify with that same clarity of thought. He wants to embody the geometric simplicity of it. In spite of the countless times he's used this technique, it still surprises him when it works. Not *because* it works, but because the form of the emergent vision can never be anticipated. And into his mind's eye comes a god-like figure, crouching naked in a golden circle, emerging through dark clouds. It shines in his mind, static and almost cartoon-like, with the figure holding a draftsman's compass, reaching down from the sky to measure the world below. Norman recognises the image as a painting by William Blake. (At some later date he'll research the provenance and learn that the design is called *The Ancient of Days*; that the celestial figure represents the forces that bind the universe together, and he will never cease to be amazed at just how accurate these mind games can be.)

The process is a standard invocation ritual but it's years since Norman defined it as such. He doesn't like to categorise his methodology, believing that the naming of names will distance an act from its intention. To him, this is a default procedure for finding direction: a question is offered and help is received. On this occasion the help is bidden in the cartoon form of a divine architect, and Norman begins to analyse his problems in the light of this consideration.

The problem is this: they have long known it's not possible to share voodoo theurgy with strangers. Not directly. Which is why they choose the more discreet activity of leaving clues, to beguile and entrap unwitting acolytes. It's arrogant and manipulative, but they believe it's for the common good: creating situations in which their arty brand of occultism might be allowed to move through the currency of other lives.Mostly, they just put like-minded people in contact with each other. Or they might set a power object in someone's path to steer them in a freakish new direction. Trying to arrange it without either party being wise to the play. Karmic Vigilantes, pushing a chosen few towards their potential by contriving treasure maps for needy imaginations...

This planned involvement with Bradley Holmeson the author shouldn't be a problem: they put him in contact with their client, Eugene Polonski, a former colleague of the scientist Bohm, and they trust the meeting will give Holmeson's ideas a new context. This is what they do. Is it manipulative? Of course! But Holmeson is looking for validation. If they handed him the answers on a golden platter, he wouldn't trust them. So instead, they invite him to walk upon gilded splinters. They make him work for his knowledge; concoct an adventure that will help to authenticate his new discoveries. They're doing him a favour. And if it turns sour, so be it. Holmeson has the grace of time on his side; he can bear the brunt of adverse fortune and chalk it up to youthful misadventure.

Norman takes the view of the mathematical overseer, and from this perspective the Earth is revealed as a swirling vision of black satanic torment and golden fire. This is the primary cauldron, the atomic conflict of energy in which all matter, and consequently all life, has been forged: through the binary interplay of positive and negative energy. Attraction and rejection, light and dark, love and fear; it all comes back to this.Finally, he understands the question he needs to ask: does the wilful inclusion of Bradley Holmeson into their necromantic plans contribute to the light or to the darkness?

When he opens his eyes, the day appears brighter. In the end, the decision has been simple. He feels morally certain. He waits for Frank to return with coffee; it's time for a livener.

Brad drinks a fresh cup of tea, sitting sideways on the windowsill overlooking the bustle of Western Road. He likes being up here; the impartial observer. Watching people from a distance, not to sit in judgement but removed from their anxieties...

There's a noise from the hallway and in walks Jane. The sparkle in her eyes and the warmth of her smile like nothing ever happened...

He looks up and says, *Hey, babe...*

His cool is measured.

She says *Hey, Moose.* And takes a gun from her purse and shoots the love-drunk fool dead. Poor Moose.

It's the final scene from *Farewell, My Lovely,* the version with Robert Mitchum as Marlowe. What Brad remembers most is that line, when Moose is finally reunited with his Velma, the double-crossing dame who ripped his heart out and kicked it into next week...

Hey, babe...

He sighs, and stares back out the window. He plans to be that cool when he sees her again.

He wants to talk to her about his bizarre morning. How the undertakers creeped him out. But he'd rationalise: people die and other people bury them. He has to be okay with that.

They didn't look like ordinary undertakers, though. The tall one had an ancient face somehow, like a Norse berserker; he had a sinewy intensity. And the short chubby dude was clearly no stranger to DMT and chicken blood. They said they were occultists, but what does that even mean...?

In Brad's imaginary world, Jane has already apologised for throwing his drugs out of the window. In primitive societies, rejection of the sacrament is considered a form of insanity. They laugh about how the Western world is upside down, and how in love they are...

Brad now has bird feathers in his hair and red ochre on his skin; he travels through a psychotropic portal towards the otherness and brings back messages for the tribe. And when he returns, Jane is waiting for him in a grass skirt and a coconut-shell bikini top...

He looks down at his hands. When he was a little kid, he had the reputation for being a dismantler. Electric plugs, torches, watches, radios, fountain pens – he used to take them apart, like a compulsion, to discover their inner workings. *What a destructive little boy*, they said, but he was breaking things open to reveal their secrets. It would seem that little has changed; he's still looking for secrets. Only these days he's dismantling conceptual science under the influence of narcotics; and now with the potential guidance of occult mentors. This has to be progress of some description.

He ambles into the kitchen. The kettle's boiling and he's been bleaching the undertakers' mugs in the sink. He rinses them several times and they still smell of bleach. Thank God. He's now washing all the surfaces with hot bleach-y water from the sink. He wants the kitchen box fresh, cleansed of third-hand-contact with the dead.

'The thing is, at some point as a *society*, we made the collective decision to legally deny the altered state of mind, or to satirise it as naïve; and yet it is our evolutionary connection to…'

He gestures at the world in general, but keeps talking to an empty room.

'It's not a hallucination, it's the very same universe seen through a different lens. Don't you get it? The brain is a lens that focuses information. If you change the lens with natural psychotropic substances, it merely focuses the brain onto a different channel, a different aspect… *So why did you throw my stash out the window, Jane?*'

He didn't realise he was still this upset. But he knows it's all connected. It's a modern malaise: without a higher vision, he believes the human condition is *bereft of meaning, bland, unbearable, cold, overly rational, diminutive and just fucking boring, don't you see…?*

He fully understands the irony of talking to a non-existent girlfriend about the reality of drug-induced visions. If she were really here, he wouldn't be so cranky about it. She'd calm him down. He wouldn't be banging on about materialism being the *end of days*; he wouldn't insist our salvation lies in chemical gnosis…

In fact, he's not sure what he'd say to her, but he'd definitely cite the occultists as authentication. They understood him. There must be an entire community out there who seek something beyond the ordinary. It makes him even more determined to become their spokesman.

Frank returns with coffee: black Americanos in takeaway cups.

'I ordered toasted sandwiches. They're on their way.'

'Okay...'

Norman takes one of Brad's flyers from his pocket and spreads it flat on the table:

The Scribbler Festival of New Writing presents:

An afternoon of readings from self-published authors.

DEATH AND PHYSICS with BRADLEY HOLMESON

An experiment in science and philosophy!

For the post-hip and currently disenchanted.

Essential information for modern living.

The New Paradigm will defend your creative lifestyle

and fill your future with optimism.

So there!

So be there!

Yeah?

Frank points to the information at the foot of the flyer. There are five different dates and venues for this upcoming mini-tour of libraries and literary groups.

'You noticed the date of his first reading, right? It's this Saturday. That gives us today and tomorrow to get organised. I want this, Norman. And I want Bradley to be our witness. Obviously not to the killing itself, we've discussed that... But he'll be a witness to its consequences. He's an author! And he's hungry for it! He'll make observations and record the fallout. Let's be honest, Norman, this is fucking perfect.'

It's rare that Frank swears. When he does, it heightens his authority.

'Okay,' says Norman. 'We involve the author. Agreed. I'm fully on board.'

They shake hands.

'And we hope it works out.'

'Of course! Nothing is assured.'

All we can rely on with any certainty is uncertainty.

The starkness of this epigram contains both the excitement and the fear of living. All things will pass. Everything will move on. Norman thinks he should write the maxim into his notebook.

The Chinese patriarchs dealt with the problem of uncertainty by doing nothing about it. They called it *wu wei*: the concept of effortless living. We assume Yin and Yang to be antagonistic, but opposites are complementary, each containing the seed of the other. Every empire contains the seeds of downfall. Every winter contains the seeds of spring. And the practise of non-action is to concentrate on the flow of energy that exists *between* the changes. Tread that sweet spot and you'll have nothing to lose; and with nothing to lose, how can we fail?

The Earth continues to orbit the sun. The day grows longer, and the traffic warden has started to walk back to the illegally parked hearse. Frank stands to leave and the scraping of his metal chair on the pavement wakes Norman from his reverie. They beat the parking ticket rap by a few minutes. They climb into the car. Sunlight floods through the black lace curtains. Shades on. Ignition. Frank adjusts the level of the sound system. The V8 lump breathes heavily as a warning to pedestrians, and they're swimming through traffic on a fading sea breeze, driving home.

Mr and Mrs Osman

For Frank, the drive home always feels like travelling back in time. Motorways become A-roads, dual carriageways give way to B-roads; then they're meandering past tall hedgerows, underneath the spreading branches of trees that make tunnels of barely remembered country lanes. To finally arrive at a one-road village in South Lincolnshire called Fenderby.

Norman lives above his bookshop on this one main street. Sandwiched between an off-licence and a deli-tearoom. His building is a timber-frame red-brick two-up, two-down. Redolent of history and shenanigans, having been at one time a ship's chandler, an alehouse; and, according to local legend, a knocking shop. His book trade is high-end, so any visit is strictly by appointment. It leaves him free to use the shop floor as a study and living room. The window display retains the illusion of this being a regular bookshop; constantly updated with leather-bound first editions and hardback children's adventure stories. At a glance, *Norman's Bookshop* is a positively charming addition to the village panorama; but few of the residents could guess that it's a smokescreen for the more profitable exchange of occult ephemera and rare narcotic potions.

The hearse has achieved an iconic status in the village, which is a testament to the off-grid sensibilities of the locals. It now sits purring by the roadside as Norman jumps out. A few familiar faces walk past, nodding in recognition. He waves farewell to Frank and heads inside the bookshop. If their arcane ambitions stand any chance of success, he needs this time to prepare. The hearse continues through the village and out onto a small gravel track that leads to the end of this inhabited stretch of land, to the deconsecrated church: the last bastion of safety before the fenland gives way to the unforgiving expanse of the North Sea.

The church is hewn from squat, hefty grey stone, as if sinking into a lake of graveyard meadow grass. Leaning crosses, broken gravestones and sad-faced angels hide among the anarchy of nettles, brambles and buddleia, the whole vista framed by poplar, sycamore, oak and cedar. The setting sun burns the clouds powder pink and bonfire orange, and almost reveals the curvature of the earth as it descends from sight.

Beyond the church, which glows faintly in the yellow-mauve dusk, Frank's view covers acres of rich, ploughed soil, interrupted only by the dykes that drain the fields. Their banks are high, some populated by broadleaf trees, some left to turf; most of them crossed by wood and brick bridges, the oldest dating back to the 1600s when the original marshland was reclaimed. It's a still and almost soundless evening, belying the fens' history of flood and desolation. This land has long been witness to darkness and cold, watery death. No surprise it holds a tradition of superstition and witchcraft, as protection was sought from the water that heedlessly pulls all of life into its embrace. Fenderby isn't on the route to anywhere else; no one drives through to arrive here by accident. This is the end of the line, a chosen destination. And this is where Frank and May Osman have chosen to make their home.

She hears the hearse arrive, and emerges from the church's interior. Waits on the porch, dressed in a long black dress and black cardigan. Stands there, watching. He pulls the hearse in close to the church wall. Steps into the settling dust, and crunches his way across the gravel path.

'Hey, Frank. Good day?'

'Long day, that's for sure. Pleased to be home…'

He walks up, holds her in his arms, and pulls her close. It makes her smile, which softens her features. Not that she has a hard face, but with a shaven head and heavy black eyeliner, her inner warmth often remains hidden from public perception.

Frank bends down to kiss her head, smiling as the bristles tickle his lips.

'I love you, May Osman,' he murmurs.

'I know…'

She squeezes him tight, and leads him indoors.

Their living quarters are built into the south aisle; a set of rooms away from the business side of the building, away from the mortuary slabs and chemicals. They walk into the kitchen, and Frank sits down at the table.

58

'Can you reach me a cold one from the fridge, May? Please?'

'Yes, Master,' she says, half curtseying, half meaning it. She slides a bottle from the fridge across the table. He catches it. Looks at her.

'This one of those self-opening beers I've been hearing about?'

She laughs and throws him an opener. He pops the beer, washes the suds down his throat. Wipes his mouth with the back of his hand.

'Thirsty! How was your day? How's business?'

May shrugs.

He says, 'What's been happening?'

'Same. Nothing new.'

'Okay...?'

'We've got a couple of people on hold. Mr Barnes: he won't be long.'

'Remind me...'

'From Louth. He wants the whole ceremony outside. Prayers and songs. I'm going to try to organise a few singers for him. I was thinking of that ceilidh band from Skeg. He even wants an outdoor pyre if we can swing it.'

'Have to check the Health and Safety on that.'

'But if the wind's in the right direction... Who's to know? The east garden's completely secluded.'

Frank isn't sure about flouting the council guidelines on outdoor cremations. May moves on to other business.

'And I saw Sal Butcher, from the village. You remember...?'

'How's she?'

'She wanted to substitute her morphine for acid.'

Franks sits up and takes more notice.

'She read somewhere that LSD would help more than the morphine, because her problem isn't just the physical pain; it's the fact that she can't disconnect emotionally from the illness.'

'You're talking about the cancer woman? Youngish.'

'Right... She's been doing her own research about treatments. She needed some means of connecting with how she felt before the illness, with the person she used to be.'

'So you bought her some acid?'

'Yes, I did!'

'Where from?'

'Welshy, of course.'

'Of course!'

'And when I explained what it was for, he actually dropped it off. So I've spent most of the day watching a dying woman converse with the living memory of her younger self.'

'Sounds emotional. How did that work out?'

'She forgave herself for becoming ill. She was holding onto a lot of blame. So there were lots of tears, lots of talking, but it was way more mellow than it actually sounds...'

'Good girl.'

'She used to call her cancer *the beast*, like it was an animal living inside her. You know? Like she'd say, *The beast is strong today*... Things like that. It was pretty gruesome. Horrible. But now she feels connected to the person she was before the beast arrived. Anyway... She's on our list. She doesn't have long. Wants a simple cremation when the time comes: *nothing sectarian*, her words, *but nothing too tree-huggy*, also her words. I'll miss her.' They're both quiet for a while.

Frank stands up and pokes around in the pantry. May follows him.

'You hungry, Frank? I might do some pasta.'

'Pasta would be good. We got any spinach?'

'Well, let's have a look...'

'Because I could make that great pesto...'

'I love that spinach pesto...'

'Right. What do we need...?'

'Ground almonds, garlic...'

'Yes, we've got that...'

'Well, okey dokey, chef...'

Frank collects the ingredients into a neat pile. May finds a pan for the pasta, and one for the sauce. She clatters them onto the stove, fills the kettle, begins rinsing the spinach as Frank slices onion and garlic, throws them into the heating oil. And he looks up during this sudden commotion of activity and declares, 'Man, we are *owning* this recipe, May Osman!' They carry on, talking about nothing; talking between each other's sentences. Finding excuses to rub shoulders, and to bump into each other in the spacious kitchen. Flirting while the meal is cooked, served and eaten. Passing the time. Avoiding the topic that won't disappear. And a couple of hours later, May gets round to it.

'And how are things in your world, Frank? How did today go? Are you decided?'

'We're going ahead.'

'Okay.'

'Yep.'

'You have dates in mind? You know Polonski is being moved tomorrow, moved into new premises…?'

'Then I think it has to be tomorrow.'

May nods.

Frank reiterates. 'I think it has to be tomorrow. Been discussing it on the way back…'

'Okay… I don't want to play the worried wife, Frank, but…'

'You couldn't if you tried.'

'You know what I mean.'

'What's up?'

'I'm not doubting your abilities…'

'Here it comes…'

'Just your motives.'

Franks stiffens in his chair. 'My motives come from the right place…'

'Because I do know what this is about.'

It sounds like an accusation. Frank doesn't like it. He looks right at her, demanding the worst. May laughs at this sudden conflict.

She says, 'Don't get upset when I say this, Frank, don't get mad – but it's kind of a mid-life crisis thing, isn't it?'

'You think I'm planning to kill someone on a middle-aged whim?'

May stares him down. He shakes his head.

'I'm not looking forward to being fifty. It's foolish, I know. But half a century is a marker. You think it's funny, don't you? You think you'll never get there because you're still – what – thirty-nine? May, that's nothing! You probably still feel invincible! I'm coming up to fifty! I need to try something new, for myself. I can't be doing pagan burials forever, and have people talk about me: *Hey, what did Frank Osman do all his life? Frank Osman the great occultist? Oh, he just buried people!*'

May is about to jump in and defend the progressive aspects of their work, but Frank avoids the argument by agreeing with her.

'It's a good living, May. I know that. And I'm thankful, and proud of what we achieve. That's a given. But... You know what I heard on the radio the other day? In a discussion about mental health? You know the main cause of depression?'

'Is it men?'

'Ha ha! Very good! You got me! No. It's unfulfilled ambition.'

May puts her hands up in complete agreement.

'You have to do your own thing, Frank. And I'm the first person to insist you do. I'm just checking you're okay.'

'Thanks, baby.'

'Because I care.'

Frank doesn't want to talk details, but he tries to put May's worries to rest.

'We can't plan for every possibility, but our involvement is very low-risk. Me and Norman: tight ship, low risk...'

'And what about this man Finnigan?'

'What can I tell you? He's a complete unknown.'

'But dangerous, don't you think?'

'Given he's a hit man, that would be his advantage.'

'And you're almost fifty!'

'Yes, heard that before somewhere...'

Several weeks ago, Frank and May accepted an obligation to have Eugene Polonski killed. A difficult decision, but they had little choice. Frank managed to source Finnigan for the job; but this doesn't imply he condones the profession of murder. It means he's using this opportunity to make his own play; to serve Finnigan his karmic deserts. It's a dark art, but Frank is assured he has the edge.'Also, I'm not going in alone. Norman is the perfect wingman. He's my back up.'

'Eyes wide open, Frank. Don't become victim to hubris.'

Frank enjoys her use of language.

'There is something of the Greek tragedy about it. Maybe always is when you're planning a devious murder. But we're just the mechanicals. Nothing to prove, nothing to lose.'

May knows Frank has everything to prove and everything to lose. But she changes the subject.

'Hey, the Polonski money came through. Showed up in the business account today.'

Frank looks to the heavens like it's an omen.

'It's *all of his savings*, Frank! Spent on a funeral.'

'But what a funeral it's going to be…'

May quietly contemplates the twisted morality of banking Polonski's money while preparing to have him killed. How easily these circumstances could be misunderstood. She can't consider it anymore. Too many chances for ruin. She needs distraction.

'Hey, Frank. What do you say we roll these old bones of yours?'

She slides her hand into the waistband of his suit trousers, and pulls him close.

'What is this? Age Concern?'

Frank is still smarting from her mid-life-crisis dig earlier.

'It's just you, Frank. Always has been. Always will be.'

Eugene 'Gene' Polonski is taking his evening constitutional, which comprises a slow walk around the ground floor of the country manor house where he lives. He shuffles from room to room, checking the locks on the windows, making sure the outer doors are secure. Through the lounge, the library and the various reception rooms. He walks up and down the hallways, across the tiled floors, carpets and parquet, listening for the changes in his footsteps. Listening for the echoes bouncing back. Listening for anything extraneous and ominous.

He finds himself in the conservatory, peering through the windows into the darkness beyond the security floodlights, out beyond the manicured lawns and geometric flowerbeds, imagining the dreadful unknown. For years this was his least favourite view, the dense treeline harbouring any amount of villainous activity. But tonight he feels less trepidation than normal, knowing that plans have been made.

Eugene Polonski looks every inch the retired university professor, in tweed trousers, baggy cardigan, collar and tie, his grey hair wild as his thoughts. And he's carrying a notebook, as always, that he gesticulates with while mulling over some singular topic. Occasionally he'll stop to pore though the pages, looking for a section to amend and annotate, scribbling at the speed of light, or staring into the future waiting for a certain thought. And this is how he continues: stopping and starting, muttering and gesticulating, all the while pondering the devious conundrums of existence.

This evening, his regular brain-food has been usurped by earthly concerns. He's thinking about his funeral, which recently cost him every last penny of his savings. That's expensive by any standards. It will be a very elaborate affair, because of his very specific needs. He's assured these needs will be fully met, and that the money has been well spent. He hopes so. It's taken months of indecision. All that remains is to write his confession, and wait.

He continues walking the rounds, welcoming the value of physical activity. It allows his imagination to untangle, and his ideas to arrive unhurried. Sometimes, when sitting at his desk, the speed of the pen loses out to the flurry of his mind; his thoughts like a tank of darting silver fish, effortlessly evading capture. And so he walks, composing his confessional:

I betrayed my friend for money, my good friend David Bohm. It is the worst thing a man can do apart from kill. This is the Judas Crime. If you think it's not so terrible, ask Jesus how he felt.

He enjoys that phrase, the notion of a *Judas Crime;* and he's tempted to stop walking and write it down, but his mind runs on…

You won't have heard of David Bohm. Very few people have. He died in 1992 so there goes your chance of meeting him. You could try reading his books but good luck with that…

Polonski chides himself for this arrogance. He must never berate the young for their effervescence and fleeting attention span. He misremembers a quote from Marilyn Monroe: *all we want is our chance to sparkle.* In the light of this, he is certain that sparkling should be a prerequisite.

Polonski can't blame anyone for a lack of understanding; instead he must further deconstruct his notions to make them popular. He must make plans. Then remembers: he *has* made plans... All that remains is to write the confession...

Everything can be traced back to David Bohm. He is the source... Polonski stops and waves his notebook in the air to emphasise this point. But there's no one listening, and no one to talk to. It's late. He must stop this procrastination. He must attempt to put words onto paper, so he heads up the stairs to his study.

David Bohm had theories on life and death, some of them very persuasive, because every misunderstood genius has the power to change the world. But how can the layperson make an informed choice between the genuine and the deluded?

Polonski has always made a case for scientific method, which he can break down into eight distinct units: ask a question, run background research, construct a hypothesis, design an experiment to test the hypothesis, analyse data, draw conclusions, modify hypothesis. Only when these first seven stages have been satisfied can the scientist move on to the eighth: communicate the results. And that's where Polonski is now; trying to communicate the results. *Perhaps if David Bohm had been better at stage eight,* he jokes to himself, *I wouldn't be in this predicament...*

Up in his study, Polonski marvels at how tidy it is. Everything in order. The results of his life's work, neatly written up in a small collection of school exercise books sitting on one side of his desk. His precious notebooks containing mathematical flow charts annotated and augmented into collages of meaning. Over the years he's worked diligently and quietly, creating these personal interpretations of Bohm's theories: the communication of the results. There's no point harbouring the secrets of the universe if they remain incomprehensible.

All that remains is to write the confession.

He opens a fresh pad of exercise paper, picks up his pen.

My name is Eugene Polonski. If you are reading this, I will already be dead…

He crosses the line out. It's a tautology. Whoever finds his notebooks will be fully cognizant of his condition. He tears this page out and throws it away.

Fresh page.

It is time for my confession. The reasons will be made clear and you will understand why.

> *I would prefer to speak these words out loud in the traditional way, as I did when I was a child, speaking before a priest. Speaking the words helps the story flow. It would be easier than this effort of writing with a pen. My hands are old, and in the time it takes to write the words, concentration wanders and the meaning is lost.*
>
> *This is my confession.*
>
> *I no longer have the luxury of believing in God, and there is no one to hear my sins.*
>
> *I am asking you to witness them.*
>
> *Whoever you are.*
>
> *Please forgive me, and save me from torment.*

Polonski rubs the fingers on his writing hand. He re-reads these opening sentences and is pleased with the attempt. He carefully tears the sheet of paper from the writing pad, and places it on one side. He leans back from the desk. He has made a good start, but his story remains elusive. There are many conflicts and starting points. There are many reasons for his difficulties, but he is beyond blame. He only means to set the record straight.

He turns to a new page in the writing pad, and continues.

I am writing this for David Bohm. For the man I wronged. You have probably never heard of him. Very few people have. He died in 1992, so there goes your chance of meeting him. You could try reading one of his books, and good luck with that. His brand of physics is so niche that even other physicists consider him something of an outsider. Yet he produced such a remarkable vision of the sub-atomic world that if it were ever disseminated into popular culture, it would revolutionise our understanding of life and death…

Friday...

These Important Things

Brad wakes up mid-morning. He makes coffee. He eats toast. He washes up. He sighs. The book reading is tomorrow afternoon. Thirty hours away. His involvement was very last-minute (via his boss, the owner of The Brighton Book Cellar, proving that success is less a meritocracy than a function of random networking). So he had ten whole days to prepare, but what with girlfriend issues, and general procrastination...

He rolls a joint of some very sub-standard homegrown that he should have binned months ago because it just gives him headaches. He smokes it anyway, more as placebo than pleasure, and thinks about a plan of action. The minimum requirement is that he talks for 40 minutes, including a Q&A session. He's understandably nervous, but it shouldn't be too difficult.

First thing: he Googles the name Eugene Polonski.

He can't believe he didn't do this yesterday, but with one thing and another... It doesn't matter; he's doing it now. He assumes he's remembered the name correctly. Wrote it down as soon as the undertakers left. He didn't dare take notes in their presence and appear too keen because their visit could have been part of some elaborate hoax. So he tried to stay cool, and he wrote the name down the moment they left.

Eugene Polonski – the man who, apparently, worked with legendary science genius David Bohm.

The search engine provides over a million results. Then he realises it's chosen to search for *Eugen Polanski*, a popular Polish footballer.

He makes the correction and tries again... Nothing. He gives up the search. It doesn't matter. If the undertakers are on the level, they'll send this Polonski character to see him, as promised. Whatever. Maybe he'd be useless anyway. Bohm would have had numerous work colleagues, in America, Brazil and Israel, before moving to England. So this Polonski could be some low-ranking lab technician, with no real insight into Bohm's ideas.

He closes his laptop and tries to concentrate. He has a copy of his book in front of him.

Death and Physics by Bradley Holmeson.

He loves the title. He's pleased with the edgy self-published design and feel; but he's never pitched the book as an idea and isn't sure how to present it to an audience. It should be simple enough: start reading at the beginning, and stop reading if there are any questions. Answer the questions as best he can, then continue reading. But what if he's heckled? What if the audience turn aggressive? He's not sure how to defend himself.

His book is an extension of a 100-year-old quantum argument: *is consciousness somehow fundamental to the structure of matter?*

He knows there's a growing sense – among a select group of scientists – that consciousness might not originate in our nervous system but in a deeper aspect of the world, as something fundamental that we tune into. It's a concept that explains various aspects of sub-atomic behaviour. But Brad isn't a scientist, and he can't play the argument out with science history and theory. In his book, he takes a more interpretive route. And that's the problem: any public discussion of transcendence, of *existence beyond the physical plane*, sounds like mysticism. And the future is secular – any hint of religion must be deconstructed, rationalised and destroyed.

He feels the onset of a dull headache, looks at the joint and remembers why, hating this sub-standard marijuana the same way a barista hates instant coffee. Suddenly, fresh air seems like a good idea, but rather than go outside he ambles into the lounge and opens a window. The wind pushes into the room, clean and cold, immediately picking up his mood. He imagines all the oxygenated goodness rushing through his blood. It's a tonic to his lethargy, but the colour of the day remains terminally overcast.

He roots about in the hallway, looking for his cycling glasses, the ones with the persimmon-coloured lenses. Back at the window, he puts them on, and the winter-grey is transformed into an alien summer. The same view but now cast in vivid new tones. He stares into the cold until his face goes numb, letting his mind wander.

The altered-reality view is easily explained. Everything we see is information carried by electro-magnetic waves, and his coloured lenses block out certain light frequencies, allowing others to dominate. It's the same with thought perception. If you think of the brain as being a lens that focuses the world, the filters on the brain-lens can be adjusted, for example, by using one of the psychotropic drugs, thus blocking out the usual everyday frequencies, allowing other information to dominate: same world, seen through a different lens.

Can he discuss this at his book reading? There are portals to transcendence, doorways to other realms, that exist and have evolved side-by-side with our primitive, forest-dwelling ancestors. There are respected professors from the best universities studying this legitimate subject of entheobotany, defined as *the study of flowering plants that make us divine*. Brad laughs at the audacity of this definition. There *are* plants that make us divine, that transport us to a more fundamental realm of consciousness, that help us transcend the daily struggle of *work, consume, sleep*. We have the means to cure our capitalist urges; it's why his book is so important.

He takes the cycling glasses off and closes the window. He can't become side-tracked by drugs and shamanism. Science has saved us from the tyranny of superstition; the new rationalism has bred a negation of anything beyond the immediate physical world. It's one of the modern tragedies that our enlightened secularism has created a new tyranny of superstition and prejudice.

Focus!

He needs this book reading to set him on a path to victory. He needs Jane to recognise his drug-free commitment. Unless he can do this, nothing will ever make sense. He must return to the source; to the work of David Bohm. And the more he thinks about it, the more he needs the undertakers to send this Eugene Polonski character to see him. He needs authentication. It might be his best chance for success.

Eugene Polonski has made remarkable progress during his years in care, and is now on such a low dose of anti-psychotics he almost enjoys the mild hallucinations that stem from his schizophrenia.

There are mysteries in the world he can explain with simple diagrams and equations. He can demonstrate how the energy of the sun is captured by green plants and made available to the food chain, and how information is transferred through space by the radiation of light waves. He can trace the evolution of mankind back to its origin as self-replicating strands of humble protein. And he harbours ideas for our continued human development. His mind is a bright, clean library of mathematical charts and geometrical patterns. As for the specific meaning of his own existence, he finds this more difficult to express.

But today is his lucky day. That's the sentiment handed down at the Ravenshead Care Home for Ex-Servicemen. He's not sure if he agrees with the logic. He's due to leave this country mansion, this place of architectural beauty, this palace of monotonous safety for an uncertain life in the outside world. There isn't a choice: healthcare cutbacks. And he's been sold the idea as if it were always his intention to be cared for in the community.

Since the news of the closure there's been a steady increase in stress-related panic attacks. Most of his peers are chemically battened down to keep the phantoms at bay. Polonski feels too old for new beginnings, but he hasn't made any trouble about the move. He's been making plans.

He sits quietly on the narrow ex-hospital bed, wearing the suit he arrived in. A 1970s sky-blue polyester leisure suit. Once the pinnacle of American West Coast fashion, it reminds him of youthful immortality.

There's a knock on the door, and Karl walks in uninvited. As if Karl ever needs an invitation. He stands over six feet tall and functions as part nurse, part security.

'So, Mr Polonski. You pack up and ready to go, I see.'

Polonski looks up and nods. He believes he's been content here, if not actually happy, although the room now looks forlorn, having been emptied of his personal effects.

'Nice suit,' says Karl, laughing. Polonski can't tell if this is a compliment or not. His relationship with Karl hasn't always been civil. Polonski has learned docility, and of course the drugs have helped.

'Come, Mr Polonski. We must to get you moved, so we get you

moved, yes? The woman is to collect you, is here soon I think. We get you waiting in the reception?'

Even after decades in England, Karl retains a curious Slav accent and syntax. Polonski remembers when he first arrived, how Karl would stalk the grounds with a crust of bread in his back pocket, and one day Polonski saw him making a sandwich from the grass cuttings on the front lawn. And now this giant man who makes furtive snacks from garden refuse is making jokes about his suit. He tries to decide which of them has retained the most of their dignity.

Polonski stands up. He holds a small case close to his chest; like a brief-case, but in that old-fashioned style, cardboard with wooden slats.

'You want I should help you with carrying?' asks Karl.

Polonski gestures to the large plastic laundry bag and the removals box sitting next to him on the bed. The bag contains his other suit, his charity shop clothes and washbag; the removals box is half full with books, stationery, photographs, envelopes, paper cuttings, a camera, a military-looking tie and a rusting enamel biscuit tin.

'Just this is all you have?'

Polonski can't imagine why anyone would need more.

Karl picks up the box and the bag and strolls out. Polonski follows, with his small cardboard case, down the stairs to the main reception on the ground floor. He waits, listening for extraneous sounds. He doesn't bother to say goodbye to anyone.

His transport is finally announced by a woman's voice. He hears his name mentioned but can't decipher the details of the conversation. Then she walks into the room, and he studies her for signs of treachery. The way she walks over to him, smiling, and offers to shake his hand in greeting. The way she says, 'Hello, Mr Polonski? I'm Stella. Stella House. I'll be helping you settle into your new home.'

It all seems too easy, and it makes him suspicious.

He's not ready to shake hands, and barely acknowledges her presence.

She studies him sitting there in his absurd attire. The trousers are so large he has to wear the waist high up, just under his ribs. His sparrow legs are lost in the abundance of cloth; and the jacket falls around his shoulders, the imprint from the hanger making the shoulders jut out as if hiding a small pair of wings. He stares at her with the face of a man who's hiding secrets that don't make sense.

She looks to be late thirties, early forties; a slender, strong and independent type, wearing an illegible smile. He can't read anything else about her except to say she looks kind, but that could be the most obvious of confidence tricks.

'You'll be safe with me,' she says.

'That's something we're about to find out,' he replies, clutching his briefcase. There is no choice. At least she has a kind face. That's all he can think. 'You could be one of the sirens,' he says.

'I'm just a social worker,' replies Stella, trying to remember what the sirens were meant to look like.

'They lured unsuspecting sailors towards the rocks, then the wreckers would come and steal their treasure.'

He speaks slowly, with a slight transatlantic accent. Stella remembers something in his file about a connection with American military, but then all the inmates here have a military past.

'There's always a danger of information falling into the wrong hands, and being misinterpreted,' he continues.

Stella nods, agreeing with him.

'Would you think our movements are being monitored?'

'Monitored?' she repeats, trying not to look at the ever-present CCTV cameras. 'Why would you think that?'

He doesn't answer.

'And who do you think might be monitoring us?' she asks, regretting the question; hoping it doesn't spin the conversation in an awkward direction.

Again, he doesn't answer.

Stella picks up his laundry bag and removals box, and leads the way into the hall. He hesitates, peering into all the dark corners.

'Mr Polonski? Eugene? Can I call you Eugene?'

That gets his attention back, but he still refuses to move.

'I'm sure people are too busy to be watching the likes of us. Come on.'

He remains rooted to the spot, hugging the small case even tighter.

'Oh! The case? Is that why people are following us? I remember you saying you have some important things in there.'

Stella House has an instinct for the route of least resistance. She walks to the inner security door, signals for it to be opened, and takes a good look around. Announces the all clear and marches him forward. Same procedure with the outer security door. And following her lead, they both slowly emerge into the open air. Halfway down the main steps towards the courtyard and her car, Polonski freezes. His movements grind to a halt. He sniffs the air like a small mammal waking from hibernation. Stella waits for him.'Lovely afternoon,' she offers, trying to break the spell.

It's true; there has been a break in the weather, bringing a barely discernible smell of spring on the chilly breeze. It's invigorating. But Polonski is struck with nostalgia, a hefty emotion that resides in the hearts of the trees and shrubs, and all the living things, as they begin their seasonal re-awakening. He feels a part of it and knows if he can actively tap into it, it will kill him now in mercy. It will surely kill him now with a clean conscience, in this happy moment. He so dearly wants to die in a happy moment, and not bring life's regrets into death with him. He lifts his arms high into the air to signal these intentions and he begins an improvised, geriatric dance. Within seconds his entire body is shaking to some inner rhythm of voodoo communication.Stella House has never been an impatient woman, but when his jacket sleeves fall back and she sees the scars along his inner forearms, the vicious white lines standing out like rope hidden under the skin, it unnerves her and she snaps. 'Stop that! Stop that right now!'

She puts the box and the laundry bag down on the ground in front of her, and claps her hands to distract him. And she continues clapping, as if shooing a goose along a country road, herding him down the steps and into the car.

They drive in awkward silence for several miles, with Stella thinking up excuses for this lapse of calm, but it's the old man who speaks first. He leans forward from his sitting position on the back seat, so he'll be heard.

'During the break-up of the Soviet Union there was a cosmonaut left in space. He was part of the Soviet space programme, living in the

Mir space station orbiting the earth. But after the dissolution of the USSR, none of the newly formed countries wanted the responsibility of bringing him back.'

'Really? Is that true?'

'Yes.'

'They left the poor man in space? How long for?'

'Long enough to convince him he'd never return. Sergei Krikalev. It was in 1991. Since then, other cosmonauts have stayed in space longer, but Krikalev assumed it was the end. So when his return to earth was finally arranged, he didn't want to come back.'

Stella says nothing. She's concentrating on her driving. Or she's pretending to while deciding what to say next. He can tell she doesn't believe the story. It doesn't matter. Polonski knows it's true. He can imagine being lost in space, floating in his thoughts. In many ways he considers it a perfect distillation of the human experience, like a short story by Borges, with nothing to do but watch the view and come to terms with mortality.'It's an analogy,' he says. 'It means I was resigned to never leaving the care home.'

She looks up at him in the rear-view mirror.

'Well, your new residence is right in the heart of the city, very urban. No doubt you'll find it busier and noisier. But you'll be properly looked after. I'll make certain of it.'

He nods in acknowledgement, but it does little to relax him.

They are still miles away from the ring road that leads to the heart of the city, and against common practice, Stella makes the decision to take a more scenic route, through the wide, open spaces of the Nottinghamshire Wolds. When she was a youngster she would take Sunday drives with her grandfather. There was rarely a destination in mind; it was just an excuse to spend time together. He drove an old Vauxhall Cresta, a huge car with a bench seat up front and a magic-ribbon speedometer that changed colour the faster you drove. She remembers standing up on the back seat, putting her head next to his, trying to see what he was seeing, and urging him to put the speedometer into the red as they trundled around these country roads. He often used to talk about things she didn't understand, but it never seemed to matter.She looks back at Polonski. He's still holding tight to the small case, lost in thought. She assumes he's on the spectrum, and wonders how many ideas are trapped inside him.

Stella lights one of her occasional cigarettes, opens the window to blow the smoke away. He flinches as the cold hits his face, then wakes up to the passing view. They drive in silence. Past giant cooling towers, billowing clouds of steam. They see a horse in a field, brown and white, standing perfectly still. The grass looks unnaturally emerald in the low winter sun. Fence posts like bones. Silver vapour trails cut across the blue. Black crows commandeer the tall branches of a leafless tree. A line of JCBs, orange and yellow, stand to attention in a plant hire depot. And traffic. So much traffic, so many separate lives.

'By the way,' he says, a good while later, 'may I apologise for that incident on the steps?'

Stella says nothing. It should be her turn to apologise, but that would imply an admission of bad practice.

'At that moment, I could have died happily. I'm not being morbid but I crave a happy death. Have you heard of karma?'

'Yes, like *you shall reap what you sow*?'

'That particular phrase is a Western interpretation, one that implies judgement. Which in turn necessitates the existence of a third party with the power to *make* that judgement. Do you see? Your understanding of karma is in accordance with Christian values.'

'Okay…?'

'The Buddhists don't believe in God. Their concept of karma suggests that in death we come face-to-face with demons of our own making. Unresolved emotions. Hidden fears. See those Buddhist paintings of ferocious creatures, with horns and talons, dripping with blood and festooned with skulls? Trampling the bones of the dead? That is what karma is: manifestations of your own sub-conscious attacking you – or leading you to salvation.'Trampling on the bones of the dead…?' says Stella.

'If we rise above the animal emotions, we're set free: *if we become like the clear and cloudless sky, we will have risen above the beast.* That's how I felt, that moment on the steps. That's why I reacted as I did. The death demons are entirely our own invention. So we should try not to die until we have a clear mind.'

He stops talking. He shouldn't be discussing post-death hallucinations. It will be written down in a report: did he seem stable? Should we review his medication?

He no longer cares what they think, but he doesn't want new pharmaceuticals forced on him; doesn't want his last days to be drug-hazed.

'So where did this interest in Buddhism come from? Was it when you were in the army? An exotic posting somewhere?'

She's trying to be jolly. Trying to lighten the mood.

'I wasn't in the army…'

'But… Oh, I thought everyone at Ravenshead was ex-military.'

'I was a G-man.'

'A *gee–man*?' she says.

'Protecting the world from the Red Peril. I was a government man.'

'What does that mean?'

'I was recruited by the Bureau. The FBI. But I shouldn't be talking about it…'

'Why not?'

'Because I might have to kill you…'

He says this as a joke. She doesn't get it. It sounds unexpectedly aggressive and, by association, unhinged. She remembers that he's on clozapine, an antipsychotic, and wonders if he's taken the day off his meds. Prior to this car journey, there was no mention of him being a Buddhist, or a scientist, let alone an FBI agent. She now regards his whole conversational tone as a scream of delusion. *Never make friends with the client group. Keep it sociable but maintain a strict professional distance.* She grips the steering wheel and begins to regret taking this longer scenic route.

Polonski notices the change. He thought his joke would introduce a more personal tone to the conversation, break the ice. He was always taught to keep his cards close to his chest. It's a generational thing. He can't just launch into his personal history and offload. These days it's a prerequisite to have your emotional life on view. Everyone wants to be acknowledged. To have their lives witnessed. But to Polonski, unprompted emoting smacks of low character.

Each of the special agents of the FBI must be ready and capable to meet any challenge. The security of our nation and the life of a loved one may depend upon him.

He never met J. Edgar Hoover, but certain lines from his speeches still resonate; he clings onto them as an excuse for past behaviour. And if his deeds are judged to be *in*excusable, then the knowledge of this indoctrination might help to explain his actions. He owed America a debt, and he repaid with unquestioning allegiance.

America has no place for those timid souls who urge appeasement at any price; nor those who chant the 'better red than dead' slogan. We need men and women with a capacity for moral indignation, men and women of faith, men and women of conviction, men and women with the God-given strength and determination to uphold the cause of democracy.

His friend David Bohm was an unrepentant Marxist at the worst time – during the Cold War. Even when he was hauled before the House of Un-American Activities Committee, he pleaded the Fifth Amendment: the right to not incriminate oneself, and the right to not incriminate others. He chose to remain silent while his colleagues were naming names, toeing the party line and blindly destroying lives. They hated that Bohm wouldn't play the game. They said he was selling state secrets to the Russians. What else was Polonski expected to do? Same as any loyal American: he took Bohm to the cleaners. Tried to incriminate him as best he could. Rid the country of the red scourge.

The traffic snarls up as they join the city ring road. It's too late to worry about it now, but they won't arrive until after dark. Maybe it's just as well. The worst of urban neglect will be hidden by cover of night. Polonski has nodded off, and Stella finds her way to the inner-city area of Radford. It's a place devoid of architectural aesthetic. The hostel itself is one of several post-war concrete blocks. Flat-roof, black paint over rusty window frames. Curtains faded in the geometrically placed windows. She parks next to the wide, paving-stone steps leading up to the main entrance.

This is a student area of the city, but the huddle outside the hostel is distinctly social-service roster. Men in charity-shop coats, of an indeterminate middle age, smoking and watching the time pass. There's a bottle doing the rounds, and muted conversation. The day is done, and the streetlights warm the scene with a dismal glimmer.

Polonski wakes up as the car draws to a halt.

It takes him a moment to recognise his situation, and decide how to proceed. Stella observes his slow patience. The last weapon of the old is their stoicism. But what would he fight against? There's no enemy. There's no conspiracy. He's been moved here due to the simple fact that this inner-city hostel is cheaper than his exclusive countryside care home.

She helps him out of the car and up to the pavement.

'It's always difficult moving home, but we'll soon get you settled.'

He says nothing. The moving isn't a problem for him. As a child he moved from Lithuania to America under more difficult circumstances, a move that probably saved his life. They didn't talk about it then, and he doesn't talk about it now. They just used to say they were Survivors. If anyone asked, they were Survivors. Of course their stories circulated during private moments. They learned of each other's fate and gave praise to God, to the goodwill of strangers and earthly luck. And they gave praise to their adopted American home, and proclaimed how things would be different from now on.

Arriving in the New World, he was still a junior citizen, even though his 12 years had witnessed more heartache and horror than would be decent for a 100-year-old. He was taught to be positive. Things would be different now. What kind of a future is it if you keep talking about killing and gassing and maiming? So they talked about the good people who helped them survive, and they talked about their bright future.

The migration of European Jews from Lithuania began in 1933, but it wasn't until October '39 and the Soviet invasion that his family sought an escape. Some of their friends travelled east, trans-Siberia to Vladivostok, and shipped to Palestine. Some travelled south to Italy and made their luck that way. There was also the possibility of travelling west, right into the heart of the terror, before heading south for France to cross the Pyrenees for Spain and Portugal.

This was our chosen route…

Polonski's thoughts turn into first-person narrative automatically. He's told this story before, and can recount the details like a patient recounts their case history.

We had papers. We visited one consulate after another, for a visa to anywhere else, exit visas, travel visas, diplomatic passes; we memorised atlases, we became experts in the most intricate travel plans, we invented routes where none had existed before because it was up to us to find a way. And, God-willing, with the help of strangers and with luck…

Persistence and luck! You heard this again and again in survivor stories, how some might happen to take a chance, to leap from a train, run into the woods, hide in the trees; how one day, on a sudden instinct, they would leave home with just a suitcase, forsaking all friends and family and worldly possessions.

When the German Army first invaded our Soviet-occupied Lithuania, they were welcomed as liberators. But they were closely followed by the Einsatzgruppen; the Death Squads. Years later it became known how the SS were treated for stress and trauma due to the sheer number they had to kill and dispose of. It became a huge problem for them. This was their answer to the Jewish Question but it wasn't easy. It was hard killing so many people in such a small time; 175,000 in Lithuania alone during the first six months of occupation. It created huge logistical problems of disposal and burial. This was still the early days of their Final Solution. They were yet to instigate the relative civilities of ghettos and concentration camps; at this time, Jews were merely rounded up and shot in pits near their homes. And bulldozers spent days burying the bodies, and flattening the ground to make sure that any left alive would be properly suffocated.

Our escape route was organised and improvised as best as it could be, through Lisbon where we shipped to New York and what a fairy tale sight when we hit the coast of America: the lights, the cars, the vitality, the excitement, the thousands of people; all that life, and modernity, and sheer optimism. If you knew how determined you must be to become an immigrant, how much tenacity it takes just to survive the journey, you wouldn't be vot-

ing for immigration limits; you would be welcoming us into your country with open arms, and you would be shouting, we need people like this!

But even in America, in my beautiful land of Hope and Glory, there was always the whiff of anti-Semitism; the atmosphere of mistrust, and jokes about gas chambers and we usually bore it all with a patient shrug as the saying goes, because sometimes sufferance really is the badge of our tribe.

For years, in his therapy groups, Polonski was encouraged to share his life story. It would explain his obligation to America, which in turn would explain his other problems. He never felt the need to have his life witnessed and his madness placed on trial, but at this moment he could easily talk about it. But he doesn't know how to begin, and it's not his care-worker's remit to ask. Instead she offers platitudes.

'Faith conquers fear,' she says, as they stand there looking at the bland misery of his new home. Stella isn't sure where this thought comes from, or even quite what it means. But she feels the need to say something personal.

'Some people travel their entire lives without finding anything to believe in, but you have faith. I'm sure you take strength from that.'

So he reaches out and takes her arm, for the stability and the human contact. They climb the steps and go inside.

Polonski is a scientist. He can draw parallels between sub-atomic physics and Eastern mysticism. He can explain the development of the Hidden Variable Interpretation of quantum mechanics. He understands the world as the manifestation of a more subtle and fundamental order of energy. He knows consciousness will survive the death of the body. He knows this not as a religious belief, but a scientific certainty. We are all individual aspects of a larger idea; and eventually we will become cognizant of this fact. And this is ultimately why he says nothing, as he climbs the steps of his new home and goes inside.

Finnigan and Blackstock

They're driving north on the M1 from London, heading for an inner-city area of Nottingham called Radford. Blackstock's Googled it: famous for being the city's main drug-and-gun-crime area... *Sounds about right*, he thinks. Also, he's discovered that Alan Sillitoe's family used to live there, back in the day...

What's that, Finnigan? You don't remember him? He's only a famous author; one of that Angry Young Man brigade, working–class scribblers, prominent in the 1950s – famous for their disillusionment with traditional British society. You remember? He scripted the likes of Saturday Night, Sunday Morning, *and* Loneliness of the Long-Distance Runner – *iconic! Black and white! Starring Albert Finney and that other bloke... Tom Courtney – that's it!*

Blackstock hasn't found an opportunity to use this information yet, but he's trying it out in his head. Mulling it over, remembering the salient facts. He can't just offer it, because Finnigan will know he's been swotting up to appear more interesting. He needs to create an opening before he can drop it into conversation. But it'll be worth it. He loves his films, does Finnigan. He's what you'd call a proper film buff.

Both men are in their late thirties; and at first glance they look like all the other businessmen on the road, in their suits and company cars, chasing vague corporate targets of better, richer, smarter. Keeping ahead of the downturn. Grafting all day just to break even. Dreaming of reaching the top percentile. But a closer inspection would reveal their silver-grey BMW to be a 7 Series; the 12-cylinder twin-turbo, a car with more grunt than your regular business commute.

Finnigan wears a dark-grey, single-breasted over a white shirt with open collar. He has the suits made by an old fella he knows down on Roman Road; been there for donkeys knocking out these bespoke whistles, all to the same early-60s design. Narrow ankle, narrow lapels, three-button, single vent. Classic. Like something the actor Steve McQueen would wear.

He takes £100 from a money clip and hands it to Blackstock, who stares at the notes while holding the car at a steady sixty. It's as fast as they can possibly move through the traffic, in spite of his creative lane changes and occasional bursts of leery Bavarian acceleration.

The driver, Al Blackstock, who prefers to be known as Mr Black, says, 'I remain reluctant to spend a ton on a fucking valet clean, Finnigan. If I put wedge into the motor, it's for mechanical consideration, not for tarting it up.'

Blackstock pulls back his thin lips to reveal sharp, yellowing teeth. It's a gesture he uses to emphasise a conversational point.

'Spend enough keeping it tip-top, anyway. S'pose I had a transmission problem or something on a job, yeah? You wouldn't be sitting on the hard shoulder thinking, well thank fuck it smells nice.'

He rubs a grubby finger over his rotten teeth, inspects the damage, wipes it on the back of his trouser leg (black TK Maxx, machine washable) and grimaces again. Blackstock believes he resembles the actor Lee Van Cleef, with his thin features and weasely contempt; so the sneer has been practised to complete the image. It's an affectation that has become an unconscious habit.Finnigan says, 'The car won't break down. Because if the car broke down I'd have to break your fingers. Get it cleaned.'

Blackstock takes the money.

'Presentation is a reflection of inner attitude.'

'Yeah…?'

Blackstock folds a sharp crease into the notes, and picks at something in-between his teeth.

'What's that about anyway? Inner presentation?'

'Inner attitude.'

'Yeah? What is that? Sounds a bit gay,' he sniggers, expecting a laugh that doesn't arrive. He still persists with this unreconstructed 1970s ideology where anything gay is automatically considered amusing.

'At the dojo…'

'Oh, right! It's a dojo thing, is it?' says Blackstock, thinking this explains everything.

'That's right. At the dojo, poor *physical* hygiene is believed to be a reflection of poor *spiritual* hygiene. Understand? If you stink, it might be the smell of your rotten soul.'

Blackstock laughs. 'Rotten arseholes, more like. And anyway, while we're on this subject, can any of your dojo mates handbrake-turn a 7 Series Beemer?'

In spite of Finnigan's efforts to find everything about Blackstock boorishly tedious, this last comment makes him laugh. And thus encouraged, Blackstock warms to the conversation.

'You spend too much time alone, Finnigan. You should come down The Beggar with the lads.'

'Why would I do that?'

'Right portion merchants they are. Right laugh.'

'Is it?'

'Yeah, right bunch of funny cunts.'

'Are they?'

'Yeah. Right laugh some nights.'

'Oh. I'll come down then. If it's a right laugh some nights, how can I keep away?'

Blackstock coughs up a clogging wad of lung snot and spits it out the window.

They drive on in silence.

Miles later, just past Newport Pagnell Services and still well south of their destination, the traffic snags and grinds to a halt. It cheers Finnigan up. He enjoys the folly of our petrol obsession. He lowers his window. Stretches his arms wide, one out the window and one slapping Blackstock in the face.

'... do that for?'

'Sorry, didn't see you.'

'Yeah, funny.'

They creep forward a few more miles, with Blackstock becoming antsy.

'This is bollocks, this is. We are stationary in the fast lane. We have come to a fucking halt in the fast lane! How can they have the... the – what's the word?'

'Temerity?' says Finnigan.

'Yeah,' says Blackstock. 'How can they have the fucking audacity to call it a fast lane if we're parked in it? Back in the day, there never used to be a speed limit on the M1. When it was first built. Did you know that? They'd use it as a test track for the Jags coming out of

Longbridge. They used to race them up and down here. Remember the old Mark II? The Krays used to drive them. All the wide boys used to drive them. Like wasisname in *Performance*...'

'James Fox.'

'Right! Like James Fox in *Performance*. He drove a white Mark II, silver spoke wheels. 4.2-litre. In fact, that's why Plod ended up driving them, because they could never catch up with their quarry. See, in those days the getaway car really did get away, because the Plod were driving Morris Minors, the twats. It's true. Saw it in a film.'

It makes Blackstock anxious to remain stationary on such a potentially fast road. He lights a cigarette and concentrates on the solace of the nicotine. Smokes it right down. Lights another one from the butt. Then he notices Finnigan looking at him.

'What? I got to smoke. You know that. The country air's too thin for my lungs. I always smoke out of town. Makes me nervous, all these delays. I love smoking anyway. Fucking traffic.'

There's no indication of what the traffic problem is. Travelling anywhere on a Friday is an ordeal. They should have left earlier.

'That cunt's gonna die of natural causes before we get there, at this rate.' Blackstock laughs at his own joke.

'How you gonna do him, anyway?'

Finnigan snatches the cigarette from Blackstock's mouth, tearing a little piece of skin from his lip as he does so. Then moves to stub the cigarette out on Blackstock's face; flicks it out the window at the last second. Blackstock flinches, thinking he's about to be burned. Some hot ash blows back in through the window into his eyes. He shakes his head nervously like a dog that's been kicked for no reason.

Before he can remonstrate, Finnigan says, 'What are you doing here?'

'How do you mean?'

'I mean... What. Are. You. Doing. Here.'

'I'm... I'm trying to drive.'

'That's right. Driving! And what were you talking about? Just then?'

'What?'

'Details! You were talking about details that I never discuss!'

'I know that, Finn. Only saying. Making conversation.'

The traffic is going nowhere, and Finnigan reaches his hand over to Blackstock, cradles the back of his head. Blackstock assumes the worst, and pulls away.

'No, come here. Come here,' says Finnigan, in a consoling manner.

Blackstock relaxes.

'There are some things we don't discuss. You know the rules. But just this once, I'll let you into a secret. I'm going to do him like this…'

And he grips the back of Blackstock's head, twists it through 90 degrees and bashes it onto the steering wheel.

'… the fuck is wrong with you!?' screams Blackstock, making no attempt to stop him, not sure if this is meant to be serious or a laugh. Then Finnigan relaxes his hold, and leans back.

'See what you made me do?' says Finnigan.

'Yeah? Well, look at my fucking face.'

He flips the sun visor down, and peers into the vanity mirror to inspect the damage.

'That's gonna bruise, that is.'

His cheekbone and forehead have already started to show signs of swelling and redness. Finnigan ignores him, wiping the hair grease off his hand with a clean white handkerchief.

Blackstock waits a minute before saying, 'You know, for two hundred I could get this motor completely spritzed, just like you said, like you could eat your breakfast off it.'

Finnigan knows he's being taken for a ride, but he doesn't seem to care. He slowly folds two more fifties out of his money clip, and holds them up in front of Blackstock's face.

'And make sure you do spend it on valet clean. Don't spend it on beak because I'll find out, and I'll hurt you.'

Blackstock narrows his eyes at the traffic ahead of him. He doesn't look directly at Finnigan, because it had crossed his mind to spend some of this windfall on a cheeky couple of grams. He tries to hide his intentions as he pockets the cash.

'Sorry about that, Finn. I know you don't like to talk about it, but you already told me it's an old bloke. So that's all I'm saying, right? It's nothing you haven't already told me, and I was just wondering about it. So, what do you reckon he's done?'

'Done?'

'Yeah, what's he done? Why are we driving up North?'

'Does there have to be a reason?'

'No one's killed for no good reason.'

'You believe that?'

'If someone's paying, there has to be a reason. No one parts with hard-earned for no good reason.'

Finnigan shakes his head and looks away. He's tired of this now. Millions of people are killed for no good reason. He watches the History Channel. He's studied footage of people dying in armed conflict, and in natural disasters. All around the world and every day, through violent or passive means, thousands of people suffer a pointless death.

Sometimes, when he's watching a documentary on genocide, he tries to imagine the individual lives that make up these vast numbers of the dead. He likes to focus on the details, to get a hint of individuality by freeze-framing rows of decapitated skulls, or a mound of reading glasses, or a pile of shoes. Once he saw a glass jar of gold teeth and tried to imagine all the people who had experienced dental decay, gone through the agony of denial before having these expensive gold caps fitted. But to witness and acknowledge every single death against the vast backdrop of all human history would be impossible. Then he remembers how much he's being paid for this one day's work, and decides that in the absence of other factors, money will always be a reason. So maybe Blackstock's right; maybe everyone has reason enough to die.

The traffic is stop-start, stop-start, and Blackstock snarls at the world every time he's prevented from gaining any momentum. He clears his throat and tries again to broach the forbidden subject.

'But if we're talking about it...'

'Yes...?'

'Which we were...'

'And...?'

'And if you really don't mind having this conversation...'

'Go on...'

'I mean… No disrespect, but what's the point of having *you* do him?'

'Meaning what?'

'Meaning he's an old bloke. A little kid could dispatch him with a stick. Probably. What's it all about?'

Finnigan says nothing.

'He must have properly pissed someone off. Why use an expert when a dodgy pavement or the cold weather will eventually do the job?'

Finnigan rolls his neck, hearing the vertebrae crack.

'I mean, what's that about? He must have pissed someone right off.'

'Imagine,' says Finnigan, closing his eyes.

When he pictures Al Blackstock in his mind, he sees a dog; thin and rangy, like that sculpture by Giacometti. But musty-smelling, as if he's been left out in the rain; hiding under pieces of cardboard, scavenging bone and offal from dustbins of kitchen waste. Finnigan picks the image up in the palm of his mind, crunches it into powder and allows the breeze to blow it away. But when he opens his eyes, Blackstock is still there.

'All I'm saying, Finn, if you ain't bothered, I could do him for you. I don't mind.'

They have stopped again. There's a sign up ahead, warning of roadworks, so this hold-up might be over in a couple of miles. It's a good sign. The daylight has all but disappeared and the headlight reflections make the stationary traffic seem almost festive. But the lack of details for this current job is eating away at Blackstock's composure. He can't understand why Finnigan's skills are being wasted on such an easy target, and consequently he has started to make foolishly arrogant suggestions. It's not the first time he's used this tactic to gain information; but Finnigan decides to show him some rare charity.

'I like you driving for me. You're good. You're very good. Dependable. Trustworthy. I like that. But that's where it ends. I don't want you talking about the job. And I don't want you talking about the killing. That is one thing I would never ask of you. It wouldn't be right.'

'Why not…?'

'You don't have the temperament. Not for killing.'

'You think?'

'You're too nice.'

'No fucking way am I too nice.'

Blackstock is seriously offended by this idea.

Finnigan explains. 'I'm not saying this as a pejorative...'

'Yeah, whatever! But I am not a nice bloke. Ask anyone.'

'I'm not being derogatory. I'm being complimentary. It's why I like you. It takes a special kind of cunt to start killing and not care about it. To not let it bother you. That's all I'm saying. It would bother you.'

'No it wouldn't.'

Blackstock says this loud, but it doesn't carry any conviction. In the face of Finnigan's certainty, he's forced to consider his shortcomings.

'Alright, I'll be honest. If it was self-defence, I wouldn't care. I could kill any fucker who was trying to kill me. But dispatching some poor sod cold, like you do? Thinking about it, I'm not so sure.'

Blackstock surprises himself with this admission. He looks upset by it.

Finnigan tries to smooth things over. 'I'm not saying you're gutless.'

'I know.'

'Because you can be a right nasty cunt if needs be...'

'Thanks, mate.'

'But it takes a special kind of cunt to kill for money. That's all I'm saying. Don't go there. You're not me.'

'Right.'

Finnigan can't explain it any better. If pressed, he might say it was something to do with karma. He knows he has this ability to do things that leave no mark on his conscience. As such, he believes retribution will never catch him. He doesn't reckon on there being a universal filing system, keeping tabs. Retribution is a reflection of our own fear. This is how he sees it. And Finnigan is no longer fearful. He believes whatever evil he might bestow won't ever come back to haunt him. He doesn't care to explain this to Blackstock, but he pauses to smile at his own certain ruthlessness.

Vital Evidence

He didn't mean to sleep, but the procedure of being checked in seemed to take forever. By the time he was shown to his room, Polonski felt wrung dry. He sat on the bed, unable to function, then rolled over and closed his eyes. On waking, he can't remember where he is, and has a notion that all familiar surroundings have been stolen and replaced with this alien, threadbare version. He's afraid to move too quickly because his bones are made of glass, but he gradually sits up, rests his feet on the floor, and looks around.

The cast-iron radiator is pumping out a cloying heat. His throat feels dry, but at least he's not cold. That's a blessing. He remembers there's something he must do. He can't recall what it is, but consoles himself with the knowledge there's something he must remember. It gives him purpose, even though the specifics currently escape him.

Everything aches. Maybe it's the gradual wearing out of moving parts. The last rays of daylight were lost hours ago. The flare of the streetlights filters through a gap in the curtains. It seems to glow slightly in a thin shaft of light; he fancies he can see the illuminated dust particles as they climb towards the heavens. Returning to the source. The allusion isn't lost on him.

He can't recall what he must do, but remembers there is something. There's a basin sink in the room; he walks over and runs the cold tap. The water comes out surprisingly clear, his anticipation being that everything will be rusted and broken. He fills a plastic beaker and takes a sip. It begins to revive him. He drinks some more, and makes a mental note to keep drinking water. Such simple things get forgotten.

He walks to the window and gently parts the curtains. His room is at the front of the building, overlooking a main road. Across the way he sees an industrial building with a corrugated roof; beyond that a disused pub with a small tower, shrubs growing up from the guttering. Below his window there are men in coats drinking and smoking. A few cars are parked sporadically, but no pedestrians. It's not a street you'd choose to walk along; no shops or aesthetic appeal, just an undercurrent of misdemeanour. He looks up to the night sky. It isn't as darkly dense as in the country; the light pollution has cancelled out the stars. He has an urge to open the window and smell the air. The latch turns easily. After hitting the frame a couple of times with the heel of his hand the window opens, releasing a shower of paint flakes and woolly grey dust. A breeze blows an excitement of eddy currents around the little room. Had it been fifty years earlier, he'd be getting ready to hit the nightlife and explore his fresh surroundings. He'd drink some beer and make new friends. How small his life looks being viewed from this end, like studying himself through inverted binoculars.

He's been shunted around all his life, adapting to unfamiliar surroundings for survival. Today is no different. Change is the undercurrent of existence. Even memory is a changeling, rewriting the past to suit our needs. While much of the escape from Lithuania remains buried, he retains earlier, brighter memories of his home there. But he doesn't dwell on it. The migration saved his life. It set his ambition to achieve. He earned a scholarship to Princeton, a feat celebrated in his local paper. Not bad for a kid from the old country. He still has the cuttings somewhere, yellowed and fading: *Immigrant Jew Awarded Top Science Prize*, and God Bless The USA for making this opportunity possible. His parents cried real tears and held a party to celebrate New World benevolence. Even later, when the Feds exacted their pound of flesh, he didn't feel compromised; he relished the chance to pay his debt.Polonski is hit with palpitations that jerk him back to the present moment. He can't entertain this former enthusiasm for the Great American Dream without acrimony; something else his capricious memory is yet to accommodate.

Then he remembers what he must do.

It throws a gust of panic into his movements. He shuts the window, closes the curtains, and scurries back to his small case. He lays it on the desk, patting his suit pockets for the key. He laughs at the futility of locking a cardboard case, something that could be cut open with a kitchen knife; the lock merely draws attention to the value of the cargo. He unlocks the case, and takes out a large manila envelope, years old and softened from use. It looks more like a paper bag, and held together by two large elastic bands. He resists the urge to open it. Instead he stands back and surveys the room, looking for a hiding place. There's nowhere that isn't immediately obvious. He puzzles about this for a few minutes before kneeling on the floor to look under the bed. He knew it wouldn't be right, but had to check. He clambers back to standing, and again regards the room. It contains a small chest of drawers, a narrow wardrobe, a low wooden armchair, and a desk with a single drawer. He circles the space, trying to make a decision, looking into all the corners. As he moves he can hear the floorboards creak, so retraces his steps to investigate the floor.Under the sink, a section of carpet has been replaced. There must have been a leak. Again with some difficulty, he lowers himself to hands and knees to lift the corner of the carpet, and where the water pipes disappear beneath the floorboards there is a sizeable gap, like the mouth of a thin-lipped postbox. The replacement board has been measured and cut wrong. Perfect.

Rummaging in the bag of clothes he finds his spare shoes; unthreads the laces and ties them round the envelope of papers. Ties the envelope onto the water pipe. Then drops the bundle through the gap and folds the carpet back in place. Exhausted, he stands up again and begins to worry about mice and water leaks. But there's nothing else he can do right now. He's done enough.

He considers venturing out of his room to explore the canteen and the television lounge. Instead he pours another beaker of water, sits back in the small armchair. Tomorrow he'll rearrange the room. He'll ask them to take away the wardrobe to make more space; bring him an office chair, and maybe a reading light. He decides to contact the social worker who moved him here; she might help arrange things. She seemed genuine. *Faith*, she said. *Remember you have faith.* That was nice. He's surprised by this thought of tomorrow. The effort of getting his affairs in order made him forget about the time he has left. It puts a smile on his face. Looking forward to tomorrow is such a rare commodity these days, he almost views it with nostalgia.He looks around the room, pleased with his progress. The minimum requirement was to put the envelope out of sight, to secure the information as best he can. He knows it sounds paranoid. If anyone wanted to steal his secrets, they would have done so. If he were on anyone's radar, he would have been found. He's hidden the information because he needs it to fall into the right hands. It needs to be found by the right people, or else it will be lost. Hence this elaborate subterfuge. All this trouble…

All this trouble began with his physics tutor at Princeton; a man called David Bohm, who even during this early stage of his career was being singled out as one of his generation's most brilliant minds. Problem was, Bohm made no secret of his political affiliations.

Polonski tries not to blame himself. Communism was being touted as a genuine threat to the American way of life, and to national security. In the physics department at Princeton this problem was magnified by the sensitivity of the work. There was a genuine fear that atomic secrets would find their way to the Russians.

Despite the political climate, these were glory days for young Polonski: America victorious in war, a scholarship to this glorious institution; surrounded by eminent names in science. This was the promise. This was the American Dream. It was everything an immigrant could hope for. It was acceptance. So of course Polonski upheld McCarthyism and joined the fight against the Red Scare. It was the done thing; a prevailing attitude of toxicity, as summed up by Princeton's president Harry W. Dodds in a speech to the student body:

Communists have surrendered their rights as persons made in the image of God… They make loyalty to one's country a despicable thing; treason in their accepted code of conduct. They are unfit to teach in schools or universities, for they are part of an international conspiracy…

David Bohm's research project – on the collision of protons and deuterons – had already proven so useful to the Manhattan Project and the building of the atom bomb that he was denied access to it. In fact, due to an astonishing and retrospective security ruling, he was denied permission to have written his thesis in the first place. Such was the climate of paranoia.

Bohm was arrested for pleading Fifth Amendment at the HUAC hearings, and consequently suspended from teaching at Princeton. He was eventually acquitted but the damage had been done, and he was banned from continuing any serious research work. Not even his esteemed colleague Albert Einstein could persuade the authorities towards clemency.

To continue working, Bohm took a teaching post at São Paolo

University. And young Polonski was given an opportunity to fight the good fight, by following Bohm to Brazil as a government man, as a field operative for The Bureau. He accepted without question.

It took years for Polonski to fully appreciate Bohm's politics, because for Bohm politics and physics were inseparable. This seems counter-intuitive, but in the material world, everything has a cause and an effect, as defined by physics; and Marxism describes society, too, as causal. Therefore, if any aspect of society appears unfair or broken, then according to Marxism, someone has decided (actively or passively) to make it so.

Bohm believed if society were organised along Marxist lines, every action would be rational and taken with regard to the welfare of the whole; and human nature itself would change. He passionately believed that a clear understanding of physics would also change our perception of the world, and contribute towards the liberation of the proletariat.

One of the difficulties Bohm had was with the generally accepted interpretation of quantum mechanics. To most people the difference of opinion between the various interpretations of quantum theory remain a cosmetic difference, and not big enough to impact on daily life. Bohm was different.

The widely accepted interpretation of quantum mechanics is called Copenhagen Interpretation. It works. It underwrites all digital technology. But it contains an anomaly: it claims the fundamental aspect of sub-atomic process to be random.

Einstein famously said, *God does not play dice with the world*, meaning he expected the sub-atomic world to be deterministic. He also said, referring to this need for a new quantum interpretation, *If anyone can do it, then it will be Bohm*.

The post-war years in America saw a growing attitude of cynicism and commercial greed. Bohm believed this was due to morality and responsibility having no objective basis. If he could overturn the Copenhagen Interpretation and prove the sub-atomic world was deterministic, it would demonstrate that our capitalistic reign of destruction was neither a chance phenomenon, nor the natural way of the world.

This is why he persisted with his revolutionary politics. This is why he took on the entire weight of the science community. This is why he ended up in Brazil with young Eugene Polonski as his deceitful shadow, working for the Yankee dollar.

It wasn't a clandestine operation. The Bureau *wanted* Bohm to know he was being shadowed. Agents once followed him in a bright-yellow convertible, for Christ's sake. The purpose of the exercise was to unnerve him *and make sure he's not selling secrets to the goddamn Russians!*

They were both strangers in a strange new land. São Paulo was ceaseless confusion and endless noise, the oppressive smell of decaying food, the insane traffic, the poverty gap. And the climate! Always too hot, too wet or too cold. But Polonski knew he was saving the world from the Communist threat. He was part of the cavalry. He began turning up at Bohm's lectures, appearing in the university canteen and common rooms, making his presence known. It felt righteous. Yet one day Bohm walked up to him and called him out. Demanded an explanation, some kind of apology. It threw Polonski, who assumed his presence was unimpeachable. It opened a route to dialogue. It transpired that Bohm was having difficulties, so he appreciated an American voice to talk to. Polonski found it disarming. And in spite of their enmity, the two men began to socialise.

There was one night during their first equatorial summer: it was storm weather, the air thick enough to cut with a razor blade, and humid; loud with the singing of cicadas, the buzz of mosquitos and a whole wealth of tropical wildlife echoing in the trees. They headed into the city for a drink. The streets shone with automotive electric blaze and the atmosphere crackled with static. They found a street just as the bars were waking up; where the night shift of peacocks would strut, and some of the city's 10,000 musicians began to hit their pay dirt.

The rains fell suddenly and hard, usurping light from strings of coloured bulbs and candlelit booths with explosions of thunderous sheet lightning. Rain like liquid pebbles smashed into their hair and eyes, plastering shirts to the skin in seconds. It had been hovering for days, and as it landed it threw human preoccupations into chaos and washed them down the drains.

They sheltered in the first bar they found, which turned out to be a haunt of fellow travellers; a motley crew of writers, bar-room philosophers and deviants of all colours. Young Polonski was on edge, surrounded by the enemy, but conversely he saw an opportunity to gather intelligence. He waited, and drank, and watched, and took note.

In the jostle to escape the rains they meet this intense, dark-suited American, a scrawny hipster with black-rimmed glasses and a journal. He calls himself a poet but Polonski marks him as a well-heeled bum travelling the continent on a trust fund while the rest of the world is busy rebuilding the damage of war, brick by brick. He introduces himself as Bill.

You want to know where I'm at? The yage experience, man. That's what I been chasing. You know? The holy vine…?

Bill is clearly high and excitable, distracted by the vivid memories of his recent adventures deep in the Ecuadorian rainforest, living with indigenous Indians, and acquainting himself with their occult ceremonies.

Polonski suspects there's something certifiable about Bill. He listens with growing animosity, but Bohm remains fascinated, genuinely entranced, chipping in with anecdotes and theories that seem to validate the man's experience. It appears that Bill, whose full name is William Burroughs, had been addicted to heroin and sought the Secoya yage ceremony as a cure. So he hooked up with an old Harvard buddy, some renowned ethnobotanist and Amazonian explorer called Richard Schultes (Polonski makes a note of this name too) and they went in search of the legendary yage, an emerald-green vine that grows double-helix-shaped coils around the rainforest trees.

Several days' march through virgin jungle to the banks of the Rio Aguarico, to a tribe of original humans, whose culture is based on communion with heavenly creatures that live along the river and in the sky. Yage is *the purge*, and *the vine of souls;* in the rainforest it goes by the name of *ayahusca, the mother of the jungle*. The shamans are its commissioners – dressed in white tunics decorated with beads, elaborate headpieces made from bird feathers; full of ancestral knowledge granted by the vine.

Bill is told his problems go deeper than the heroin; his addiction is an outer manifestation of fierce trouble. He's burdened with a psychic disease, attributed to the Western syndrome of the empty self: our religion of destruction and insatiability.

Young Polonski can't hold his tongue: *The American Dream is not an affliction, you Commie beatnik fuck…*

And Bill, cranky after ten days of heroin withdrawal, loses it. The yage helped him go cold turkey but he's ragged, and on the edge of social tolerance. He snarls his words, *Where else in the world would this happen? Where else does a society exist where a bunch of wise old dudes would stay up all night for days on end, singing incantations to guide you through the spaceship travels of your subconscious?*

Polonski makes a snide face, and Bill's rebuttal hits a crescendo: *You want to know why they do this? To reveal the wretched conditioning of your psyche, to heal your innate self-destruction! They see through the veil of ego illusions, man! They inhabit both worlds. They know! This is an act of compassion, my uptight little friend, pure fucking compassion!*

Bohm doesn't react to the vehemence of Bill's words. Instead, he picks up on the phrase *the spaceship travels of your sub-conscious* and begins to riff with it. Polonski remains silent for the rest of the night. He feels abandoned; even though he and Bohm are enemies, he assumed they were both rational men. He can't believe this doctor of science is entertaining the mystical ramblings of a drug eater.

Bill is now describing the yage ceremony, sheltering in a vast thatched lodge where all the villagers sleep at night in one ship of safety. They pass the noxious red hooch around the circle. Shamans blow datura smoke in their faces, they sing improvised melodies, they spray water on them, guiding them towards the visions. But the drink tastes like forest rot. The purging is physical, graphic and violent, and enlightenment is only earned after hours of vomiting, shitting and fever sweats.

And not everyone earns the visions; some just get the purge. Of those called to the yage, not all are chosen; but Bill was granted the insight: *The consciousness of the forest had deigned to meet me face-to-face…*

Polonski can't take any more of this hipster narcotic-whimsy. He stands to leave, tries to bid farewell, but Bohm doesn't notice. Bohm is erupting in a flurry of enthusiasm for Bill's story.

So, Bill… You have a plant that allows a glimpse into The Mystery. *Yes? Because this is what we're discussing isn't it?* The Mystery! *Don't you see? This is what science is talking about, too, but you have taken your search from a very different angle, using remarkably different procedures and protocols – but the aim is identical. You have heard of Watson and Crick, I'm sure – the two British scientists who recently discovered the structure of the DNA molecule. It is a snake-like string of coded data, full of information. A double helix! The same shape as your vine that reveals the answers…*

There's something captivating about Bohm when he's fired up. He can't match Bill's volume or anger, but he has more charisma because of it. He's informed. Excited. Tangential. And non-stop. Polonski sits back down, settles in for the evening, as Bohm surmises that the vine and the society who worship the vine, must have evolved side by side. *For the Secoya to have such knowledge of rainforest chemistry, there must be some form of communication, some sentient connection between the plant and the human.*

Bill starts to laugh: *That's how they tell it! They claim they have learned everything from the plant itself.*

Bohm suggests the plant-human interface could be DNA: common to all life and imprinted with information that is passed from cell to cell via photon emission, creating a global network of spectral energy.

They call it the mind of the forest, says Bill, *but if there is a collective sentience it's beyond the range of instrumentation, or you bastards would have found it and be making money out of it…*

Bill laughs, thinking he's snookered the scientist.

Bohm replies, *Absence of evidence must not be confused with evidence of absence.* He's ahead on the banter; enjoying his erudition.

It is not by chance your visionary vine has evolved alongside people who know how to use it; not by chance that humans have discovered a botanical portal into the spiritual aspect of existence...

It was on this particular night in Centro São Paulo, during a spectacular tropical storm, that Polonski began to question the assumptions of his life. It came at him like a slow-motion lightning bolt, on a percussive wave of samba that stretched back to West Africa: on the horns, the swinging hips and the swilling tequila of that night, Polonski realised he might be fighting for the wrong side. Brazil was so carefree! It was so bright. So *La-La-La!* It sparkled! The people around him seemed to sparkle, and connect with something deeper than flag-waving and empire-building. For if there *is* a Mystery, and one so *credible* it can be discussed by drug-heads and theoretical scientists alike, then his own rigid assumptions must be flawed.

The year was 1954. The Cold War was in full swing but Polonski felt the entire world begin to swing, from black and white to Technicolor; from mono to multi-cultural diversity. And he realised Bohm wasn't the enemy. He was a visionary, a humanitarian, and criminally misunderstood.

It was at this moment Polonski's mind began to cleave in two.

Old Polonski stares at his reflection in the mirror above the sink. He can't remember becoming this old. But it's not just that. It's not that he thinks he should look younger – he has the impression that his inner-reality has remained the same, while the body has aged around it.

He should have taken a self-portrait every day of his life. He's 86 years old; multiply that by 365 days per year... He sits at the table with pen and paper to do the maths. Not counting leap years, that's 31,390 days he's been alive.

If he could have taken a photograph of himself every day, and ran them together at 35 frames per second like a moving-image film, his life would be over in 15 minutes. End to end. But only the body would age; the ageless him would shine through his eyes, like it shines now through the reflection in the mirror.

There's nothing else to Polonski's story. He continued with the Bureau, but his resolve had been broken. So while working for the Special Relationship in England in the mid-1960s, he allowed the safety of mental illness to beckon, to draw him into its embrace. He was a service veteran. He was cared for. Years later he learned that Bohm had succumbed to depression and ended up in Maudsley psychiatric hospital to have his exquisite brain fried by electricity. In the end they were both broken by ideas. It doesn't seem fair. But all things pass.

When Lao Tzu left civilisation to go and die in the mountains, he was followed by some of his students. They urged him to write down his teachings because everything up to that point had been verbally communicated. He did. He wrote 81 brief chapters, like miniature poems. Polonski would have liked that: to be so revered; to have translated his life work into succinct nuggets of wisdom instead of instigating all this secrecy and pantomime. But once a spy, always a spy…

He tears a page from a spare exercise book, picks up his pen and begins to draw. It's a scratchy style, but the lines are accurate and assured. He draws a cowboy riding a wild-eyed horse racing across a vast desert, away from snow-topped mountains that peak above the clouds. Dust billows from the horse's hooves. The cowboy is holding something hidden under his long coat.

Underneath the picture he writes, *Polonski carries a diamond, from the mountains to the world below.*

He leaves the drawing on the table. It might be too cryptic to be seen as a clue. It might be thrown away and the notebooks never found, but he's finally too tired to care.

Finnigan Goes to Work

'Like I said, you can't reckon with the traffic.'

'It doesn't matter.'

'No, all I'm saying, it was traffic build-up. Driving anywhere Fridays, what can you do? Wasn't me made us late…'

'Late?'

'Later than we would have been. Not like you had an appointment or nothing…' Blackstock sniggers at this idea, that they had an actual appointment, but he catches Finnigan's eye and decides to keep a lid on the frivolity. There's something amiss with Finnigan that he can't reckon.

'Just saying, I drove as best I could. Given the circumstances.'

'Okay, you've driven. Job done.'

'Yeah, but…'

'But nothing… Leave it.'

Blackstock bites his tongue. Eyes forward. He can't stop thinking about Finnigan's earlier comment, about him not being man enough for killing. It might be true, but it's eating at him. Perhaps this is what Finnigan senses. This resentment. Because, truth is, Finnigan does feel unnerved. He likes having Blackstock drive because he's loyal as a dog and connects him to the endless wealth of common humanity; but he hates him for these same reasons. And if not Blackstock, what else to kick at? Feels like he's forgotten something, but he stares through the windscreen at nothing.

It's dark enough for streetlights; and there's a constant hum of traffic from the nearby ring road which blends into a silence of its own. The car is parked 150 metres from the hostel. Finnigan walks to the boot and takes out a gas board jacket. He puts it on over his suit. The jacket is large enough to disguise his body shape. The collar unzips to release a waterproof hood that he pulls over his head. He takes out a shoulder bag full of paraphernalia, should he need to embark on some emergency-gas-call-out ruse. He takes a handgun from the side pocket of the bag. Its compact shape fits snugly into his palm. A Walther PPK first-generation, ex-British Special Forces, so it's seen action. Also, it's James Bond's weapon of choice, so it's a nod to the theatricality of the job. They want an assassination, and that's how it'll look: clean and purposeful, like a statement is being made.

'… the fuck is all this about anyway, killing a harmless old man?' he whispers under his breath as he inspects the gun. Slips the magazine out, checks the breech before slapping the mag back in place. Shakes his head, shocked to realise this is the sort of question Blackstock would ask. Always looking for the whys and wherefores. This isn't him. He needs to focus. He drops the weapon into his jacket pocket. It doesn't matter what the reason is. It has never mattered.

Not my place to make reply, not my place to reason why, I'm just here to do or die, into the valley of death I ride…

He repeats this mantra to clear his mind: *Not my place to make reply, not my place to reason why, I'm just here to do or die, and into the valley of death I ride…* The origin of these bastardised lines isn't lost on Finnigan. He knows what happened to the Light Brigade: *Boldly they rode and well, into the jaws of death and hell…*

He loves the do-or-die of the poem, the valour of carrying out an order regardless of outcome. He saw the Tony Richardson version, starring David Hemmings and Trevor Howard: the futility and the triumph of war encapsulated in one doomed manoeuvre; the extraordinary grit of these highly trained men riding wide-eyed towards death without question. *Without question.* That's what he loves about his Tennyson misquotation: *Not my place to make reply, not my place to reason why, I'm just here to do or die…*

He breathes the night air. Cools his mind. Sits back in the car. Turns to Blackstock and says, 'You know what to do?'

'How can you ask me that?'

'Habit.'

'I always know what to do. I'm ready for anything.'

'Okay.'

'Okay then…'

Finnigan opens the car door and leaves. And neither his fastidiousness nor Blackstock's raw Van Cleef instincts can pinpoint the problem.

Finnigan walks down the pavement, past the front door of the hostel. Sees a couple of old fellas smoking roll-ups and muttering; mellow now, having seen life past another day. He avoids eye contact. Clocks the front entrance is security-locked. Assumes there must be a night-time curfew, with a bell to the night porter inside. Without hesitation, he continues round the block and locates the service area at the rear of the building. It has a ramp and stairs leading to the service entrance. There's a security camera but it's been angled away from the ramp, no doubt to allow the staff the luxury of half-inching kitchen supplies undetected. It's a good sign, and there's no evidence of any security alarm. Only problem: the doors are locked from the inside. He figures there'll be a quick-release panic bolt, as on most fire doors. No lock on the outside… So much easier if there's a lock to pick. He reluctantly reaches for the crowbar. Waits for a few moments, hoping for some random noise to disguise his efforts, but waiting at a fire door with a jemmy in hand eventually becomes more incriminating. He takes a breath and levers the door open with a juddering scrape of metal and splintering wood. Then he's inside.

He holds his breath again, listening for a reaction to the break-in. Nothing. Hides the crowbar, slips a Maglite from his pocket and continues on through the stock room, out into a corridor leading past the kitchens. A service door leads him to the hallway of the main entrance. He's standing hidden in the stairwell. Looks through the stair railings across to the reception desk, which is built-in behind a security booth, currently unmanned. There are lights on in the adjoining office. Night watch is evidently hunkered down for the time being. Across the hall there's what sounds to be a communal lounge, its door wide open with Sky Sports ringing out, some voices joining in. He stands tall and walks forward, rounding the foot of the stairs. Allows himself a glance into the television room. Sees a flat screen bolted to the wall. Counts about nine blokes in there, comatose from the sports action. It makes him wonder at this complete lack of security, but what would they be expecting? Anyone destined to rob this place would be the staff and the residents themselves.

He starts up the stairs. Brisk pace. Not running, just purposeful. He knows the room is on the second floor. The number confirmed in a call he made from a payphone earlier in the day, with him playing the concerned relative. He soaks in the minutiae of everything around him, noticing everything and dwelling on nothing. The walls are painted council magnolia, now tired and grimy. The wooden banisters sit on wrought iron stanchions firmly bolted to the stairs, the handrail worn smooth by years of touch. He can smell forgotten lives, like old flowers. There are dust balls in the corners of the stairs and the anti-slip mat is loose in places. On the first landing a radio noise creeps from under a door, accompanied by low voices. He sees a fire escape at the end of the corridor. Continues up to the top floor. It's darker here. Some of the landing bulbs are out. Another fire escape at the end of the hallway that must link down to the first floor and to the ground. He moves soundlessly into the gloom, reading the door numbers. Four along, and he finds room 203.

He listens at the door, tries the handle, and finds it unlocked. He gently pushes the door open, waits momentarily for a sound, and hearing nothing he slides inside, out of the hall light. There's a figure lying on the bed. Still wearing his outdoor clothes. He looks asleep. He soon will be. One, two, three, four, five soft thuds jerk this frail shape into a spastic dance and it's over. Too fucking easy. *Not my place to reason why, I'm just here to do or die…*

Sliding the warm gun into his jacket pocket without letting go of it, he turns back to the door. Steps into the corridor. Reaches to pull the jacket hood back up, and before he manages to he hears a noise behind him instantly followed by a sharp stabbing pain in the side of his face, in his cheek, like a hornet sting. His hand moves up to investigate as he looks around him. Down the corridor he sees a stocky black dude in a suit, holding some kind of long stick. Staring at him. Then he checks the other side of the corridor, and sees another man, also in a black suit; a tall white fella striding towards him from the shadows. He snatches at the pain from the side of his head, looks down and in his hand…

Frank and Norman have been in the building for a couple of hours. They were able to roughly estimate the time of Finnigan's arrival, having organised it through their third-party contact. They didn't see Finnigan as the main problem. The difficulty was gaining a legitimate and innocent entry to the building; but the best subterfuge is always based upon fact.

Months ago, May Osman received a random call from The Ravenshead Care Home for Ex-Servicemen. One of their residents had died, leaving plans and enough money for a lavish send-off. He was a veteran of the Korean War, seconded here at the end of that campaign to head up security at Greenham Common. But he wanted his last journey to be redolent of his halcyon days. Consequently, the Coupe de Ville Funeral Home granted him this last wish. And if he remembered to look down from above on his special day, he would have been proud to see his earthly remains being transported with vintage-Cadillac style. Since then, May Osman has maintained a working relationship with the care home.

The story Frank and Norman sell to the man on reception is that they're catching up with old friends and potential clients. They have a list of three names. It's a risky ploy, but it works out. Top of their list is an 80-year-old warhorse, late of Bletchley Park. Moved here a few weeks ago. And they strike lucky: his room is on the same floor as Polonski's. It was a 50 percent chance, there being only two residential floors in the building, but they accept this fortune as a positive sign. Their decoy is a cantankerous, gravel-voiced amnesiac, but they arrive at his door with smiles, a bottle of malt, some smokes, a wealth of informed conversation and a small phial of curare paste.

It isn't long before their new friend is dozing, thankfully achieved by his enjoyment of the whisky, rather than coercion by muscle-relaxing poison. All they do now is wait. Keep a watch on the corridor. Wait for Finnigan to show. Check the plan. Double-check equipment, which includes homemade darts, an industry-standard blowpipe, a 2.5-litre oxygen tank and a portable ventilator It all fits into an attaché case – even the blowpipe, which Norman has adapted to break down into sections.

The success of their plan is largely dependent on Finnigan. If he recognises the danger for what it is, they are certain he'll play into their hands. If he chooses to run, things could get awkward. They'll have no option but to abort. It all depends on Finnigan choosing the certainty of survival over the uncertainty of escape. Sometimes the most haphazard plan will win because it is so unexpected. This is what they are relying on...

Finnigan looks down at his hand and sees a small handmade dart. It takes a long three seconds for him to fully comprehend the implications. The anachronism of being attacked with a prehistoric weapon has slowed his reaction time. He makes the correct assumption that he's been hit with curare. The bitter, acrid smell on his hands confirms this. He calculates he has about 50 seconds before the drug renders him completely immobile. He needs to cover two flights of stairs to reach the ground floor. If he then heads for the front door he'll be seen on CCTV, but disguised by the hooded jacket. If he takes the longer route he won't be seen at all but he'll be cutting it fine. He needs to be in the car. Once in the car he'll have maybe three minutes before he dies. The poison doesn't kill directly, but it leaves him with a maximum of three minutes before he suffocates.

Curare attacks the nerve receptors, dismantling the signals from the nerves to the muscles. All voluntary muscle responses, including breathing, are shut down. The heart continues beating, the consciousness remains intact; but being unable to consciously work the diaphragm, the victims soon drown in the air around them, unless breath can be forced into their sleeping lungs.

It takes another four seconds for Finnigan to make this assessment. From the dart hitting him to this moment has already taken eight-to-ten seconds. Thirty-five left before the capacity to move is taken away. Forty seconds before he stops breathing.

The men in suits are closing in. This isn't a problem. He's decided to head for the front door where Blackstock will be waiting. He needs to avoid any more delay; he needs to avoid active confrontation with these suited men. Four immediate possibilities for action line up clearly in Finnigan's mind: show the gun and bluff; shoot to maim; shoot to kill; drive his straight fingers up into their chest cavities and rip out their hearts... He hasn't yet been incapacitated by fear, or by the poison. Not yet. 34 seconds...

If he can reach the car, and Blackstock remembers his CPR, then all is well. 33 seconds...

His escape route blossoms like a fractal pattern of possibilities, spawning a fresh array of outcomes. But as he steps forward, one more option is offered. The man in front of him is holding an oxygen tank. He's working the regulator and Finnigan can hear the faint hiss of gas feeding into the attached facemask. 32 seconds...

He can feel his muscles begin to ache. The facemask is attached to a neoprene bag. He recognises it as a manual resuscitator: the piece of equipment that will save his life. The man is offering the facemask to him. This means they don't wish to kill him. 31 seconds...

They plan to save his life, but for what purpose? 30 seconds...

His limbs are growing heavy, as if they're filling with wet sand. He looks behind him, and the other man is closing in, barely two sword-lengths away.

Finnigan can't tell if the poison is affecting his perceptions. He's sure his thoughts will remain sharp until a lack of oxygen creates an altered state of consciousness, but by then it would be too late anyway. In spite of this, he has an intuition that these men are watching his thoughts forming. They seem to be one step ahead. He understands the game, and attempts to blank out his thoughts to allow instinct to take control.

Action without premeditation. He attempts to fill his head with white noise, knowing he can do this, but by dwelling on these matters he wonders if he's already lost. His actions are written on their impassive faces. His thoughts return to him like vocal feedback, revolving faster, distorting and turning in upon themselves: a psychic trap, spinning an effortless web.

29 seconds...

The ventilator is being held in front of him like a peace offering. He becomes intrigued by their motivation. He doesn't feel afraid of them, just curious. And this curiosity becomes his fate. He's outpaced them to the top of the stairs. He knows he can reach the car, but begins to doubt Blackstock's ability to react in time. He imagines the indignity of having Blackstock pressing his foul lips around his own, breathing his stench into his own lungs to save his life. And it would necessitate stopping the car to perform this brutal task. He knows a dose of curare might only last about 20 minutes, but during that time he would need constant attention. He would need constant air pumped into his dormant lungs, which would leave both him and Blackstock open to pursuit and capture.

He has 28 seconds left to make a decision...

The man with the oxygen is directly in front of him. Finnigan lets the gun drop back into his pocket, and slowly reaches for the man's throat. No! Shoot him and take the oxygen! Of course, shoot him, and take the...

27 seconds...

He feels sluggish now, as his muscles relax even more, tranquilised at such a basic level of operation. But he refrains from killing the man, because he is instinctively curious about the man's motives. Finnigan now believes he needs their help; but he can no longer tell if this thought is his own, or if it has been projected at him. And this effortless capitulation is reflected in the dark centre of the tall man's eyes.

26 seconds...

There isn't enough time. He should have run immediately. He engaged his reason instead of trusting his lizard brain for survival. But perhaps this *was* the fight or flight decision handed out by the amygdala, bypassing the conscious process. Perhaps this was pure survival instinct. For as soon as he saw the Ambu bag and the oxygen, the primitive part of his brain must have known that surrender was the quality decision.

25 seconds...

He drops his hands from the man's throat, and consciously reaches out for the mask...

According to Al Blackstock

Blackstock hates sitting in the car while the excitement continues elsewhere. But he revels in the knowledge that someone, somewhere is being dispatched. To describe it as erotic would be wrong; but knowing what he knows, knowing what's happening, elevates him to a state of heightened awareness, a trepidation he can feel in all his limbs. It connects him with everything he sees, and he tries to imprint the details in his mind for possible future reference. There's an overweight white bloke on a cheap mountain bike trundling past his car. One of the streetlights on the opposite side of the road begins to flicker. A small flock of birds disappears behind a rooftop. Two middle-aged Asian women walk towards him, both in bright saris covered with dowdy woollen coats, carrying bags of shopping from a cut-price superstore. He imagines that everything he sees is witness to his terrible importance, and it fills him with a lust for life. He looks at his reflection in the rear-view mirror, confirming this.

The hostel is about 200 metres ahead of him. He watched as Finnigan walked straight past the front entrance, checking it out before disappearing round the corner at the end of the road. Blackstock hasn't seen him return and assumes he must have found a less obvious point of entry. It is therefore possible that Finnigan might re-emerge from anywhere. His mobile earpiece is in place should he need to drive and speak. His hands rest lightly on the wheel, sweating slightly. His stomach feels tight. He keeps checking the rear-view should Finnigan reappear in that direction.

Opposite the hostel is an old industrial premises with a small drive leading to its main gate. He sees a couple of cars parked there, up on the kerb. A van and what looks like a long black estate car. He can't see it too clearly because it's partly obscured by the security railings surrounding the yard. Thinking about it, though, he wonders if it doesn't look like one of those old-fashioned hearses, the ones with the flamboyant chrome styling. It might even be a working vehicle, meaning that someone must have died in one of the houses on the street; now with undertakers in attendance. It makes his heart jump. He doesn't know why. He hopes it doesn't spoil things for Finnigan, having coffin lifters larking about while he's trying to accomplish an honest day's work, but it makes Blackstock smile to know there's murder taking place and already here's a couple of undertakers on the scene. *How did they know?* he laughs to himself.

The Asian women have disappeared into a building behind him. Nothing else moves on the street. Blackstock cracks the window open and lights a cigarette. He has considered the possibility of walking into the building himself, in case diversionary tactics are needed. He doesn't even know what that means. Finnigan is effortlessly capable. He doesn't need help; he needs Blackstock to stay in the car and wait, like always. This is his best tactic, to remain dependable and behind the wheel, ready for anything. What could he achieve by abandoning the car?

Blackstock hopes that Finnigan gets a bloody move on because, Jesus H. Christ, what the fuck is keeping him? He's offing an old bloke in a minimum-security hostel; it's not a difficult hit. It's only been 12 minutes, but his guts are beginning to squirm, and he reminds himself it's always like this. There's never anything to do but sit in the car on full alert. Watching. Thinking. Ready. Every job is like this, and every job has been accomplished with a lack of fuss. This won't be any different. But what the fuck is keeping him?

Blackstock lights another cigarette from the one he's smoking. He doesn't notice himself doing this. He hawks up a gob of filth from his lungs, and spits it out the window, pleased with the trajectory. He concentrates on his problem. Then tells himself that he doesn't have a problem. There is no sign of trouble, but he thought it would be swift. This always happens. Time moves at a different pace when on a job. He watches a cat squeeze through the security railings of the industrial yard and pad leisurely across the road. He feels jealous that cats have such an easy life. Ginger with white markings, and fat. Still agile but overfed. Fucking cats. It leaps onto a garden wall and saunters along, before dropping down the other side. He can't understand why anyone would bother to keep a cat. He hears the constant murmur of traffic from the ring road beyond the houses on the right. He thinks it's curious that he's only just noticed this traffic noise. What else has he missed? Is there some other important thing that would indicate why Finnigan is so fucking late? Relax! It's been 15 minutes – but why would it take that long?

Has Finnigan double-crossed him? He doesn't even know what this would entail, not in practical terms. Who else would Finnigan team up with? Who else understands Finnigan as well as he does? He smokes and tries not to think about it. He feels resentment for being put through this anxiety. If he was allowed to do the killing for once, these worries wouldn't vex him so much. There's nothing to do but wait.

And remain alert.

And wait.

Twenty minutes, and Blackstock is anxious. He checks his phone: plenty of signal. He has Finnigan's number at the ready and dearly wants to talk to him. He wants some reassurance. It would be completely wrong to make contact. He imagines the grief that would transpire if he called Finnigan during a job; if he called him for no good reason, if he called or texted for reassurance. And it's the prospect of the violent recrimination that would follow that makes him forget about the phone.

He takes another cigarette out and puts it into his mouth, but doesn't light it. He holds it between his mean lips; clamps it between his teeth as he grimaces. He decides not to light it until he sees Finnigan safely back in the car. He imagines how cool he'd look to have an unlit cigarette between his teeth as he's making their getaway. It would make him look relaxed and confident. That's why he's here. That's why he's the perfect driver. Relaxation and confidence.

Twenty-five minutes, and Blackstock is out of his mind with worry. There's a slow drift of old men in and out of the hostel by the front entrance. So he assumes Finnigan must have had difficulty accessing another entrance. Or maybe he has been waylaid by some deception with strangers. He can't believe Finnigan would be in trouble, because that never happens. He recalls a previous job, some years ago, where he was kept waiting for about an hour-and-a-half because the target hadn't shown, and Finnigan was happily drinking in a bar, blending into the background causing less suspicion than if he'd rushed in and out. Perhaps this is one of those times.

Forty-two minutes and there's movement at the far end of the street. Blackstock sees three figures walking round the corner. Heading towards the car. They pause in the light of the hostel's entrance. He recognises Finnigan. Relief sweeps through Blackstock's chest, mixed with confusion. Who are these other two men and why would Finnigan be walking with them? And why the fuck is he waiting with them in full view? And what is he holding? He's holding something up to his face, like a gas mask. This is fucked. He turns the engine over. It purrs into life immediately. He slides into first, holds the clutch just as it bites, keeping the car stationary, waiting for the exact moment to move. Waiting for Finnigan to give a signal. But Finnigan does nothing, just holding this mask to his face – like what…? Is it a disguise, or what? But he's not hiding or running or anything, just standing there by the front steps of the building, like a figurehead on a concrete ship. Blackstock is watching with all his might for a signal, a sign, a movement. But there is nothing. Finnigan does nothing.

The men standing with Finnigan are wearing black suits. They seem to be talking to him. Blackstock tries to understand. He remembers the hearse parked over the road. So perhaps he was right, and these other two *are* undertakers that have been called to the hostel or a nearby building. And for some reason Finnigan has made contact with them. But why, why, why doesn't he leave?

Blackstock studies the two undertakers, if that's what they are. He sees one of them holding an attaché case. Finnigan is standing in between them but none of them are moving. They don't even appear to be talking – so *What the fuck is all this about?*, Blackstock is screaming to himself. This can't be coincidental. This has to be meaningful. But what it means, he cannot tell.

In his brain, Blackstock is screaming with the most violent anxiousness because he needs a signal, a sign, a movement, a look in his direction and he'll send the car hurtling over to the kerbside and rescue Finnigan from whatever predicament he's in. But how can he do this without a signal? How can he react to nothing? He considers that

Finnigan is testing him. He knows this was an easy job; this was the job he could be tested on without causing any alarm. If he was ever to be tested, it would be here and now, but as the seconds mount precariously one upon another, Blackstock gets the feeling that something is seriously and weirdly wrong. Nothing in his life is weird. Nothing in his life is worthy of puzzlement. Things are either on or off. Yes or no. Things are black or white, but this…?

… Christ sakes, Finnigan! Look at me, look at me, look at me!

Without further thought, Blackstock slips the clutch intending to creep the car forward because something has to be done; but within a couple of seconds it seems he's kissing 30 or 40mph and the sound of the engine racing makes the men in black suits look over in his direction. Blackstock is aiming the car right at Finnigan. He's looking at all three men, maintaining eye contact, but they give nothing away. They are all looking straight back at him, emotionlessly. It gives Blackstock the nausea of bad fear, which builds in his belly. And still Finnigan does nothing to save himself.

Approaching the front of the building, Blackstock pulls a handbrake turn and swings the wheel so the arse of the car slides towards the kerb, leaving the nose looking into the road for a clean escape. He does this instinctively. Finnigan is still staring at him but shows no hint of recognition, no reaction, no signal. There is nothing to be read on his face. It makes Blackstock realise he was correct to come steaming in. He will rescue Finnigan from this terrible predicament. The tall, suited man is still looking at him but Blackstock manages to pull his gaze away. He is concentrating the way a dog would do, summoning all his strength to pull his master from the burning building. This is how essential his actions appear.

Blackstock is now out of the car and racing towards Finnigan. And Finnigan has taken the mask off his face and is giving it to the smaller of the suited men. Blackstock races around the front of the car and onto the pavement, surprising himself with his speed. Everything is incredibly clear. Lucid. Fresh. His muscles are pounding and his heart is hurting and he grabs Finnigan with both hands. He grabs him by the arms and pulls him back towards the car. He's concerned to stay out of the way of the other two men. He knows he could take them in a fight, but even as he thinks this, he knows he's wrong. He must keep out of their reach. There is something not right about these other men; he must keep out of their reach to save Finnigan. He must not get caught in a grapple with them, not even in this current state of explosive energy. He will tire in a few seconds and it will be over. All he's good for is driving. He knows how good he is at driving. He must get Finnigan into the car and to safety. So he leads him, manhandles him, back towards the passenger door. He keeps looking back at these other two fucking bastards. Expecting them to make their move and ruin his life, but they do nothing. They do nothing! And by now Finnigan is standing by the passenger door. Blackstock wrestles it open and tries to throw Finnigan inside. He is shouting at him. Realises he's been shouting at him all this time because he looks drunk, or stoned, or smashed, or like fucking hypnotised or something... *the fuck have these two freaks done to him?*

Blackstock has somehow wrestled Finnigan safely into the car, into the passenger seat, and his heart almost bursts, right there, with pride at a job well done. But he still has to drive to safety. He races back around the bonnet of the vehicle. They are almost clear. Soon they will be on the road, burning miles between this place and safe home. He reaches the driver door. He had left it open but the door is now closed. He reaches for the handle, he pulls the handle but the door is stuck. He pulls again on the handle and feels resistance. What is happening? His energy is at its lowest ebb. Panic brings tears to his eyes. In through the window he can see Finnigan has locked the driver's door. He sees Finnigan has locked the door as he slides over to the driving seat.

Blackstock cannot understand this sudden role reversal. But he resigns himself, and feels relieved that, okay, maybe Finnigan will drive. Maybe he does have a plan. So Blackstock signals to Finnigan, *Should I run to the passenger door?* He's exhausted by this activity, and by all the unknowns; but everything will be explained once he's inside the car...

He will never be inside the car. This realisation is becoming brighter in his mind. Finnigan is cutting him adrift. He will never be inside the car. The men in black suits are walking back towards the building. This is a relief; their presence is diminishing. All that remains is the fear, the incomprehension…

Finnigan has gone rogue. Blackstock *has* been cut adrift. He knows this for certain because he sees Finnigan settle himself into the driving seat proper. Even taking the time to adjust the rear-view mirror. So Blackstock stands in front of the car to get Finnigan's attention. He bangs down on the bonnet. He's shouting. Finally, there is eye contact and recognition. It burns a glimmer of hope in Blackstock's imagination. Finnigan beckons him to the driver door. At last it will be explained. He can adapt to a changing plan. He can always accommodate change once it's explained. That's all he needs; to be included.

He peers into the driver's window and, *thank God*, the window is being lowered, and Blackstock realises this was all a test. Finnigan will explain things now and they can both laugh about it. But Finnigan says nothing.

Blackstock shouts, 'What? What's happening? I don't fucking understand!'

And Finnigan gestures for him to come closer, and as he lowers his head towards the open window, Finnigan punches him almighty hard with his left, smack in the middle of his face.

Thirty seconds later – or it could be a couple of minutes, he doesn't know – Blackstock awakes to relative calm. He's lying on his back in the middle of the empty road. He opens his eyes. The sky is dark and empty. He rolls his head to one side as a group of dispossessed gather on the steps of the hostel. They're pointing at him, discussing him. There's no sign of Finnigan or the undertakers. A siren sounds in the not-too-distant. Blackstock knows he has to go. However bad things are right now, they'll become worse if he's found bleeding and abandoned at a murder site. He sits up, spits out the taste of his own blood. He fingers his face to inspect the damage, almost not daring to touch it because it feels so swollen and wrong. He spits again, enjoying the sight of his blood on the tarmac. He breathes hard to summon the strength, staggers to standing, resting his hands on his knees. Blood and drool drip from his face. The siren sounds closer, and Blackstock lifts the darkness of his heart to the heavens and howls for the most rabid revenge on all his transgressors.

A View From Above

Before his work with the Bureau, Polonski was happily resigned to being an unknown technocrat. He dreamed of a skill-based job with nothing to prove, just small daily problems to solve; something he could disconnect from at weekends to enjoy suburban life. He wanted a house to call his own, a garden with a tyre swing rope and apple trees. He expected the whole Norman Rockwell picture postcard bit. At Princeton he was always more Middle America than his richly cossetted Rothko-Pollock colleagues. In fact, when he arrived in America aged 12, Rockwell was his only vision of the future. His dreams were pure apple pie and white picket fences.

Meanwhile, Einstein as a child imagined riding a train at the speed of light – a daydream that led him to his theory of relativity.

Isaac Newton had wondered if the planets fell through space at the same rate as the apple falls into his hand – a daydream that led to the theory of gravitational attraction.

And David Bohm was obsessed with a light so powerful it could penetrate all matter. He dreamed of a light so intense its colour transcended blue and ultraviolet into some unknown colour beyond. He dreamed of fingers of light that could reach into and probe his own brain.

Looking back, Polonski wishes his life could have been as important; that he might have been consumed by visionary aspirations. He was always dependably middle-of-the-road. Never had the illumination that forges a life's path. He even regrets his two failed suicides. Had one of them been successful, he would now be living a new life, returned to the world with these experiences behind him, and he'd be stronger.

In these later years his life regrets and private shame (the misjudgement of Bohm) have manifested as night terrors. Negative emotions become dark phantasmagoria, threatening to undermine his morale. But he's learned the skill of confronting dream fears by retaining a degree of awareness during sleep. It takes positive intent but his

REM dreamtime has become increasingly lucid, often manifesting as another coherent reality. So when the footsteps creak outside his door, when the sliver of light cuts into his room and the shadow slips inside, he can't immediately tell if this is a dream or a waking reality. He doesn't know which world the shadow inhabits. But as the microseconds become a yawning chasm of cognizance, he knows these moments are his last and can't believe how quickly this time has come.

He's scared to move, and incapable of mounting any defensive reaction before a succession of dull mechanical noises attack his body. The pain is overwhelming and all-consuming. The shadow leaves, and the remains of life escape through the punctures in his chest and head...

He knows the attack should have killed him, but when he regains consciousness he doesn't consider the logic of it; he just accepts it. He's standing on the doorstep of an old country mansion. There's the yellow glow of a gaslight, the emerald green of winding wisteria, the blue-black of clear night and a pair of heavy wooden double doors in front of him set between ancestral patinated stone pillars. He doesn't recognise where he is. He looks around and the surroundings fade into the dark and the murky mustard fog. All he can focus on is the doorway, the threshold. He tries to find a geographical context, but there are no clues, no obvious landmarks. He has to accept it as reality and follow where it leads because there's no immediate option. And it is so vivid, so luminous...

Inside, he is led through a richly carpeted hallway into a smoking room, like a post-Imperialist gentlemen's club, with flock velvet wallpaper, leather armchairs and an atmosphere of power and gentility. He seems to recognise some of the figures that surround him, not quite believing he's been allowed access to their exclusive company. Everyone is smiling, like they know a secret he's yet to discover.

Words are called to his mind, and he can't immediately tell if he's being spoken to or if the words are passages from his own memory.

All life is suffering, caused by our attachment to the transient: that's the first precept of Buddhism. He knows this like he knows his times tables or his alphabet. Why would anyone think it was important to remind him? To understand the world we must relinquish its outer form and seek the unity beneath. That seems obvious.

Matter, as it were, is condensed or frozen light: that's a quote from David Bohm. He knows that one too, and the memory of it makes him laugh. Underlying the world of things is an ocean of energy. Our fundamental reality isn't a collection of disparate objects but an undivided whole: a constantly evolving energy flux that brings matter into form…

Deep down, the consciousness of mankind is one. This is a virtual certainty because even in the vacuum, matter is one; and if we don't see this, it's because we are blinding ourselves to it.

The voices are coming at him intense and fast, and it's overwhelming because he's still not sure where he is. It feels like he's definitely been invited here, but he can't remember why. Did he apply for membership of a new club? Because this feels like one of those informal interviews where the applicant is judged as much by attitude as by having the right connections. He's being judged by his ability to fit in, but where does Polonski fit into this exclusive gathering? He can't tell; but he dearly wants his place by the fire.

He notices there's a fire burning in the stone hearth, and he's not sure if it's there because he's just thought of it or if he's thinking about it because it's actually present and real. The fire makes the scene feel like an old-fashioned Christmas. The quality of the light, that's what's distinctive; a deep, golden colour flickering against the leaded glasses of ruby port sitting on the deep walnut of the table. The glow of the light! It makes the whole scene feel like the Norman Rockwell paintings from his youth that he loved so much. He saw his entire and perfect life predicted in those paintings. Even his old age was set out, as one of the crinkly gentlemen in overalls and shirt sleeves puzzling over a broken radio set while a cherry pie cools on the windowsill, his still-beautiful wife pulling up in the drive in her wood-sided station wagon…

Some of the men around the table slap him on the back, as if they can hear the thoughts he's having. He likes this place. He wants their acceptance, these bright captains of secret ideas. He tries to join in with the first thing that comes to his mind that will persuade them of his authenticity.

He says, *Of course, you know that David Bohm used to take a copy of Hegel's* Science of Logic *with him everywhere he travelled… Lenin suggested that all good Communists read the German philosopher G. W. F. Hegel.*

The voices in the room subside. They look at him like a child trying to recite a poem for the grown-ups, slightly patronising but agreeably supportive. He tries not to worry. He'd like to stay here. He finds their attention genuine. He wants to fit in. *You see, the State of Being is secure. But Hegel realised that any concept when pursued to its limit will engender its opposite. Therefore, Being must also contain the State of Non-Being. But how is this accommodated? The resolution must be in the movement itself. The resolution of thesis and antithesis is transcendence. Therefore, we are always in a State of Becoming…*

His new friends are smiling but he's not sure if he's winning the interview process. Is it too presumptuous to be discussing Hegelian dialectics? He can't even remember why the subject came to mind, and has a sudden gust of panic that there's something he's missed. He used to think Hegel was just more words to tie the mind in knots, but Bohm would rhapsodise at length, *We are always in a state of becoming…*

What kind of a brain can translate pure philosophy into mathematics? Bohm understood that the true unchanging reality of existence is not change itself, but the movement of change. He called it the *Holomovement*; a constant flux of information encoded as light…

Polonski can't gauge how this meeting is progressing. The entire experience is beginning to look a little shaky, like interference on an old television. And why is he talking like this, so pompously? What's he trying to prove?

Within the everyday world of things lies a manifestation of something hidden, a realm of conscious process. This is not to say that Bohm has found

God within the Schrödinger equation. It is to say he has found a theoretical precedent within physics for a subtle realm that lies beyond physics…

It. Eventually. Dawns. On. Polonski. He has been preoccupied with *ceaseless change and the evolution of forms* because he has arrived at the interface: this is what his thoughts look like. At last! He is finally having a vision. His thoughts exist as energy on the invisible spectrum. This light is the potential of everything. So bright and fluid, like bathing in perfect white noise. An ocean of energy and information, a perfect white light in which he floats and dissolves. Like an emptiness manifesting in bliss.

This place then and these people, these charming people he's surrounded by, they must be extensions of his own personality? Or are they part of something else? He's standing on the edge of creation. And with this new objectivity he tries to control the vision with positive intent. Shadows are moving behind him. Are they shadows of his fear? Phantoms painted by his divisive past? They're souring his pitch. He tries to shrink into the background of this Norman Rockwell vision he's created. He could be like a mouse in the corner that no one ever sees, melting into the incidental. If he remains unobserved he might stay in the warmth of this benevolence. He feels sick to his core, and yet there's no aggression, but neither is there a choice. They're waiting patiently for him to leave.

Ceaseless change and the evolution of forms…

The most important thing is to keep this memory safe. The most profound secret is the journey itself. The secret is hidden in the medium of the message. He prays this memory will save him as the song of the siren calls him down.

As soon as the idea is planted, its reality grows; his salvation seems like another lifetime away. The lure of earthly thought is pulling him in. Instinctively he attempts to protect himself, to cloak his personality in some imagined form. He needs to become like the warrior. He imagines himself as a bandit with a rifle and gun belt. He's riding a silver horse across a desert of broken skulls, hiding the knowledge of his journey like a talisman, keeping it close to his heart so it might serve him in the world of blood and visceral judgement. These ideas are palpable. He descends from the golden mountains; the atmosphere becomes heavier, and weighs him down. He was drenched in sunlight, but is now descending through porous grey clouds. His horse's hooves reverberate across rocky plains. The sirens intone their song like countless saffron monks praying in unison; their chanting vibrates through the planet's crust, setting atoms in motion, calling him back, echoing in his mind. He sees the room that he died in. He recognises the body, cooling on its blood-stained bed. The implication hits him hard. Having tasted immortality, he has returned to the dogs, to eke his existence among the bones of mortal torment.

He is back in the room where he died. He sees two grave-faced men attending to a third who is slumped on the floor, propped against the wall. They're using medical breathing equipment to force oxygen into his lifeless lungs. It's a beguiling sight. The third man is comatose, but evokes an air of latent strength, like Superman poleaxed by kryptonite; and Polonski is captivated.

The choice is binary: safety or death; life or the void. Put in these terms, there's no choice to be made. And what happens next, happens naturally. Polonski knows that his journey is over. He gently manoeuvres the remnants of himself into a hiding place behind the third man's eyes; and his significance dissipates like the curling smoke from a cigarette.

Post Mortem

Norman is visibly agitated, expecting yet another thing they hadn't planned for to come and slap him in the face. Because they hadn't planned on Finnigan having a driver – *so what else have they missed? Goddammit! When did necromancy become so difficult? Why am I even doing this? I could be in the bookshop, I could be selling books and drinking coffee and whatever… Fuck…!* he thinks to himself.

Frank grabs Norman by the arm, trying to shake him free from these negative thoughts, trying to hurry him across the road, away from the hostel steps. There were no loud noises to draw spectators from inside the building; there was just the sound of the car accelerating and pulling that handbrake turn (*which was one cool manoeuvre, by the way,* Frank admits quietly).

No gunfire, no fighting. Not much of a crowd. No problem. Yet Norman is freaking out, so Frank is trying to walk him across the road to the hearse without causing a situation. For a man who does yoga and whatnot every day, Norman can display a whole heap of tension.

The driver is still lying in the middle of the road. Looked like he was out cold for a moment, but he's stirring. Too dazed to notice them crossing the road a few metres upwind, but for some reason Norman is dawdling like he wants to pick an argument with the man… *the hell is he doing?*

'Move it, Norman, get across the road, get to the car, regroup. Leave him.'

'We should have known he had a driver.'

'We didn't know…'

'We should have known. What else have we missed?'

'Get in the car. We'll talk about it.'

Norman assumes it's all too late. It's done. The gig is up because they were visibly waiting with Finnigan on the hostel steps, standing there with the guilty party for what seemed like half a lifetime. They would have been seen waiting for Finnigan to shake a tail feather and vamoose. It was all so badly executed. And then the driver roars up out of nowhere... And now there he is, flat out in the road creating even more problems. Norman has the urge to stride over and take issue with the man. He's not thinking it through, but he finds enough composure to leave the driver be, and to follow Frank across the road.

They reach the hearse, which is exactly where they left it. The hearse is hunkered down in the tall shadows of the security fence bordering the industrial yard. It gives a measure of concealment, and a clear view of the hostel entrance. They jump in. Frank puts an unlit cigarette between his lips. He hands Norman a hipflask. And they stare straight ahead through the windscreen to watch the episode continue...

Blackstock stirs himself into action. However bad things are now, they'll get worse if he doesn't retreat – although he appears to be savouring the moment: swaggering like a broken animal, spitting copiously, spitting blood; almost wanting to be noticed before he lopes away, head down with a broken face.

'What do we do about him?' asks Norman.

'What can we do?'

'He saw us.'

'And then what? You think he's going to make a statement?'

'He'll get caught, and he'll make a statement.'

'What makes you think he'll get caught?'

'He looks the type.'

'Yeah... He does. But I hope he gets away. That was cold – left lying there punched out when he tried so hard to save his buddy...'

Frank almost starts laughing. It's the tension after finishing the job, or it's because Blackstock's downfall is so tragically human.

They had allowed for the effects of the curare to last about 20 minutes. That's the standard recovery time after a single dose, and that was the window of opportunity they allowed for their necromantic endeavours. The point is, as the curare poisoning wore off they expected Finnigan to skedaddle; to bust a groove. That was the expectation. But Finnigan was too spaced out. He was dissociated from events.

Couldn't find a foothold. Probably why he hung on to that ventilator – because it connected him with his world before the thing happened…

Which means the thing *must have happened.* Their bold experiment into necromancy must have worked. Which means they needed Finnigan to escape into safety. It was all part of the plan. They couldn't just abandon him. They had to see him escape back into the world.

Norman takes a sip from the hip flask.

'Nice. Medicinal.'

'It's the Elijah Craig…'

Norman doesn't care about the brand of heart-warmer he's drinking. He has another bang at it. Coughs a little. Screws the cap on and leaves the flask between them on the front seat. He stares out at the night as the police siren creeps closer.

'Is it wrong?'

Frank smiles. 'You mean like evil-wrong?'

'Yeah, evil-wrong! Is it evil-wrong?'

'That depends on who's judging us.'

'True.'

'It's just heritage. With our skill set, it might be considered evil to do nothing.'

'Maybe…' says Norman.

'Modern culture has no conception of what we're doing. That's why we're safe: they have nothing to charge us with.'

'You think…?'

'Of course! What *could* they charge us with? If they caught us in the act, what would they say? That we were singing to the body of a murder victim?'

Norman wants to explain they weren't just singing to the body of a murder victim, which – by the way – he *would* consider dubious enough had they been caught, and certainly a questionable offence in most of the civilised world. They were in fact singing to the dead man's consciousness, it having been liberated from his body…

'Like sirens…' says Frank, as if he's hearing Norman's thoughts. 'We were acting like sirens, calling him back down.'

Norman appreciates the image. The sirens of Greek mythology would call the unsuspecting into potential danger, hypnotising them with song, taking them in a new direction. They both know their method is more than just intoning words, but that's what it would look like to outsiders. They both know the consciousness, once released from the body, will drift aimlessly; it's why the Tibetans intone over the body of a loved one, helping to direct their journey towards a beneficial rebirth.

Frank and Norman's endeavour is slightly different, slightly less benevolent: the plan being, to sing the dead man's consciousness down into the body of his murderer. See what happens. See if the killer's karma is affected. See the sparks of regret and recrimination fly. See if Finnigan can find redemption. This is their great experiment, and expressed in these terms it sounds criminally insane, and borderline evil. No one could deny how wrong it sounds. Which is why they try not to express their metaphysics in everyday language, because the subtlety of their procedure and any sense of compassion will become lost in translation.

'So what do we do?' asks Norman.

Blue flashing lights race across the ring road and come hurtling into view.

'We wait. We see what happens.'

'But we should leave now, right? Before…?'

A solitary police car silently cuts into their vision, with flashing blues. A few of the old fellas are outside on the hostel steps, ready to throw conjecture, give their version of events. One of them reckons he has the registration number of the BMW that was somehow involved in whatever just happened.

'We can't leave,' says Frank. 'We've already been seen. There's CCTV all over this part of town. No doubt filming us right now. I say we introduce ourselves to Plod and get it over with. That way, we're absolved. We're innocent citizens doing our civic duty.'

The police car remains in their foreground, lights blazing into the night. Two policemen step out of the car. Look around them. Blackstock has reached the end of the road and disappeared. The police adjust their belts, and walk into the hostel; for now, ignoring the old men on the steps, their most reliable witnesses.

'So here's what happened,' says Frank. 'We were visiting potential clients...'

'True.'

'We interrupt a man in the completion of his homicidal duty...'

'Also true.'

'We can only give the vaguest description because of his hooded jacket – he was armed, blah blah blah – and he kept us semi-hostage inside the room, before marching us out onto the steps there, while he organised his escape.'

'And what about the ventilator? Could they trace that back to us?'

'Why would they? He carried it with him. A bizarre fetish of the criminal mind. Proves the man was dangerous. Remember that scene in *Blue Velvet*...?'

'With Dennis Hopper.'

'Same deal... In fact, the weirder the gunman appears to be, it takes the attention away from us.'

'That's good.'

'We were here in pursuit of our legal and essential services as bona fide undertakers. *Here officer, take our card, and contact us if we can assist any further.* Big smile, move on.'

'Okay... One thing, though...'

Norman points to Frank's shirt collar. Frank investigates, and pulls up what looks like a necklace of rough string. Hidden under his suit jacket, it's decorated with small hessian bags of herbal potions, tree bark, a wizened and desiccated baby monkey skull, some manky-looking lion's teeth, and the foot of a monitor lizard. All tied together with grass and beads and rusted wire. It was a purchase they made some years back in New Orleans, from a dude calling himself Dr Jonathon Vudou Bokor, who traded on stories of once being a witch-doctor in Benin, hounded into exile by bad jungle karma.

Frank is unnerved by his remiss. Not the best portrayal of Middle England innocence, wearing a juju power object around your neck. He's even slightly abashed at using it as a serious totem. In many ways, it's his four-leafed clover, or pig's head on a spike: his lucky charm.

He places the talisman into a velvet-lined lead case, like a Victorian syringe case. The necklace is signified with occult intention, but he closes this connection after use: lock the evil behind a leaded door buried deep in the back of the mind, and throw away the case, throw away the key. Burn it. Burn the connection, until the next time... It's a science he improvises to some extent.

He lights a cigarette.

Norman says, 'What do you think is going to happen with Finnigan?'

'That's the experiment. We don't know how it's going to play out, but if the voodoo is good... We've set the trap, now we wait and see.'

Frank smiles.

'And you think he'll contact the writer?'

'The Boy Holmeson...? If the clues hit their target, he'll pick it up and run with it.'

They feel on the verge of something magnificent. In the jungle there'd be drinking and dancing and the banging of drums.

'And who'd have known you'd be so handy with a blowpipe?'

'Practice... I really put the time in on that one.'

'Certainly paid off.'

'Good work, man.'

'Likewise, brother.'

They look at each other and shake hands.

As they step out of the car, Norman buttons up his suit jacket, brushes it straight. Frank throws away his cigarette. They walk calmly towards the melee to proclaim their status as innocent bystanders, Norman slightly nervous but led by his business partner's heroic chutzpah.

As they cross the road, Frank and Norman are silhouetted by the police car's headlights. They cut a confident style; holding their cards close to their chest, because what happens in the morgue stays in the morgue.

Finnigan Wakes Up

Finnigan is functioning by instinct to escape a dangerous situation; not so much as a participant, but as an observer of his activity. He drives an endlessly dark road, lit by the light from his eyes. The road is a grid matrix that he navigates according to the geometric patterns in his mind. The car handles like a spaceship, hovering inches above the planet surface, travelling at unknown speeds through a black tar night. Flashing white lines torpedo by underneath him. The vehicle must be fitted with tractor beam or force-field technology, because the ride is velvet smooth. And as he becomes aware of these thoughts, he feels unable to gauge the level of reality he's experiencing. It makes him nervous, signified by a cold shiver of paranoia that rushes up his spine. So he lets go of the wheel to see what happens...

He watches the car take charge and steer itself; beginning to veer left following the natural camber of the road surface. It crosses both sets of white lines, moving towards miscellaneous foliage and a safety barrier. His foot is heavy on the accelerator, because what's the point of this exercise if he's not moving at pace? He hears the holler of an air horn from somewhere behind him, accompanied by repeated flashes of dazzling bright lights. An intuition warns him to take the control back from blind chance. He sees this intervention as a positive step. He corrects the car's trajectory, feeling its momentum fight against his will. He swerves it away from the gritty section of hard shoulder, kicking up gravel and detritus into the undercarriage. Then he's back following the white lines, and the juggernaut monster behind him sounds its air horn again, and blasts him a second time with its blinding lights. Pinpricks of panic stab at his eyes; he rubs the water out of them with the back of his hands.

He becomes aware of his breathing, and feels a pounding in his chest. The physicality of this makes him shout. Not words, but noises. He shouts noises to counteract the bewilderment. He is unable to recognise his surroundings, but has established that active control is necessary. He is fully certain that he's alive and must control his reality, meaning that quality decisions are essential. He narrates the details of control, to further establish leadership. *Hands on wheel... Relax*

shoulders… Tension… Breathe it out, eyes forward… In control, like fly-
ing, this is good… This is good… Stay focused…

Imaginary details are superimposed on his functional reality. He can
see the muscles in his arms through the material of his jacket. Sees the
stark white bones in his hands. His attention traces the line of the car
bonnet, which has the nose of a shark. He blinks hard, tries to focus,
but the vehicle has the nose of a shark, now showing rows of teeth,
cold air racing across fleshy gums. The rush of air maintains the car's
stability; streams of vaporised minerals pass into its gills through the
air ducts and into the cabin, invigorating his lungs and blood-stuff.
His growing confidence makes him weave unreasonably fast through
the traffic; overtaking on both sides, swerving from lane to lane, as
other vehicles sound their alarms in solidarity with his progress. He
races on ahead, encouraged by their support.

Wide-eyed and hyper-aware of his vision, he stares at the sights
around him. Everything seems sharper, almost gleaming. Clearly
defined. He stretches his muscles to feel their vitality. He can sense
their strength; feels the fluids coursing round his body. He notices a
mirror above the window glass, being surprised by the face staring
back. Not sure if he can recognise it: unstable like a speed-freak on
a mission; sunken eyes and hollow cheeks below a shaved head. If he
saw this face on another person he'd worry for his safety; not to say it
looks unfriendly, just too eager for involvement.

Up ahead a sign informs him that *Tiredness Kills*. He has no idea what
this means. Without knowing how, he lowers the driver's window
and faces the night wind. His eyes grow moist. The sky is a dark, vast
expanse and he feels large enough to touch it.

Another sign reads *Services: 1 mile*. Again, he quite can't imagine
what services are being offered, but he's intrigued. He wants to
explore this newfound enthusiasm, this excitement. The roadside
messages are written specifically for him. Of course, there's a giant
white arrow painted on the road, leading him off the three-lane highway. And more signs declaring: *Services!* Then on the circular slip

road: a set of lights in three colours. The top one is lit and shines red, warning him to wait. He can't remember how he knows this, but it's the correct thing to do. The lights change to orange and green, and other cars surge forward, so he joins them. He feels in less of a need to outrun them now, letting his vehicle adjust to their pedestrian pace.

He negotiates several more turns following the main flow and finds himself in a vast car park. He copies the symmetry of parking etiquette, and steers between two white lines, engine off, and steps out onto the planet surface. Adrenaline and stress-inspired hormones pump through him; muscular twitches ripple across his limbs. And he walks, cool as a reptile, towards the bright lights of the main building.

Once inside, nothing could have prepared him for the sickly stench of so much plastic and electricity. The array of primary colours hits him like hypnotic oppression. He fronts it out, holding his head high, eyes gleaming. He looks like a concussion victim seeking new friends. And this nagging pain in his throat could be evidence of a raging thirst. He needs rehydration, pleased to have deduced this information without any help.

In the main concourse, a small line of maybe eight people… He doesn't recognise them as customers waiting for attention. They're standing next to a curved plastic counter, which covers a display of garish cake slices. Beyond the counter, things look more industrial: a steaming coffee dispenser, like a fetish machine of nozzles and buttons. Next to this he sees a metal counter with a huge shiny steel sink, into which is cascading gallons of water. The tap is set high up, and the water reverberates as it crashes down.

Finnigan walks around the counter and plunges his head under the tap. Twisting from side to side, letting the water cool his thoughts, rubbing strong warm hands over his scalp, then turning to gulp at the running water. He remains unaware that he's become the centre of attention, even as he faces the queue, shaking water from his head. He fails to notice the stern middle-aged barista woman marching out of the kitchen, holding a toasted panini in metal tongs. She sees him, drops the sandwich, then recovers enough composure to jab him in the ribs.

'Oi…! Whatdoyathinkyordoing…?'

He spins round, backed up against the sink. She continues to poke at him with the tongs, as punctuation to her words. 'You – are – not – allowed – this – side – of – the – counter.'

Finnigan flinches every time he's prodded, and in spite of her determined aggression he laughs at her. She stands back to get a good look, hands on hips, before launching another assault. He seizes this chance to escape, but rather than rush past her, he improvises a gymnastic leap over the counter, scattering the onlookers. It's a dazzling feat of strength, and he lands it with arms outstretched for an Olympic ten points, prompting a small murmur of genuine approval. One or two customers are holding their phones up, recording his random flamboyance.

He looks directly into the camera lenses; unaware of the chaos he's creating. He thinks it's all a joke. He feels better than James Brown. Why bottle it up? He wants everyone to know he feels like a sex machine. So he throws a few shapes, kung-fu style…

Away from the serving counter, a commotion is brewing: three uniformed men bowling towards him, moving in from different directions, co-ordinating their approach on walkie-talkies. Advancing from all sides, with sanctioned disapproval…

'Come on, then!' he hears himself shout, throwing his arms out wide. The first one wades in with a confident attack; somehow misses his target, loses his footing and spins to the floor. Finnigan remains out of reach. The other two follow a similar pattern of lunge, spin and fall. Finnigan isn't being aggressive. These are his defensive strokes: sidestep, turn, and catch the men off-balance, lowering them to the floor. But they learn nothing, picking themselves up, making repeated attacks.

'I'd stay down if I was you, mate. I can do this all day. What's your game, anyway?' He genuinely doesn't know what they expect from him.

Their attack finally loses its momentum, because public humiliation is an exhausting business. They attempt to contain him from a safe distance, as the barista woman arrives with her mobile.

'We've had enough of this…' she declares.

Finnigan raises his hands in playful surrender.

She waves the phone. 'I'm calling the police.'

'Don't bother yourself, love. Only wanted a splash of water. I'm done.'

Finnigan walks towards the exit. They let him go. It's the clever play. They can't get near him, let alone hold him, so best let him leave.

Outside, Finnigan walks straight to his car. He needs a new plan. He's a stranger in a strange land, and needs a place of refuge. He takes off the large Gas Board jacket and throws it on the back seat. It falls to the floor with a clunking sound. Picks it up again and checks the pockets. He finds a small handgun with silencer attached, recognising it as a PPK. He unscrews the silencer and places it in his suit pocket. Presses the magazine-release button with his thumb, drops the magazine out and checks it. It's half full. Or half empty. The significance of this makes him assume the worst. He puts the magazine in his pocket with the silencer. Then removes the safety, pulls the slider back, and pops the round out, emptying the chamber. He catches the round as it flies into the air. Makes a visual check of the chamber, and stares at the empty gun. He can't remember owning a weapon, can't remember why it was used. He looks around him, acting relaxed; just a man checking his armoury, nothing to see. He presses the ejected round back into the clip, slides the magazine home. Returns the safety. It doesn't surprise him that he can check and clear the Walther without conscious effort. Gives him a measure of self-assurance to operate it so easily. He tucks it into his waistband, and pats himself down for further clues. There's a money clip in his trouser pocket. He brushes the notes with his thumb, seeing a healthy fold of fifties and twenties. Replaces it and continues searching. Finds nothing. There is nothing else to prod his memory. Nothing but a folded sheet of printed paper. A5 size.

Finnigan walks away from his vehicle, towards the glow of the car park lights, still looking around for potential dangers. Then he holds the paper up under the light and studies it. It's a flyer, announcing what looks like a theatrical event.

The Scribbler Festival of New Writing presents: an afternoon of readings from self-published authors...

There's a photograph of a man's face, superimposed on a Yin-Yang symbol. *DEATH AND PHYSICS, with BRADLEY HOLME-SON...*

It gives an address and a time.

He doesn't recognise the man's face. He has no idea what the words mean, but it's his only clue. He stands waiting under the light. A battered Volvo warhorse of a vehicle pulls up nearby and parks. The car looks as damaged as the occupants. Finnigan watches as an old chap struggles to get his arthritic frame out of the car door, then walks round to hold the passenger door open for his equally decrepit wife. But the way they complement each other's needs is somehow life affirming. He walks over to them.

'Where am I?'

'What do you mean, where are you?'

'Where am I?'

'You're in a motorway services.'

'And that road outside, the big one, where's it heading?'

'The road? That's the M1.'

'Where's it heading?'

'North and South. This side's going South.'

'Okay then.'

He shows the man the flyer. He says, 'This event. Am I too late?'

The man doesn't question the oddness of Finnigan's requests. He's old enough to have seen everything. Nothing left to surprise him. Or perhaps his frailty only allows him to acquiesce. He searches for his glasses, and studies the information. He asks questions of his wife, and turns back to Finnigan.

'This is a poster for tomorrow. It says you need to be there by two in the afternoon.'

'And where is it? Will I get there in time?'

'You should do. It's only in Leicester.'

'And where is that? Is it south of here?'

'Leicester? You're almost there. It's the next exit.'

After the debacle of his previous human encounter, Finnigan tries to be neighbourly. He reaches for his money clip, peels off a few notes.

'Here...'

'What's that for?'

The old man doesn't understand.

'It's for you. For your help.'

'You don't need to do that.'

'I want to. Buy something nice for the old lady.'

It's more money than they've seen in a while. The old man can't understand it. He remains there, blinking, expecting this to be a trick. He holds the money in his outstretched hand, ready to return it. But Finnigan's thoughts have already moved beyond the money.

'So this Leicester, is that near here?'

'Look… There's a postcode; you can put that into your sat nav. You got a sat nav? It'll take you right there. No more than thirty minutes, I would think.'

He turns to his wife. 'Leicester city centre, June? How long from here, the man wants to know.'

'Oooh, no more than forty-five minutes.'

'No more than forty-five minutes,' the man repeats to Finnigan.

'Okay then.'

Finnigan smiles at them. Walks back to his car, pleased to have handled things so well.

Saturday...

Sometimes Nothing Else Matters

Bradley Holmeson is 100 miles away from home, heading up the motorway towards Leicester for his book reading gig. He's been preparing for days but remains uncertain how his spiel will be received. It's billed as a book reading with Q&A, but he wants to escape the rigidity of the page. He wants to create something more theatrical; so he's prepared a few set pieces and is using the journey to rehearse. In the privacy of the car he can imagine bantering with his audience, chasing humorous tangents…

He goes through the running order, glancing at the crib sheet next to him on the passenger seat. It's making him tense, the anticipation, but he's enjoying the challenge of trying to balance all this information in his mind. He has no idea how the reading will be received. He knows several copies of *Death and Physics* have been found and haggled over at various bookshops, because he's had emails of encouragement from readers. They all mention the enjoyment of arguing over a price with the bookseller, but so far no one has mentioned the content. It confounds him that people can buy his book and not mention the content. So far nothing has propelled this literary adventure into the viral frenzy he expected.

He's had a couple of emails from bookshops, questioning the practice of leaving his product on their shelves; requesting he pursue more traditional channels of distribution: sending copies to agents and publishers, waiting months for photocopied letters of refusal. He doesn't have the resilience; all his dreams are embodied in this random tactic of leaving copies in bookshops, hoping some influential person will find the book and champion it.

He checks the time, knowing he should have left home earlier. It's going to be tight, but he should make it if he can find easy parking. He just wants it to be done. To get this first show done, under his belt, so he can assess where it's going. If people are intrigued by the ideas, he can confidently promote the hell out of it. He can relax, and finally phone Jane; blame their separation on his need to succeed – that the tension between them is due to this urge to create something worthwhile. He doesn't want to be an outsider to success. He doesn't want to be one of those writers who are marginalised by the weirdness of their ideas. He wants to be mainstream weird, like Philip K. Dick, or Robert Anton Wilson, or the provocative non-fiction of Daniel Pinchbeck. He wants acceptance, and money; he wants a continued life of writing unorthodox ideas into public consciousness. But in his heart he suspects he'll always be an outsider, because he doesn't have the skill or detachment for mainstream acceptance. He'd love to write genre bestsellers, but fears he doesn't have the ability.

'Fuck!' he shouts to the world in general. He needs influential friends to admire and promote him. And he wants Jane to adore him unconditionally. It's not much to ask. If he were successful she'd condone his preoccupations; or at least she'd understand them, and resign herself to his semi-recreational drug use. If he had success, these idiosyncrasies would be a requisite for his achievement. Like his friend Tony, who spends all day at the pub, writing. He was mid-divorce until he sold a series to Channel 4, and now his wife drops him at the boozer on her way to work.

Brad's phone rings, startling him. He assumes it's the venue calling to see if everything's okay for this afternoon – but it's Jane, finally calling him after all the messages he's left. But why now, when he's so busy?

He picks up his mobile while attempting to plug in the hands-free set, shouting 'Hold on, hold on, just doing the hands-free thing, hold on...'

Then: 'Sorry about that, I'm driving. Yeah? Hello?' He answers like he's being so cool, and almost pretending he doesn't know it's her.

She says, 'Have you taken my car?'

'Say again?'

He heard her, and is stalling for time.

She says, 'You bloody have, haven't you? I was about to report it stolen. I might still do, actually.'

'Jane, Jane, Jane, listen...'

'No, you listen, I was just about to report it stolen!'

All his cool deserts him and the attitude returns.

'Really? You'd have me busted for nicking your car, when you completely know I just borrowed it?'

'Well you *didn't* borrow it, because if you had, you would have asked me to borrow it, and I would have said no because I need it myself today, therefore technically you *have* stolen it, and I'm absolutely within my rights to call the police and tell them it's been stolen and it would bloody serve you right, Brad, because you just take liberties with people sometimes, you really do, without ever considering their feelings, almost as if the whole world were invented just to circulate around you and your own bloody needs.'

She has to pause for breath. He now regrets answering. He can hear her start up again, so he says, 'Listen I, er... Oh I think the signal's going... I can't hear you...' And he throws the phone to the floor of the car – on the passenger side. He doesn't know why he does this because the phone is still on. He can hear her talking. So he has to drive blind, holding the wheel precariously while grappling to get the phone back. He hears her saying, 'I know you're still there, Brad. What do you think you're doing?'

He rings off, and shouts, 'Fuck, fuck, fuck, fuck, fuck, fuck, fuck, fuck...'

He swings the car onto the hard shoulder, puts the hazards on, and with the engine running he climbs out and strides up the steep incline of grass verge, still shouting. He's holding the dead phone tight in his hand, looking for somewhere to sit down. Finds a damp patch of stubbly grass, squats on his haunches and lights a cigarette. He checks the time for no reason. It's just gone 11.30. She phones back, like he knew she would.

'Did you just hang up on me?'

'No. I did not just hang up on you.'

'Yes you did.'

'Alright then, I did! Yes, I did! And I'm sorry. I've been tense. I've got this show in a couple of hours. I've been working hard as hell to get it right, and I'm tense about it, and nervous, and I didn't mean to steal your car, and I miss you Jane, I really, really miss you, but I couldn't talk to you because for the past three days you've had your phone turned off.'

'And why do you think I had my phone turned off?'

Brad holds the handset as far away from him as he can, and screams, *I'm sorry!* at the top of his lungs. Then he slowly brings the phone back to his ear. It's quiet, but he can hear her breathing. He feels like crying with sheer frustration, trying to breathe his anger away and speak softly…

'I'm sorry we argued. That's why I've been trying to call you. And I didn't know you were going to need your car.'

'Well I was going to stay with my mum.'

'Fuck, really? Stay with your mum? Things are so bad you have to stay with your fucking mum?'

'She's not been well.'

'Oh, well, that's good, I mean… You know what I mean. I hope she gets better, okay?'

'Where are you?'

'I'm, like, fifty miles south of Leicester. I'm doing this little festival gig…'

'What gig?'

'I'm sure I told you…'

It's freezing cold out there on the hard shoulder, and uncomfortable. He's starting to shake with the release of tension as much as with the temperature. He's aware of being late for the gig, but there are things that must be said. He concentrates on getting this done as seamlessly and honestly as possible.

'I left it too late to take a train, so I took your car. And I've been wanting to speak to you for days because when you left it was so sudden… I know I've been preoccupied with work, but when you walked out I wasn't being rude. I wasn't being nasty. I was trying to be nice… What did I even say? I called you an inert gas.'

He can hear Jane laughing but trying not to, and he immediately knows everything is going to be fine. There can be nothing unspoken between them. Opinions might sometimes clash but they always find common ground. Like clouds hitting each other, or pieces of random music synchronising. Like the sum of their parts is greater than the individual components. He can't express it as well as he'd like, but there's a shared experience that exists both in his mind and in hers, and so it exists in the space between them. There is something they both cherish, that exists in the space between them. That's what he wants to say. And this is the most important thing, because if they believe in it, everything else will make sense.

Hearing her laugh slows the whole day down. They talk about the shining brilliance of the inert gasses, and they laugh some more. She apologises for throwing his hash out the window, but he doesn't laugh quite so much at that. They miss each other. He stumbles back down the incline of the hard shoulder, the noise of traffic making conversation difficult, but he can't hang up again. He should get driving, and concentrate on his material, but he delays for the pleasure of hearing her voice, to hear all the conversation she's been saving up…

She knew he was doing his book reading today, which is why she phoned, knowing how important it is to him. She knew he'd taken her car, and she also knew that once they spoke and cleared the air, everything would be okay between them. Her love for him is a hormonal response. But it seems more than the serotonin rewards of lust, and the oxytocin rewards of nurture; it's something she might never admit to because it's so non-rational…

It came to her after their argument: how when they first met she felt a thread pulling them together. How else to describe it? The picture had always been there in her mind: they'd been talking about Australian aborigines, how *dreamtime* was considered a fundamental reality, and how the ancestors sang the world into being; and she recognised the intangible connection that exists between the two of them; a thread stretching through atoms of space had been sung into existence, like an ancient dream of certainty.

But she doesn't mention this.

She's a rationalist.

If we all submerged ourselves in the mystical hereafter, nothing would get done.

'Do me a favour, Brad, keep it light… I know you like that quote from William Blake, *I must create a system, or be enslaved by another man's*… But most of his contemporaries thought Blake was mad. Seriously. And try not to bang on about the science stuff because, honestly, most people just want a nice story. Keep it light, and everyone will enjoy it more. Even you, probably.'

'I don't know how to keep it light. It's all about the physics, that's the centre of my argument…'

'So maybe the proof isn't important…?'

'But it's the *most* important thing… It's what everything revolves around. Without the science, there'd be nothing. *We are one consciousness experiencing itself subjectively*, remember? I can prove it.'

'You're wrong.'

'I'm not, I can prove it!'

'No. You're wrong because you think you *need* to prove it. You think other people care, and they don't.'

'But they should care…'

'Then make friends with them. Be light and fluffy and make friends, and *charm* them into buying your book. Let them make up their own minds. If you steam in all guns blazing, you'll sound like David Icke lizards-on-the-moon crazy. Is that what you want? To be an evangelist for the crazy people?'

'No…'

Jane has a notion that it's unseemly to talk about belief in public; that it's a private contract between oneself and the gods that flick your switch. She's certain most people have their own understanding of life and death, and have made peace with it. Yet Brad is convinced he's found *an objective truth* without realising that *everyone* believes they have an objective truth. The fact that his belief is apparently verified by a forgotten interpretation of quantum physics is immaterial! How does it help? Even if it *is* a stand-alone truth, someone will use it to gain power, because all doctrine is destined for selfish purpose…She talks him down from his ivory tower; and Brad knows he wouldn't take this argument from anyone else. It's why he loves her: because she will save him.

When he rejoins the motorway, he feels there's nothing left to prove. If things are okay with Jane, everything is right with the world. He hardly needs to go through with the book reading; he could turn back right now – the public display of his ideas was only necessary as proof of his conviction.

A Festival of New Writing

Finnigan wakes up in the back of his car, aching from the cramped conditions. It takes a moment to adjust to this new situation. The windows are steamed up, and there's a smell of fish supper. He can't remember why he was sleeping in the car. He clambers out to stretch his muscles awake, standing in this urban wasteground, breathing in the new day. He recalls the drive here as a dark, nightmarish escape from events that remain hidden. This lack of knowledge would terrify most people; instead, he finds it liberating.

He turns his attention to the current surroundings: the car park is an undeveloped industrial site, the size of a small football pitch, almost empty of vehicles. Surrounded on three sides by the brick and concrete of commercial buildings, and fenced in on the fourth side.

Looking back in the car, he finds the paper wrappings of fish and chips, and walks it over to a rubbish bin. He notices he's wearing a watch and examines it closely, listening for memories. An aviator's Breitling, heavy enough to be used as a weapon. He stares at it, although nothing more is revealed. Then he walks back to the car and empties his pockets for further clues. There's the money clip, and small change. He remembers having money. He can't remember anything else.

He looks inside the car, and in the door pocket he finds a small bunch of door keys, a white handkerchief and a handgun. There are no memories of these possessions. On the passenger seat is a flyer, advertising a book reading. He remembers setting the sat nav to the postcode on the flyer. He makes the assumption that the venue must be close by.

The watch tells him it's almost midday. It's unlike him to sleep so late, but he can't be sure if this is true because he can't remember any details of his former life. Sleep seems like a waste of time, the day being so fresh and bright. He feels its vitality and has an urge to move, so he locks the car to embark on a recce. A few minutes' walk brings him to a main shopping street. He sees a sign – Granby Street – and re-checks the flyer in his pocket. Same street the event is on this afternoon. The sat nav brought him to the right place. This bodes well.

The past is blind to him, but the future stretches endlessly forward. He passes a sports shop, and decides to purchase running clothes and hi-protein snacks. He's following instinct, and doesn't question the decision.

Back in the privacy of his car he changes, then goes for a run around the city centre. The movement relaxes him. A balm. It builds his energy and confidence in a situation that remains unknown. He runs past the bustling shoppers, sidesteps the fat, the ill, the ungainly, rejoicing in his supremacy. He runs for about an hour without appearing to lose breath. It's incredible. He buys water on his way back to the car and rehydrates. Eats a handful of the hi-protein bars, and stands alone in the car park. Takes off the running shirt and vigorously dries himself. It's amusing to him, to be half-naked in a car park. He has no concern about his apparent vagrancy; he feels carefree and footloose. The sky is his new home.

He changes back into his suit, wanting to blend in with the literary crowd. The event sounds highbrow. But by the time he finds the venue, it has already started. He'd walked past the address several times, missing it because he couldn't recognise the building. The venue is an Indian restaurant. A literary event in an Indian restaurant! He expected a wood-panelled room in a library, or an anteroom of the town hall, something more fit for purpose. So he's missed the start of the talk, but is still allowed admission for full price.

He's lead to a function room above the restaurant. The earthy aroma of spice and rice accompanies him up the stairs. Given the location, he now assumes it must be some crusty alternative-lifestyle thing; but he's surprised once again when he enters the room. The audience is decidedly middle-class, and middle-aged. He spots a couple of goths and longhairs, but in general it looks genteel and earnest. And it strikes him: how strange to be this lucid, but have no memory of who he is. No memory of past events, yet he retains this innate confidence to size up a situation to his advantage. He doesn't question this. Just accepts it. Finds a chair at the back of the small room, settles in for the talk.

The man on stage, who Finnigan clocks as the author Bradley Holmeson, is 30-something with demob hair and a suit jacket. He's holding a page of notes while berating the audience with an aggressive deconstruction of organised religion, including some banter about the ex-pope being a Nazi and paedophile-denier.

It's a shocking first impression for Finnigan. Everything the man says is a gross extension of the truth, but the audience are enjoying the hyperbole. They don't seem to mind his cartoonish movements and hectoring tone. It's actually making them laugh. Then it dawns on Finnigan this might be comedy, which would explain the author's posturing and idolatry. Finnigan has never been a fan of comedy – he doesn't understand the point of it – and he begins to wonder if his presence here might be a mistake; if the flyer is a red herring, leading nowhere...

The author is now describing religion as an invention to subjugate the working class: a promise of salvation in return for obedience and hard work. It sounds contentious, but he's preaching to the converted. Finnigan can't remember having an opinion on religion, but he's bored by the negativity. He looks around the room, and sees a table by the door with wine and beer; it looks like a good idea. He walks over and leaves £10 for a bottle of warm Cobra. A helper rushes up to find some change but he waves them away. Sits back down with his thoughts. Was the flyer for this show planted on him, or was it random? He can't see how any of this could be relevant to his current situation: he's adrift with an empty memory and a loaded handgun. He sips the beer, and tries to relax as the author continues his diatribe...

'For a lot of people science has replaced religion. Am I right?'

They murmur their assent.

'Of course it has, because science is rational! You've abandoned the superstition of religion and replaced it with the rationality of science. I understand that. You believe in science, yet half of you can't wire a plug...! That's not important, by the way. I just thought it would be funny...'

His deconstruction gets a small laugh.

'My point is: if you know nothing about science, you're using it as an article of faith, which means you're as misguided as any religious disciple.'

This changes the mood.

He's undermining their secularism. They don't know why.

'I'm not saying science has all the answers. It doesn't. Have you heard of the Groucho Marx Paradox? *A universe simple enough to be understood is too simple to produce a mind capable of understanding it...*

He allows the epigram to hit home, and Finnigan reconsiders the author's game plan. The earlier religion-bashing must have been to get the audience on side, claiming science is our rational salvation. He's now suggesting this attitude is flawed, and Finnigan can't guess where the argument is heading, but he's enjoying the unease in the room.

He shouts, 'Amen, brother!' in a loud, clear voice. It seems appropriate. Several faces turn his way, and he waves his beer bottle at them like, *Don't worry about it, I got this covered.*

Brad turns to the voice in the audience, and continues.

'There isn't an equation that explains the purpose of evolution...'

'You explain it then!' shouts Finnigan. He doesn't mean to interrupt, but he's keen to know where this is leading. He scans the room for support, but this time his roving eye is studiously ignored.

Now Brad feels a gust of panic. He takes a glug from his bottle of water, steps back from the light to look at the heckler. He sees a man in a well-cut suit, with a shaven head and glad eyes. The man is evidently unstable. Brad tries to placate him.

'We don't know the ultimate purpose of evolution. But we do believe scientific rationalism describes the world. Although, when you get into it, science is just as divisive as religion. There are so many different ways to describe the world using science, and we're currently stuck in a particularly destructive outlook...'

'Okay... Let's cut to the chase. Where's this leading...?' shouts Finnigan, who has forgotten he's in a room with other people. The rest of the audience are content with the heckling, because it's turning the author's monologue into something more palatable. But every interruption throws Brad's concentration. He can feel the pinpricks of fear-sweat. He tries to keep it conversational...

'Cut to the chase...? If that's what you want, okay, I'll cut to the chase. I'm talking about perception. Like, how is perception actually achieved? Like, how does the process of awareness actually work? Because when you break it down, our mind exists not *in* the brain, not in the brain *cells*, but in the spaces *between* the brain cells – at the end of the neurones, between the dendrites, that's where the actual process takes place, that's where sentience is created...'

Brad shakes his head in apology. He didn't mean to do this. He didn't mean to freak out and make outlandish statements that no one will understand. He's missed the entire build-up to his argument. He tries to backtrack. And the audience try to follow his contention that underneath our everyday world of matter, there exists a more fundamental dimension of reality. A level of energy-process that David Bohm calls the Implicate Order.

He then sidetracks with a brief run-down of Bohm's life, trying to give credence to his argument that sentience exists on a more fundamental dimension of reality than the physical body, and therefore...

Back in the audience, mention of the name *David Bohm* gives Finnigan a sense of dread. He can't explain it. He struggles to remember why this name should appear so important. He can't see the connection, and drops head into hands to search his own fractured past.

Meanwhile, Brad has bailed on the technical explanations and is now trying to sell his big idea on personality alone, bluffing it like a preacher craving blind devotion.

'Therefore... the thing we know as our own mind is actually a small part of a vast sentient sub-atomic force field...'

This statement doesn't get the *Wow* of amazement it deserves.

He sees a young couple near the front, and watches the man turn to his girlfriend with an exaggerated sigh, like, *Oh, for fuck's sake...*

Brad desperately tries to defend his reasoning. 'You said you believe in science, well *this is science*... I know it sounds weird, but *all* quantum physics sounds weird! This is proper fucking science... I mean, if you were Jewish you could eat it, because it's kosher! Listen: Western science has direct parallels with Eastern mysticism! Can you even dig that? Geographically and culturally the exact opposite, but they tell the same story…!'

'What story?' shouts Finnigan, suddenly back in the picture.

'I've just fucking told you!' Brad shouts back, with approaching hysteria.

His game plan was simple: to deconstruct religion; explain and dismiss our destructive Cartesian-Newtonian paradigm; introduce the work of David Bohm; and set the platform for a new vision of reality, based on Karl Pribram's Holonomic Brain Theory which, when considered in the light of Bohm's Holographic Universe Theory, implies consciousness will survive the death of the physical body. Simple! He's researched it. The facts are there, based on the actual process of sentience. This is the bold and beautiful backbone to his talk. But it doesn't create the blinding light of revelation he expected. It's actually causing a mixture of boredom and derision.

Brad doesn't want confrontation; he wants peaches and cream. He wants to forget this event ever happened. He wants to go home. So he cuts directly to the selling of merchandise, hoping to make a few quid before heading home.

He picks up a copy of *Death and Physics* and waves it at his audience.

'See my book? Hand-produced limited editions, on sale at the door for a fiver-a-pop. And look, a cheeky little sub-title: *How to use sub-atomic science to justify a low-achieving artistic lifestyle*. Now. This is what we're talking about…'

'Hello… Excuse me… Excuse me…' A middle-aged woman in waxed cotton jacket and walking boots is waving her hand to gain attention.

'I'm sorry for butting in, but I think we've created a precedent for dialogue.'

She gestures towards Finnigan, smiling at him before continuing.

'I would like to know – I mean, it's all very interesting and left-field – but I would like to know why you feel the need to *justify* a creative lifestyle.'

'I'm sorry?' Brad doesn't understand the question.

'The sub-title of your book: you said it was a *justification* of an artistic lifestyle. And I wondered why.'

Brad can feel his mind unravelling.

'I... Maybe I haven't made myself very clear...'

'No, no...' says the woman. 'It's been very clear. And robust.'

The greybeard next to her nods in agreement.

'But we're not sure why you feel the need to *justify* creativity.'

Brad smiles at the woman. 'Perhaps I'm trying to justify my *low-achievement*. We all have a certain peer pressure to succeed, and—'

'But I think you are succeeding. You're here, aren't you, talking to us? You've written a book.'

The woman is trying to help, like a teacher in a Steiner School: encouragement through positive reinforcement. But she's undermining the remains of his authority.

He explains. 'It's a joke. I sub-titled my book *a justification of low-achievement* as a joke...!'

'But what does it mean...?' the woman asks.

'Have you understood *anything* I've been talking about?'

He doesn't mean to sound quite so sarcastic.

The woman holds her hands up in a shrug. It's a genuine response; she hasn't understood that much. And it raises a huge laugh from the rest of the audience because, in truth, they haven't understood too much either.

Brad feels giddy, as he teeters on the brink of failure. But he doesn't give up. Not yet. He spells out his final argument, not quite shouting, but determined.

'What have I been talking about? That consciousness exists on a more fundamental level than the physical body. Therefore, when we die, some aspect of our memory-stuff remains. Yes? Meaning that in the final analysis, pursuing creative interest is more important than chasing money. The mind is like an iPod, a virtual iPod, and we spend our lives filling it with experiences. The better lives we lead, the more *creative* lives we lead, the better memories we'll have when we're dead. Don't you see?'

This is his stunning conclusion. It's met with silence. Fucking silence! They're staring at him, almost angrily. Even the Steiner teacher looks confused. What can they do with this information? Is it religion? Is it science? It's certainly not funny, even if it was meant to be. They don't know how to react. And into this awkwardness comes Finnigan's voice. 'Are you saying you know what happens when we're dead?'

It cuts through the tension. Suddenly the game's back on...

'I'm saying that in death, we will come face-to-face with our consciousness...'

'That's Buddhism, right?'

'Partly...'

'So you're talking about karma?'

'That wasn't my point, but yes. When we die, we'll be confronted with fears and desires; with our past deeds. For example, if you killed someone...'

Finnigan stands up. 'What do you mean *if...?*'

People laugh.

Brad ignores them.

'This is what karma is: face-to-face with our deepest thoughts. If you killed with a clear conscience, you'd be a psychopath, but it wouldn't mean it was your destiny to be killed in return.'

'That's a relief,' says Finnigan to the audience. This elicits another laugh, which Finnigan acknowledges before continuing.

'Here's a thing, though... What about Hitler? According to your theory, if Hitler had a clear conscience, and truly believed everything he did was for the common good of mankind, would he have gone to heaven?'

The laughter dies down.

Finnigan asks his question again.

'If what you're saying is true, did Hitler go to heaven?'

Brad believes he's already described the concept of heaven and hell as a construct of emotional memory, rather than a geographical place. However, this cartoonish idea of Hitler arguing his way into a picture-postcard heaven makes him laugh. It's childish and offensive. He finds it incredibly funny. And he no longer cares what happens next, because he's finished his talk. He'd planned a Q&A session, but he can't face any more interaction. Fuck it, he's done. Finished. It makes him happy to be finished. And because he's happy, he laughs some more. And because he's laughing, the floodgates of pure relief open up, the delight floods through his veins, and he keeps laughing.

Finnigan meant the question as a genuine enquiry. He thought it was a good question. *Will evil go unpunished in the author's version of heaven?* But it now looks like the prick upstart is laughing at him. *At him!* He doesn't like it. He's not sure what to do, but starts striding towards the stage, unbuttoning his jacket. He allows Brad to see the handle of the Walther, jutting out from his waistband. Brad can't believe this is happening. There is a man with a gun walking towards him. Finnigan is now pointing the gun directly into Brad's face. It smells like a car engine that's been burning oil. This is real. It's happening right now. Brad holds his breath, focusing on nothing but the gun barrel.

'So if I killed you now, with a clear conscience, that would be okay, would it?' Finnigan holds the gun steady, inches away from Brad's head. Holds it there as he turns to face the audience. He is in complete control. The audience don't know if the gun is real or not. It looks real, but this is still theatre, right?

'Anyone seen this man before today?'

He speaks with a calm assurance.

'Take a good look at him. This man standing before you is a disseminator of seditious ideas.'

A few people laugh.

'Ideas that threaten to undermine our security, our belief in God, and our moral fibre. And I'm here to take him in.'

'… the fuck are you doing?' whispers Brad.

He knows the gun is real.

Now it's Finnigan's turn to smile. To cover his amusement, Finnigan throws the gun into the air. It spins several times. He catches it clean, with the barrel pointing at the side of Brad's head. The gun remains motionless. The audience are motionless. Finnigan surveys the room. And as he looks at them, one by one, they stand up and begin applauding. They don't understand what they've just seen. It could be a satire on the dangers of radicalism. Or the dangers of capitalism. Or a prose poem to the future possibilities of holistic science. But it doesn't matter. Each person in the audience has their own interpretation, and they're happy with it.

They were duped into thinking the heckler was real, but he was part of the show! A brilliant piece of choreographed theatre, even down to this bizarre ending that leaves the author looking so bewildered his body refuses to function. And to the sound of applause, the gunman clamps an arm around the author's throat and drags him effortlessly from the room.

This Emergent Idea

Somewhere between being on stage and being dragged out to the street, Brad loses consciousness. He half remembers blacking out to the sound of laughter and applause, and has now woken dizzy and nauseous on a street corner with Finnigan still laughing at him.

'How was that stranglehold on you, mate? That was vicious, right? I don't know my own strength. I really don't.'

The cold air is biting into Brad's face. He's been left in a sitting position, propped against a wall like a ventriloquist's dummy. He recognises the pavement under him, slowly focussing on its quality of roughness and stain. His mouth feels bone-dry. There's a headache brewing under the surface. Too early to risk standing up, half expecting permanent damage to limbs or motor function, he twists his head sideways towards the voice and sees the gunman no more than a few feet away. Staring at him. Sniggering under his breath.

Brad turns away and lifts his hands to his neck. He breathes slowly, trying not to cough. His head is throbbing and he detects the taste of vomit. He tries to clear his bruised throat and spit away the nausea, but even this activity keeps the killer amused: sitting on his haunches, rubbing his face with both hands, trying hard not to laugh.

'Your face,' he says. 'If you could have seen your face, you'd know how funny this is.'

Finnigan stands up straight, trying to get a grip. Then looks back at Brad and the torrent of laughter begins once more as a rush of noise; he's shaking his head like he can't believe it himself. There are tear tracks on his cheeks.

Brad feels too weak to argue the point, but this boundless hilarity is getting on his nerves. He waits for the merriment to subside.

'Seriously, though, what is so fucking funny?'

'Your face!'

'What about my face?'

'Don't do it again. Don't start me off.'

'What?'

'That look when you think I'm about to kill you.'

'You almost did kill me, you fucking mentalist. It really hurt!'

Brad shouts these last words, and his voice breaks into a hoarse croak.

'I was joking,' says Finnigan lightly. 'I'm not really the anti-terror squad. It was a joke.'

'Yeah? I can't see anyone else laughing.'

It's true. They're alone on this street corner, just 50 metres from the venue.

Finnigan moves nearer to get a better look at the lad's injuries, but Brad flinches away.

'You're scared of me, aren't you?'

'Of course I'm scared of you. You've got a gun. You pulled a gun on me, then half-strangled me to death. I'd be stupid if I wasn't scared of you.'

'Good point. But you have to admit, that face you pull when you're scared? You might not be aware of it, but mate, that is proper funny.'

'And the more you mention it, the more it pisses me off. So don't rile me, okay? If I get riled I'll attack you in blind rage and you'll have to shoot me. So let's try to avoid that, yeah?'

'Really? You want a piece of me?'

'If I could stand up without feeling sick: yes, I bloody would have a piece of you, you steroid-pumped fuck-knuckle.'

Finnigan hops from foot to foot, rolling his shoulders, like a boxer warming up for sparring.

'Okay,' he says. 'Let's do it. This is go-time.'

'I said don't provoke me,' shouts Brad, croaking. 'Alright? Please! Do not provoke me. I go crazy when I'm provoked. You wouldn't like me. And I can hardly breathe. Jesus, I feel sick… Have you got some water? Or cigarettes? Please don't say you left my baccy up there. Someone's gonna have that away if it's left lying around.'

Brad pats himself down, and finds his tobacco in his jacket pocket.

'Thank God…'

He starts to roll a cigarette. His hands are shaking. He tries to style it out. He looks across at Finnigan who is suddenly lit in silhouette by a shaft of afternoon sun blazing between the buildings. It gives him the appearance of being on fire. Brad slouches back against the wall and lights up. He sees a couple walking towards them, who smile and nod in recognition from the show; but Brad doesn't acknowledge them, or signal for help. He leans there, looking drugged out. Finnigan doesn't respond to their approach either. He remains utterly unconcerned. So the friendly couple drop eye contact and steer a wide berth.

Finnigan says, 'Come on, mate, let's go.'

'I'm fine here.'

'You've got every right to be scared of me. That's good. Like you said, only stupid people have no fear.'

Brad shrugs.

'You scared of death?' asks Finnigan.

'Bit of a leading question, given the circumstances.'

Finnigan watches him smoke. 'First cigarette after a near-death experience always tastes the best.'

Brad ignores him.

'So answer my question. Are you scared of death?'

'Depends how far away it is.'

'Yeah?'

'At one point back there I was scared, but I kind of accepted it.'

'Go on.'

'I could smell the gun. I had the impression it had been fired. Recently.'

'Listen to the detective.'

'You asked.'

'So... Are you scared of death?'

'You mean *my* death. You're asking me if I'm scared of dying.'

'Are you?'

'What are you driving at?'

'Answer the question.'

'Okay, it depends how much it's going to hurt. I'm scared of the *pain* of death... As for the event itself, I like to think I have that sorted. So in answer to your question, I'm more scared of physical pain than physical non-existence.'

Brad doesn't think he's being threatened, but there's something inevitable and sneaky about death. He looks away from Finnigan to watch his surroundings zoom into sharp focus: between the tops of the buildings he sees the pale blue sky and scudding clouds, swooping birds in formation; the buildings themselves alternatively lost in shadow or blazing silver and gold in the distant winter sun. Multi-storey, post-war concrete and steel, rows of faceless windows; all the petty parochial history these rooms have seen, so important at the time.

Slow verbs. That's what Bohm called this apparent permanence of cities and buildings. Brad tries to imagine not existing. He can't quite do it. His imagination can't imagine itself not existing.

According to the mechanistic paradigm, everything will eventually be destroyed and ruined. It's the second law of thermodynamics: if you buy an old car it will break down, but if you buy a new car it will break down, because *everything* is destined to break and die. He was never able to come to terms with it, because something exists within us all that can never be guessed at by the sum of our parts. The clues are there. He's researched it, and there are systems that reverse this law of destruction.

He's fully aware this compulsive search for something lasting might be an evolutionary fail-safe; an inherited attitude to stop the human race from running crazy with the prospect of its own godless demise. But within the definition of emergent systems he's convinced that human life is that *chaos of simple events* and our shared consciousness is the *emerging higher-level order* – although the only way to prove this idea would be to die and send messages back from beyond the veil. But what form would the messages take, and who would believe them?

Finnigan's voice cuts through his melancholic reverie.

'So you've got the death experience under control, have you?

You'll have to tell me about it one day; I'm very interested. Maybe another time, eh?'

Brad can see the gunman is taking the piss; and right there he makes a decision to never talk about his ideas in public again. They're too paradoxical. This unswerving belief in the evolution of collective sentience is matched only by his conviction that God does not exist, but arguing this point still sounds like he's looking for religion. *A universe simple enough to be understood is too simple to produce a mind capable of understanding it...*

Brad can't tell what Finnigan is thinking. All trace of mania has drained away, leaving a rumpled sort of gentleness.

'If you're ready, there is one thing I need you to do.'

Finnigan helps Brad into a walking position. Brad feels the strength of his hands, and knows the futility of struggling.

'What do you want me to do?'

'A simple little favour.'

Brad is unsteady on his feet but feels assured that he'll live, for the time being. The uncertainty was worth it for this sense of reprieve.

'You need a lift somewhere?' asks Finnigan.

'No, I've got my car.'

'Where'd you park?'

'Just over the road there, in that parking bay...'

Finnigan pats him down, looking for his car keys. He finds them, and dangles them in front of Brad's face.

'I need to take your motor.'

'Is that all you wanted?'

'Maybe it was.'

'Thing is, it's not my car. It's my girlfriend's.'

'And...?'

'Once she finds out I've given it away... Christ! We've been arguing recently, and...'

'I'm only gonna borrow it.'

'Suppose I don't tell you which one it is?'

Finnigan walks Brad across the road.

'One of these?'

Brad shrugs.

Finnigan walks along the row of cars, pressing the button on the key fob. Eventually a little white Nissan bleeps in reply, indicators flashing.

'Of all the things still working on that bloody car,' says Brad.

Finnigan turns round to throw Brad a different set of keys. He misses the catch, picks them up from the road.

'A BMW? You're swapping my girlfriend's piece of crap Nissan for a BMW?'

'Needs must, mate. Do me this favour, yeah?'

'Have I got a choice?'

'No. And another thing. You don't have to, but it might help…'

'What?'

'Torch it.'

'Your car?'

'Seriously. Torch it.'

'Why?'

'Fingerprints. You'll find it over there, in that car park.'

With that, Finnigan has no further thought for the present situation.

Brad shouts, 'Hey… What was your interest in my show anyway?'

Finnigan turns back, confrontational. 'What…? Because I work with my hands, you don't expect me to appreciate a bit of theatre?'

The way he says *work with my hands* gives Brad the fear again.

'I'm just asking… why were you there?'

'That's something I need to find out,' says Finnigan vaguely.

Then he turns to go. He wants to be away from here.

Now the obvious danger has passed, there seems so much left unsaid. Brad shouts after him again.

'Also… I mean, what's your name?'

Finnigan laughs.

'Nice try, mate. Nice try. I'll be in touch.'

Brad can't quantify the level of danger he was in, but as Finnigan steps into Jane's car and drives away, he feels weak from the tension. The encounter has ended almost as abruptly as it began. He decides he doesn't need another cigarette. He might even give up. He wearily ambles back to the venue.

The audience has left, and the venue organiser is setting up for the next reading. Someone has gathered Brad's belongings into a neat pile by the door. Then the organiser sees Brad and breaks into a satisfied grin.

'Great show, Bradley, great show. So visceral. So real!'

'You have no idea,' mutters Brad.

'You had us all guessing at the end, wondering where it was going to turn. And you sold a few books as well. There was a lot of interest. Where were you?'

'Any chance of a cup of coffee, do you think?'

'Seriously, where did you go? I've got another show to prepare for, and—'

'Yeah, I know. And thanks for collecting my stuff.'

The venue organiser sends one of his helpers to find Brad some coffee.

'You can't just disappear like that, Bradley, you really can't. And the stunt with the gun? I know the audience liked it, but really... It's a *literary* festival! You can't charge off-piste like that and expect me to be completely happy about it.'

'It was... It was unrehearsed.'

'I'm not denying the audience liked it, but to just disappear like that? I had to field all the enquiries myself.'

Brad isn't in the mood for this, but the organiser is going to have his say.

'I had to take the money for you, for the books. No doubt you would have sold more if you'd actually been here in person. We thought you'd at least come back for a curtain call, you and your friend. I thought he was very good. Played the part perfectly, if a little aggressive for this kind of an event. But I took the money for you, for the books – five copies – so I owe you twenty-five pounds.'

He continues in this vein, and Brad can hardly concentrate. He waits for his coffee, just wanting the organiser to leave him alone. He needs to collect his kit, and his thoughts. Find somewhere quiet. Make some notes. He needs to phone Jane… That makes him anxious, having to explain why he's just given her car away.

Half an hour later, Brad is in the car park, playing the same trick with the key fob – waiting for the madman's car to reveal itself, which it does: a silver-grey 7 Series Beemer. Looks new. Clean. Why swap this for a crappy Nissan? Then he remembers what the man said about fingerprints. It's reasonable to assume the car's been used as a getaway vehicle for some nefarious deed. Does anyone use that phrase anymore? *The getaway car!* He shakes his head. At least it'll get him home, and in some style. He opens it up. It looks new but doesn't have that new-car smell; more like cigarettes and fish supper. He finds some sweaty joggers on the floor along with a Gas Board jacket. Nothing makes sense. He doesn't care. Throws his stuff on the back seat and climbs in.

He's looking forward to driving home, and foolishly wonders if he could keep the car, because maybe it's off-the-radar, registered to some bloke long-dead. Or he could report the incident, and in return for his honesty keep the car as a spoil of war. He shakes his head. *Spoil of war? You're not starring in a bloody pirate film, mate…*

It's naïve to assume he'll keep the car forever; but perhaps he can keep it until Jane's is recovered. He still needs to explain it to her. Fact is, he stole her car and then gave it away. Difficult to pretty-up a story like that. However it's told, he remains complicit.

What the fuck am I doing? How many people were at the gig? Thirty, and five books sold. This is not going to win the revolution. He decides to cancel the rest of the book readings and embark on another plan. If only something could propel him into notoriety, they'd all be offering him book deals. The TV chefs and reality stars: they always have book deals. Has the world gone mad? Is it not bad enough we suffer them on the box, without letting them invade the bookshops?

Even in his little independent bookshop back in Brighton, they bow to the pressure of selling units of celebrity product every Christmas. Is it a reaction to godlessness? Is the adoration of fame a surrogate-religion? And what are they famous for? For being famous! Like a snake eating its own tail, and here we are *worshipping* them. He sighs with incomprehension. But sitting here is getting him nowhere. He adjusts the driving seat and the mirrors. The engine turns over effortlessly, with a suggestion of the power that the car is capable of. He rolls out of the car park onto a one-way high street and starts looking for the ring road, for the journey home.

The mind is a process, not an object.

He should have explained this. When you cut a brain open, it looks like a dense and heavy piece of kit. But zoom in deep, right down to quantum level, to a scale where the nature of atoms is revealed, and it becomes a cathedral of light: a vast space in which matter exists as an energy matrix. This is where the memories are stored, in the space between the atoms; where experience becomes encoded, as the bio-photons sparkle with light, creating ripple patterns of intense complexity; a repository of dreams, of imagination, of memory, unbound by the limitations of physical matter, an ever-changing flow of electrical-information; and existing, according to quantum definition, beyond time and space.

He's enjoying the drive.

He'd love to own a car like this. To have the money necessary to keep it tip-top, never worrying about your ride breaking down. That's the best way to stay ahead of entropy. By being rich. And what better way to express the capitalist dream than being *pointlessly* rich?

The late Walter Benjamin (a little known German philosopher) defines capitalism as a religion of destruction, devouring everything in its path, from the lives of wage-slaves to natural resources, chasing wealth for the sake of wealth, chasing the money in the vain hope it might protect us. And we're so stuck in this outlook. The built-in obsolescence, the craving to stay young; consume or die. That's why his book is so important, describing a wider perspective: if the consciousness continues beyond the veil, there's no need to fear death, thus putting an end to our capitalist cravings...

Brad makes a mental note to find out how these dead German philosophers always manage to get published, because he has tried the traditional route with *Death and Physics*. Just once. It was a meeting with a friend of a friend publisher, who explained it was *impossible* to get weird science published without a whacky angle or *a personal story* attached to the material – implying Brad would have to hitch-hike around the world on a journey of discovery or some such before anyone would even touch his book.

The publisher described how even Stephen Hawking's recent book was a difficult sell. Brad started to explain how his own book was completely different, based on the Deterministic Interpretation, the Holographic Universe etc, whereas Hawking was an advocate of Copenhagen Interpretation. And the publisher just lost it, stood up in the middle of their meeting and shouted, *Are you trying to outdo Hawking?*

Brad had to beg the man to sit back down – he actually wrestled him back into his chair – in the desperate hope of being understood, aching for recognition…

Sounds funny now.

He must see Jane. She'll be back in Brighton later tonight. He misses her. He misses her like… Like a Vegan misses honey… Like pollen misses the bee… Like a naked body misses touch. Whatever. He craves her warmth; the security of lying in her arms. Quietly. There's too much to be said, and he shudders at the expectation of an in-depth about his life choices. They have their entire lives to talk. What he needs now is blissful silence; such an easy favour to bestow.

An hour-and-a-half later he's passing Toddington Services on the M1. Not too far from the M25 turn-off, which means he's almost halfway home. And on the hard shoulder he spies a couple of skulking police cars. It's lucky he spots them because he was driving way too fast – it's so easy to race a quality motor without noticing. He drops his speed to legal requirements, and smiles at the coppers as they attend to the business of stopping innocent people in fast cars from enjoying themselves.

Brad knows nothing about the ANPR network in Britain. He wouldn't be able to tell you what the acronym stands for. He'd probably deny the functionality of automatic number plate recognition technology even if it were explained to him, claiming it was an urban myth to scare drivers into paying their road tax. But the national ANPR data centre is fed from hundreds of thousands of cameras and deals with 50 million reads per day; reads which are checked against lists from the police national computer – lists of vehicles the police are interested in. There are also mobile number plate recognition systems in traffic-intercept cars, so any vehicle of interest will be flagged up on the inboard computer screen, and can be tracked around the country in close to real time.

Brad sees one of the policemen holding what looks like a speed camera. He laughs about how ironic it would be if his car were stopped for no tax. It amuses him so much he doesn't see these officers of the law frantically conferring before running back to their vehicles and heading after him in distant pursuit. He's unaware that a firearm unit is now being mobilised: a team of gym-hardened men with the authority to pick up weapons and take appropriate action. They train all day for moments like this.

So half-an-hour later, as he's rounding the M25 and becomes aware of them flashing their blues in stroboscopic unison, he actually slows down to let them past, feeling sorry for the hapless chump who's about to get busted...

Back on the Road

Finnigan is less confident than he dares to admit as he drives away. His enthusiasm for confrontation is on the wane. It's only a matter of time before the car he's driving is reported as stolen, and he's still no wiser regarding his predicament. So he drives like a tourist, slow and wide-eyed, trying to pose a minimal threat to other road users. He heads for the ring road, for the outskirts of town, avoiding the motorways, and follows the smaller roads into the countryside. Not that he could encourage any proper speed from this borrowed motor even if he wanted to. It's a laborious drive, but homely with its clunky gearbox and soft brakes. He likes the dice hanging in the windscreen, though – it's kitsch, and in the end it all comes down to chance.

He drives for 30 or 40 minutes in an aimless direction: hills, cows, muddy roads, village crossroads, naked trees, expanses of meadow, pedestrians with dogs, cyclists with yellow waterproofs and skinny tyres. There is much to see, but the afternoon is painted long and grey, and turning to rain. Soon enough these satellite towns and hamlets become a story he no longer cares to read. On a sudden impulse he heads into the car park of a random country pub, finds a secluded corner and turns the engine off. He lowers the seat back and rests for a while to consider his options.

Again he empties his pockets looking for clues. There are no surprises. He turns the Walther over in his hands. The incident with the author makes him smile. He didn't understand everything the bloke said; but he'd like to read a copy of his book one day, to see if it made any more sense than his talk. He slides the handgun under the driving seat, cracks the window open for an inch of fresh air, and closes his eyes.

He can visualise the perfect functioning of his body even in the smallest of movements. The blood, bone and muscle, how it all fits neatly together, but he can't clarify his thoughts. It's a problem he needs to address. But he has the impression that events will resolve themselves. He feels looked after. It's a strange one, because normally his sense of security is due entirely to physical prowess and a threat of menace; whereas this current sense of confidence is like innate certainty.

He feels a sense of coherence. The assurance of a pattern unfolding. He can't capture it. He tries to gauge what it is, and sees shapes forming, but they're out of focus and ephemeral. Like trying to recall the words to a song you've once heard in a dream. He needs to reboot. Restore his factory settings. He needs something to help drown out the incomprehension.

The car has a radio-CD player. He tries the radio. The stations are pre-set; he presses the buttons, trying each one in turn. Too much babble. He considers playing a CD. He looks in the door pockets and glove box, and finds a choice of one. A pirate copy of something: the handwritten dedication reads, *Raindogs. For Jane x.*

It seems appropriate, because the afternoon has turned to persistent rain. So he loads it and turns up the volume. The music is nothing he can recognise: angular rhythms and discordancy. But it sits well with his mood. It has edge and attitude, and progresses stridently enough to override the turbulence in his mind. Then the voice comes in, like whisky on warm gravel, like a salty seadog spilling his gourd: years from home, miles from hope, the wreckers and the wretched, playing at love and adventure like a hand of cards while the whole world turns and we turn with it, stamp our feet, clap our hands...

The songs are continuous and abstract, connected to reality by the authority of the voice. Finnigan pushes back in the driving seat, stretches his legs out by the sides of the pedals. Tries to find a position of compromised comfort, knowing he can't maintain this vigilant wakefulness. The music is something he can surrender to; its stride should help to quieten his own.

Finnigan is asleep to the applause of the rain on the car roof and the roar of the singer's voice. The song lyrics plant ideas in his dreams, its chorus distorting into a new mantra: *you can always find a million in a shovel load of coal...*

He's dreaming in vivid cartoon colour, holding a piece of coal in each hand, clenching his fists. His arms are naked, the veins and sinews standing out, distorting tattooed images of anchors, guns, bleeding hearts and bluebirds. The dream weaves a comic-book story featuring the iconic Superman performing a feat of strength by producing diamonds from coal. Finnigan's dream-self emulates this trick, crushing the coal into a diamond lattice. His hands simulate the weight of millennia pressing down on ancient buried forest. The coal cracks and splinters, its carcinogenic dust falling from his fingers. He perseveres through the pain until the sweat and blood drop to the floor, mixing with the black dust.

It's a dream prompted by a misheard and random song lyric. In some later waking moment its memory will rise vivid in his awareness, and appear prescient. On such tenuous threads can articles of faith become written. Dream lucidity argues the coal-crushing feat is impossible, therefore dream logic deduces it must be a coded message. His determination is an omen: he will squeeze the coal until his fingers bleed and his skin tears to show signs of stigmata. He sees through the cells of his body, and from within the blood and dirt of his hand shines a crystal lattice of invisible strength, the diamond's radiant strength derived from inner purity.

Two slender hours of sleep roll past like days. He awakes calmer in thought, to an obsidian black night. There are gaps in his memory but he assumes these will heal as any physical scar will heal. He steps out of the car to stretch. Behind the pub, the slow rise of a tall hill, soft with turf and punctured with craggy outcrops of grey rock. He walks towards it. Skirts around the back fence of the disused beer garden and begins to climb.

He enjoys the effort of conquering the incline, and once he reaches the higher ground, he can see it gives way to a long stretch of moorland. As the view widens so do his perceptions. It feels like an alien landscape, being the antithesis of urban sprawl, where he would never be at the mercy of his darker thoughts; a place where he is larger than other people, and judged by a talent to intimidate. There is no threat in the urban world because it's populated by inferior beings. But out here on the empty, dark hill, the shadows of his memory have no buffer zone.

It's not the presence of God we find in these desolate places, but the knowledge of our insignificance. Lesser men would presume the existence of God to make sense of their frailty. Religion was invented to give mortality a reason and create a meaningful context, because the blind earth will soak up our death in the blink of an atom.

But there is a presence here, in this isolated place; and its vast loneliness is somehow consoling to Finnigan. The solitude is clearing his mind, the wind blowing through the spaces in his thoughts. He has nothing left to rely on but his instinct. There is a power here, infinitely stronger than himself; and he sets his intention to survive its overwhelming indifference.

He heads back to the car park. He needs to move, to stay ahead of the unknown. The little car starts straight away. He bounces it over the potholes and out onto the road. Following instinct, he turns left. Heading south.

It's a blustery night and the car lurches spasmodically with the wind. He sees tarmac and distant darkness. Giant pylonic men hold electricity cables in their rusting steel arms. The side of the road is home to rabbits and weasely mammals, nightcrawlers and arthropods, all fighting for survival. Weedy shrubs of thorn and bramble lay discarded from God's garden and scrabble for a foothold among the dirt grass and the fly-tip refuse.

The road widens into a two-lane, and juggernaut lorries capture him in their invisible slipstream, trying to lift him towards death. Faster cars race past, headlights making the sparse trees dance, lighting up the empty landscape before his eyes readjust to the moonlit shadows.

As he hits the motorway the lights become bright and plentiful. The road is wide, and signed for London. That's where he's going. He arrived here by random logic. Even now he doesn't recognise it as the road home, a journey he's made a thousand times before. He assumes he's being guided. And following this rationale he is led by twists and turns, via green lights and one-way streets towards the north of the city: dense urban conurbations with road junctions that break out into nasty rashes of ugly shops and pubs. Then private brick houses, rows of flats, schools and empty playgrounds; and night buses that illuminate the pallor of tired faces. Quiet now, with sparse pedestrian activity...

Without planning to, he drives the car into a side street and parks up. Leaves it there. He walks down a long road of blighted trees, tall brick houses cut into flats. He spies on occasional lit windows, revealing safety behind deadlocked doors. Then he comes to a row of closed shops with a flashing green light. Investigating, he finds himself outside a late-night mini-cab office. He presses a button on the speaker-phone.

'Where you going to mate?' asks the metal box.

'I need a drink.'

'Don't we all. What destination?'

'Destination?' He rolls the word over in his mind.

'Where are you going to?'

Finnigan has no idea where he's going to, but a place name comes into his mind and he's given no reason to distrust it.

'The Beggar,' he says.

'The Beggar? What is that? A pub?'

'That's it.'

'Whereabouts? What area?'

Finnigan hesitates, and hears the controller ask his drivers for information. A minute later he comes back with, 'You talking about The Beggar on King's Cross Way?'

'Yeah, that sounds right.'

'Then you're lucky Vik's on. He knows where it is. Be right with you. Call it twenty quid?'

Vikram is a burly Indian bloke, middle-aged, in a tatty sheepskin driving coat, roll-up in his mouth.

'This way, mate,' he says.

Finnigan follows him to a non-descript four-door, and climbs in up front.

'So, The Beggar on King's Cross Way, yeah?'

'Yeah, that'll do.'

They've only been driving for a couple of minutes when Finnigan sees the picture. How could he have missed it? It's decorated with multi-coloured fairy lights, powered from the cigarette lighter socket.

A 3D colour postcard of a skinny long-haired man, dressed in a white robe; his arms are outstretched, his oversized heart shining through his chest cavity.

'Who's that?'

'Only the Son of God, mate,' replies the driver. 'We're not all Muslims, y'know.'

'The Son of God?'

'It's Jesus, innit? You winding me up?'

He remembers this from the dream: the stigmata. The Son of God has these same wounds on his hands. He has light shining from his head and his heart.

Without knowing why, Finnigan says, 'But aren't we all sons of god?'

Vikram doesn't warm to this topic of conversation.

He says, 'Look, mate, do you want this ride or not?'

'To The Beggar?'

'To The Beggar, that's right.'

'Yes.'

'Okay. So leave it with the ethnic stuff, yeah? Some of us happen to fucking believe in Jesus, okay? It's only there for good luck; let's not chance it.'

'Right.'

'Right. Let's find this fucking pub already.'

They drive in silence, but the glowing light of Jesus's heart continues to make Finnigan smile. It's a meaningless coincidence, but it gives him the courage to assume he's moving in the right direction. The pattern that will reveal itself, like a diamond lattice; like a trail of coloured sand leading to the heart of the mystery.

The Beggar is a members-only drinking club. It stands opposite a railway bridge, near a row of arches and industrial units. Wind whistles through the overhead wires of the railway line. The old pub sign *The Blind Beggar* still hangs outside the premises; creaking like a stretching gallows rope. Underneath this, a *Welcome* sign remains in place, but it's no longer an invitation.

The window shutters are closed, as an assumption of class and privacy, and the entire building is painted a uniform matt black.

Finnigan pays the cabbie more than necessary, and steps into the night. The cold wind blows; he feels the skin shrinking and tightening around his skull. He has no idea why he's here.

He waits for the cab to leave before rapping on the door; looks up at the security camera and grins. The door slowly opens, revealing a huge man in a black overcoat. He has a boxer's nose, a 1950s crew cut, and he makes slow methodical progress like a giant on ketamine. He's holding a newspaper, which he folds and places on the desk behind him. Then he turns back to the doorway, and studies this intruder.

Finnigan tenses.

The doorman gives a smile of recognition.

'Finnigan!' he says, quietly surprised.

Finnigan looks behind him. There's no one else there.

The pugilist repeats himself. 'Finnigan! The fuck brings you here?'

The doorman has a face from Finnigan's past. He towers in the hallway, and moves forward to wrap Finnigan up in a manly embrace. The man-hug turns into a subtle pat down. Finnigan allows this to happen. Then the doorman steps back, and once more blocks the hallway.

'Can't allow the shooter, though. House rules. No hardware. It'll be safe with me.' He nods and winks as he says this. Finnigan allows the Walther to be taken from him. It looks like a toy in the doorman's hands; appraises its balance and action. 'Nice piece! Must be ex-army. Old-school. Special Service issue, yeah?' He releases the clip, and hides the weaponry on a shelf under his desk. He turns back and welcomes Finnigan in with an imperceptible gesture. Walks in front of him down the small hallway painted black and blood red, and leads him towards the inner door.

Finnigan allows this information to settle. His name is *Finnigan*. He has been recognised and accepted. A diamond shines brightly in his mind. He appears to be starring in a film that is writing itself in real time.

The Whole Truth, Etc.

There's a joke that goes: *Did you hear about the coke-head who got arrested? The police let him go because he wouldn't stop helping them with their enquiries.* Brad will be reminded of this during his own police interview. After being left alone for a couple of hours with nothing but police-cell graffiti for company (*Terry sez good luck lol*), he will realise an inability to stop talking. He'll experience a mental free-fall, made so by shock, low blood sugar, and by the unique situation of talking to the police under guilt-free conditions. In days to come, he will spontaneously laugh at the memory of it. At the time however...

The circumstances of his arrest were film-trailer vivid. Seamlessly crowded onto the hard shoulder by three squad cars; and officers with guns – *with fucking guns* – surrounded him. He followed their instructions, emerged slowly from the getaway vehicle with hands behind his head, allowed them to manhandle him to the tarmac and cuff him. His face pressed into the road surface, a knee in the small of his back while being officially cautioned. It was probably the caution speech that made this event the most surreal, because it's a speech everyone knows from watching cop shows and has lost all power of meaning. But whispered into your shell-like by paramilitary lawmen, with the world lit by motorway traffic racing past your head, and the reds and blues flashing on the cold road surface... This is real: *You do not have to say anything, but it may harm your defence...*

Etc.

It left Brad literally pleading, 'No, I want to say something, man. Seriously, let me talk...'

He called his arresting officer *man!*

But they didn't want him to talk.

They wanted him to shut the fuck up.

They wanted to throw him into their car and drive him away.

So he tried not to talk, and he tried not to say *fuck*, as they drove him back up North.

'You're driving me back up North? You fucking fuckers!'

'Shut the fuck up!'

After the obligatory two hours in a holding cell, he's led into an interview room. The attending officers introduce themselves as Detective Sergeant Johns, who sits across from him with nonchalant propriety, and Detective Constable Vincent, a surly female subordinate who hovers near the door, as if anticipating the suspect making a sudden bid for freedom.

The entire procedure is being filmed and recorded; and Brad boldly resists the offer to have a lawyer present because (paraphrasing his defence): *This is a bullshit mistake, and you'll soon realise it's me who's the victim here! I mean, what am I even being charged with…?*

And so on.

Brad made the assumption that having legal representation would only delay matters, and thus delay returning home. He also knows that staying calm would help to get things done, yet he remains on his high-and-mighty. He remains the belligerent victim until he's shown the disclosure document: that takes the wind out of his sails; seeing photographs of a man recently murdered. Throws the situation into a clear focus. Makes him feel quite faint. And although his status isn't being openly discussed, it's this impromptu giddy fit that almost certainly relegates him from suspect to witness.

Brad doesn't have a point of reference for true-life murder apart from browsing reference books on warfare. It's a stage that boys go through: a fascination for photographic evidence of dead people. Vietnam. Auschwitz. Rwanda… Pre-internet, this experience was a special library trip: hunting down graphic, photo-reportage evidence of real-life death. So the collection of colour prints on the table shouldn't shock him; it's just one more dead person: wizened, blood stained and frozen in pain.

It's not the images that distress him so much, it's the realisation of having been in close contact with the alleged perpetrator. Then he reads the name printed on the accompanying notes. Eugene 'Gene' Polonski. There's a moment before it hits him. Like when you hit your thumb with a hammer – that millisecond before you feel the pain, before you know how much trouble you're in.

Brad pushes his chair away from the table, leans back with eyes closed and breathes out. Needing time to think. This man Polonski should have been at his book reading. Now he's dead. Presumably the man who killed him took his place. It leaves Brad with the certainty he's somehow complicit, and he becomes paranoid this fact is written on his face. It's this implication that precipitates the nausea, this fear of his certain involvement.

He looks across to DS Johns. 'Why are you showing me this?'

Johns is slowly collecting the prints together, studying them as he does.

'To give you some insight into the man we're dealing with. See the close grouping of wounds to the chest, and one in the head…? Professional work. But then we have a report that the car, the one you were driving, was seen racing away from the murder scene, causing undue attention… So we remain unclear regarding the type of person we're dealing with.'

'But you can't think it's got anything to do with me?'

'As of now, we're gathering information. That's why you're going to be helpful. That's why you're going to answer our questions without any more histrionics. We need to know why you were driving the car; we need a description of the man who gave you the car, because presumably there was some exchange? We need a full breakdown of events…'

As Johns reels off a list of all the information he wants, Brad realises they've reached an understanding. Now that he's stopped bleating on about his supposed innocence, he realises they assumed he was innocent all along. The air around him clears; and DC Vincent is sent to fetch a sugary brew, to revive him – 'and not because she's a woman, but because she's the closest to the door'.

Johns points this out with some clumsy flirtation in Vincent's direction. Brad doesn't react to the laddish humour. He doesn't react to anything. Stares at the empty table regaining composure, while Johns stares at him. Looking for signs.

Brad is fine-tuning his attitude. *They haven't asked me about the victim. They haven't asked me if I know the victim – which I don't. And they haven't asked me if I've heard of him, which actually I have… But unless they ask me specifically if I recognise his name then I know nothing; I do actually know nothing…*

Finally he looks up and says, 'I'm going to tell you everything I know. Sorry if I was shouting earlier. I didn't realise what this was about. It's been a long day; but now I know how important it is… Having seen the evidence, the photographs, I'll tell you everything. Has she gone for some tea did you say…? Yeah, let me have some tea; I'm still a little shaky from the… That was a shock, the photographs. I mean, I was only up in Leicester for a book reading, a literary event; that's where it all started, completely random, can't understand it. I was being heckled by this man, presumably the man you're looking for. And the reading was going well – a bit under-rehearsed, but you need to get the material in front of an audience before you can begin to judge it, so for the first few gigs you're not really selling the material so much as internalising the response to it…'

And so begins his free-fall. A free-form exposition of events: energetic, tangential, mostly pointless, but constant. Sipping the tea as punctuation, leaving no room for interruption, channelling all his energies into manic helpfulness to distract himself from the knowledge that he knew the dead man's name. He gives them as detailed a description of Finnigan as he can muster, from the cut of his suit and the warmth of his hands to the superiority of his car. It's all going very well. His complicity is at zero percent probability. He actually begins to enjoy the attention.

Then Johns turns the spotlight on the details of Brad's book reading event, the place where Finnigan first appeared. And with Brad's consent he asks for his belongings to be brought to the interview room. The video recording has been paused. It's all looking quite informal. He allows Brad to find a copy of the book. Johns takes it, turns it over in his hands as if appraising the quality of the printing.

'Right… You're in Leicester for an event to promote this…?'

He waves the book in the air. Studies it again, as if he can't quite place the meaning or the genre.

'What is it...?' he says. '*Death and Physics...?*'

Suddenly Brad isn't sure if he has the energy to explain the reasons behind his book. Is it even possible to discuss existentialism with a policeman without sounding sarcastic? He gestures his reluctance to get into it, says, 'Ah, fucking hell, man, where do I even begin?'

'Mind the language, lad,' says Johns, nodding in Vincent's direction, because she's a delicate flower whose sensibilities must be protected.

'Yeah, sorry...'

He continues as best he can.

'It's kind of a revolutionary manual, a seditious treatise, if you will...'

Brad laughs at this pretentious summary of his book; a laugh misinterpreted by the brick-house Vincent, who steps up and screams in his face, 'Exactly what is the joke, Mr Holmeson?'

It's the first time she's spoken to him directly.

'Thank you, DC Vincent, thank you...' says Johns, waving her back to a position of servility. He throws a look at Brad as if to say, *How can any man be expected to fully understand the emotional boiling pot that is the female of our species?*

There's a studied scruffiness about Johns; he's seen what life has to offer, and has chosen a path of effortless mediocrity and minimum input. But Brad's grateful he's keeping Vincent under control; she could do some damage if left to run feral.

Are they winding him up by playing this nonchalant-cop, angry-cop routine? Practicing their moves? Whatever game they're into, he needs to make a greater effort to be understood.

'You know the way Zen monks would paint themselves looking miserable in self-portraits? Exaggerating their condition to undermine it? The first truth of Buddhism is that *all life is suffering*, so they'd portray themselves looking as depressed as possible, but actually they were being satirical...?'

'Is that what you're doing? Being satirical? Causing a stir? Exposing the folly of those in authority...? I assume you're disseminating this material yourself?'

'I'm not an agitator, if that's what you think. I'm not one of those anarchist types...'

'What are you, then?' screams DC Vincent, out of nowhere. This double act they're playing is really kicking in.

'I'm an Existentialist!' shouts Brad, right back at her.

'A what?' She takes a step nearer and Brad flinches, rushing to explain himself.

'There is no God, and therefore no given meaning for life, yet we spend our lives looking for meaning. Right? That's Existentialism! We look for meaning in a life with no meaning. It's absurd. Life. Life is absurd.'

Johns begins to look genuinely interested.

'So the book is an experiment in content and form,' continues Brad. 'I self-publish, and I distribute... and I encourage readers to contact me, to do the social-media thing, y'know...?'

'And *has* anyone contacted you?'

'Nothing! Apart from a few complaints from the bookshops I left copies in...'

Brad rubs his face in his hands. His standard reason is that he's chasing a literary adventure based on existential hypotheses. But as in all talent shows, every contestant has a back-story.

'I sometimes get depressed...'

'Don't we all?'

'No, I mean really... beyond-all-reason depressed.'

Johns senses a new thread of honesty uncontaminated by attitude. He's finally breaking the lad down.

'And what have you got to be depressed about?'

'The lack of inherent permanence in life, I suppose...'

'Go on...'

Brad can't believe he's attempting this level of candour.

'Evolution has granted us an exceptional sense of self-awareness, but housed in a system that will break down and die. We're all going to die! Resulting in our most evolved aspect – our mind-stuff and our thoughts – being destroyed and lost. Making sentience utterly pointless. After all we go through to become caring, informed adults, trying to keep our shit together. All the experiences we share and cherish. Everything wiped out in the blink of an eye. We're good people; we deserve better...'

Brad wouldn't say this if it wasn't true.

'Sounds like you're looking for religion.'

'I know it does. But I'm not. I'm looking for certainty, for something I can prove. So that's what the book is – an attempt to define a new paradigm that demonstrates a possible permanence of consciousness.'

Johns maintains eye contact, and listens attentively as Brad goes into the details of his quest from depression to the cure: seeking a proof, which is tied up in brain theory, bio-photons and neural resonance. Johns isn't sure if he's following every turn, because the need to undermine Copenhagen Interpretation is beyond his remit. But he did ask. And halfway through a brief history of holograms (as the cornerstone of the Holonomic Brain Theory), he's heard enough.

'Alright! Let's fast-forward to the money shot. You've created a paradigm that apparently demonstrates how the consciousness will continue to function after the death of the physical body. Okay! What next. What are you hoping to achieve?'

Brad is surprised the man has to ask. Isn't it obvious?

He says, 'It's a scientific theory that removes the fear of death!'

He blurts this out like he's holding a coveted key to world peace. There is no question in his mind regarding the importance of this discovery. He wants to say it's the salvation of the human race. But he doesn't, because surely this is implied?

DS Johns doesn't share Brad's enthusiasm. He doesn't have a breakthrough moment. He doesn't experience what the Japanese call *sartori*. Instead he pulls a puzzled face. It's a very theatrical manoeuvre. And he waits for Brad to continue, and dig himself deeper.

Brad tries to put his argument into an easier context. He says, 'Have you heard about the near death experience?'

Johns says, 'You mean like after a heart attack? When people claim to remember the experience of being clinically dead?'

'That's it! And they all have the *same* experience. Positive emotions, unconditional love... Acceptance by a greater power, yeah? That's what I'm describing in my book! This so-called higher power these near dead people experience isn't God, it's loads and loads of other dead people. Existing beyond the physical plane. Existing as thoughts. Consciousness. It's the collective consciousness of everyone dead, existing on a different frequency...'

Johns isn't swayed by Brad's high-pitched enthusiasm. He says, 'It doesn't work though.'

'What doesn't work?'

'Your book! I mean, the science of it might be mathematically perfect, but your book doesn't work.'

Brad begins to panic. He's tired. But he wants to make himself understood. He speaks very slowly, trying not to sound patronising.

'If science proves that consciousness exists beyond death, it *removes the fear of death*. Don't you see? Fear of dying is the main cause of every human problem.'

'Your book doesn't work because it hasn't worked on you.'

'Why would you say that?'

'People who have a near death experience claim they return to life with a relaxed inner-peace, and a new kind of wisdom. And, being honest, looking at you, I don't see it.'

This statement hits Brad hard, because he knows it's true.

Johns continues, 'I once read somewhere there's a strong statistical probability of alien life existing in the universe, but it doesn't matter how many books I read about it, I'm not going to believe until I experience it first hand. Do you get my drift?'

Johns ends the interview looking disinterested, but in reality he's transfixed. This is one of the reasons he became a protector of the peace: to study and then destroy the weirdness in other people's brains. He'll be putting it down in his report. *Get a job. Contribute to the economy. Pay your fucking taxes...*

Such is the empathy that Brad has inspired in the man.

'DC Vincent,' shouts Johns. 'I think we're done here. We'll need to sort out some transport for Mr Holmeson. Get him home.'

Brad says, 'What transport are we talking about?'

'Rail warrant,' explains Johns. 'One-way ticket. Token of my generosity.'

And he walks out.

Vincent follows him.

Brad is alone with his thoughts. His mission has been blown out of the water. His book doesn't work. It isn't ever going to work. He should be relieved. He can draw a line in the sand; burn every last copy. Give it all up, and go back to being normal. He can't go back to being normal. But there's a shadow lurking in the periphery, a creeping fear that something will draw him back in... It takes a few moments to remember what it is. When Johns asked him, *Has anyone contacted you?* Brad hit a blank at the time. Now he remembers with a sickening thud: the undertakers! Those bloody undertakers contacted him.

There's something happening here and he doesn't know what it is.

As David Bohm might say, *Beyond all the politics and commerce, there remains a mystery to be defined.*

He picks up his bag, walks towards the door. Towards the dawn train. It's a new day, he's a free man, but he's up to the gills in this.

Lizard Skin

The doorman has given Finnigan his name back; but like a ship-wrecked man, it's the recognition of finally being rescued that panics him: the realisation of how deep he was lost. He grabs the doorman by the arm, hard enough to stop him dead in his tracks. The doorman stares at Finnigan's hand, observing this reckless breach of etiquette. Finnigan lets go, and apologises.

'No offense, but I need a favour. Something you need to tell me…'

'And what would that be?'

'How do you know who I am?'

'Everyone knows who you are, Finnigan.'

The doorman speaks softly and surely, but his words don't help. He peers into Finnigan's vacant eyes. 'What happened? We heard you had some trouble in the Midlands…'

Finnigan remains non-committal.

'You don't remember me do you? You got concussion or something? What happened? It's Jackie! Name's Jackie. We've known each other for years.'

A fraction of fallen memory slides into focus.

'Jackie…? What can I tell you? I'm sorry.'

'I've known stranger things happen, Finn. Head trauma. The brain is a delicate machine. But because of the history between us, because of my respect for you, take a word of warning… You do know Al comes down here? You do remember that, don't you?'

'Al?'

'Blackstock. Al Blackstock. He comes down here regular. We all heard what happened…'

'Mr Black?'

'Who else?'

Blackstock. Of course! He was always talking about going down The Beggar. And with this information, other snapshots of Finnigan's past scatter into view; a brief kaleidoscope of history that throws him off balance. He leans against the wall to offset this curious sense of vertigo.

Jackie watches, assessing the situation before continuing.

'Don't get me wrong. We like Al down here. Or tolerate him. Part of the furniture. When he's on a job, he's tight as a gnat's. As you're aware. But once affronted, he turns into a right gabby cunt. I'm not choosing sides, because it is not my business. Just saying… He's got a fucking hard-on for you, Finnigan. Thought you should know.'

'Why are you doing this?'

'You've earned it. And we like to keep a tidy house.'

'He's not here, is he?'

'No. But it's early doors.'

'Thanks, Jackie… Appreciated.'

'Just doing the right thing.'

They shake hands.

'Give me a heads-up if he shows, Jackie. If you hear anything.'

Finnigan presses a couple of notes into the man's hand. Jackie protests, but allows himself to accept the cash. He pockets it, and leads the way to the bar. Waits for the clamour to settle before announcing: 'Have a look… It's only *Finnigan!*'

Part greeting, part warning.

Finnigan strolls in. Like stepping into a dream. The bar is another photograph from his past, decked in gold-embossed wallpaper and mahogany; a décor once considered very classy. One side there's a pool table, an open coal fireplace; on the other, a scattering of mismatched tables and chairs. Situated between these two ends, a well-stocked bar where a handful of men are sat on bar stools. Hard looking men of uncertain age, between late-youth and early demise.

They avoid direct eye contact, reaching for their pints, waiting to see how the land lies before committing to dialogue. An awkwardness smoothed over by Eric, standing behind the bar; an East End whippet of a man, with flattened nose. Finnigan clocks him for the governor.

'What's this, Finnigan, business or pleasure?' Eric asks. 'No – before you answer that, what are you drinking? On the house.'

'Water would be alright,' replies Finnigan.

'Can't turn up out of nowhere and ask for water. What you drinking?'

Finnigan concentrates, and walks towards the bar. The other drinkers give him room. Some leave the bar to sit at tables; seeking ringside seats, should things take a turn.

'Water and scotch. Separate glasses.'

Eric busies himself at a leisurely pace. Watching Finnigan. He can see something isn't clicking.

'Remember me, don't you, Finnigan? It's Eric! Haven't seen you since Ruby's funeral, bless her heart. How you been?'

'Been okay, Eric. Finnigan's been okay.'

They notice Finnigan referring to himself in the third person, but no one calls it. Eric places two glasses on the bar.

'Whatever the reason, pleasure to have you grace my establishment, Finnigan. Your health.'

Eric raises a glass of red wine from the bottle he keeps permanently open. In reply, Finnigan nods thank you. He drinks the water for thirst. Then turns to face the room, and salutes them with the malt. Knocks it back like medicine. Most of the men join in the toast. It makes him feel more feared than liked. He turns back to Eric.

'Might need somewhere to stay. One or two nights, no more.'

There's a heavy silence, as the men wait for Eric's reply. In turn, Eric glances at Jackie for approval. He turns back to Finnigan, giving his business face.

'Stay here if you need. It's a courtesy I extend to some of my regulars. If they need to lay quiet.'

Finnigan stares at him.

'Is that what you've heard, Eric?'

'I don't know what I've heard. It's a figure of speech. No questions asked. If you want the room, I can extend that privilege.'

'Just like that?'

'The room's there... We know you.'

There's a murmuring as the men cast judgement on this arrangement.

'Appreciate this, Eric. Just till Finnigan gets his head right.'

He turns back to face the drinking men, and with arms open wide, non-threatening, says, 'My round?'

Finnigan lays a couple of fifties on the bar, and one by one they drift across to collect their drinks as Eric sets them up. It's an old boy's club of reprobates and chancers, and they regale Finnigan with their endless banter. Every story populated by ghosts of past glories, reckless encounters, manly bonding through depravity and violence. Finnigan hears his name feature in all these accounts. His glass is never empty. He drinks, and listens, and piece by piece the building blocks of his personal history tumble into place. He's led through their nostalgia like a lizard crawling back into its own discarded skin. Memories of bonhomie and casual savagery, clammy with the nicotine breath of his former cronies. And unconsciously he begins to showboat, swaggering and throwing shapes as a mirror to their stories. This is how they choose to live…

A young black dude he doesn't recognise sidles up. Gym-sculpted and keen.

'Still training, Finn?' he asks.

'Training?'

'Heard you was into the Small Circle style. Been learning a bit of jujitsu myself…'

'Try him,' shouts Eric. 'Go on, Jimi, try him!'

'You serious…?'

Jimi tries to retreat from direct involvement, but the men see a sporting opportunity and persuade the kid to chance his luck. Finnigan smiles, and steps up to the challenge; advancing without hesitation. Jimi places a hand on his chest to slow him down.

'Whoa, brother, let's make some room, yeah?'

Finnigan takes hold of Jimi's hand, levering the small finger sideways… Within seconds the kid's on the floor. Effortless self-defence. The audience hoot in derision; but Jimi remains encouraged, looking to learn some new moves. He goes to push the tables back, making some fighting room, as Finnigan advances again.

'Seriously, Finnigan, hold on, yeah?'

Jimi offers a handshake, to confirm this is still a friendly encounter. Finnigan accepts, and with his other hand digs his thumb into the pressure point by the elbow. Jimi's knees buckle. Incapacitated. Like magic. Back on the floor…

The kid bounces up laughing. Impressed by these simple moves.

'Is that what you want to learn, or something less restrained?'

Finnigan takes off his jacket, limbers up and executes a roundhouse kick, landing it millimetres from the side of Jimi's skull. Classic kung fu; athletic and cinematic.

Jimi tries, but he can't get it right.

'I ain't got the flexibility… Look at me: it's pathetic…'

'Your technique's off… Set the feet, flex the hips, then… Bang! Snap the leg out…'

They go through the move again, Jimi improving each time.

'Get the basics right, and everything follows… Practise five hundred times a day, both sides… and do that for twenty years; you'll be as good as me.'

'Is that right?'

'No. You'll never be as good as me.'

The look of failure on Jimi's face is genuine. So Finnigan forces him back, to stand his ground, to practice the move again, giving him no choice. It turns into a physical dialogue, to the exclusion of their audience. But the longer he continues, the dimmer the room becomes. Someone must have lowered the lighting; he's in the same room but it's a darker place. And as he demonstrates his moves, forgotten crimes begin to bleed into the present moment, hallucinations as real as acid…

The first time he attacked his stepfather, it opened his world to the pleasure of violence. Not just the swagger of supremacy, but fighting for honour. His poor strung-out mum, everyone's favourite when she was banging away on the amphetamines, but made a victim by her needs; her friends a bunch of freeloading wasters. He fought with all of them over time, asserting his territory, finding his space. He can see blood on the faces of strangers, his mother crying for peace as he strips her friends of their dignity, leaving them damaged… Sometimes so wasted himself, it seemed he was fighting a nest of snarly-toothed nocturnal monsters, their black nails and insipid skin like giant, hairless rats… He remembers it now for the first time, how it started; always good money for a soldier. Always a fair exchange for some heinous deed…

He takes a breather, leaving Jimi to slink back to the outskirts of his interest. He demands a malt, and then another, and then the bottle.

Like swallowing the breath of dragons, trying to douse the memories. The men notice this change in Finnigan's fortune. No longer the returning hero; merely another drunkard being demolished by the weight of his past.

His mind is fizzing, his ears singing with cerebral distortion. It would seem the Laphroaig has claimed another victory, but this is not how he plans to live.

He walks unsteadily to the fireplace, wading through the furniture, pushing tables and chairs aside. He picks up two hefty pieces of coal from the scuttle. Weighs them in his hands. Turns to face the room. Begins to squeeze down hard on the black rocks, attempting to crush them, to change their molecular structure. He wants the world to witness this: *At the heart of sentience is a diamond. This flesh is a vehicle for the light. We live like dogs, but we shine like diamonds. See how it shines between us. Look at my hands...*

Words echo through Finnigan's mind. He can no longer tell if he's thinking them, or shouting out loud. But he will demonstrate his true worth by crushing the coal into diamonds. His teeth are bared, entire body tensing with the effort, groaning with the exertion. After less than a minute, he sees blood begin to seep through his fingers. And to the audience, this is incomprehensible. *The fuck is he doing...?* No one likes a man who can't take his drink; they're incapable of understanding this bizarre display. And yet he persists.

He relaxes his grip briefly to look at the results of his endeavour. Black dust mixed with blood from the cuts to his fingers and the palms of his hands. But the coal itself remains unchanged. He tries again, squeezing the rocks with all his superhuman might, eventually falling to his knees defeated by the task.

You can always find a million in a shovel load of coal...

He can't believe he's failed.

Jackie steps to the fireplace. He pats Finnigan on the back. He encourages a round of applause. He demands the men show appreciation for his effort. Then he bends down to unfold Finnigan's cramped fingers. Removes the pieces of coal. Shakes his head at the blood.

'Come on, mate. Let me show you where this spare room is.'

A simple change of location can resolve a bad trip. It's classic drug-knowledge. If all turns dark, change location. *Move to another room. Move outside. Walk through the portal.* It's an obvious piece of symbolism, but effective. And this is what Jackie's doing, leading him through the portal, as he talks him back to earth.

The upstairs flat is designer-minimal. Straight white lines, block colours, chunky, clean surfaces, and birch-ply furniture. A haven of solitude, like heaven designed by Philippe Starck.

Jackie leads him into the kitchen.

'Wash that dirt out your hands, Finnigan. That'll fester if you leave it.'

He runs the warm tap, and finds some antiseptic gel and towels. Finnigan allows Jackie to direct him through this procedure. The washing of the hands: concentrating on the pain as he recognises the hands as his own, that he's cut them, torn patches of skin off, scraped the coal dirt into the flesh. He is still dazed, but less confused.

The onslaught of malignant memories that threatened to destroy him are returning to their hiding place; but thus confronted, his past can now bed down in a less corrosive form. He's stronger than his past, yet it felt so real; like walking back in time. Like time travel. But he's back in the present moment. Tired but brighter. There are nagging pains in his forearms, deep in the muscles. What the fuck was he doing? Trying to make diamonds from coal? He laughs to himself. That was way out of line. Psycho-crazy. But leaving him with stigmata? Was that the point? Is it a message?

He feels a hand on his shoulder. Jackie passes him a clean towel. Passes him a tube of Germolene antiseptic. Finnigan applies it to his bleeding hands. It has a good, clean smell that evokes memories from his earliest childhood, where some days the biggest trauma was a grazed knee or an insect bite. He's so used to reviling his upbringing, but he now temporarily concedes it wasn't all bad growing up; some days the sun was out, there were picnics and football in the park. Children deal with whatever's presented to them, knowing nothing else. His mum did her best. He wouldn't be here without her; and he's strong enough to conquer these new challenges…

With his hands washed, and wounds attended to, Jackie leads Finnigan away from the bathroom, to give him a full tour of the flat. Talking him down to the safety of the present.

'Knock yourself out, Finnigan. Pleasure to have you here. Whatever's happening, get some rest, yeah?'

Closer and closer to the here and the now.

'See that phone? Red one? See that red phone…?'

He insists Finnigan focus on the phone.

'That's a direct line to the front door. That's where I am most of the time. Anything happens, I'm on that phone.'

Finnigan nods, looking at the gauze and bandage on his hands, pressing the medical tape firmly in place. 'That's right, tape it up. We don't want you bleeding all over the guest room, now, do we?'

Jackie's parting shot.

'And keep your ears open for that red phone… Anything happens, that's your lifeline!'

The spare room, clean as a private hospital bed; cool linen sheets calling him like a favourite girlfriend. But he turns back to the kitchen; pours himself a tall glass of warm water, mixes in some salt; walks to the toilet and chugs the salt water down to make himself vomit; to purge the remains of the alcohol. Then he strips and hits the shower. It's an effort, because his hands are bandaged. So he lets the water cascade over him. Washing away the sins of his youth, cleansing the space between the atoms…

He dries, and marches towards the bed. The red phone is his only concern. If it rings, he must be awake and ready. If not, the world can forget he was ever born. He climbs between the virgin sheets and crashes.

Downstairs, from the privacy of the gents, Maltese Dave is putting a snide call through to Al Blackstock. Maltese is providing information for previous favours, and because he's a grass. He describes Finnigan as lying low, staggering drunk and gone doolally. He tells Blackstock it's a perfect opportunity for reprisal.

The call finds Blackstock at home, and leaves him with something of a dilemma. He didn't reckon a chance for revenge would be offered so quickly. He looks at himself in the mirror. That business with Finnigan has left its mark; the injury spreading like a disease across his cheeks and up to his eyes, bloodshot and watery. The broken nose has been re-set; in a couple of weeks it won't look so damaged, but right now his face is a riot of bruise, blood and plaster. No doubt the lads at The Beggar will take the piss on witnessing his hideous visage, but he has to put these considerations aside. He can't miss a surprise confrontation with Finnigan.

Blackstock has a few emergency grams of cocaine hidden away. He keeps it in a small wash-bag in his sock drawer, along with his passport and several thousand in sterling and euros: his rainy day stash. He takes out the little plastic coke bag. Of course, his nozzle is too mashed up to think about snorting, but he needs a livener and sharpish. He needs a confidence boost. He can't rush in looking desperate and beaten, not without medication.

He opens the coke bag, plunges a moist finger into its midst; sucks on the finger rubbing it into his gums. Way too much: his whole mouth goes numb, his throat expands, leaving him barely enough room to breathe or swallow. But it *is* waking him up. He snaps the bag closed. He lights a cigarette. He tries to stretch some of the tension from his neck and shoulders.

Blackstock strides about his flat in a turmoil of anxiety, knowing he must make the right decisions. He needs to be prepared. He draws heavily on the cigarette; nicotine on the cocaine feels so good to him. He throws on his jacket, walks to the hallway mirror to look at himself. Wipes some drool from his thin lips with the back of his hand. He needs back up, and wonders who to call at such short notice. He needs to arrive with an entourage. No one would consider flying solo into this situation. It's a position of strength to arrive with a posse, and he is so fucking ready right now.

He turns away from the mirror, picks up his car keys, pockets the bag of coke and a bubble-strip of Diazepam, and he feels ready. He is so fucking ready for this. He knows who to call for back up. Starts dialling as he leaves the flat and walks down to his car. There are obvious reasons for revenge, but his core need is the betrayal. He shudders with dread at the enormity of this decision to front up to Finnigan; and he heads out into the night.

The Diamond Terrifyer

It takes Blackstock about an hour to collect his three-man crew; jobbing hard boys, beaten down to 70 quid a pop for the night's work. They remain silent in the car as he races them through deserted North-East London rat runs. Road surface glistening with rain. Green lights all the way. He feels like the Sweeney, with his boys, behind the wheel of this rebuilt '78 Granada. Regrets the loss of the Beemer, obviously, but it was a working car and pissed away to chance; something else he'll be arguing with Finnigan about. That, and the face he's been left with.

The crew are briefed once more as they park up outside The Beggar. Blackstock then strides to the entrance while his posse hang out of range of the CCTV. Inside, Jackie hears the buzzer. He peers into the security monitor. The image of Blackstock is grainy but unmistakable. He lifts the internal phone, and waits a good 30 seconds for Finnigan to pick up in his room.

'You got a visitor…'

He makes sure the warning has been registered, lowers the receiver.

Then he shouts into the bar, 'Eric…! It's Blackstock!'

Only then does he deign to stroll towards the front door and throw the latches. As he does, Blackstock pushes straight past, bowling on through to the bar. Jackie allows this to happen. Obviously this manoeuvre has been planned: if Blackstock rushes past it'll force Jackie to follow, because Jackie won't abide a lack of common courtesy. But this time Jackie chooses to stay put, waiting by the door, knowing revenge rarely travels solo. Right on cue the three stooges lumber up, expecting a free entrance. Jackie stands in their way.

'Alright, ladies… No rush, room inside for everyone. It's all quite mellow in here tonight. Let's keep it that way, shall we?'

This gentle admonition has the required effect. Some hired men don't need much excuse to drop their guard; they file inside with a studied air of decorum, line up in a semi-circle behind Blackstock.

Most of the evening's carnage has been tidied away, leaving a few diehards propping up the bar, talking the talk. Eric is pottering about making good. They were warned about Blackstock's imminent arrival, and therefore underplay his entrance to wind him up. No one mentions his face, but they all have a sidelong butcher's.

'Heard anything, Eric, have you?' demands Blackstock.

'What should we have heard?'

'News of Finnigan, as it happens. Little bird told me he was staying here.'

Eric and Jackie keep schtum, but judging by his body language and past history, it's Maltese who squealed.

'I know he's here!' declares Blackstock. No one denies or confirms this.

Then he's talking to Eric, in a discreet and business-like manner. 'Cunt stitched me right up. No doubt you heard about it?'

'Only what you let on yesterday... You phoned us, remember?' says Eric, still wiping down his surfaces, unconcerned.

Blackstock repeats his story. He always was gabby on matters of disrespect and revenge. He turns his back on Eric to address the room.

'So we're out of town Friday... He only takes the wheels, and leaves me with this face...'

'Oh yeah. Hadn't noticed...' says Maltese Dave, trying to win some credibility back.

'Fuck off, Dave...' shouts Blackstock.

The other men stay silent, knowing the biggest wind-up is to say nothing. Waiting for him to snap.

'I got no idea what's going on. He's been a cunt. A slag...'

Blackstock bares his yellowing teeth. Habit tells him he still looks like a Hollywood hardman; but when he pulls the grimace, it cracks his broken lip and makes him wince. The men just stare at him.

'You shower of cunts... Stop staring, for fuck's sake. He got lucky, that's all. Don't fucking laugh...'

But no one's laughing. They're holding it together because it's funnier that way.

He turns back to Eric.

'Get us a fucking drink, Eric. Voddy on ice. Large one. Look at the state of me. This is a proper need-to-know: he upstairs, is he?'

Blackstock is leaning over the bar, shouting spittle into Eric's face. Jackie places a hand on Blackstock's shoulder. It's a sobering influence. He continues with a more contrite tone.

'I only brought the boys coz I want this cleared up, Jackie. I don't intend any trouble…'

His humble best, with the weight of Jackie's paw on his shoulder.

'It won't get messy. I just want answers… And I know he's here coz Maltese told me.'

The men at the bar finally break their joke of silence; punching Maltese on the arm and slapping his head because he's a grass and everyone knows it. Blackstock's men remain nonchalant but imperious; still expecting to earn their money the hard way.

'So have a word, Jackie, raise him out of his slumber. Do the right thing…'

Jackie turns to Eric, saying, 'Get the lads a drink, Eric. They promised to keep it nice.'

Eric organises a free round as Jackie stands between Blackstock and his crew. Not aggressive. Not smiling.

Upstairs, Finnigan is moving. He was spark out. Now he's alcohol-befuddled but awake, listening for clues. He hears Blackstock's voice, that distinctive moan… Remembers punching him out, but can't remember why. He heads downstairs from the flat, and forges an entrance into the bar with open-handed gestures and an apologetic grimace. The way he creeps through the doorway is almost comical; he's on tiptoes, hands out in surrender. It's like a weird game of chess, the players subtly adjusting their position to seek advantage and safety.

Blackstock is immediately on the back foot. He looks to his crew but doesn't have a plan. He just has a sense of moral compensation. He knows he's owed, but Finnigan is overplaying the remorse, like the entire episode was a joke. He keeps making these deferential gestures; and his hands are bandaged, with crusty bloodstains showing at the palms. It all distracts Blackstock from his mission, so it's Finnigan who speaks first.

'You don't half bruise easily…'

'Do what…?'

'Looks a right mess, mate… Hope that wasn't me. I don't remember. Gone a bit vague, as it happens…'

'Vague?'

'What if I told you I was sorry…?'

Finnigan keeps advancing at an oblique angle to hypnotise the wounded beast. Blackstock edges back against the bar. This plan to surprise Finnigan at his most vulnerable was never going to fly in reality. Blackstock finds himself turning to Eric for support.

'He told you what went down, Eric? Has he? Because I don't fucking know, do I? Leaves me stranded, on a job! Who does that?'

Blackstock turns back to the looming presence of Finnigan, and gears himself up for assault.

Finnigan remains placatory. 'What can I do? How can I resolve this? You want to fight me, is that it?'

'Fight you?'

'Will that resolve things?'

Blackstock lunges forward, fists swinging. 'I'll fucking kill you…'

Finnigan leans back to sidestep the attack, and Blackstock's momentum finds him stumbling into an empty table and chairs. Another loss of dignity. He turns to his hired men. 'Don't just fucking stand there… have him!'

Jackie attempts to hold Blackstock's men in check, but given their financial investment, he resolves to let the move play out. If blood needs to be let, then it will be, in spite of any objection he could mount. So Blackstock's crew move on Finnigan, and although he spins and dodges their advance, he finally allows himself to be held by the arms, as an offering to Blackstock's anger.

'Alright, Al. I'll give you this one. Do what you have to… This one's on the house.' He's not even struggling. He makes himself a standing target, as a gesture towards reconciliation. Blackstock finds it disarming. It doesn't seem right having nothing to fight against; but Finnigan wants this done, and tries to provoke a reaction.

'Anyway… Suits you, that face.'

'Come again…?'

'Your face… Damaged goods, mate… Reflects the personality.'

Blackstock lashes out, aiming for Finnigan's head. Automatically, Finnigan shifts his weight at the last second, and Blackstock connects with one of his own men. Blackstock throws another good punch, and again Finnigan can't stop acting defensively, easily deflecting the attack. It's a learned response. So Blackstock rushes in with both hands, takes Finnigan round the throat; screaming and spitting; squeezing the breath from him.

Jimi attempts to even the odds, but Jackie holds him back. Blood must be let. It is the way of things. Blackstock leans in, putting power to the strangle hold, and Finnigan head-butts him in the face. Not hard; but a broken nose doesn't need much attention to worry it. Blackstock falls back against the bar, eyes filling with water. He should have known this would happen.

Finnigan blows his breath out, incredulous.

'You really were trying to kill me!'

'You think I'm not up to it?'

Blackstock steps up and punches Finnigan in the stomach, followed by a flurry of open-handed slaps to the head and face. Finnigan isn't fighting back, but neither is he immune to the hurt. He allows the punishment to rain down. There are calls for Finnigan to be released to level the playing field, but Jackie refuses intervention. And within 90 seconds Blackstock is exhausted. He stands back, catching his breath. Finnigan is allowed to fall to the floor. Blackstock steps up for a kick to the ribs, but Jackie hauls him away.

'Oh, bad form to kick a man when he's down, is it, Jackie? Have a look from my point of fucking view, will you?'

He attempts another kick, and Jackie pushes him across the room.

'Fuck you, Jackie. Ain't your argument.'

'My gaff, my rules.'

Blackstock's minders step back up to the plate… It's about to get messy.

Finnigan attempts to call order. 'Whoa! Okay… This is between me and Al… Eye for an eye…'

Blackstock acknowledges this and waves his stooges away, letting Finnigan stand up and stretch his limbs.

'I think you cracked a rib, mate,' says Finnigan.

'… do more than crack a fucking rib. I am in the right here.'

'You're the moral arbiter now?'

'I'm holding the advantage, if that's what you're saying.'

'Always someone else's fault, isn't it? Always someone else to blame…'

Blackstock reaches over the bar and picks up Eric's lemon slicer, a hefty nine-inch Sabatier. He turns back to confront Finnigan. It's a mood changer.

'You think I don't dare?' screams Blackstock. 'Seriously...?'

Jackie moves in, but Finnigan stands in front of him.

'Leave it, Jackie. It's not your fight.'

Jackie raises his hands and retreats, leaving Blackstock to wave the blade in Finnigan's face.

'You seriously think I don't dare? Because this is all I've thought about... I was a good man. I did good...! We were a good fucking team, Finnigan. I done my best...'

Finnigan is inching closer.

'Don't fucking move, I'm telling you,' screams Blackstock. He grips the knife ever tighter, dropping it level with Finnigan's torso. Finnigan doesn't look worried. He's taken a steady, balanced posture, anticipating the attack. Talking quietly, getting under Blackstock's skin.

'I know what I've done, Al... I'm facing up to it. Seeking the True Path. This hell you're in is of your own making...'

Finnigan is in position.

'You made choices. You're making one now. But you don't have the clear light. All you got is bitterness and revenge...'

Blackstock lunges with the knife. A short, swift move, aiming for Finnigan's guts, but the attack is clearly signalled. Finnigan defends himself by raising his left knee, turning to connect with Blackstock's knife hand. It deflects the blade away from his body. He drops his left foot, spins through a complete 360, and delivers a kick with his right that catches Blackstock hard in the chest, throws him back against the bar top. Finnigan moves in to lift Blackstock's attacking hand out of range. He delivers short, sharp punches to abdomen, chest and head. And Blackstock gives up; dropping the knife into Finnigan's grasp.

Blackstock knows it's over. He allows Finnigan to place a firm hand on the back of his neck. He does this because he has no idea what's coming next: a hefty slap to the forehead. It doesn't look like much, not compared with the earlier body shots; but Blackstock's head cracks back and he collapses, out cold, falling into Finnigan's arms.

And as Finnigan heaves the unconscious body into a chair, he comments on the result.

'What looks like the killer blow, that tap to the forehead, that was foreshadowed by the bodywork, by those brutal hits to the lungs, liver, heart; creates a nervous overload in the brain… See how I placed my wrist on the back of his neck? That's the point I was attacking: all those nerves in the neck. So one tap on the head, and boom… Out go the lights.'

His matter-of-fact manner defuses the need for retaliation. Finnigan is punch-weary, but in control.

'I could bring him round using the pressure point below the nose there; stimulate cardiac rhythms and restores consciousness… But I don't want to do that.'

Finnigan surveys the scene as he makes this pronouncement. He watches Blackstock's men retreat to the sidelines; their part in this unfolding confrontation is over. No doubt they'll make it up to Blackstock under easier circumstances. The room is clearly in Finnigan's hands. And when he asks for rope, Eric provides it. And as he hog-ties Blackstock to the chair, no judgement is made. Jackie and Eric have decided that Finnigan must see this through.

Twenty minutes later, Blackstock wakes to the vision of his men tucking into a platter of bacon sarnies while he remains tied to a chair, and clearly tied with a certain amount of ceremony. There's symmetry to the knots and bindings, leaving him immobile and vulnerable, like a violent form of shibari. The only thing to ruin the style of the ropework is the way his left hand has been gaffer-taped to the arm of the chair, secured in a closed fist but with the pinkie loose and exposed.

Finnigan sits close to Blackstock, nursing a mug of tea. No one has referred directly to the hostage situation; but as Blackstock finds the energy to struggle against his bindings, Jackie decides it's time to call the proceedings to order.

'Now… Gentlemen… We know something happened between Finnigan and Al up in the Midlands. We're aware there is bad blood, and blood must be let – as I always say. But for me and Eric… This is our gaff, so please' – he turns to face Finnigan – 'furnish us with the facts.'

It's Finnigan's turn to stand up, and present his case.

'I know this doesn't look clever. It's disrespectful. But any trouble, any expense you might incur, will be doubly repaid.'

Jackie nods in appreciation of Finnigan's opening statement. Then counters with, 'That said, you appear to have one of our drinking companions held in a hostage situation; does not bode well for our continuing sense of trust.'

'There is no issue with trust, Jackie. Who else could I turn to?'

Finnigan throws the kitchen knife in the air, testing its weight, catching it clean. The motion of steel is mesmerizing.

Eric says, '… fuck's sake, Finnigan, that's my citrus knife.'

'I told you, Eric, I'll make good. I just need a few words with my man…'

'What are you doing?' Blackstock whimpers.

Finnigan slaps him. 'I'm doing that every time you interrupt.'

He smiles at his audience. 'Friday night, we're out of town… Transpires it's a set up. Who else knew but me and Blackstock?'

'Don't mean to say it was Al, Finnigan,' responds Jackie, reasonably.

'That's what I intend to find out.'

Finnigan isn't sure where this is going. Since his memory went haywire, he's been free-styling with words that arrive unbidden to his mind. He has no idea where the words hail from. But he assumes the more he allows their full expression, more chance he has of discovering some clue about his current predicament.

Blackstock shouts: 'Tell him, Jackie, tell him. I'm not a grass. Why tie me up?'

Finnigan stabs the tip of the knife into the wooden arm of Blackstock's chair, aiming to miss the exposed finger.

'Heard of the yakuza?'

'Oh sweet, fucking Jesus…' moans Blackstock.

'…course you have: that film with Robert Mitchum…'

'I never did nothing. You know that…'

'Remember that scene where Mitchum owes his yakuza boss a debt of obligation…'

'Listen to me, Finn. Seriously…'

'Minutes ago, you were threatening to cut me.'

'I never meant it. I'm just a gabby cunt; you know me.'

Finnigan places a gentle hand on Blackstock's face, pushing on his broken nose.

'Okay, okay, okay…'

Then Eric pipes up, realising what's about to happen.

'No…! You cannot cut his finger off in my bar. There are rules. Health and fucking safety…'

'Eric… If there's any hope for mankind, we must believe the likes of Al Blackstock can be saved.'

'Saved?' screams Blackstock. 'Saved from what?'

Again Finnigan tests the weight of the knife.

Blackstock keeps pleading.

'What have I done wrong?'

'We have all committed wrongs. Admit that and our sins will be forgiven.'

'What the fuck are you even on about?'

Finnigan knows this theatricality is a product of ego, and ego is the enemy of true compassion. He's sure Blackstock is innocent of double-dealing; but he hopes that by continuing in this vein, some memory of the event will be salvaged.

'Have you got religion, Finnigan? Is that what this is about?' asks Malone, piping up for the first time this evening; his broad Belfast accent exaggerated for maximum effect. 'Because if you have, you've chosen the wrong fuckin' meeting.'

This cuts through Finnigan's tenuous hold of the moral high ground.

'We were told the Saviour would return!' Finnigan roars.

The men are silently mugging complete incomprehension.

Jackie calls it: 'Saviour? Seriously! What are you driving at?'

'The Truth that lives in all of us…'

Finnigan sweeps his hands over the assembled throng, including them all as conspirators.

Malone picks up the baton.

'I'm not sure what your point is, Finnigan. But don't all religions subscribe to the sacrifice of the Only Begotten, so mankind might be saved? The Son of God, in return for salvation; that was the bargain, but I don't see any evidence.'

The room is silenced by Malone's apparent erudition. No one points out the glaring mistake that not *all* the religions subscribe to the sacrifice of the Only Begotten. They take it as read.

Finnigan stabs the knife into the table to gain control. Blackstock struggles to free himself; fighting so hard the chair begins to shuffle across the floor. Finnigan places a hand on Blackstock's head, to calm his anxiety. *Only by suffering ourselves can we truly empathise with the suffering of others. Only then can we realise our commonality.*

These are the words in Finnigan's mind; but his spoken words come out as more holy roller.

'Relinquish this illusion of personality! The source is universal. Radiant and innate! We rise above the beast as we embrace the clear light!'

Finnigan hears these ideas spill from his mouth, believing he understands their meaning.

'There is no heaven or hell, but what we create through our own endeavour. There are no gods or demons, but those of our own design...'

Finnigan has a reputation, but how long can they take this bull-shit?

Malone says, 'Right: enough, Finnigan. We all use religion for our own ends; and when the car bombing's done, don't we all expect redemption?'

'Could someone please untie me, you bunch of fucking pricks,' screams Blackstock.

Finnigan is rapidly losing his authority, so he raises the knife above his head. 'This illusory body which we hold precious, I dedicate in sacrifice...'

He brings the kitchen knife down on Blackstock's exposed fin-ger. And with some spurting of arterial blood, the severed digit flops to the floor.

Finnigan knows he could have played this differently. He's just giving rein to a new enthusiasm, and the outrageous theatricality of it makes him laugh.

The men assume Finnigan is laughing at the act of violence;

and in this they recognise their own shortcomings. Yet the smell of blood unleashes a basic malevolence. They rush Finnigan, moving as one. He drops the knife but remains merciless in retaliation. His moves are automatic; his mind on distant thoughts, acknowledging that mankind is doomed.

The fighting is hard and swift; and over within a couple of minutes. It's been a long night. Yet in spite of Finnigan's worries for the future of the human race, they each believe they've learned something. There is brotherhood in the room. Something has been achieved.

Finnigan regains enough composure to recognise that Jackie is the final barrier to a safe exit. He takes a step forward, but Jackie stands impassive.

'We don't have to do this, Finnigan.'

'No?'

'I'm not backing down. Just saying there's another way.'

'There's always another way... What I've been trying to teach these bastards.'

'Really?'

'We always have a choice. Appraise the situation from the other man's point of view. It's the foundation of hope.'

'If you say so.'

Finnigan turns to Eric, who has remained behind the bar, guarding his optics.

'I'll make it good, Eric. Count on me.'

'I'll be honest with you, Finnigan. I'm no clearer about what went down. But I'll send you a bill for the tidy-up, be sure of that.'

Finnigan turns back to Jackie. He sees a reasonable man whose first call is to seek the route of least resistance. A man who is able to put ego demands to one side, and find a solution of mutual benefit. It's a position of strength: we suffer, we recognise each other's suffering, we try to relieve that suffering. The three steps towards empathy, the cornerstone of salvation and the road to enlightenment.

'I've been a fucking idiot, Jackie. All I can do is apologise.'

'Don't worry about it, Finnigan. It'll make a good story. You best not stay in town, though. You were never very popular, even before this.'

They shake hands, and Finnigan makes his exit.

Outside: it's too early for the milkman, too late for another drink. He vaguely remembers where he left the borrowed car. Might take all night finding it, but there's no hurry. He sets off on his solitary walk, when there's a call behind him.

'Hey, hold up…'

It's Jimi, loping up the road, big fat grin like he's 12 years old and just seen his first kung fu film. Finnigan lets him catch up.

'That was wicked.'

'You mean the way I made enemies of everyone who knows me?'

'Yeah, that's rough, man. But… Let me ask you, right? When Blackstock went for you with the knife? How come you use the knee, man? That was whack! The fucking knee!'

Finnigan says, 'Come at me with a knife, like he did.'

Jimi mimes the same underarm thrust that Blackstock attempted, and slowly, almost balletically, Finnigan repeats the same defence move he used earlier: pushing aside the attacker's knife hand with his left knee, landing the left foot firmly on the ground, pivot through 360, lean back, and kick to the chest with the right foot.

He then explains. 'You've got a knife: I want that knife away from me, then I want you far away as possible.'

'I see that. I see that. Thanks, Finnigan. Hey… At the end there, when they was all coming for you? That wasn't me. I was trying to stop them. Just so you know.'

'I know. I saw you.'

'So, like… If you ever need back up?'

Jimi stands smiling with his arms open wide.

'Thanks, Jimi. But I'm by myself on this one.'

'Karma, right?'

'How do you work that?'

'You just fucked off all your mates. Now you're on your own. Cause and effect.'

Finnigan looks up to the sky. Wonders about this.

'Karma is what you confront when you die. That's what all this leads up to. Like an end-of-term report…'

'I hear you, man, coz you don't half keep banging on about it.'

'Nothing else is important… Don't die 'til you have a clear mind.'

Before Finnigan sets off again, Jimi reaches into his pocket and takes out a card. He presses it into Finnigan's hand.

'My number… Whatever. No reason, just… Just so you know. I'm with you, bruv.' And Jimi touches his fist to his heart.

'Take care and shit, yeah?'

Finnigan looks at the card. Who carries business cards? *Jimi Brown, Rich Town Music, Sales Technician.*

Jimi slides off down the road, throwing punches at shadows. Finnigan walks in the opposite direction. He's blown his chances with Blackstock. Should have sat down for a head-to-head, might have learned something. Opportunity wasted. This judgemental fervour he's in is ruining his chances. And he's left the Walther back inside The Beggar. Too many mistakes! He trusts Jackie to lose it for him, but it could have been useful.

In spite of this, Finnigan feels quite optimistic about the future. He's getting his mojo back; enjoying the theatricality of his behaviour. It's a path of discovery, and a pattern will emerge. He just needs more time.

Next move? Find where he parked the stolen car. Take it back to the owner. Ask more questions. Someone has to know something.

Sunday...

Sunday Morning at Home

Ex-Detective Inspector Graham Walsh came back to life just after midday on Thursday on a metal gurney, as vicious hands pinched his cheeks and voices implored him to wake up. The new world assaulted him with an aroma of bleach, urine and pain. A cocktail that remains in his senses, even though he's back at home recuperating.

Waking up from the anaesthesia, he was told how *lucky* he'd been; how his poor lifestyle choices had led to a heart attack, car crash, broken ribs, bruised face and successful triple bypass. Lucky, lucky, lucky! They cut open his chest, stretched his ribs apart and grafted healthy blood vessels from his leg onto the diseased arteries, increasing blood flow to the heart.

He should have stayed under the watchful eyes of medical professionals, but the sloppy hospital food, the indignity of bedpans, the relentless conversations about how fucking *lucky* they all were: Christ! The detailed personal histories of strangers; people he wouldn't care less about even if he *did* know them. The constant debate about cholesterol half choking them all to death; followed by hopeless resolutions of new health regimes: no alcohol, no fry-ups, no ciggies, no strenuous activities. And watch your blood pressure when considering amorous intent, the nurses all joked, as if lecturing a room of former Casanovas. He couldn't take it. So this morning, after their paltry excuse for breakfast, he found his clothes, got dressed, called a cab; and no one noticed when he left.

It all looks depressingly similar when he arrives home. Following the accident, he'd hoped for optimistic insights into life's greater meaning, but the gloom of Chez Walsh gives him the shudders. And the complete lack of fabled visions during his near death experience confirms the worst: life is a brief and pointless blossoming before an eternity of nothing.

He didn't expect a welcome home party, but he thought Mrs Walsh might be here. Of course, she doesn't know he's discharged himself. He'll face that problem on her return. She'll be at work, fund-raising for her latest cause. Even on a Sunday, those mistreated Spanish donkeys still need the benefit of a whist drive.

He's standing in the lounge, looking at himself in the gilt-framed mirror above the coal-effect fireplace. His face looks longer; yellowing bruise on the side of his head; bloodshot eyes; and broken skin on his nose. He's in sore need of a shave; that's something she'll mention. *No need to let standards go, just because you've had a heart attack.* Maybe he'll grow a beard. The thought cheers him up. He chances a beard would make him look like Sean Connery on a golfing holiday.

It's so *tidy* everywhere! There's a mundane order, everything accessorised into blandness. And cold! The central heating must be set for her work timetable, rather than his 24/7 descent into geriatric beard-growing. God, he hates this moment. It's why he bought the car. To escape this. He almost daren't think about the car. He was told the insurance company had brought it home, to wait further instruction. £500 excess, and loss of no-claims, but he could easily have it rebuilt. In fact, the car might be looking at a longer lifespan than he is. *God's teeth*, he needs counselling. Mrs Walsh will know someone. She knows everyone, and he can't understand why this annoys him so much.

He walks back to the kitchen, stands in front of the adjoining garage door. He has to man up and assess the damage. He prepares for the worst, but the sight doesn't shock him as much as the anticipation. It doesn't look too bad... No – it looks bad. The entire off side is totalled: she'll need new front and rear wings, new door, new bumpers, plus indicator lights and miscellaneous trim. But as he shuffles around to inspect the rest of the vehicle, things don't look so bad. The main damage occurred when he spun into the concrete embankment. It depresses him, though, seeing his favourite dream this broken. He resolves to have her rebuilt, no matter what. After all, it was the heart attack, not the crash, that almost finished him. Car probably saved his life.

Back in the kitchen, he pulls up a chair and sits down. What do people do all day? What's his remit? Toss about in the garden? Do crosswords and sudoku to keep his mind active? Daytime telly and watercolours? The garden was always Mrs Walsh's domain, anyway. And why does he insist on calling her Mrs Walsh? He remembers it was once a sexy pet name. Jesus! He never saw himself lacking imagination, but *Mrs Walsh?*

He stands up, opens some of the kitchen drawers, then realises he's looking for cigarettes. Is that why he's so pissed off, because he hasn't had a smoke for four days? He concedes it's a good thing. Pours a glass of water, takes it into the lounge along with his bag of blood thinners, antibiotics and painkillers. He's exhausted, and lies down on the sofa without taking his shoes off. A small victory...

Then he remembers the pet name incident. She'd returned home late from some do-good thing, a formal dinner. A glow in her cheeks from an evening of alcohol, sparkling conversation, and benevolence; must be 20 or 30 years ago. She was wearing this tight, shiny two-piece suit, and stood in the doorway, half in silhouette; posturing, but pretending not to. Slowly taking off her earrings, and she dropped one; a sparkling diamond stud. He can remember exactly where it fell. He said, *I think you've dropped something, Mrs Walsh,* and she smiled at him; slowly bending down, the silk skirt pulling tight around her hips, rustling over the stocking tops. Knowing how provocative these simple gestures can be. And they fucked right there over the arm of the sofa, and she was watching him in the mirror, smiling as he lost control.

He curls up into the beige-floral embrace of the cushions, and blinks back a tear. He sighs. Then allows it to happen. He lets go, crying like a child, having spent his entire life guarding against such moments.

When he wakes, he's calmer. Slightly embarrassed by the outpouring of grief. They warned him at the hospital these episodes might happen. Having your chest ripped open, and your dead heart exposed to the world, makes you prone to such things. He moves back to the kitchen, and makes a brew, has a wee, takes more pills, discovers a homemade cake... Victoria sponge! Then he staggers back to the lounge, and sits in front of Mrs Walsh's desktop, with tea and the thinnest sliver of cake imaginable. He logs on, and types *American hearse* into Google.

0.3 seconds later he has 153,000 possibilities. *1974 Dodge Coronet...* He checks it out. The vehicle is called Rock In Peace, and driven by Estonian Goths touring Europe.

He explores a link to *American Coach Building*, and ends up on a page advertising *Essential Guide to Becoming a Coach*, meaning baseball, netball, etc. Computers have a great memory but they can't read his mind. He backtracks to the original search.

Convalescent Soldiers in L'Ouverture Hospital express their views, as they take an American Hearse Driver to court.

Poems by Emily Dickinson...?

American Funeral Vehicles. Sounds useful, but it's an advert for a book.

He scrolls down.

Wayne's Rides, Home of the Hot Rod Hearse: try before you die.

There's a photo of a huge bearded man, tattooed to the gills, grinning from the driving seat of a 1970s Cadillac hearse. There's something about this one. The styling is too modern, but...

He closes his eyes and watches the shadow of the beast as it appears to fly over his head, crash-land on the road in front of him, and tear into the distance. He knows that memory and imagination are interchangeable. The hearse didn't fly over his head.

He concentrates back on the screen. Then from somewhere he gets a whiff of her perfume. He closes his eyes as the memory explodes in a rapid succession of fleeting images: her skin, their youth, the sun's warmth, together outside, like animal inevitability. Naked. Outside. A secluded hill, the Sussex Downs. Spring... Greenery all round, blue skies, her skin.

The images hit him where it hurts the most: right on the scar tissue. He can't believe it happened. Can't believe they ever had that sense of spontaneous intimacy. Naked out of doors, sex in public, what urgent madness, fucking insanity...

Tragedy is, they lost the knack of communication. They forgot how to talk about fucking, and so eventually stopped fucking; and, what's worse, they've become content with it. They can't even talk about *not* fucking.

He takes a forkful of the cake, raises it to his mouth; and before he can eat it, he realises this is what he could smell. This was the trigger to that sudden erotic memory. It wasn't a trace of her perfume that led him to imagine her naked skin; it was home baking. And slightly saddened by this, he pushes the cake away and returns to the screen.

There are hundreds of nut-jobs who hold a preference for driving a hearse. From the photos, it's normally young people behind the wheel. Being ironic. Laying claim to their invincibility.

He finds a site dedicated to death's head logos. He finds a site dedicated to bicycle hearses. Motorbike hearses. He needs more pictures. He clicks on images. This is better. Why didn't he do this first of all? But the problem with scrolling the images, the information isn't always obvious. He doesn't care who took the photo. He doesn't want to get sidetracked by hunting through a photography website. He keeps scrolling…

There's something familiar about this one. Something he seems to recognise. He clicks for information.

'69 Cadillac, Traditional Landau Hearse. Designed for death, deserves some fun!

What is it he finds familiar? The grille? The grinning chrome mouth? It can't be; he didn't see the grille. He returns to the main page. Finds a 1968 Cadillac with outrageous fins and flamboyant, rocket-shaped chrome-and-glass tail-lights. He's getting closer.

He refines the search to *Cadillac hearse*. In 0.28 seconds he finds 17,600 sites:

> *The Rides of Dracula*
> *E-ville de Ville*
> *A Cadillac called Pasternak*
> *Grave Rides*

Nothing triggers his memory until he sees, on Cohen's Movie Cars website, the grand vision of a menacing 1965 Cadillac hearse. His freshly overhauled heart threatens to miss a beat. He recognises the weird, whale-like curve of its roof, like a humpback in vinyl; the tall, red tail-lights and chrome stylings… He feels the bile bubbling in his gut. This is the one.

The next move is easy. He phones an ex-colleague and begs a favour. And it *is* a favour, because any search put through the Police National Computer must be logged, with specific reasons given, as such entries are randomly checked for legitimacy. A search is put through for the registered drivers of any 1965 Cadillac Coupe de Ville Hearse that can be found. Walsh leaves his mobile number, and the PNC is put through its paces.

Out in the non-pixelated world, the Cadillac Coupe de Ville hearse is parked in its usual spot, by the deconsecrated church in Fenderby, South Lincolnshire. And today, the small gravel parking area is overflowing with top-marque vehicles. Inside the church, an invited audience of occult collectors, with Frank and Norman curating the sale of the mordant, the bizarre and the fully functioning esoteric artefacts.

The tables and cabinets in the oak-lined study display the sale collection, which features hand-carved mahogany Ecuadorian skulls; a 200-year-old post mortem dissection kit, complete with bone saw, flesh hooks, head spikes, cartilage knife and chisels. A ritual drinking-skull, with brass-lined interior, engraved with a pentagram and the black goat. A glass jar containing human finger bones. An Edwardian undertaker's embalming kit. A Tibetan thighbone trumpet. Plus all manner of grimoire and occult books. Some of these items are from Frank and Norman's own collection, now put on sale. Others were bought purely for trade. Pride of place is a Victorian rubber sex doll, originally used for therapy in a home for the mentally ill.

The collectors are an equally ethnic mix: tweed suits brush shoulders with velvet cloaks, leather jackets, and bare tattooed flesh; pince-nez and piercings, all with money to spend. Frank and Norman know almost everyone here, and treat the occasion as a PR exercise for their bespoke-pagan funeral services, as much as a collector's sale. It's a niche world, but full of opportunity.

Norman is deep in conversation with a tall, slight fellow sporting a vampire haircut and eyeliner; a studious Nosferatu, currently appraising a book called *Death and Physics*. He's listening to Norman's pitch.

'Self-published. Limited edition of five hundred. First print run. All numbered and signed. The author has been hiding them in book shops, leaving the buyer to haggle over a price.'

'So you want me to haggle?' asks the young man.

'You'll be able to move them on. It's pure occult. On the surface it looks like sub-atomic physics and Buddhism; but the commentary is pure naïve occultism.'

'How many do you have?'

'I can let you have three.'

He leaves the young man with that thought.

Frank is extolling the virtues of a Brion Gysin Dream Machine to a young man with silver jewellery and headphones around his neck. He's gently handling the device, which really doesn't look like much. A cylinder of heavy white card, with geometric slots cut into its side. It looks old enough to be original. Frank explains that it was made to have a light bulb suspended in its centre, while spun on a 78rpm turntable; describing it as a kinetic sculpture, designed to induce visions. He then places the cylinder back in the cabinet next to letters of provenance.

He says, 'Gysin said the experience made him feel he was *high above the earth in a blaze of glory…*'

He likes to leave them with a story. It's more persuasive.

Norman is now chatting to one of the tweed suits; an older man with long grey hair tied in a ponytail. They're discussing a witch's bottle: a small glass bottle containing hair, rusted pins and dried urine. Traditionally used as protection against malign influence. It was found suspended in the cavity wall of a nearby cottage during renovation. The grey-haired tweed says, 'It might just be what I need for the house in Norfolk.'

Frank crosses the room. He wants to confer with Norman on the afternoon's progress. They decide to regroup outside with a cigarette.

Norman wipes the witch's bottle with a linen cloth, and locks it back in the display case with the other morbid delights; and he turns away, leaving the buyer to make a decision.

Frank catches May's attention. He smiles at her, in full appreciation of her style: Hobo Jones T-shirt, studded jacket and biker boots; adding a touch of rock-and-roll glamour to the funeral game. He walks past, whispers in her ear, 'Keep your eye on things, May… We're stepping outside for a smoke.'

May shrugs like, *of course…* And she turns back to the room, assuming command like a dominatrix in a crèche; severity and compassion in equal measure.

Outside, Frank and Norman light up.

'Might have a sale on the doll. There's been a lot of unhealthy interest.'

Norman grimaces. 'Be glad when you've got rid of that thing. Gives me the creeps.'

'Also… Found a buyer for *Le Dragon Rouge*…'

Norman makes his *I am impressed* face.

'We just need to argue about the price…' says Frank, meaning he hasn't actually made the sale. 'What about you, Norm? Any business?'

'Was just talking to Tarquin…'

'The vampire-looking dude?'

'Book dealer…'

'Yeah? Get him to bid for the *Le Dragon Rouge*…'

'Ha! Way out of his league… He's looking for small returns on minimum investments…'

Franks laughs. 'Where have I heard that before?'

'He's taking a few copies of that *Death and Physics*…'

Frank stares into the distance. 'You been thinking about it?'

'Trying not to…' says Norman.

'You don't think we should pay him another visit? The author?'

'No…'

'See if he's heard from Finnigan. See what's happening with that?'

Norman is not keen to shake the hornet's nest. 'I like my life too much... Way I see it, we're finished with that. It's done.'

Frank stubs his cigarette out and throws it in the bin by the church door. 'Aren't you even the slightest bit curious? Find out what happened to Finnigan?'

Norman faces Frank directly. 'I have pushed the entire episode as far from my mind as possible. I have severed connection using golden scissors, rolled the remains into a ball and cast it towards the fire of a billion suns....'

'So that's a *no*, then?'

Frank smiles. They shake hands. They go back inside to join their guests.

Walsh is asleep on the sofa when his mobile bleeps, letting him know a text has arrived. He rolls over, reaches for his glasses and reads the message: *1965 Cadillac Coupe de Ville hearse, registered to Frank Osman @ Coupe de Ville Funeral Home, Fenderby, South Lincolnshire.*

It surprises him to discover the car is a bona fide funeral vehicle. Why was it driving so fast? So recklessly! He still clings to the idea it was the hearse that caused him to crash, rather than the heart attack. He feels certain that if he investigated, he'd find evidence of collision.

He's not sure how to proceed. This isn't a sub-plot in a novel in which the retired detective overcomes all manner of adversity, and triumphs. This is a remnant of his depressing life. He isn't a pulp fiction detective. He won't be solving any mysteries. He won't make a miraculous recovery and save the day. What needs saving anyway? No one's dead. He crashed his car, and wants someone to blame. If not for this particular incident, then for his entire useless fucking life. He has to stop and remind himself that relentless negativity is a product of his medicinal drug cocktail.

He hauls himself off the sofa and back to the computer; types in a search for the *Coupe de Ville Funeral Home*. Immediately, on screen, there it is... There's the car parked innocently outside some old country church. He doesn't need any more convincing. He jots down the phone number, and without considering his actions, picks up his mobile and starts to dial.

This being a Sunday, he doesn't expect anyone to answer. He's not even sure what the tone of his message is going to be: random vitriol to help vent his ruptured spleen, or a coherent explanation of the incident? To his surprise, an articulate young woman answers.

'Hello? De Ville Funeral Home. May Osman speaking… How can I help you?'

It completely floors him.

'Hello? I… I… I have a friend…'

'Of course. Take your time…'

'I have a friend who hasn't been well. And he wanted a… He loves cars, you see, and he wanted something special…'

'I understand.'

'It's quite random really, I saw your car, your hearse, purely by accident…'

'The Cadillac?'

'Yes.'

'Can I send you some brochures? Or direct you to our website?'

'Send me something, please. Do you have a pen? Send it to Graham Walsh. That's Detective Inspector Graham Walsh…'

He gives his address, and vainly hopes the driver of the hearse gets to hear of this interaction. He hopes the title of *Detective Inspector* is enough to put the frighteners on the scrote who drove into him. But in truth, he doesn't know what he's hoping for; and exhausted by the task of being alive, he hauls himself upstairs for another nap.

Homeland Security

Rex D. Boyd is running to work, as he does every day of the week. Hoodie up, head down, zoning out. From Notting Hill, Ladbroke Grove, Bayswater Road, the long way around Kensington Gardens, past the Serpentine, through Hyde Park and into Grosvenor Square. He doesn't notice the other pedestrians or the traffic. He doesn't luxuriate in the city's green open spaces. It's no longer a decision to run the ten-mile round trip rather than cab it or take the bus; this aerobic endurance is pure bull-headed routine.

In spite of the weekly miles he doesn't look like a runner, doesn't have that effortless style of a track athlete. For Boyd, running is more about punishment; covering the hard miles like a boxer who knows that to go the distance he needs stamina and mental power. The first few months he'd run this route carrying a rucksack of rocks, but it began to feel like the journey to Calvary, or a flagellant in the Muslim Shia processions commemorating the martyrdom of Husayn ibn Ali. His running isn't a public demonstration of piety, nor is he looking for atonement. He merely craves physical exhaustion to keep the memories at bay. These days he ups the ante by running with a diver's weight belt, discreetly worn, giving him something to fight against.

The exercise can't stop the memories completely, but the repetitive movement allows him to run through the burning sand and the smoke. And sometimes the memories are welcome. The victorious invasion of Kandahar! Operation Enduring Freedom! He was there with the Airborne, and what in hell is wrong with attaching an enemy combatant to ceiling hooks by his thumbs? This is Standard Operating Procedure: humiliation and casual beatings are by the book. Just don't broadcast it to the world. Don't allow the media to judge these actions out of context. Would a linebacker be reprimanded for breaking the bones of his opposite quarterback? Not unless he relished the damage caused. Enthusiasm for interrogation must be kept on the low down. He was too successful, too zealous; and of course he should never have published those pictures on Facebook. The folly of young manhood became the architect of his career demise. Something he berates himself for every day, pounding his feet on the London streets, driving his indiscretions into the past. But oh, to be back in the desert…

Special Consular Services have offices in the American Embassy, providing a variety of emergency and non-emergency assistance to American citizens in the UK. Boyd cools down, standing to attention behind his workstation, and waits for the desktop to start up. A towel round his neck, two-litre bottle of Evian in his sweaty hands, he rehydrates. Must rehydrate! Learned that much in Afghanistan.

He loves this early-morning solitude of the office as much as he hates his co-workers, the college men with their five-year plans. Suited and connected, they talk the dynamics of international business, media communication strategies, cultural awareness, global economic governance… Boyd knows how fortunate he is to have secured a desk in this office following his very public fall from grace, but these fucking career jockeys! He puts the water down and throws a few punches into the air, up on his toes, teaching his absent colleagues a lesson in Krav Maga.

The desktop eventually coughs up the latest emails. Boyd scrolls down, seeing the usual remit of lost passports, wrongful arrests, stolen traveller's cheques. Occasionally he'll have a random road-death, some of his countrymen being blind to the left-handed British traffic. It happens. Death Happens. Shit Happens. The Special Consular Services are there to clear it up: the deaths of American citizens abroad, in all flavour of natural and accidental causes. So the communication from DS Harry Johns of Nottinghamshire Police completely bemuses him:

Re: Polonski, Eugene.

Boyd skims through the email. *American ex-serviceman…*

This is the story of a violent murder. And the initial report has arrived along with his regular bag of tourist trauma. It's the best news Boyd has received for a long while. It could have gone to the Department of Homeland Security, or the Secret Service, or the National Threat Assessment Center. But luck isn't entirely random; it's the ability to recognise opportunity and act on it. He decides to hold onto this, make his own enquiries before alerting any other department. Boyd can smell intrigue, and he makes a call to have Polonski's military service record delivered to his desk. He hits the showers before deciding his next move.

After an interminable wait for the milk train from Nottingham, a tube across London, then another train from Victoria, Brad finally arrives back in Brighton by late morning. Emotionally and physically drained. He makes coffee, and rolls a joint in preparation for crashing out. All he wants to do is sleep, but being back on home soil he takes his time, luxuriating in this renewed sense of safety. He lies down on the rug in his living room, stares at the ceiling, and thinks about running a bath… But all he's really doing is waiting for a phone call from Jane.

He'd phoned from Victoria station, hoping to catch her, but what he caught was voicemail. He left a brief message, explaining her car had been stolen. He resisted the temptation to go into more detail. Of course, he wanted to replay the entire ordeal, because we all secretly need someone to witness our suffering; and we all have a need to feel loved.

The old Persian rug he's lying down on is musty, rough to the touch, and not particularly pleasant to lie down on. But it reminds him of a scene in the film *The Big Lebowski*, in which a rug is said to *really tie the room together*. He likes the phrase, and believes his rug also *really ties the room together*, and by association he assumes a small measure of Lebowski's cool.

The rug has been passed down to him through two generations. He imagines the hands that wove the wool, in a hot dusty town like Isfahan, or up in the hills near Tehran. He actually has no idea where these rugs are woven or where this one originated, and is creatively entertaining the only two Iranian towns he can name.

Prone. Flat on his back. Breathing and stretching. He's concentrating on a yoga position called the corpse pose. To anyone else, this looks like lying down. The key, so he's been told, is to concentrate on the inhalation, visualising the exchange of rich oxygen into the blood, and holding this exchange before pushing out the exhaust breath along with its psychic disturbance and poison waste: letting go, and clearing the thoughts.

He tries to relax even further, by concentrating on the pull of gravity, the heaviness of his body. Imagining the wooden floor supporting him with the strength of the forest it was hewn from.

He stretches his arms and spills the ashtray, knocking a half-smoked joint onto the rug. He sits up and relights it, rubbing the rogue ash into the rug's moth-eaten weave. As he inhales he remembers another relaxation technique. In this one, you imagine standing in the rain, and feel the water pouring right into your body, through the spaces between the cells of the muscles and nerves, washing away all the tension, the badness, the darkness, everything negative; feel it all rinsing away, draining through the pores in the skin, dissipating through the cracks in the floorboards, into the foundations of the building, down into the deep, dark earth. A constant pure rain that washes away your sins...

Boyd stares at the bundle of papers on his desk. It's so rare to have a paper file rather than a digitised version. This Polonski character has been out of service for so long, his records are faded paper facsimiles, enclosed in a buff-coloured folder. He skim-reads the facts:

> *Eugene Polonski. Sequestered to the FBI 1949.*
> *Parents: Lithuanian Jews, immigrated to America to escape the pogroms.*
> *Born: 1929.*

Christ! That makes him 87 years old! Boyd re-checks the date of birth. Who would murder an 87-year-old? And he was shot, assassination style, according to the preliminary police report. Killed on the very day he was re-housed back in the community, after 40-something years in a care home. He reads on...

Polonski arrived Stateside 1941, age 14.
Honours student.
Scholarship to Berkeley, majoring in physics…
Studied under David Bohm…
Followed Bohm to Brazil in 1951, aged 24, where he reported
his findings back to the Bureau…

So Polonski comes to the States, and is persuaded to work as a field agent, to keep watch on this David Bohm character.

In 1957, he follows Bohm to Bristol, England…
Sectioned in 1973, at 46 years old, where he remains to the pre-
sent day, at The Ravenshead Care Home for ex-Servicemen in
Nottinghamshire, England.

The Special Relationship is alive and well. But who is David Bohm? And there's no evidence of Polonski's reports to the FBI. Boyd makes a note to seek these out. He turns back to his computer and types a search for *David Bohm*. Pages of entries pop up. Again, Boyd skim reads and makes notes of the salient facts:

David Bohm, born 1917, Pennsylvania…
Hungarian Jewish immigrant father, and Lithuanian Jewish
mother…
A Theoretical Physicist who contributed innovative and
unorthodox ideas to quantum theory, philosophy of mind, and
neuropsychology…
Teenage agnostic. Graduated Pennsylvania State University in
1939.

Worked under Robert J Oppenheimer at Berkeley California
where he obtained doctorate…

Holy fucking shit! He worked with Oppenheimer!

Involved with radical politics… Joined Young Communist
League and Committee for Peace Mobilisation. His friend
Joseph Weinburg suspected of espionage.

Oppenheimer wanted him working on Manhattan Project at Los Alamos (1942) to help design the atom bomb. Security clearance not approved.

Remained at Berkeley. His doctorate proved so useful to the Manhattan Project it was immediately classified…

Jesus! What a fucking mess! So radical, he didn't have security clearance for his own work.

Assistant professorship at Princeton… Worked with Albert Einstein… Called before the House of Un-American Activities Committee in 1949, pleaded Fifth Amendment… 1950 he was charged for refusing to answer questions from the Committee, and arrested.

Acquitted in May 1951, but already suspended from Princeton. Einstein wanted him as his assistant but the university didn't renew his contract.

Recommended for post in São Paulo University in Brazil.

Relinquished American passport.

Visited by physics alumni, including Richard Feynman, Louis de Broglie, Isidor Rabi, Leon Rosenfeld, Carl Friedrich von Weizsacker… blah blah blah…

Boyd double-takes on the name Albert Einstein but doesn't recognise any of the others. He gathers they must be cream of the crop, prize-winning originators; and all of them consorting with this known Communist sympathiser:

1955 Bohm relocated to Israel…

1957 relocated to UK as research fellow at Bristol University…

1961, Professor of Theoretical Physics at Birkbeck, University of London, working with Basil Hiley to expand his theories on the Holographic Universe and Holonomic Brain Theory with Karl Pribram…

Retired in 1987, but kept working on his papers… series of meetings with Dalai Lama…

OMFG! The Dalai fucking Lama is involved!

> *1991 admitted to Maudsley Hospital… underwent electrocon-*
> *vulsive therapy.*
> *Died Hendon, 27 Oct 1992 aged 74.*

The brain of Rex D. Boyd is expanding at a rate commensurate with the expansion of the known universe. This is a ticket to higher places. It's immediately clear that the dead man Polonski would have been privy to David Bohm's work; and him being a Marxist, all manner of sedition… All manner of weird revolutionary science!

And then he's assassinated!

It has to be an internal plot to silence Polonski. But what secrets would he have left to spill?

Boyd re-reads the police report. Then phones DS Harry Johns in Nottinghamshire. He's eventually put through.

'Is that DS Harry Johns?'

'Make it quick…'

Boyd explains he's in receipt of the intel on the Polonski investigation. He informs Johns that he'll be doing everything in his power to search for next of kin, for service records, and for anything that will help Johns in his task of solving this case swiftly and decisively. This is now a high-priority Embassy concern and anything Johns needs, etc.

Johns thanks him, and briefly reports on his own investigation. He gives Boyd the details of the social services woman who last saw Polonski alive. He agrees to share forensics, and two witness statements: one from a pair of undertakers who confronted the alleged killer at the murder site, and another from a man who was found driving the killer's car.

This second witness, Bradley Holmeson, is described as a freelance writer; and there's mention of a seditious home-published pamphlet he's been distributing.

As far as Boyd is concerned, this phone call could not have gone better.

Brad is fast asleep on the rug in his lounge when his mobile rings. It's a London number he doesn't recognise.

'Hello?'

'Is that Mr Holmeson?' asks a clipped American twang.

'Yes? Who's this?'

'This is Mr Rex D. Boyd from the American Embassy in London…'

'And…?'

'And I would like you to come in for an interview, at any time of your convenience, but preferably today.'

'Ha ha ha… Whoa! Seriously? Who is this?'

Boyd repeats himself, word for word.

Brad still doesn't get it.

'You want me to come up to London for an interview? What for?'

'It is a matter of some urgency, Sir. Homeland Security.'

Boyd allows his gravitas to hang in the airwaves, assuming he's about to hear some lame excuse that will confound this initial enquiry. Also, he's not calling from the Homeland Security department but, had the initial report been sent to its rightful place, the call *would* have been from there, so…

By now Brad is standing up and pacing the room.

'Okay, okay, let me… Tell me what this is in reference to.'

'In reference to the murder of a fellow US countryman, an ex-serviceman. We need to debrief.'

Had Boyd called about a less serious matter, Brad would have laughed out loud at the phrase *We need to debrief*. But the word murder has captured his full attention. It brings back images he's been supressing. Seeing the photographs in the interview room… It didn't faze him at first. But during the journey home, he kept flashing on the human details: the finger nails, the calluses and blemishes on the hand as it reached out across the blanket; the trace of veins under the opaque white skin; the face drained of emotion; the whole body a discarded husk. And the stains of dried blood, crusty and thick, coagulated in pools on the mattress and the floor. Thinking about it now brings on another swell of nausea. He has to concentrate to stand upright. He knows it's delayed shock, and drops to his knees before the fall. He places the mobile on the floor in front of him. It's still talking. He hangs up to better concentrate on not being sick.

Rex D. Boyd hears the phone go silent. It doesn't surprise him. He makes a note to find Holmeson's address and have a face-to-face.

Next on his list: Ms Stella House, from social services. After a few exchanged voice messages, Boyd is talking to her directly. He notes the softness of her voice, the guarded precision of her words, and her reluctance to give any concrete information. They discuss Polonski's move to the hostel, and the state of his mental and physical health. But she offers no opinion on the killing, apart from shock and bewilderment.

'What else?' he asks.

She says nothing.

He asks again, and waits...

Slowly, slowly, catchee monkey.

She says, 'There's no reason I should tell you this, but he told me he was being watched. It's ludicrous because he is, I mean he was, suffering from paranoid personality disorders.'

'But given the circumstances of his death...?'

'I know. It leaves me confused, because he sounded deluded, like a fantasist. But in retrospect, in the light of what's happened, there must have been some coherence to his ideas...'

'What ideas?'

'Well... He anticipated his death. He mentioned more than once that he was being watched. I didn't take it seriously. He'd been in care half his adult life. So when I heard that he'd been killed, and in such a ritualised way... It made me wonder, was this meant to look purposeful, maybe like a warning...?'

Boyd says nothing.

'And there's something else. He had this little case with him, which he said was full of important things. That was the phrase he used. It was why he believed he was being followed.'

'Important things...? And what do you think he meant by that?'

'I don't know. There might have been mention of notebooks? Work notebooks?'

'Okay. So he had a small case that might have contained important documents of some sort?'

'Yes…'

'And you're assuming that's why he was killed?'

'I don't know. At the time I didn't think anything of it, but now…'

Boyd scans the reports for mention of a small suitcase of documents, anything to substantiate this new information. He finds nothing. He double-checks the details of the hostel where Polonski died, and thanking Stella for her time, he hangs up, and Googles the train times to Nottingham.

Brad can't remember climbing into bed, but that's where he is when his mobile chirps again. It's mid-afternoon. He checks the caller, then…

'Hey, baby,' he whispers.

'Brad!'

'Hold on, hold on,' he says, reaching for cigarettes and lighter. Sparks one up, while propping the phone on his shoulder.

'Jane… So good to hear from you… So pleased you called… Listen, I'm devastated about your car, really, if I can explain…'

'I got my car back,' she says.

This information immediately curtails his confession.

'You got your car back?'

'Yes. It's brilliant. Well, it's not brilliant it was stolen, but the police found it, and brought it back.'

'The police came to your flat?'

'Yes! Just now. The policeman who found my car brought it back to me, so I thought I'd drive round to see you. I'll have to be quick though, I need to get to work…'

'Oh God…'

'I thought you'd be pleased.'

'I am pleased, Jane. Pleased you got your car back, but this policeman who came to see you… Was he carrying any ID?'

'What do you mean, ID? He was the police! He had my car. He had all the details, so no I didn't check his ID.'

'Okay… When was this?'

'Just now! What's going on?'

'And was he like, a regular, uniformed policeman?'

'Brad, he brought it back. Everything's fine.'

'Okay. Just answer the question, Jane. Was he in uniform?'

'No, he said he was a plain-clothes officer, but…'

'It just seems unlikely, y'know?'

'Brad? It's good! Lets you off the hook for having it stolen in the first place.'

She's trying to be jolly.

Brad continues. 'I've had cars stolen before, Jane. And they've never been delivered back by the police.'

'Well, mine has.'

'What did he look like?'

'Brad! For God's sake! What is it?'

'I just have a bad feeling about this, Jane. Please… Humour me. What did he look like?'

Jane describes the policeman to Brad. He swears under his breath when he hears her description.

'And what did you tell him, this plain-clothes officer?'

'Tell him?'

'The policeman! What did you tell him? He must have asked you questions?'

'Well, yes, he said he wanted to contact you because…'

'How does he know about me?'

'Because you're the one who lost my bloody car, Brad, for fuck's sake…'

'And you gave him my address?'

'And your mobile number. He said he needed to contact you.'

'Why?'

'To check I was who I said I was. Otherwise he might have brought the car round to the wrong house or something. He got my address from the reg number, and… Oh, I see what you're saying.'

'That's right.'

'Why would he need to speak to you, if he had my details from the DVLA?'

'Exactly!'

'So you don't think it was a policeman?'

'I can't tell you who I think it was.'

'Who do you think it was?'

'I can't tell you.'

'Who was it?'

'It might have been this random murderer I seem to have become involved with.'

The End of the Mystery

Brad recognises the inevitability of Finnigan arriving at his front door, but when the doorbell rings, it still gives him a fright. At some point later in his life, he'll wonder why he didn't run. Why didn't he hide? Why didn't he call the police? At least have a shower and feel prepared. But he does nothing.

The doorbell rings again…

Brad is ever on the look-out for positive signs revealed by random events; but for the last 30 minutes or so, during the time it's taken Finnigan to walk over, there's been nothing. He sat on the rug, waiting expectantly. Made coffee. Smoked a cigarette. Looked at the sky. Sat back on the rug. Nothing happened: the world of meaningful phenomena playing dumb. He considered this absence to be the sign itself, that he's being advised to sit still and welcome his fate. But maybe he's just exhausted. Maybe that's the reason he did nothing.

There's a scene in a book by Ken Kesey where one of the characters is so physically exhausted he makes an error of judgement, and thus fails to save his brother's life. When Brad read that some years ago, he didn't understand it. The book is called *Sometimes A Great Notion*, Kesey's version of the 'Great American Novel'. In this particular scene, two brothers are working hard all day, felling trees. They're rolling the logs downhill towards the river where they're floated to the sawmill. It's a while since he read the book, but this is how he remembers it playing out: one of the brothers becomes caught under a felled log, trapped in the river, his legs held on the river bed. It's a tidal river, and the water is rising. The other brother should have run back up the hill to the truck, and found a length of hosepipe; something to use as a breathing tube. They know the river will become too high for the trapped man to keep his head above water. But they've been logging all day. He's exhausted. Instead, he concocts an absurd plan that is destined to fail, and his brother drowns. Why didn't he get the hose? Why didn't he call for help? Why didn't he drive the truck to the riverbank and haul the log away from his brother's legs? Because he was too tired.

Brad clambers to his feet, again spilling the ashtray, and bends down to rub the ash into the rug. He walks to the door and peers through the peephole; sees a small, dark eye looking right back at him.

'Hello, Bradley!' says Finnigan through the door.

Brad freezes. Why is this happening?

'You've got to tell me who you are. I need to know your name.'

'Finnigan… Name's Finnigan.'

'You can't keep doing this, harassing me like this.'

'I'm sorry.'

'What do you want?'

'I need to talk. It's important. Important to me.'

'What's important?'

'Open the door, mate. Come on. I feel like a rejected girlfriend or something, talking through a closed door like this…'

Brad hesitates. Still hoping for a sign to avert the tidal waters of inevitability. Nothing. So he takes a breath and opens the door. And Finnigan walks into his flat. It looks like he's been sleeping rough. He needs a shave. There are stains on his jacket that could be blood. Aside from that, he looks bright-eyed.

'Still got that worried face, Bradley! Hope that's not because of me,' he chuckles.

'Never mind that. What are you doing here?'

'No way to treat a friend.'

'Friend?'

Finnigan makes a placatory gesture. 'What else? The brotherhood of man is greater than our individual desire. Together we achieve greatness, but alone we die. Am I right, Bradley?'

As Finnigan advances into the flat, Brad finds himself retreating. They end up in the lounge, with Finnigan still riffing on this theme of friendship.

'There is nothing of value, but that which is shared; no home but the earth, no opposition but the smallness of our hearts…'

He continues making expansive gestures as he talks, and no doubt would have continued all day had Brad not interrupted.

'Seriously, though… What do you want?'

Finnigan stands there, saying nothing. He's gesturing with his hands; either trying to summon the words, or for the simple enjoyment of striking postures. Brad can't read his mood. Perhaps this mania is a prelude to malevolence. However the cards fall, Brad is resigned to see it through and put an end to it.

'You said you needed to talk. That's why you're here. So let's focus on that, yeah?'

Finnigan focuses. Breathes out.

'That's why I like you, Bradley. You get to the heart of things. You're right. We need to talk.'

'Okay then. You want a cup of tea or something? Wait here; I'll go and put the kettle on.'

'Good plan, Bradley. Good plan.'

As he walks to the kitchen, Brad begins to relax. Maybe he can help. Maybe he does have information to share. And anyway, he likes meeting people that make his life seem less vanilla. He knows a Finnish woman who spends half the year living in near darkness; he knows a gay man who didn't come out until he was married with children. He knows where to buy good weed, and cheap coke; he knows a garage that could write you a dodgy M.O.T.

It might be too much to say he *enjoys* Finnigan's company, but different social opportunities allow him to feel superior to people who only have mates from the office. Undoubtedly the correct course of action would be to double-lock the door, and phone the police. Speaking of which, he needs a legitimate excuse for not doing so, should matters turn legally compromising.

They're sitting at the kitchen table with cups of tea. And Brad finds himself broaching a subject he can't ignore.

'You know I was shown photographs of the body?'

'They stopped the car then?'

'Yes they stopped me in your car, and came at me with guns! Like it was me who...'

He can't finish the sentence.

Finnigan looks genuinely contrite. 'Sorry... But I did tell you to torch it. I remember that much.'

'Shouldn't you be hiding out or something? You know I had to give the police a description? They know what you did.'

It's a dangerous gambit, but he has to get his cards on the table. If this is going to be resolved, he can't pull his punches. Finnigan puts his tea down. Looks him right in the eye. Takes his time.

'I can talk about the killing, if you want to talk about it. Everyone wants to know about the killing. Generally they're too scared to ask. I'll tell you anything you want.'

Brad says nothing.

'I always said, if someone wants a person dead, there must be good reason. It doesn't affect me.'

Finnigan turns away, walks to the window. Brad watches him, wise to the need for silence. Letting the man speak.

'But recently things have taken a turn. Not better or worse. It's like I'm seeing the world from the other man's point of view; and for once I don't feel the need to exploit that to my advantage.'

'That's good though, right?'

'Like I said... Not better. Not worse. Just different. Things appear to have more depth. More resonance. And I have the illusion everything is happening for my benefit. I am the centre.'

'Is that rare for you? Being at the centre of things?'

'What is rare, is that I now realise everyone feels that way. To a degree, everyone is at the centre of their own world. It blows my mind. The level of importance I have about my life; you think it's just you, but *everyone* has that!'

'Yeah... The Golden Rule: trying to see the world from the other man's point of view.'

'... give you an example: I see you're scared of me, which is why I'm being careful to explain myself.'

'Instead of doing what?'

'Instead of dissing you as a pencil-squeezer, and taking advantage.'

'Thanks...'

'I mean it. I *am* able to see things from your point of view; what's more, I find it interesting. That's why I'm here... My life used to be black and white. I relished it. No one could be trusted. I was invisible darkness. I enjoyed it. Loved it. Manipulating people. It's easy. In a way I'm still doing it, because here I am in your kitchen.'

'And this is what you want to talk about?'

'I got to talk to someone. Might as well be you. You've read books. You're a clever cunt.'

'I'm a fucking idiot. I let you into my flat.'

Finnigan laughs. Leans across, and says, 'I want to talk about the need for pain.'

'Seriously…?'

'Double serious. One of the things I've been pondering… Way I see it, we need pain as a response to danger. You burn yourself, you feel pain, you take your hand out the fire. Survival. But now, when I see pain in another person, I'm starting to understand what they're going through.'

'We're social creatures. And it benefits the group to recognise each other's state of mind. It's the mirror neurones, in the brain.'

Finnigan is impressed.

'Hear that? *Mirror neurones!* I knew you'd have the words to describe it. That's why I came to see you. You're an author. You know things.'

'You're talking about empathy. Only… you've discovered it a million years too late.'

Finnigan can't tell if Brad's taking the piss; and Brad wonders if he's overstepped a line. He continues… 'I'm serious. It's how we evolved. What benefits a *part* of the group, will benefit the *whole* of the group. You could argue early primate groups had a moral code. Not consciously, but empathy is a precursor of morality… It's how we protect ourselves.'

Brad gets up to make more tea.

'This what you wanted to talk about? Or is something else going on? Not that I'm trying to get rid of you…'

'Mate… there is so much going on. I can't explain it. I'm a riot of new ideas, which is why I need to talk, and hope the meaning of things will be revealed. That's why I'm here. You give good conversation.'

Brad looks at Finnigan and recognises a genuine need. 'Okay… These feelings of empathy… Is it like remorse?'

'The opposite. I feel no remorse for the things I've done… Because I know that's what you're getting at.'

Brad doesn't want to dwell on Finnigan's past. He watches him pace the room. A former psychopath learning empathy, it's like the dawn of early man.

'Alright, Bradley, here's the thing: you see someone suffering, you feel their pain, and it causes you to empathise, right? Compelled to help. Like the Boxing Day tsunami, if you remember? People said how could God allow so many innocent people to die and suffer?'

'But God doesn't exist,' says Brad.

'This is my point! God doesn't exist. Because why would God allow such a ruthless bastard as myself to continue living?'

Finnigan laughs to himself. 'The tsunami was a blameless natural disaster. But after the event, what happened?'

'People stopped going to Phuket for their holidays?'

Finnigan is disappointed by the reply. 'Don't let me down. How did people react?'

'I suppose they reacted with compassion.'

'Exactly! Compassion! Therefore: suffering creates compassion. And how is God defined? I'll tell you. As a compassionate force! Therefore, after the tsunami, God was created in the minds of strangers...'

'Meaning that God is a secondary evolutionary principle to mankind?'

'There you go again... Putting words to my thoughts.'

It's rare to have a conversation that recalibrates your theory of the world. Finnigan has deduced that if God can be said to exist, it must be as a by-product of human evolution. It seems obvious now, but Brad doubts he could have devised this idea by himself. He reaches for a pen and paper to make some notes.

'You mind if I write that down?'

'Do what you need to; you're the writer.'

As Brad scribbles a couple of sentences, he says, 'Where are you getting all this?'

'Well... That's the other thing I need to talk to you about. Where the fuck *am* I getting all this?'

Rex D. Boyd has spent the afternoon on a train to Nottingham. Using the InterCity wi-fi, he's been swotting up on David Bohm. And the question that entrances him, more than the reasons for Eugene Polonski's elaborate death, the thing that really intrigues him, is why the work of this David Bohm has been marginalised for so long.

Boyd doesn't pretend to understand the details of Bohm's physics, but he can see the man had some genuinely futuristic ideas. In the decade after the end of the Second World War, America actively sought the cream of Nazi German scientists, the rocket experts especially, to come and work in the States. It was an official programme called Operation Paperclip. These war criminals had past deeds exonerated in the quest for America's technological supremacy. A pragmatic strategy to prevent them from defecting to the Eastern Bloc, or even to Britain... But if they were prepared to go to all that trouble, why not nurture their homegrown talent as well? At the time Bohm was a leading authority on plasmas, and the burgeoning science of nuclear fusion. He could have led the States into a new era of nuclear fusion power plants, not to mention the expertise he could have brought to building the hydrogen bomb. It hardly makes sense. Was Bohm merely the victim of McCarthyist bullying?

Boyd is aware that America needs enemies: create a perceived threat, keep the voting public in a state of fear, and win the right to go to war. It's the same with any imperialist power...

He recently heard the voice-over to a Vietnam War documentary, listening to it while he was cooking, and initially couldn't tell which American war was being discussed. It could have been one of so many, the 'enemy' being a malleable commodity; the rhetoric remains the same, as evidenced by the current debacle with Militant Islam.

Boyd closes his laptop down.

Why did the entire physics community sideline Bohm for so long? Was it just because he was a Marxist? The easy answer is often correct. McCarthyism was like a 1950s version of political correctness. The scientific community distanced themselves from left-wingers and the politically suspect. Also, Bohm had the temerity to question the Copenhagen Interpretation, which was seen as the ultimate betrayal of scientific truth.

From what Boyd can understand, Bohm's interpretation of the quantum world wasn't seriously considered until the 1990s. So maybe he was just 50 years ahead of the rest of the world…

Boyd's mind is rambling, looking for a position of advantage. But it's surprising to learn that the science community is as full of prejudice as any other discipline. He would have assumed science was a non-partisan search for objective truth. Apparently not…

He arrives in Nottingham late afternoon, and catches a cab to the murder site. He's making this journey in his personal time and at his own expense. He wants to get a flavour of Polonski's murder. That's what he keeps telling himself. But the social worker mentioned Polonski was carrying a small suitcase; the contents of which could likely be documents of some kind. No such documents have been found. Either they don't exist, or they have been stolen. The final option is that they remain hidden on site. This is the prize he's seeking, but it's such a long shot he keeps putting it out of his mind. He's here to analyse the murder.

The hostel looks bleak. Old men on the front steps, grey as the surrounding concrete. Boyd walks past them and into the building. He carries enough ID to blag access.

Upstairs, the police have done and dusted. The clean-up crew have cleaned. This is no longer an official crime scene, but Boyd pulls on some thin latex gloves anyway. It only seems right. He takes out a pocketknife. Every soldier has a favourite brand of weapon, and Boyd carries the brutally simple, single-blade Douk-Douk, also favoured by the French Foreign Legion.

He pushes the door open with the knife.

Hovers in the doorway.

The room as welcome as a mortician's breath.

If he listens carefully he'll be able to hear the distant clamour of war, because proximity of death always takes him back to the sand and the burning oil fields. He puts his past in its place and studies the scene. A solitary window allows enough streetlight for his initial appraisal. He imagines ghostly traces of fingerprint powder on the surfaces; although in reality it has all been wiped away. He must be noticing the residue of cleaning fluids.

The room is almost completely bare. There's an old iron bed-frame; no mattress. A table. A chair. A wardrobe. By the side of the bed the carpet looks fresher, having been bleached clean of dripping bloodstains.

He flicks on the light, and steps into the room. And using the blade he begins to poke around, opening the wardrobe door, pulling the curtains aside...

There's nothing left to see. The room has been emptied and sanitised. So he stands with his back to the window, trying to decide where he might hide a stash of important documents. He told himself this wasn't the reason for his presence. But it's the only thing he can think of.

He crouches down and peers at the underside of the table. Then under the chair and behind the wardrobe. He tips the wardrobe on its edge to look underneath; could be a good place to gaffer-tape some papers to. But, nothing...

The only decent hiding place for papers would be under the carpet. He takes his shoes off, and walks the room in his socks, feeling for lumps and bumps. He finds nothing but the damp patch by the bedside. Then takes a closer look under the sink where a section of carpet has been replaced... Lowers himself to the ground, next to the sink outlet pipe, and prises up a corner of the carpet. Nothing... But he sees a gap in the floorboards near the copper pipes; he feels around with the knife, catches something snagging on the blade. Peering into the hole with a pocket flashlight, he finds the end of a shoelace tied round the copper pipe; an anchor line that drops straight down.

The manila envelope he pulls out of the space is so old it feels like skin. He looks up, wanting someone to witness the precision of his methodology; someone to acknowledge his success. He photographs the moment in his mind for posterity, and for his forthcoming report.

'Okay. My turn to ask you something…'

This is Brad talking. They're still in the kitchen. It's been intense. Made more so because he's been rolling spliff, almost as something to do with his hands, while witnessing Finnigan offload the breadth of his new perceptions. It's only some old Moroccan hash he's had lying around for months – a real harsh smoke and a dull high – but it's been jollying their conversation along a treat.

'Let me ask you something,' Brad repeats, exhaling blue smoke, passing the joint to Finnigan. 'What do you know about David Bohm?'

Finnigan looks puzzled. 'Not sure that I know a David Bohm.'

He takes the joint, draws on it.

'You reacted to the name during my show, remember?'

Finnigan puts his hands up in surrender, blowing smoke to the ceiling.

'Can't remember too much about that; me going to your show. Only yesterday, wasn't it? Seems way longer… Things were unravelling…'

'But you reacted strongly to the name David Bohm. And…'

'Who is he, then?'

'Who *was* he, you mean. He's dead now…'

'Don't look at me, I never touched him.'

Finnigan laughs at his own joke. It takes Brad a moment to twig. He keeps forgetting the truth of Finnigan's past.

'You want to know where these aberrant thoughts are coming from, right?'

'Yeah.'

'So this David Bohm might provide the clue.'

'How's that?'

'Well, first of all… What did you know about the, er, the victim?'

'The target…? Some old bloke. Never need to know much, apart from description and whereabouts.'

'So where did the job come from? If you don't mind me asking.'

'I don't mind, Bradley. You know that. I'm trying to be – what's the word they use nowadays…? I'm trying to be transparent. I get these jobs through a contact. A criminal defence lawyer, as it happens.

And the less we know about each other the better. We have a symbiotic relationship. That's how he describes it.'

'Living off each other to mutual benefit. As opposed to a parasitic relationship, which eventually kills the host.'

'That's what he said. Mutual benefit.'

'So you had no knowledge of the old man?'

'Not directly.'

'I've got this weird theory…'

Finnigan looks at the joint they're smoking, and shrugs.

'Hey… Don't shoot me down because we're getting stoned. You know Jesus used to get stoned, and he had some good ideas.'

Finnigan laughs. 'How do you figure that?'

'Okay. I don't know if Jesus *was* a stoner, but he's become the poster boy for a stoner revolution, yeah? With the long hair and sandals? All that peace and love…? But the point I want to make is that he was preaching the words of the Zadokites, who lived in caves and ate hallucinogenic mushrooms…'

Finnigan waves this conversational thread away. He's got enough to deal with.

'Get back to what you were on about…'

'Okay. The man you killed… He used to work with David Bohm, a Theoretical Physicist. Helped to develop what's called the Holonomic Brain Theory…'

Finnigan begins to zone out, leaving Brad to explain the formation of light waves: how they carry information which is then decoded by the brain, turned into mathematical transforms, and how our actual thoughts are produced as yet another set of electromagnetic waves, specifically encoded as interference patterns within an ambient energy field. Which by definition proves that our thoughts inhabit a plane of spectral energy existing beyond space and time as a discrete part of the so-called universal consciousness.

Finnigan stifles a yawn. 'You think I've got the dead bloke's memories?'

Brad starts to laugh. He desperately wanted to explain this theory with the clarity it deserves.

'I've heard some stuff in my time mate.'

'But you believe in *chi*, right?'

'Maybe.'

'You must do! I mean… I assume you've studied some form of martial arts, right?'

'Alright. I concede that point.'

'So you'll know that the quest in Eastern philosophy is to seek a fundamental unity in all things? And that's what Bohm did! He created a scientific model that mirrors the Eastern paradigm. This separateness we experience as individuals is an illusion of personality… Your problem is that you're experiencing some bleed-through of ideas from…'

Brad gestures to the world around him.

Finnigan says, 'Maybe from the… What did you call it? … *interference patterns within the ambient sub-atomic force field*?'

Brad admires Finnigan's ability to repeat these words back to him; and sighs in despair, because in doing so, Finnigan has made the theory sound improbable, like a science fiction wish fulfilment.

He gives up on the deconstruction of quantum mechanics. Moves away from the kitchen table, staggers into the lounge, calling Finnigan to follow him. They stand in front of the bookshelves while Brad scans the titles.

'What are we looking for?'

'I want to give you a book. I never do this. I never lend my books because… It doesn't matter why. But there'll be something here that will turn you on to what I'm talking about.'

He picks up *The Holy Mushroom* by J. R. Irvin, and thrusts the book under Finnigan's nose, as if to prove his earlier argument.

'Look… Evidence of hallucinogenic mushrooms in Judeo-Christianity.'

He puts the book back, and hunts for another title, *The Rainbow and The Worm* by neuro-biologist Mae-Wan Ho. He flicks through the pages looking for a particular passage.

'I'm not giving you this one either, because I'm still trying to read it. It's really difficult. That's the problem. If the science is too easy you don't believe it; but if it's too difficult, you have to take the arguments on trust. But check this out…'

He reads aloud from the book: '…*much of our personal memory may be stored in an ambient, collective quantum holographic memory field delocalised from the individual… in the universal holographic medium of the quantum vacuum… Fully consistent with the romantic idea, increasingly validated by the foundations of quantum theory, that all nature is interconnected, and that the separateness and discreteness of things in the common-sensible world are illusory.'*

Finnigan looks nonplussed.

'It's what I've been talking about!' Brad returns the title, and scans the shelves. 'Mate, books are brilliant! There's definitely something here for you.'

He runs his finger along the spines, then shouts, 'Here we go! *The Holographic Universe* by Michael Talbot… You can have this one. I'll get another copy. It explains everything I've been talking about. David Bohm. Karl Pribram. The Holonomic Brain Theory. Everything. Written in the 1980s but still knock-out. Gets a little hippy-dippy near the end, but it's bloody marvellous. Here: it's a present.'

Finnigan looks quite moved. Astonished that anyone would go to this trouble for a book he might never read. He gives it a cursory glance, then grabs Brad in a solid man hug, growling with enthusiasm.

'You're a good bloke, Bradley. Thanks for your time.'

'Yeah… I've had enough as well. Go home! Seriously, Finnigan, even hit-men must have homes to go to.'

This reminds Finnigan for the first time since this whole incident began that he does have a home to go to. He'd forgotten it was an option. The mention of it allows another section of his past to drop into place.

'And get some fresh clothes, man, seriously. You're wearing a bespoke suit with blood stains.'

Finnigan looks at his fading elegance. 'You're right. I should go home. Get organised…'

They walk towards the front door of Brad's little flat.

'So what are you going to do? Lay low, or something?'

'Considering going abroad. I've got money. Maybe I'll be like David Carradine in *Kung Fu*. Remember that show? Might be before your time; on telly in the '70s. All about this wandering Shaolin monk, beating people up and helping strangers. Sounds like my style. Might help to redress my karma. Put me in touch with the…'

Finnigan gestures to the universal energies that supposedly surround and feed us all. He laughs again at this shared joke.

'Thanks, Bradley. We all need someone to talk to. It's been real. And the book – I'll get round to reading that one day.'

Brad follows him to the front door. And with that, Finnigan's down the stairs and gone.

Brad moves back to the lounge to lean out of the window, trying to see Finnigan as he crosses the road towards the sea. He's sure he catches a glimpse, before the man becomes lost in the surge of other lives bustling through the afternoon. It leaves Brad with a feeling of melancholy. Anti-climactic. It's probably just exhaustion, but he senses he's let Finnigan down somehow. Not that he owed him anything.

He must sleep. Takes his phone into the bedroom, leaves another text for Jane: *Panic over! Everything okay! Love you xxx*.

She'll be at work, with her phone on silent. He kicks off his shoes, and climbs into bed fully dressed. Sets his alarm for two hours' time; should be long enough to revive him. He leaves a notebook and pen on the floor by the bed, but he's too tired to write anything down. Sometimes the act of capturing one's thoughts seems so futile. Bohm was fond of the admonition, *Whatever we say a thing is, it is not*. It's a reflection of the opening passage from the *Tao Te Ching*: *The truth that can be spoken is not the eternal truth*.

And yet Brad feels he could have done better by Finnigan, in helping to explain his meltdown. Regarding the physical *cause* of his condition, Brad can't begin to fathom. Of greater interest to him is the nature of the phenomenon: somehow, Finnigan's brain-machine seemed to be resonating with a dead man's thoughts. As a dabbler in theories of neuroscience, Brad assumes this anomaly could happen.

Thoughts are written in code and constructed of light. It's how we have evolved: to be a vehicle for consciousness. Each physical vehicle has its own unique resonance, its own signature mind waves;

but suppose the brain-machine was somehow thrown out of sync and retuned…?

Brad slowly fades into a doleful sleep, where his thoughts roam a familiar landscape of dream world quandary. It's the classic Catch 22 of human sentience. The fact is, we *all* have insights into the sphere of ultimate meaning, but due to this being a subjective experience, we will never agree on what the ultimate meaning actually means.

It's heart-breaking to think that the fundamental essence of life and death remains beyond the scope of words; that every separate definition only distances the idea from its mathematical truth. Brad would like to believe it's possible for The Mystery to be deconstructed; but he knows it would have to be done through science, and by someone with a greater expressive skill than his own.

Boyd has the envelope in his hands. This is the mother lode. The key to the mystery. It's what Polonski was killed for. Boyd has no preconception of the form this information will take, but expects plans, conspiracies, names and addresses. Or equations. Pages of code…

He's reluctant to handle the envelope too much, so he lays it on the table and teases it open with the knife blade. Inside, he sees a collection of old school notebooks. He carefully slides them out. He's on the threshold of something extraordinary. He carefully turns the pages of the first book and the contents hit him like an insult.

Cartoons.

Garish cartoons.

Page after page of pen-and-ink drawings, coloured and over-coloured, as if trying to force the visible spectrum into new levels of depth and complexity.

He opens the other books, and they're all the same: impossible to focus on. Mythical beasts, flying men with numerous arms, astronauts and copulating figures, and death. Lots of death: bones and rotting flesh, fierce creatures feeding on human remains. Some in the Brueghel style, some Tibetan-mystical, all nightmarish…

Five notebooks of the stuff, bursting open with additional pages created from newspaper cuttings: topics like UFO sightings, insect communication, religious miracles, and scientific revelation. It's frighteningly intense, over-written with notes that make no immediate sense. Brilliant, slashing lines of colour join sections of writing; heavy deletions, arrows joining one footnote to another. It disappoints and scares him to be in possession of something fizzing with so much impenetrable insanity.

Boyd leaves the building as subtly as he arrived. The envelope safe in his laptop case. He waits on the front steps, taking it all in, waiting for his cab.

A few of the old boys are still sitting there smoking, chewing the fat.

'You here for the killing?' says one.

'Social services,' he says, lying without thinking.

'I heard them, y'know. Heard them… Two of them in black suits, like undertakers. Looked like they were in charge. They waited with him, with the fella that had the breathing mask…'

'Did you tell the police?'

'None of their business.'

'Why you telling me?'

'Because I saw them.'

'Could you identify them?'

'Of course.'

Kung Fu Like John Carradine

On Brighton beach, between the transparent blue twilight and a powder-pink sunset, Finnigan sees an image of the Virgin Mary in the clouds. Clear as a tattoo on the bicep of a Puerto Rican street punk, and large as the sky. Her ink-stained tears are falling for the suffering of mortal flesh.

This is someone else's dream.

Finnigan is not given to sentimentality but he accepts The Virgin's iconic capacity for absolution. He is motionless and transfixed, experiencing some form of mental disintegration.

Retain this knowledge at the moment of death.

He knows the vision is only appearing in this form due to his own cultural conditioning. He could easily be witnessing Jesus, or Krishna, or Princess Leia.

But he remains motionless, staring into the sunset. The vision of Our Lady shines back. He must retain this moment and hold it close at the instant of death. It looks beautiful up there, no longer weighed down by the expectations of matter. He could cry but vanity won't allow it, yet his cheeks are wet...

Flow my tears, the murderer said.

Pedestrians wash past him like dreams.

Finnigan's rational mind assures him this is not a religious conversion. This is merely an insight. He is being blessed. He is being nurtured. It is our saving grace.

All that matters is the piece of yourself you leave in others, and the piece of themselves they leave in you.

Finnigan can feel Brad's book in his hand. He barely recognises the receipt of presents as a social activity, but he accepts it as an idea poised in space, as an intention from the giver to the recipient. All that matters is the piece of yourself you leave in others, and the piece of themselves they leave in you.

The book in Finnigan's hand might have the words to explain this. At the most fundamental level the physical form is composed of energy that has coalesced. And, after the disintegration of matter, the waveform survives. Across the planet three people die every second. Like changing channels.

We exist as evolutionary sentience.

He sees the people around him rushing like phantoms, and wants to call out to them.

There is more meaning than is evident.

You will not be cast adrift.

Everyone has the capacity to be saved.

This would be the perfect moment for a clear death. And to retain this knowledge at the instant of death is power.

Brad is woken from a dark, dead sleep by the shrill voice of his mobile cutting into his awareness. He assumes it must be Finnigan.

'Yeah…'

'Brad. Hi. Can't talk coz I'm on a cheeky cig break. I got your text but I'm just making sure everything's okay. I've been going *frantic* with worry about you, about what I did, are you *okay*, did he…?'

'Jane…?'

'I can't believe I was so *naïve*, imagine falling for that! And who *is* this man pretending to be a policeman? I mean, God, did he actually *kill* someone…?'

'Jane, it's fine… I left you a message. Did you get my message…?'

'Yes, but…'

'Look, it's all fine… It's all over. I'll tell you everything when I see you, okay? You still at work?'

'Yeah, still here, will be for a while. Recording Phil Jupitus for this poetry thing. Did you know he used to be a poet? Porky the Poet. It's a revelation…'

'Okay. Tell him hello from me.'

'But you don't know him.'

'Doesn't matter. Tell him I like the cut of his jib.'

'Er, okay… You *sure* everything's alright?'

'Yeah. Been a long few days… Look, get back to your recording. Where are you? Salford?'

'Yeah, for Radio 4.'

'That's a long way.'

'I'll be back tonight, but late. I'll see you tomorrow, okay? We'll catch up.'

'Cool. I'll make some food.'

'That'll be nice. I like your cooking.'

'I like cooking for you.'

'I like you cooking for me.'

'And I like… er, you. I like you. So there.'

She laughs. 'Me too. You, I mean. I like you too.'

He laughs. 'Okay…'

'Okay…'

'Bye, baby.'

'Bye.'

Al Blackstock stirs himself awake from a codeine and vodka blackout. He's fully dressed, face stuck to the vinyl sofa cushions. Takes him a moment to register his predicament. Face throbbing, missing finger screaming. Revenge alight and blazing with righteousness. First things first: coffee, painkillers, cigarette; and then the journey to retribution. His plan is simple. Find Finnigan, and create an opportunity for payback.

He has a car tracker, a GPS device that sends alerts to his mobile. Bought it at one of those nerdy electrical outlets. Used it once on a job with Finnigan. How ironic, he thinks: this device will now allow him to track Finnigan and follow him to a suitable location for the showdown. He just needs to fit the device to Finnigan's car, monitor his movements and bang! He is monumentally pleased with the simplicity of this plan.

Blackstock lives in an ex-council flat on the Alfred Estate, East London, and although much of it is now privately owned, the location still has that council feel: overlooking the train lines on one side, and sandwiched in by the busy A200 on the other.

Both Finnigan and Blackstock lived here as kids. It has been witness to most of their childhood experiences: grazed knees and broken noses; loss of virginity and dignity – and the loss of the straight and narrow. They both spilled blood here, and can't remember a time when they didn't know each other, hence their mutual sense of trust.

Like much of East London this estate has been ravaged by gentrification. It isn't what it used to be. The whole area now teeming with hipsters and such, with their vegan food and yoga studios; young people getting their shit together. It's not for everyone.

Finnigan left the estate, but not the area. Lives only ten minutes' walk away. But Blackstock still lives in his childhood home. His mother's long gone, but the place is full of reminders. The cracked and broken fixtures; the plastic chairs and Formica-topped kitchen table that were once so modern. He rarely thinks about his mother, unless it's to blame her for his current circumstance. Had she made better choices...

He occasionally finds a long silver hair under the sofa cushions, or in among her clothes in one of the wardrobes. It used to fill him with remorse; these days it just makes him angry. When he sorts Finnigan out and takes control of his business contacts, he'll be happy to let this place burn to the ground.

He puts the kettle on for coffee; necks a couple of codeine with water from the kitchen tap. Goes on the hunt for the tracker. It's all falling into place. Lucky he had the foresight to lift Finnigan's Walther from The Beggar during the commotion. Lucky he knows Jackie's hiding place for such items. But it's not luck, is it? It's destiny. Working with Finnigan, he always knew if he could bide his time, he'd eventually prosper. Be elevated to a higher status, to higher ground, where the rewards are endless and the kudos gold-plated.

Finnigan has taken the train home. Direct from Brighton to London Bridge. It's night, and he takes a short walk home through the heart of the East End. Straight down Tooley Street, up the junction with Jamaica Road, and left into Shad Thames. He loves the names in this part of London. This tiny acreage is a window on the city's past. Built from the graft of Empire: Saffron, Java, Cinnamon, and Tea Trade Wharfs; Vanilla Court, Sesame Court, Cardamom Building...

On and on…

His own building is right by the river. He can spit into the Thames from his living room windows. He bought the entire top floor, back in the day when feral dogs roamed the streets and were known to savage the sleeping forms of the homeless. He remembers the headlines as a kid. Filled him with awe and respect for the dominant forces of nature. It's different now, of course: first the yuppie boom, then the crash. He's waiting for the wild dogs to return, for the bricks and mortar to crumble, for the insistence of time to lay waste the arrogance of progress. Ozymandias, where are you now?

Finnigan no longer cares where his thoughts are coming from… *Look on my works ye mighty, and despair! Nothing beside remains. Round the decay of that colossal wreck, boundless and bare the lone and level sands stretch far away…*

He concedes this area of London seems resistant to time and the folly of mortality, but everything will return to the source. He loves the breadth of this new attitude, knowing it won't last.

This is the direction of his future life: a change of clothes, handful of cash and a passport. Travel the road, watch the world spin; dispense compassion in any form he chooses. Redress his karma. It'll do until the luck and the money run out.

His building is a redbrick and stone warehouse, originally built to house mercantile goods arriving by boat from the colonies. Now it's home to the rich, the exclusive, and him. He walks up the stone stairs, four flights to the top. Inside, it's brutally sparse. One huge space with cast iron columns and tall steel-framed windows. Light from outside casts geometric shapes on the wooden floor; the shadows move as he walks into the semi-darkness. He loves the moody solitude, the simple order.

Being back home, Finnigan finds the familiarity of safety. He recognises who he is, but his plans don't change. It makes him even more certain. He'll leave first thing in the morning. Take the shuttle to France, and see what happens. A new adventure, until the luck and the money run out, which they will do sooner or later. He can't see himself with old bones.

He empties his pockets onto the kitchen counter, strips down, puts the bloodstained clothes in a bin liner, leaves it by the door. Takes a shower. Washing away the past, preparing for the new. He walks to the bedroom area. No separating walls in this gloomy mausoleum, just as he wanted it. Spartan. Basic needs. The single closet is housed in one of the building's recesses. He'll be sorry to leave his threads behind, but he needs a new look. Decides to pack a suit, a couple of white button-downs, but the rest will be workout clothes: sweats and hoodies. He has to decide which suit will best survive being left rolled up in a hold-all. Chooses a golden-brown two-tone; three button, no vent, narrow lapels, narrow ankles. Looks good anywhere, even over a T-shirt with running shoes.

There are a couple of loose bricks in the wall at the back of the closet. He removes them, and takes out a bundle of notes, passport and credit cards. All a man needs. Done. Walks to the fridge, checks the date on the milk and fixes a protein shake. Drinks it while staring at the book from Bradley. Doesn't pick it up, just stares at the cover. Washes up, and lies down on the bed. Drifting off. What else to do?

Then he has a thought: it would be nice to return the favour to Bradley. He decides to send him an envelope of cash, by courier. He reckons he knows the man for the job. He gets up from the bed, walks to the counter where he left the contents of his pockets and finds Jimi's number. Calls him.

'Jimi...'

'Yeah? Maybe it is. Who's calling?'

'Finnigan...'

'No way! Finnigan, my man! Never expected this, bro. To what do I owe this pleasure...?'

'Need to ask you a favour. Meet me at my place 6.45 in the morning?'

'Whatever you say, bruv...'

Finnigan leaves his address, smiles at Jimi's unrivalled enthusiasm, and once again hits the sheets, this time for a solid five hours of untroubled sleep.

Blackstock has driven over to Finnigan's place. Parks nearby, and peers up at the top-floor windows. He sees no lights on, and no sign of life. Even so, he waits a good half hour before making his way to the basement car park. He has the keys to this part of the building; a necessity Finnigan agreed to, should he ever need access to Finnigan's motor. Doesn't have keys to the apartment, obviously. In fact, in spite of their 20-year working relationship, he's only ever been to Finnigan's castle on two occasions. The man doesn't like visitors.

Once inside the car park, Blackstock hunches down and hunts out Finnigan's motor: a black Audi A5. It takes less than a moment to crawl beneath and fit the tracker to the underside of the chassis. Job done, he walks away very pleased. Out into the night air, and back to his own wheels for the wait.

Blackstock hasn't given up on confrontation, but sitting alone in his car he soon feels his resolve being tested. It's not just that Finnigan is a formidable opponent, but it's so fucking desperate to be out here in the cold, resorting to these underhand methods. Uncomfortable and depressing. And literally every inch of his body is causing him pain. He deserves a break. Deserves a chance at the top. And for this to happen, he needs to know who Finnigan is working with. He lowers the driving seat, rubs a little coke into his gums and hunkers down for the long wait.

All the main players are asleep, each wrestling with their dreams and shortcomings. Everyone except Boyd. The early hours find Rex D. Boyd wide awake, as his peculiar metabolism dictates. He's been waging an intelligence war with terror since the Second Gulf War, a business venture initially captained by George Bush senior. Boyd was working for the knucklehead son, the dolt of the family firm. It's how Boyd sees things, to be part of an extended American family. And he'd be the first to admit the war on terror isn't going to be won by force; that, in fact, force only serves to feed the beast. He's more interested in changing the paradigm. His interest in homeland security is more visionary than the college types'; he has a mind for the hidden machinations of subversion, hence his interest in the Polonski case. Any spilled American blood is his own blood; the name of every fallen man is engraved in stone to be remembered. He seeks retribution, but remains fascinated by the mindset that underwrites the act of terror.

He's ahead thanks to the recovery of the notebooks, but a whole night of studying has yielded nothing but confusion. His 'to do' list contains two imperatives. One is to find the undertakers who had contact with the alleged killer. The other is to interview this Bradley Holmeson, the author apprehended in possession of the murderer's car.

Boyd has made the (right or wrong) assumption that the key to this incident is Polonski's collection of notebooks. He's jotted down three questions: who knew about the notebooks?

Why was it important to kill Polonski?

Why not just steal the notebooks?

It's clear to Boyd that the overall tone of David Bohm's work is anti-capitalist. And if you want to discover the real machinations of the world, you follow the money. But he can't decide who would be threatened by any information that Polonski would have to share. It seems so nebulous. Polonski, the ex-Bureau man who followed Bohm into exile, has been killed; theatrically, assassination-style. So is it a whistle-blowing statement, to highlight the treatment of Bohm?

Keep chipping away at the clues, and the reason will reveal itself.

Boyd decides his next move is to visit the author Bradley Holmeson. See him face-to-face. See what he has to offer.

Monday...

Friendly Fire

Al Blackstock awakes in pain: knots in his back and shoulders from sleeping in the driver seat of his motor. It takes some attention away from his more serious problem. He's been here all night and has seen nothing of Finnigan. People come and go from the building, but no one that could be labelled as criminal associate. He concedes he might have missed some activity while he was asleep, but at least he knows Finnigan hasn't moved his car. He also knows from previous jobs that a stakeout has none of the excitement and glamour that fiction would have us believe. It's insufferably tedious.

He clocks a pizza van arriving at the building's entrance; looks like a Citroen, one of those small-wheelbase delivery vans. He doesn't stop to consider the anomaly of this; that takeaway deliveries are normally via motorbike. This is the type of van used to supply the kitchen with produce. But he doesn't notice this. He looks at his watch: 6.45am. Looks back at the van, with its hazard lights blinking. He knows it's unusual to have pizza delivered for breakfast, but who can account for the dietary habits of the rich and privileged? The driver jumps out, completely hidden behind hoodie, baseball cap and padded jacket, and bounces up to the intercom with a stay-warm bag balanced on his hand. Blackstock feels the rumblings of hunger, and considers calling it a day; getting something fried and heart-stopping at a nearby cafe. He steps out of the car to stretch and smoke another cigarette.

The pizza boy bounds up the four flights and raps on the penthouse door. Finnigan lets him into the apartment. On glancing around, Jimi gives full rein to his enthusiasm.

'Some place, Finnigan! Check. This. Out. I knew you was a classy dude, but this… This place is so sharp, scared I'm gonna cut myself.'

Finnigan smiles. 'I see you brought breakfast.'

Jimi looks at the pizza bag. 'This…? I got you fooled, bro; I got you fooled. Part of the disguise, yeah? I got a pizza van downstairs. Bought it off a mate months ago when his pizza place got closed down. My crew take the piss, but if it fools Finnigan, it's gonna fool everyone, yeah?'

Finnigan steps forward to shake his hand. Jimi ignores the handshake and goes in for a man hug. Then he steps back, keeping a respectful distance.

'And what's with the get up, bro? You usually so proper, all suited and booted; and now who is this I see before me?'

Finnigan shrugs. Too complicated to explain. But he throws a shape like a gypsy king, letting Jimi see the full glory of his new clobber: random trackie bottoms, big hi-top sneakers, white vest and a black leather waistcoat; bare arms displaying a scattered arrangement of prison-style tattoos.

'I'm going on holiday,' he says.

'Is it? Okay, bruv, say no more, say no more…'

'That's why I need you to do me a little favour.'

'Give the word, Finnigan, my man. Be a pleasure to help, any way I can.'

'I knew you'd say that. Why I called you.'

Jimi nods in appreciation.

Finnigan crosses to the kitchen area, picks up an A4 padded envelope.

'Need you to deliver this to a friend of mine. Down in Brighton.'

'South coast? Nice. I could do with a day out of town.'

'This friend of mine, he doesn't know about it. So you got to give it to him personally. Put it in his hands. Make sure he takes it and opens it in front of you.'

'I can do that. Easy done. Give me the dude's details, and I'm set to go.'

'Bloke called Bradley Holmeson.'

Finnigan jots the name and address on a piece of paper, hands it to Jimi.

'Here you go…'

'You got a postcode? I can put it in the sat nav.'

Finnigan shakes his head.

'It's in the centre of Brighton, just off the main drag, the central shopping street.'

'Cool… I'll find it.'

'Appreciate it, Jimi.'

Jimi bangs a closed fist to his chest. Finnigan slaps him on the shoulder. Then he takes a few fifties from his money clip and puts them in Jimi's palm, with a handshake.

'Petrol money, and something for your trouble.'

'That is sound as a pound, Finnigan. That is sound.'

'You're doing me a favour. No one else I could trust with an envelope of cash.'

There's nothing else to be said, but Jimi takes his time, walks around the apartment looking out the windows at the view of the river, turning back to enjoy the calm of the space. Everything is in its place – the gym equipment, heavy bag, loose weights; glass-brick shower cubicle, and what looks like a sauna cabin – all fitting neatly into the architecture.

'This place is boss, Finnigan. I tell you…'

'I'll be sorry to leave.'

'Not forever though, right? Not that I'm prying, but not forever?'

'See what happens. I'm feeling expansive. Need to get out the city. Stretch the legs, stretch the mind… Maybe I'll stroll across Europe; chance my luck as some kind of wandering kung fu pilgrim, a real-life John Carradine… Who knows?'

Finnigan laughs at the adventure of it.

'Don't entirely understand it, coz I love the City; but sounds righteous. Anyway, I got this address, I got the package, so I am out of here, yeah?'

Jimi turns back to shake Finnigan's hand, and as he does, he sees the flyer to Brad's show, sitting on the kitchen counter where Finnigan left it.

'Hey. This the same dude, right? Same name.'

He picks the flyer up and reads it.

'*Death and Physics*? Really? That is some heavy shit right there. You into this?'

Finnigan isn't sure what Jimi's getting at.

Then Jimi sees the book Brad gave him, *The Holonomic Universe*. He holds the book up, and scans the back cover.

'Nice one, Finnigan… Never had you down with science and shit. You seriously into this?'

The question hits Finnigan. 'Say that again?'

Jimi looks up. He notices a change of mood.

'Say that again, son. What you just said.'

Jimi puts the book down.

'Ain't saying nothing, bro. Except didn't think you was a connoisseur of science.'

Finnigan is staring at him, intense and angry.

Jimi raises his hands, placatory. 'Are you vexed, Finn?'

'Not with you.'

'Okay then, I'm just loitering, yeah. You got a schedule to keep. I'm out of your hair as of right now.'

He waves the parcel in the air. 'Consider this one thing you don't have to worry about.'

Jimi walks over to the door, less sure about things than when he arrived. Finnigan's change of mood was abrupt and cold.

'Wait!' Finnigan shouts.

Jimi stops, saying nothing.

'Why would anyone think I was a connoisseur of science?'

'No, I said you wasn't.'

'Then why have I got this book?'

Jimi is naturally talkative as a means of navigating his everyday life. A constant stream of inquisitive chatter, but he's also learned to hold his tongue. Let the other man take the floor. He watches Finnigan pick up the book and slam it back down on the counter.

'What the fuck is this?'

He points at Jimi: 'You are so fucking right. This is not something I'm into. I accepted it, because I was immersed in it…'

Finnigan turns away, deciding how much to admit. Turns back to Jimi.

'Visions! I was having fucking visions yesterday! I'm on Brighton Beach, and I'm seeing a vision of the Virgin fucking Mary. Except it wasn't her, was it? No! It was a manifestation of consciousness. Resonance. Emotion made manifest! It was the world revealed as spectral fucking information… Are you following this?'

'Can't say that I am, Finnigan.'

'No! That's right! This is not common knowledge. I see that now. I have been beguiled by the words. But the question is not *why* are these foreign words in my head; the question is, *Who deemed it necessary?*'

Finnigan is raging with the affront of this situation, banging his fist down on the book.

'Slight change of plans. I'll be travelling down to Brighton with you. Need to ask this Bradley fucking Holmeson a few more questions.'

'Whatever you need, man. Long as you don't mind slumming it in a pizza van.'

'Where you parked?'

'Right outside, boss. On a double yellow... So I'll see you down there. No rush.'

'Give me two minutes.'

Jimi leaves, pleased to put distance between himself and Finnigan's mood swing.

Across the road from Finnigan's building, Blackstock is emptying his night-time piss bottle into the kerb, prior to seeking out some breakfast. He sees the pizza boy jump down the steps and into his van. He expects the kid to burn the tyres, and cause unruly havoc in the morning traffic. Always ready to judge the youth on their driving habits. But the van stays put. It's curious. Blackstock is still bleary-eyed, and he waits to see what happens.

Minutes later, Finnigan appears. He assumes it's him; same body shape – but not the style. He's dressed like a fucking pikey warlord. Blackstock thinks he's seeing things; too much codeine, not enough sleep. But he knows this is Finnigan climbing into the pizza van. Then he watches the van reverse into the road. The abruptness of Finnigan's potential escape freezes his bones. He could tell himself it's too late, get some breakfast and some kip; wait for another time. That's what he'd like to do. But he finds himself rushing back to his motor, jumping in and ducking down as the pizza van pulls up to the junction of Jamaica Road. He watches it join the traffic. Then he's turning the engine over, and on the chase.

Nine-thirty and Brad is wide awake. He was up early to phone The Brighton Book Cellar to blag the day off. That sorted, he scrambled some eggs, brewed a pot of coffee, then dashed round with the vacuum cleaner, gave the bathroom a spruce-up, wiped the surfaces, changed the bin bags… Been a while since he's done this: taking pride in the place. But Jane's coming round, so: single man make cave nice.

His mobile is buzzing on silent on the kitchen table, shivering with each muted ring tone.

'Hello…?'

'Bradley Holmeson?'

'Yeah…? Who's this?'

'This is Rex D. Boyd of the United States Homeland Security, Sir, I have previously attempted to contact you…'

'That's right…?'

'I know you were debriefed by Nottinghamshire Police…'

Brad smiles at that word again. Tries to give a fuck about the phone call.

'I've told everything I know to the police.'

'This is a separate investigation, sir.'

'It might be, but any information I have to offer is going to be exactly the same.'

'Are you refusing to co-operate, sir?'

'No! Just read the police report. All I have to say will be right there. It was a very thorough interview.'

'With respect, Mr Holmeson…'

'What respect? What respect are you giving me? I've already explained, I told everything to the police. I'm sorry… I'm done with this. And I'm going to hang up.'

He hangs up. Slightly regretting his phone manner. He expects Rex D. Whatever-His-Name-Is to phone back. But the phone remains ominously silent. He wishes he had the patience for these things.

At the other end of the line, Boyd is staring at his inert mobile. He's on the train but knows he didn't lose signal. The Holmeson character hung up on him. Again. You do not hang up on a representative of the American Embassy. It's an admission of guilt. Boyd knew it was an outside bet boarding the train to Brighton, but he now believes he backed a winner. He looks at his watch. He'll be there in 17 minutes.

Brad finishes his coffee and picks up wallet and keys. Jane's coming round for *elevenses*, she said. He smiles at the euphemism, and is humorously compelled to buy cakes to complete their little joke. He rolls a joint to accompany his stroll to the shops, smiling with anticipation. She makes him feel good about himself, or she makes him be a better person. It comes to the same thing.

At 9.50am the pizza van arrives in Brighton, and pulls up outside Brad's address. Jimi stays at the wheel, while Finnigan races up the main stairs, finds Brad's flat and bangs on the door. No answer. He waits. No answer. Back downstairs to the van.

'Park it up somewhere, mate. Come inside. You don't mind a wait?'

'I'm easy, bruv. Two minutes, yeah?'

Jimi drives off in search of a space; Finnigan waits at the entrance, in full view of Blackstock, who is hiding in his car on the corner of a side street across the road. It wasn't a difficult drive for Blackstock, the pizza van being so distinctive. He was able to follow without being obvious, without getting too close. He waits, and watches. Then he sees the pizza kid return, and disappear into the building with Finnigan. He leaves the warmth of his car to lean against a nearby wall; blending in with the lost and lonely men who pepper this part of town, hoping the fresh air will keep him alert, trying to decide his next move.

Blackstock's success in tracking his quarry doesn't surprise him. He's fully aware of his skill base. But why is Finnigan being driven by some kid in a pizza van? What advantage does Finnigan hope to gain by this? Blackstock knows he holds his trump card of surprise, but his confidence is being eroded by jealousy and confusion.

Jimi and Finnigan wait in the stairwell for a good 25 minutes, not saying much. Jimi knows when to keep schtum, and Finnigan is exuding an extraordinary level of brooding tension. As they wait, there is a slow trickle of human traffic up and down the stairs. Then Finnigan nudges Jimi's attention towards a middle-aged, crew-cut man in a cheap suit, looking at the numbers on the doors, carrying himself with bullish authority. Finnigan clocks him for ex-services.

He finds Brad's door and rings the bell; waits for an answer, and turns to see Finnigan and Jimi sitting in the stairwell.

'You looking for Bradley Holmeson?' asks Finnigan.

Boyd answers with his own line of questioning, 'And who might you be?'

They clock Boyd's accent.

'I'm his lawyer,' replies Finnigan.

'His lawyer...?' says Boyd, pulling a theatrically confused face. It's a direct challenge. No one calls Finnigan a liar. He stands up, walks towards him. Jimi follows, on cue, and walks down the stairs to block Boyd's exit. Finnigan is now standing face-to-face with the stranger, who fronts up; puts his game face on. Both men are quietly confident of their ability to win this situation, whichever way it might turn.

'Any business you have with Bradley Holmeson is my business,' says Finnigan. 'So you may as well spill the beans, me old mucker.'

'Spill the beans? Is that how British lawyers address the public these days?'

Finnigan steps back, so as not to crowd the man. Doesn't want to freak him into defensive violence.

'You septic?'

'What do you mean, septic?'

'Septic tank, Yank! From over the pond.'

'Okay. Rhyming slang...'

'You catch on, old son.'

'And who are you really, sir?'

'No. Question is: who are you? You turn up looking for dialogue with my man, without even an introduction. I call that rude.'

'Well fucking rude, boss.'

Boyd turns to clock Jimi, bouncing on his toes. Enjoying this confrontation. He's loving how Finnigan can banter like this, to unsettle anyone. Waiting for the right moment to strike.

'I'd put you down as ex-services,' continues Finnigan.

'82nd Airborne. Two tours of Afghanistan, prior to that...'

'So what happened? Dishonourable discharge? Been a naughty boy? Power of the torture room get to you, did it?'

Finnigan has no idea how near the mark he is with this last comment.

Boyd takes a small step back and says, 'Okay friend. Let's start again. My name is Rex D. Boyd and I'm here on the official business of the United States Embassy.'

He announces this like his high status is going to win the day. But Finnigan laughs at him; laughs in his face.

Then Finnigan breathes in deeply, closes his eyes for a second, concentrating. He throws a couple of shapes to disorientate Boyd, before stabbing him in the chest with two straight fingers. Jimi is moving up the stairs to take Boyd down, but Boyd is gone; gasping for breath, in a weird faint.

'Finnigan, man, what was that?'

Jimi has caught Boyd under the arms, his body a dead weight.

'Wasn't sure it would work. I took a chance. I was showing off.'

'Right. But what was it?'

'Call it *dim mak*... Also known as the Touch of Death.'

'Touch of Death? Telling me you kill someone like that?'

Finnigan shakes his head in mock despair, talking under his breath.

'They always want to know about the killing...'

He turns to Jimi and says, 'I'm not sure it would actually kill him, but it'll do serious damage if I don't resuscitate. Right now all the life is slowly flowing out of him.'

'That is whack...'

'You want me to teach you?'

'No. I'm good.'

Jimi is struggling to support Boyd's weight, which is becoming heavier by the second. The man is falling into a complete collapse. His head and limbs are cumbersome like a crash test dummy. Finnigan watches, enjoying the results of his attack, before helping Jimi with the body. They drag Boyd over to the wall, prop him up, and turn their attention to the door of Brad's flat.

'How are you with locks?' asks Finnigan.

'You wanna break in?'

'Can't leave buddy boy out here can we? Need somewhere safe to bring him round. Not healthy to leave a man in the throes of death touch.'

'I can't do locks, bruv. Not my bag. We'll have to force it.'

Finnigan shrugs. Then reluctantly aims a kick with the flat of his foot at the edge of the door, right by the lock. There's a splintering sound. They both look round, expecting someone to hear. There's no discernible reaction. Finnigan attacks the door again, and three kicks later the doorframe gives way, and he stumbles into Brad's flat.

They carry Boyd inside, clean up the worst, and hold the door closed with the safety chain.

Brad returns home laden with cakes, vegetables and beer. He did a proper shop, cooking for two later. Planned the whole day around her like a special date, giving him a daffy, adolescent grin. He's so looking forward to seeing her; his high only slightly dented by the sight of some homeless dude, sitting on the pavement by the corner of his road. Just sitting there, glaring at him through a bruised and bloody face; one hand wrapped in a filthy bandage. Brad hurries past, trying to avoid eye contact. He's pleased to reach the safety of his building. Then he walks up the stairs to his floor, and sees the damage to the door.He simultaneously shouts *Fuck!* and drops his shopping. The case of mini beer bottles crashes down and smashes on the concrete of the communal hallway. He hears voices inside. Whoever broke the door, they're still here; so he runs up the next flight of stairs, giving them the opportunity of a clear escape. He's trying to remember if he's up to date with his home insurance, when he hears a familiar voice.

'Sorry about the door, Bradley. Needs must. I'll see you right.'

Finnigan strides into view. Holding his arms out to the prodigal son. He's wearing a vest and leather waistcoat, revealing a depth of body tattoos. No artistic grace, just a ragbag of images in faded ink.

'… the fuck are you doing here?'

Jimi appears by Finnigan's side.

'Everything okay, boss?'

'Give him a hand with his shopping, Jimi. And best clear this mess up, yeah?'

Without a word, Jimi attends to the task. Finnigan disappears back inside the flat. Brad follows into the lounge where he sees a man handcuffed to his desk chair; comatose, drooling, and deathly white.

'What happened to him?'

'What do you think happened?'

'Don't fucking say you killed him.'

'Told you: I given that up. But I have disabled him.'

'You've disabled him?'

Brad entertains a vision of limbless bone sockets.

'It's temporary. Worst he'll have is nausea, headaches, a little bruising.'

'There's a blessing. Yeah? I'm being sarcastic! What the fuck are you doing here?'

Finnigan stands next to Brad, both of them looking at Boyd's sorry state. Then he grabs the back of Brad's neck and shakes him from side to side, like you might with a scampish puppy.

'You ever heard of *dim mak*?' asks Finnigan.

'Not unless you eat it with fried rice.'

'That's why I like you, Bradley. If you don't know something, you make it up.'

'Is that why you're here?'

'No. It's why Mr Boyd of the American Embassy is out for the count.'

'That's Boyd? That's Rex D. Boyd...?

Brad throws his hands to his head, and shouts, 'No...! He thinks I'm involved! And now...? Fuck this is bad. This is very, very bad.'

'Why would he think you're involved?'

'Because you're here! And you've killed him! Not killed him, but... Does it matter? He's from the American fucking Embassy! What have you done?'

Jimi comes back into the lounge with the remains of Brad's shopping.

'All cleared up outside, boss.'

Then he turns to Brad. 'Most of that beer is gone though, mate. You should have kept a tight hold of that and let go of the vegetables, yeah?'

Brad says nothing.

'There's a few bottles left, though.'

Jimi hands them round.

Finnigan says, 'Bradley, this is my man Jimi. And Jimi, this is the Science Boy we were talking about.'

They nod a hello, with Brad pulling a face at the moniker *Science Boy*.

Jimi peers at him.

'You don't look much like a Professor… No disrespect, but you don't.'

They clink a resigned hello with their beer bottles.

Finnigan claps his hands.

'I suppose we'd better bring Mr Boyd back to life. Then, between us, we're getting to the bottom of this.'

'Amen to that, bro,' says Jimi, taking a long pull on the warm beer.

Finnigan turns to Boyd; still handcuffed to the chair, still looking deathly pale, with pained shallow breathing. Twists him sideways to get a clear view of the man's back.

Brad casually whispers to Jimi, 'What happened to Finnigan? I thought we were cool?'

'Have to ask him, man.'

Finnigan looks up from attending to Boyd.

'You're asking me what happened?'

He pulls the flyer out from his pocket and waves it in Brad's face.

'This is what happened! How did this get in my hands? Eh…? Who thought it necessary…?'

'Mate, haven't we been through this?'

'Then we'll have to go through it again. Step by step. Strap in.'

Brad says nothing.

Finnigan gives his attention to Boyd, while commentating on his actions. 'Some people don't believe *dim mak* exists. We call it death touch, but the literal translation is less dramatic. In Chinese it means *touch meridian*, referring to an attack on a pressure point: stabbing with the fingers, using what looks like a non-lethal blow to disrupt the body's chi.'

He turns to Brad. 'But you'd know about all that, wouldn't you, Science Boy? You got an explanation for everything, don't you?'

He slaps Boyd sharply on top of the spine several times. Miraculously Rex D. Boyd begins to look alive. All he remembers was being full-fronted by the force of a lorry driving into him; a heavy, flat punch, after which he collapsed. He felt the vitality drain away; turning his body to clay, suffocating him from inside. His last vision of life was Finnigan's grinning face. He has little sense of what happened, but becomes aware of the constrictions being knocked out of him. Finnigan is holding him up, and literally knocking the infirmity out of his body, like dislodging a fatal blockage. He stumbles back into Finnigan's arms, and feels perfectly safe. Finnigan smells like a lumber yard full of freshly cut pine. It must be an alpha-male thing.

'*Dim mak?*' croaks Boyd.

'You probably didn't think it was real, either, did you?'

Boyd shakes his head.

'Bradley, get him some water.'

Brad rushes to the kitchen. When he returns, Boyd is sitting more upright, still handcuffed. Brad holds the glass for him to drink.

'So you're Bradley Holmeson?'

'Listen, this is nothing to do with me.'

'Kinda looks like it is, don't you think?' says Boyd.

'Tell him, Finnigan.'

'And you know his name. Seems like you're all buddied up, Holmeson.'

Finnigan turns to Boyd.

'Bradley is only here because it's his flat; his main concern in this matter is to humour me and stay alive.'

'So why is he involved?'

'By random choice, or celestial design. I don't think it's vindictive. He doesn't have enough malicious wit to manipulate other people's lives. But I do think he knows something... And that's what we're here to find out.'

Brad turns to Jimi and quietly says, 'I already told him everything I know!'

Jimi gives him a look that says, *You better get with the programme.*

Boyd shakes his head, and speaks directly to Finnigan.

'I'll level with you buddy, I do not know as much as I'd like to know. Reason I came down here was to find out more. But as we're in a sharing mood, I will give you all my intel in exchange for my liberty.'

'Then we're all in accord,' says Finnigan.

'So why don't you start by telling us who paid you to kill Polonski,' says Boyd, slightly sarcastically.

'You ain't in much of a position to bargain.'

'Right. But you don't deny killing him.'

Finnigan opens his arms out wide. 'When have I ever denied killing him? Why don't we start by discussing who he was? Who deemed it necessary for him to die? And why the whole fucking production number? I could have made it look natural. But no! *Make it look like a message; make it look like someone's teaching him a lesson...* You know what I mean?'

'We have to absorb what is useful, and reject what is useless,' says Boyd.

At this, Finnigan's mood brightens. It's bizarre what little things can tip the balance in a game of trust.

'That's Bruce Lee, right?'

'Absolutely... How he created his own fighting style.'

Finnigan decides that Boyd might be on the level. He doesn't free him from the cuffs, but pulls up a chair and says, 'Okay then... Let's absorb what is useful, and reject what is useless.'

They begin to parley; and Boyd runs through a CV of Eugene Polonski's life. Finnigan listens, but none of the information rings any bells. So Boyd begins to theorise about the whys and the wherefores.

'It seems to me, the most obvious reason for the man's death would be to supress information, yes?'

Finnigan agrees.

Boyd says, 'Right. But look in my bag; the laptop bag. You'll find a document folder with a notebook inside...'

Finnigan gestures for Brad to do this.

'It's one of the notebooks I discovered at the murder scene. You tell me how useful it is.'

Brad walks over to the desk, waiting for someone to tell him this could be a trick. No one does. He finds the document wallet, and gently takes out the contents: an old school notebook.

'Open it,' demands Boyd. 'Open it, and tell me if your left-wing radicals have their shit together! The guy spent half his life in a mental home. And your brilliant David Bohm ended up in the Maudsley!'

Brad looks at the contents of the notebook. He has the same reaction that Boyd had. Complete incomprehension. Like an insult to intelligence, just page after page of vivid colour madness.

'What exactly is this?'

'One of Polonski's notebooks! You really think that's what he was killed for?' Boyd shouts this, confirming that the discovery of the notebooks was a great disappointment for him... A personal affront.

Finnigan walks around the desk to see the evidence, and he's immediately struck with a wave of nostalgia. There's something familiar, like a forgotten scene from a film... Is it just the style of exercise book, or has he seen *this actual notebook* before? He leans against the wall, slides to the floor, sits on his haunches poring through the pages, trying to decipher their meaning.

Boyd continues, 'We have to assume someone believed these notebooks to be useful. And we have to decide who would *benefit* from their recovery...'

He looks for a response.

Finnigan is lost in shotgun images from Polonski's life, which reads like an epileptic travel guide to another dimension.

Boyd turns to Brad.

'What do you think, Holmeson? Who would benefit from these notebooks, assuming the content was in any way coherent?'

Brad can't think of an answer to Boyd's question.

'Because I know what this is about...' continues Boyd. 'I was up half the night researching it...'

'Okay, what is it about?' asks Brad.

'You're claiming that science can prove another plane of existence beyond death.'

'*Prove* is a very loaded word.'

'Okay: science has proposed an interpretation of phenomena that would suggest, etc, etc... Right? Well, if that's true, why isn't it a main news story?'

Brad is astonished by Boyd's apparent naivety.

'How could this ever be on the news? This is the complete *opposite* of the news...'

'How do you figure that?'

'Because the news *maintains* the power structure... This story, if it ever became publically acceptable, would turn the world on its head... This is a story about liberation...'

Boyd contemplates the possibility of this information becoming accepted knowledge. He can't see it happening. But he appreciates the power it would have. The most potent weapon in modern warfare is ideology; abstract concepts that people are willing to die for.

Brad continues his rant.

'How could they *ever* tell this story on the news? Do you think they'd save it for the light-hearted segment at the end? Something to laugh at: *And finally, it seems the hippies were right, as scientists define the after-life as a spectral zone of ambient sub-atomic energy...* Then they'd look at each other, the two newsreaders, and exchange some smug banter: *So you can forget the stocks and shares, Margaret, I'm off to Peru to eat the yage vine and confront my karmic obligations...*'

'Okay, let's not get sassy...'

Brad smiles at the word *sassy*. There's something he likes about Rex D. Boyd. Such a unique dichotomy of homespun accent and military training. Yet underneath this conservative bearing he seems to have a genuine interest in the paranormal.

Boyd pulls his reasonable face.

'Can I just get your opinion, without the invective?'

'Sorry, Rex... Can I call you Rex...? It blows my mind: we have anesthetised every mystery the world has to offer, and outlawed the means to get there.'

'I don't follow...'

'There's no room for wonder. For *What if* or *Just suppose...*? Y'know? We've lost our sense of the underlying mystery, because every single thing has to be explained, rationalised, categorised and marketed. And we're so fucking *sure* of ourselves, and yet we're scared shitless of dying. I include myself in this. I admit it. I'm scared of dying. That's why I'm in the middle of this mess right now, because I wrote my book, *Death and Physics*. And I wrote it because I'm scared of dying and want to discover something more than just...'

Brad waves his arms at the present physical reality, takes a breath before continuing.

'... this militant rationalism, this secular backlash we've cornered ourselves into... It forces us to ignore an essential part of our heritage, which is to communicate with the hidden dimensions...'

'Isn't it always the same? If I had ten dollars for every nutjob who knew the secret of life and death... I tell you, buddy, I wouldn't be handcuffed to this chair, for a start.'

'But you are...'

'I accept that...'

Boyd is trying to appear non-threatening, as a ploy to being released.

'If I could applaud you, Holmeson, I would. Very extemporaneous! But we're gathering *information*. And the questions I have are these: who would benefit from the content of these Polonski notebooks; and what exactly is the message they're trying to express?'

Brad answers carefully. 'I think the story they're trying to tell heralds a new era in our perception of the human condition.'

'Right... So back to my other question: who would benefit from the notebooks being found?'

As soon as Boyd says this, Brad knows exactly who would benefit.

Boyd can see the thought falling into place.

'What are you thinking right now?'

'The Undertakers,' he says under his breath.

'Tell me about that,' demands Boyd, with an authority that would like to suggest he isn't still handcuffed.

'They were here!' Brad says this out loud, somewhat incredulously.

Finnigan wakes up to their conversation.

'Who did you say was here? Undertakers?'

'Yeah...'

'Two weird blokes in suits? A stocky-looking Caribbean fella, chubby face, and a tall, skinny white dude? Shaven heads. Cultish.'

'That's them...'

'You know them, and you didn't tell me?'

'I don't *know* them. They had a copy of my book. And they took a flyer for my book reading show, because they said...'

Brad doesn't continue this sentence. He remembers how the undertakers promised to send someone to his gig. How could he have forgotten this? They were going to send this Eugene Polonski to see him; but Finnigan turned up instead...

Boyd is now concentrating on Finnigan. 'You were seen with them, with these undertakers, on the steps of the hostel building...'

Finnigan nods: 'They were waiting for me...'

His memory of the event is deep underwater. He doesn't mention the curare poisoning and the ventilator mask. He's trying to remember the exact moment he lost control of his mind.

Meanwhile, Brad is trying to understand what the undertakers expect to gain from this.

'How do we get in touch with them, these undertakers?' asks Boyd.

Brad says, 'I've got a card somewhere... They left me a business card.'

He rummages about on his desk, and finds it. Holds it up triumphantly.

Finnigan steps up and snatches it out of his hand. *Coupe de Ville Funeral Home.* He reads the address, calculates the journey time, then grabs Brad firmly by the arm.

'Right... You and me! We're off to find some answers. Put an end to this. Time to put your money where your mouth is.'

'Why me?'

'Because you've been banging on about it ever since I've known you.'

'Banging on about what...?'

'You're the chosen one, Bradley. The undertakers came to see you before Polonski was killed. They chose you to witness these events. But all you can do is spout your clever ideas. What's the real test…?'

He speaks with profound intensity.

'Do you *believe*, Bradley? In your heart? You strong enough to test your faith? Because that's what we're going to find out…'

Brad can't refuse. Not physically, because he's not strong enough. And not intellectually, because he knows what Finnigan's driving at. He never imagined it would come to this, to put his life on the line for a belief. *We're not humans having a spiritual experience; we are spiritual beings having a human experience.* It comes to him in a gust of illuminating sanity. Reincarnation and rebirth are necessary to reset the machine; like cleansing the palate. It's our birthright: the continuing evolution. Fucking damn it.

Finnigan bustles Brad towards the front door.

Jimi, who has been diplomatically silent all this time, says, 'What about me, Finnigan? What am I doing?'

'I'll have to borrow that motor of yours, mate. Sorry it's turned out like this. Take it out of that wedge I put in the envelope. Give Boyd a few hours, then let him go. I'd like to say I'll be in touch, but this might be the end.'

Jimi isn't sure if this is good or bad news.

'Whatever you say, boss.'

He watches them leave.

In the silence that descends on the flat, Jimi turns to Boyd and says, 'Just you an' me, bro. Get you something?'

'You know, a cup of sweet tea would sure hit the spot.'

'Coming right up, my friend. Sorry about the handcuffs and shit, but I'm playing it straight by my man Finnigan. What a day, yeah?'

Left alone, Boyd worries about Finnigan's plans. Worries he'll never see him alive again. In spite of everything, he admires his style. The tea takes ages. He thinks he can smell reefer burning in the kitchen. That'll explain the delay. He knows this situation can't get any stranger, and then an angel appears in front of him. An angel with ginger hair and green eyes.

Jane

Jane can see things are not as they should be: Brad's door has been smashed in. Walking up to it, she can feel the hallway sticky with beer and broken glass. Undeterred, she walks into the flat, picking her way through the debris; and in the lounge she finds a trim middle-aged man handcuffed to a chair. She ignores the faint odour of weed emanating from the kitchen, and introduces herself to Boyd.

'Hello... I'm Jane. Brad's girlfriend. And you are...?'

'Hi there, Jane, a pleasure to meet you. Rex D. Boyd's the name. Excuse me not getting up, I'm currently handcuffed to...'

'I can see that. Is Brad around?'

'No, that he isn't. I, er...' stammers Boyd. 'You just missed him. Possibly Jimi might be able to help. You'll find him out back making tea.'

Jane ignores the fact there's a stranger in the kitchen making tea. She studies Boyd's face.

'You don't look well.'

'That'll be the after-effects of *dim mak*, Jane. Thanks for your concern.'

'*Dim mak?*'

'Yeah, I'm as astonished as you; I never realised the more esoteric forms were actually so effective. I've read about it, of course, but today my eyes have been opened... I'm sure I'll be fine once I get out of these restraints and get the *chi* circulating properly.'

Jane circles around Boyd, picks up a few of the empty beer bottles and drops them in the wastepaper basket. Takes off her coat. She doesn't appear particularly phased by the situation, but that's just her way of coping with it.

'So where is Brad, then?'

'Ah...'

'You know but won't tell me, is that right?'

'You seem to be taking this very well, Jane; finding a strange man seemingly held prisoner in your own flat.'

'It's not my flat. Brad lives here, not me. If this was my flat we'd have used coasters for the beer bottles and I'd be saying something like, *WHAT'S GOING ON? HAVE YOU ALL GONE FUCKING MAD?* But it isn't my flat, so I have the luxury of not caring.'

'Really? You really don't care?' asks Rex.

She laughs. Throws herself down on the sofa. Not rushing to discover what's been happening. Wanting primarily to maintain her dignity, while slowly assimilating the situation – there could be a very simple explanation, and she doesn't want to look uptight. She flicks the hair away from her face and studies the form of Rex D. Boyd.

'You're American?'

'What gave it away?' says Boyd, exaggerating his accent, trying to keep the mood light.

'Hmmm,' she says, as if this explains everything.

A noise from the kitchen, and Jimi appears, joint in his teeth, and a cup of tea in each hand.

'Oh… We have a visitor. Sorry, sweetheart, can I get you a cuppa? Thought it was just me an' Boydie here.'

'You must be Jimi.'

'Yeah… Given name of James, as in Brown; but I go by Jimi, as in Hendrix.'

He smiles a charming smile, and offers her the joint. She gracefully declines. It seems they're avoiding the one unspoken question. So she calls it.

'I don't want to stop whatever this is, because I'm sure it's *necessary*… but I do have a question. Where the fuck is Brad? Is he part of this? I suppose he must be. But where *is* he?'

'He's not here.'

'He assured me that whatever was happening, had now stopped happening… It looks like he got that wrong. Have you any idea where he is?'

Jimi and Rex exchange a look.

'What? Tell me!'

Jimi says, 'He left a little while ago, in my car. My pizza van, to be exact.'

'Is he in trouble?'

'Don't think so. Me and Mr Boyd talked about that, yeah?' Jimi lies.

'I can assure you he's not in trouble with us, ma'am.'

'And who the fuck *are* you? Exactly? Has anyone phoned him, to see if he's alright?'

Jane takes out her phone, stands up to dial; then paces the floor waiting for a reply.

While waiting, she says, 'I had to look after Pete Doherty last week. He didn't make as much mess as you lot.'

Boyd explains to Jimi: 'Jane books the talent for radio pro-grammes…'

Jane looks at him like, *How would you know that?*

Boyd replies. 'Sorry, Jane. During my investigations I looked at Brad's Facebook page, followed the clues. I actually Googled you prior to meeting Bradley this morning.'

He turns back to Jimi.

'She once wrestled Steve Tyler to the floor – you know? From Aerosmith?'

'Allegedly,' says Jane over her shoulder.

'Allegedly, whatever,' replies Jimi. 'You ain't so big, but you is hardcore, girl!'

Jane ignores the compliment. Looks at her phone.

'No answer!'

'He'll be safe with Finnigan. He's a good man.'

'Really? Has anyone informed the police that my boyfriend has been driven off in a pizza van by a suspected murderer?'

Boyd says, 'Agreed, this is a sensitive situation; but we are assured Bradley will come to no harm. I could put out an APB on Jimi's van, try to monitor the situation. Not sure if that would help, but Jane, please understand that my churlishness in this matter is caused by being handcuffed to the chair, robbing me of any authority.'

Jane continues her cross-examination.

'What about you, Jimi? Didn't you think calling the police would have been a good idea?'

'I'll be honest with you, girl, strange as it seems, best to let Finni-gan resolve this his own way.'

'And how will he do that? He's a murderer, isn't he?'

'No! Contract killer. He's not a madman or nothing. Seriously, he's a well decent bloke once you know him…'

'Jane. As soon as I am released from this chair, I can have a small task force follow them – covert operation, hi-tech unit. This is what we train for…'

'Well, Rex, looking around, your training hasn't been put to much use so far.'

She gives him a sarcastic smile.

'Where were they heading for? Do we even know that?'

'I could find the intel on that one, Jane. In my laptop bag…'

Jimi says, 'Some place in Lincolnshire. An undertakers'…'

'Lincolnshire? So they'll be taking the M23, M25, M11, A14 through to the A1 probably. That's a good five-hour journey, should give me time to catch them up. And you say they were driving a pizza van?'

'Red and blue van. Says *Pizza* on it, yeah? Can't miss it.'

She takes a card from her purse.

'Here's my number. Text me the address when you find it.'

'You go steady, girl. You don't want to mix it with Finnigan. Not when he's got a mind to do something; he don't stop.'

She says nothing, grabs her coat and leaves.

Blackstock's patience has finally won the day. He has waited and waited; and watched as Finnigan re-emerged from the building, this time with someone else in tow. Some tousle-haired bloke. They both look rushed and tense. Finnigan bundles him into the pizza van, dashes round to the driver seat, and they pull out into traffic. Blackstock makes the decision to follow. He was tempted to take Finnigan down there and then, but it would have been foolish. Waving shooters in a residential street might be okay for Nottingham. Anyhow, he wants this close up and personal. He wants the pleasure of seeing the tables turn. He wants to witness Finnigan's remorse.

Brad watches the familiar townscape rushing past. He knows all these roads and buildings. They each hold memories of some sort, mostly banal. He lights a cigarette, cracks his window open to let the smoke escape. They're heading north, and soon hit the A23 proper: the carriageway out of town, leading to the motorway. In the opposite lane, driving south, a long queue of commuters, slowed to walking pace due to road works.

'Modern tragedy, don't you think, Bradley? The traffic jam? The car a victim of its own success?'

Brad can't respond. He's trying to imagine what life would be like without him. He remembers a documentary about lungfish, capable of surviving for months or even years, encased in dried-up mud, waiting for rain and floods to release them back to life. Is there any awareness during that time of desiccation? And what degree of awareness do lungfish have anyway?

He studies the faces of the other drivers. He wouldn't care if they all died; yet he assumes they regard their lives with as much importance as he does his own. So why do they look so disposable?

'Am I going to die?' he asks suddenly.

'We're all going to die, mate.'

'I mean…' He struggles to get this next question out. 'I mean, are you going to kill me?'

'No.'

'Is anyone going to kill me?'

'I can't answer that.'

Finnigan places a hand on his shoulder.

'But speaking for myself, I'm done with the killing. In fact, it's more than that. I feel resolved. Absolved. Clear… I know I've created wrong in the past, but I'm facing up to it. I'm strong enough to face it. That's why I need to meet the undertakers one more time. I have a sense of what they did, and I want to know what they know. We're just here to do or die, Bradley. And into the valley of death we ride. I feel certain. Eyes wide open.'

Brad looks again at the other drivers in their tedious traffic jam. 'Can't you settle for a quiet life, like that lot over there? Nothing to worry about but what's for supper, and what's on telly?'

'Who's to say I've not tried?'

'I was only asking.'

'All my life people have made assumptions based on my appearance. The violence shines through me. It's a talent. I nurtured it. Never let it worry me. It's my advantage.'

Finnigan looks at his bare arms, a testament to dedication: the sweat it took to build the muscle; the blood mixed with coloured ink.

'Truth is, my mother was a lost cause. She did it proper: took the Magic Bus to Marrakech, trying to find herself. Came back to Canning Town, and got lost in smack. You know the story. And when people are sinking they hold onto anything for a life raft. She got into Buddhism; taught me all life was suffering, and I accepted it. I ran with it. If people are stupid enough for someone to want them dead, it was never a moral issue. I told myself they might reincarnate as a better person.'

'You seriously believe that?'

'It's what I told myself.'

'But do you believe it?'

'The most important thing is that even the ignorant and depraved have a chance to be saved. And that's something I *do* believe.'

'I have learned, Bradley, that the privilege of being alive is to seek transcendence through decisive effort. You understand? I was born into nothing, and my fighting skills were my saving grace. I fucking embraced it. But I realise there are still challenges ahead. That's why I need you. To be my witness.'

'A witness to what?'

Finnigan looks at him and says, '*The Lord of Death will lick up thy brain, drink thy blood, eat thy flesh, and gnaw thy bones; but thou will be incapable of dying… Although thy body be hacked to pieces, it will revive… and the repeated hacking will cause intense pain and torture.*'

Finnigan clearly enjoys his recitation.

'What is that?' asks Brad. 'Sounds familiar.'

'*Tibetan Book of the Dead…* For a philosophy that touts itself on peace and love, Buddhism can be a right bitch.'

They drive in silence, and Brad has no idea what's expected of him. The fear is that Finnigan is seeking some kind of death-adventure; like comrades-in-arms, expecting to cross the veil, seeking transcendence as an ultimate expression of defiance. He prays for strength when the time comes.

But Finnigan is distracted… Looking out the window into the other lane, slowing the van down. Driving alongside them, in a fully restored Ford Granada, a broken-faced psychopath. Brad recognises him as the sorry individual from earlier in the day. Now he's driving with one hand, shouting at them, and waving a gun.

Finnigan allows the pizza van to be forced off the road. He looks for somewhere to stop, and heads into a *Works Traffic Only* section by the hard shoulder; all cordoned off, a scene of continuing roadworks. There are various hi-vis engineers milling about, but they don't pay much heed, assuming this to be a breakdown, or some other road-side emergency. Finnigan pulls the van to a halt and exits, leaving the engine running and the door open. Brad tentatively follows his lead. They stand either side of the van, and watch as the leery-faced Granada driver marches towards them. He stops three metres away, at the apex of their Mexican stand-off.

Finnigan turns to Brad.

'This is Al Blackstock. We used to run together. He prefers to be known as Mr Black. Named himself after a character from *Reservoir Dogs*…'

'Shut it, Finnigan,' says Blackstock, taking a step closer.

'… although, tragically, there isn't a Mr Black in *Reservoir Dogs*. He just thought there was… And, Al, this is a mate of mine, Bradley Holmeson.'

'Didn't drive all this way for fucking pleasantries,' snarls Black-stock.

Finnigan seems pleased to see him.

'This is priceless, Al. You followed me all the way to Brighton?'

Blackstock is holding the Walther close to his side.

'You are going to fucking pay for what you did!'

'Ironic. Me and Bradley were just driving in search of retribution ourselves. And now *you* show up. It's perfect. This is my time. I'm ready for it…'

Finnigan takes a step forward; arms outstretched. No threat.

'This is real, mate… You ready? You man enough to deliver me?'

Blackstock senses a trick. He doesn't believe Finnigan would give up so easily. There's someone shouting at them from further up the hard shoulder. One of the roadworks engineers slowly trudges his steel toe-caps towards them, to deliver the mother-of-all-bollockings for *fucking about like twats on his piece of prohibited carriageway*...

What he doesn't realise is that this bolshie intrusion is about to accelerate matters to a swift and brutal conclusion.

Finnigan's intentions are clear. This is what he meant by true belief. In contrast, Brad feels pathetically insubstantial. He has a glimmer of dying here too, accompanying Finnigan on this adventure. But it's only a glimmer. He's not prepared. He doesn't have the fortitude. Not yet.

'I don't have to do this, Finnigan,' says Blackstock. 'All you got to do is apologise. Fucking apologise for what you done.'

'That's where you're wrong, Al... All our life we were a team, right? Still are, don't you see? This is my time. Prove to me you're man enough...'

Brad doesn't want this to happen. In spite of his intellectual certainty, he remains full of doubt. Finnigan takes another step forward. Blackstock retreats, assuming he's going to be caught out like all the times before.

'Back off, Finn; I will fucking do it.'

'That's what I'm relying on... Relying on you, mate. Do this for me, while my mind's right...'

Blackstock hears more shouting, and footsteps behind him, but he daren't look round and lose concentration. He can't allow the indignity of being caught again. He raises the gun and fires twice into Finnigan's chest. It throws Finnigan backward a few steps; the exit wound splatters in the air like a cheap meat firework. Brad feels the sound reverberate in his own body. He worries that the spray of blood has reached him, staining his face and clothes. He quickly checks. All clear. Looks back up, transfixed. Finnigan remains upright for longer than seems possible. Defying the inevitable. Almost savouring the intensity. Then he falls to his knees, and drops awkwardly, face first onto the hard road surface.

Blackstock panics; overwhelmed by his actions. He throws the weapon out of reach; allows the road workers to advance and wrestle him to the ground. He gives them this chance to be heroes. It's all Brad remembers.

Finnigan drifts above his body, witnessing the babble of voices, the commotion, Blackstock howling in remorse, Brad on his knees. A scene of raw human emotion that looks so urgent and necessary, and Finnigan loses himself in it. Everything a trigger to his own emotional state, his regret, his lost opportunities, his morbid fear of kindness… It all comes flooding in. He believed he was a superior man, had the chops to deal with this. The negativity appears all around him like cells in a Petri dish, multiplying exponentially, dark bubbles of living thought, drowning him, dragging him under.

He was aiming for a clear death, without reckoning on this nightmare of recrimination. He could have lived a better life. He could have done more. He made choices out of fear, and can't forgive himself. He thought he was prepared, but remains swamped in the sticky, choking, bubbling cloud of nullity. His name is being called. He turns deaf to it. His name is being called but it means nothing. He looks up, surprised to see the sky above him. Transparent blue. His name is being called. He forgets the struggle and floats towards the voice, the sky fading to invisible light.

Back on the ground: a closing sequence from a blockbuster wide-screen. Flashing blue lights reflecting off glass and steel. Uniformed officials pacing themselves through the mundanity of human anguish. Blackstock in handcuffs, in despair, being led to the custody of a police van. Finnigan's body, motionless on a gurney, lifted into an ambulance. The traffic has all but stopped moving, drivers rubber-necking the incident. And the image the audience will remember most is that of a ginger-haired woman holding a tousle-haired man in her arms. By the side of the road. Sitting on the kerb. Hugging. Trying not to cry. Holding each other because their lives depend on it.

One Week Later...

The Funeral Songs

One week later, and Brad is pulling on his black suit. It's a little tight on the waist, but he plans to ride it out; keep the jacket buttoned up. He checks himself in the bedroom mirror and straightens the creases with his hands. There's something in the jacket's inside pocket: a pre-sat nav paper map outlining the journey from his front door to a little village in Cambridgeshire, to an old country church that hosted the funeral of his Auntie Maureen several years ago. After the service they mingled in a mock-Tudor function room in the village's only hotel, drinking tea and eating the sandwiches and cakes people had brought with them. His parents were there, along with uncles, aunts, cousins – some of whom he was meeting for the first time. Strangers bonded by blood; made benevolent to one another by these twin accidents of birth and death.

His Auntie Maureen was buried, and he threw a guitar plectrum into the grave; the only object on him that carried any disposable significance; a little something to connect him with the forever.

He sat with her remaining best friends, four sprightly old flowers in their eighties, all in long, pleated frocks and lace-up leather shoes, smelling faintly of lavender and old photographs. He listened to their stories of girlish escapades, cycling to village dances, Saturday jobs at family shops that no longer exist, giggly trysts with boys no longer alive, holding hands in a local cinema that is now a carpet warehouse. Entire lives lived in full, but not entirely forgotten.

He shakes free from the memory. Needs to get his groove on. Bad form to be late for a funeral; plus, he's arranged to meet Rex D. Boyd for one of his classic debriefing sessions before the event.

Jane is working today, at Broadcasting House in Langham Place. She arrives in her funeral blacks, planning to meet Brad at the service. Not quite sure why she volunteered to partner him there, except it draws a line under the events of the last ten days. Brad described how Al Blackstock broke down after firing the gun; an image that stayed with her. Fascinating and repulsive, howling like a gun dog over Finnigan's body. Compared to this brutal man-love, Brad seems charmingly normal.

Jane checks her reflection in the darkened glass door of her office: Antique black-lace dress, cinched at the waist, black stockings, and black brogues. She smooths the dress down, hoping Brad will notice the effort she's made. He's back in the centre of her universe, around which satellite-needs continue to spin and turn. Her race to save him that afternoon still bursts into her mind at oblique moments. It was so compulsive. Her need to help him, the urgency; the sudden memory of it makes her laugh out loud in the middle of meetings, or waiting in the canteen queue. She felt like John Connor's mum in the first *Terminator* film: an ordinary person dealing with an extraordinary situation. Jane had had no choice: it was beyond logic. It must be love, and that's what shocked her the most – the depth of her emotion.

Boyd sits in the Princess Louise by Holborn tube station. He's wearing the uniform of the 82nd Airborne – the steam-pressed, box-fresh dress version. In spite of the peacocking, he manages to blend in with the lunchtime crowd. His insistence at having Holmeson attend the funeral was originally an exhibition of vanity: his vindication, after being caught spark-out and handcuffed to Brad's goddamn office chair… But there are other loose ends that need tying up.

Holmeson arrives late. It doesn't surprise Boyd, although he tries not to judge.

'Hey, Rex…'

'Holmeson.'

'Can I call you Rex? Now we're in civvy street?'

'I'd prefer Boyd. Keeps this formal.'

They shoot the breeze for a few minutes; then Brad gets a round in and carries the drinks back to their quiet table. Boyd leans in, getting down to business.

'I'm sure you know… This conversation is under the radar.'

'Okay…?'

Boyd has developed a sense of melodrama. Perhaps he had it all along; but he looks over his shoulder before divulging the next piece of intel.

'I met with the undertakers last week.'

Brad feels slightly marginalised by this news.

Boyd continues. 'We both know what we think we know, right? About what happened?'

'Not sure if we're on the same page…'

'We're on the same page!' Boyd snaps back. 'You know what happened!'

Brad is still in the dark.

'With *Finnigan*? You *know* what they did! And I *know* you know! And these undertakers…? They are knee-deep in this.'

'In what?'

Again Boyd looks around him before whispering, 'Weird. Paranormal. Practice.'

Brad looks underwhelmed. 'Mate, I've seen their website. That's not a secret.'

'No. Here's the secret…' He pauses dramatically. 'I will be joining their cabal in the not too distant future.'

Boyd has the gleam of the zealot, making this announcement. Deadly serious.

'Rex…! Firstly, what does this have to do with me? And secondly, what do you even mean: *join their cabal*? I can't begin to understand that.'

'They know things, Holmeson. I want in…'

'But why tell *me*?'

'You have a healthy cynicism, but you're open to ideas – am I right?'

'I guess…'

'Right. It's settled.'

'What's settled? What do you expect me to do?'

Again with conspiratorial glances, Boyd reaches into his attaché case and pulls out an A4 envelope, leaving it in the middle of the table.

'Don't look now. It's one of the Polonski notebooks. I want you to study it. Let me know what you find.'

This swings the conversation back in Brad's favour.

Boyd continues. 'He was killed because of these notebooks. That much is certain, trust me. But what the notebooks contain...? What they represent...? I'm hoping you can help with that.'

Boyd takes out a business card, scribbles a number on the back, places it on the envelope.

'My personal number... Keep it under your hat – all of this!'

Brad pockets the card, takes the envelope.

Boyd whispers, 'Don't ask me how, but I feel neural pathways opening up... This occultism... It talks to me, Holmeson, you understand. And I want the whole picture.'

He laughs self-consciously, then sits back upright as if nothing just happened.

Brad leans back from the table to get a clearer perspective. There are particulars that Boyd isn't divulging; so he jumps in the deep end, demanding answers.

'Who wanted Polonski dead?'

Boyd pulls a quizzical face.

Brad says, 'What? Surely that's the heart of the mystery?'

'The answer to that question... The answer is actually not important. However, you'll be surprised to learn the truth.'

'So tell me. That's why I'm asking!'

'The truth is a malleable commodity...'

'Say again? How are *facts* malleable?'

'Don't get British on me, Holmeson. It's how it works; something you idealists find hard to admit. We present a public version, while continuing with the private enquiry. Same as anyone! All the public need to know is that an ex-serviceman was killed, the details are confusing, but *thank Christ* our security forces are here to protect our citizens.'

Brad can't deny the logic. He says, 'So Blackstock's taking the can for everything? Even though he didn't kill Polonski.'

'That's why it's perfect. He can't reveal the details because he doesn't know any. Yet he was witnessed discharging a lethal handgun, firing at Finnigan... Same weapon that killed Polonski. We'll get a conviction...'

Boyd is on a roll with this, loving the intrigue; leaning in to whisper, drawing Brad into his deceit.

'If the public knew the whole story, the likes of you and me – we'd be eating rice and beans on some goddamn chain-gang.'

Brad changes the subject.

'What's the news on Finnigan?'

'Still in some sort of coma. The injuries from the shooting, the physical injuries… I mean the guy was built like a tube train, right? Built to last. So physically he's healing. But the head problems…? Who knows? Mentally he's in some sort of hinterland, because he's registering brain activity…'

Brad acknowledges this with a bemused shrug. They drink to Finnigan's health, to his recovery.

Silence.

Then Boyd says, 'When you're in combat' – he starts this like he's sharing a holiday anecdote – 'you never hear the bullet that kills you. The only way you know you haven't been killed is that you're still alive.'

Brad remains motionless.

'You can hear the ones that miss. Bullets travel faster than sound, so you hear them making a snapping noise as they break the sound barrier…'

Boyd waves his hands, demonstrating bullets flying past his head.

'And the only way you know you haven't been killed, is that you keep telling yourself you're still alive. You understand…?'

'Where are you going with this?'

'That's where Finnigan is. He doesn't know he hasn't been killed.'

Brad wonders if this *is* what Finnigan's achieved: a glimpse of the next world, while keeping a cautious foothold in this one.

Boyd continues, 'So until he figures that out, the guy's a vegetable.'

'That's your medical opinion?'

'Sarcasm! That's good… why I like you, Holmeson.'

Again, he leans in with a gesture of complicity, peering over his shoulder before saying, 'All the wrong we do in the world is related to a fear of death. Of course it is! We think this life is our only chance. But the story these undertakers are selling? I've been studying it. If we can take the fear of death away – I mean, I know you're into this, the science behind this? If science proves the continuum of conscious-ness… It's fucking revolutionary!'

Brad toasts Boyd's enthusiasm, drains his glass, bangs it down on the table to signal the end of this metaphysical speculation. He doesn't have the energy to get into it, not with Boyd so excitable.

'Your round, I believe?'

Boyd glances at his watch.

'No can do. Got a dead hero to bury.'

He stands, pulling his uniform straight. Rattling his medals. Brad knows there are questions to ask, but he has Boyd's number. They formally shake hands.

'We'll be in touch,' says Boyd.

'Of course we will. I'll see you in half an hour at the funeral.'

'About that… We don't know each other outside of official cor-ridors. We have never spoken about these matters.'

'What matters?'

Boyd allows himself a smile.

'Okay, partner.'

'Okay, then.'

They shake hands again, and Boyd marches out of the pub with-out looking back. Brad settles in for a read of the Polonski notebook.

Ex-Detective Inspector Graham Walsh studies the funeral invitation. He asked to attend, on the pretext of observing their form as funeral directors. A very unsubtle piece of subterfuge, but no one called his bluff.

He walks out of Chancery Lane tube station and double checks the address, then studies the street map by the station entrance. So… Exit left, walk down High Holborn, left into Charterhouse Street, left again into Ely Place, and there it is: St Etheldreda's Church.

He checks the time. It's a long walk for a heart-attack victim. He'll be late for the service, but it doesn't matter. Not here to salute the passing of a comrade. Of course, that's the line he fed to Mrs

Walsh. He can't be sure she believed him, or even if she cares. He's been in a desperately bad mood recently, on account of the medication as much as the visions of mortality. She's been insisting he get out of the house and get some air. Well here he is, sucking it up. And in spite of the cold, he's perspiring. He wipes his brow. He steps out of the tube station, finds his bearings, and sets off towards the venue.

The need for closure has been playing on his mind since he woke up in a hospital bed ten days ago, but he doesn't know what form this is likely to take. He can't decide how he's going to play it. He's still not certain what to blame for the car crash. Was it the driver of the hearse, or was it merely the heart attack? It's something he'll never know with any measure of certainty.

At least he's out of the house. What else is he going to do with his time? Get a dog? Take up bowls? Sit in the library? It all smacks of knowing the vital years have passed. He reminds himself it's not the cards you're dealt, but how you play them. The things he's seen… There's always a reason for mindless brutality, but sometimes it's too deeply buried. He always did his best to restore the status quo. But occasionally accidents just happen, leaving no one to blame. Sometimes it's easier to ignore the reasons why, and devise a punishment to fit the occasion.

Brad still can't figure out why someone would think it necessary for Polonski to die. And he can't believe Polonski was killed on account of the notebooks. He's studied the volume in his possession, and in spite of Boyd's certainty, Brad is sure the content has no intrinsic value, and holds no vital secret. It's too obscure. It reads like a 40-page, cryptic 3D crossword. It would take weeks of commitment to study it thoroughly. Might be a nice winter project, but he's already decided he can't afford the time. There are so many genuine books in the world, full of carefully edited information. Why attempt to decode this madness, and risk falling into its grasp?

For Brad, the value of the Polonski notebook is its inspiration to endeavour. And as such, it will remain unread in his museum of favourite books. He's already planned where: on the shelf between his first edition of William Gibson's *Neuromancer* and his photocopied transcript of Philip K. Dick's speech at the 1977 Metz science fiction convention. It seems fitting that Polonski's work should rest between cyberspace and mystical science fiction.

So three Jim Beams to the wind, and feeling good about the future, Brad is sailing down Old Holborn towards the funeral, letting his thoughts unfold. The meeting with Boyd cheered him up; because underneath the man's service training and his *God Bless America*, Boyd is radical to the core.

To scientifically prove the continuum-of-consciousness *is* revolutionary, as Boyd said. It's so easy to become blinded by details, and forget the aim. Brad knows his own book, *Death and Physics*, became bogged down with details. The subject so important to him, and the research so difficult; the more he laboured at it, the more uptight he became. He's been tense for months; and when the body's tense, it limits the more imaginative possibilities. Must learn to let go. The task of turning ideas into words can blind us to the ideas themselves.

Brad had a college tutor who would relish opportunities for boredom; moments where the imagination has no immediate function. Like being stuck in a shopping queue, held on the phone, or on a train journey with nothing to read: moments where the mind is forced to let go. Brad can't let go for long enough, trying to hold on to each significant moment. Every nascent idea, phrase, image, quote, and reference, has ended up in a notebook somewhere. And when he's dead they'll become landfill; or, depending on his status, they might be saved on a bookcase, referred to as *the dead author's notebooks*, remaining impenetrable and pointless as the Polonski volume he carries under his arm.

From Holborn to Charterhouse Street, he lets his thoughts reach the sky; floating between the bricks and mortar, the spires and office blocks. Above the din of mechanical living; beyond the reach of urgent mundanity. Then he turns left into Ely Place, and is brought back to earth by the sight of a Coupe de Ville Cadillac hearse parked outside the church.

Frank and Norman present a petrol-head vision of funereal splendour, like a painting by Vince Ray: velvet-collared drape coats, narrow dress trousers, lurid dayglow socks peeking above the black brothel-creepers. This is burial service with insolence; their sartorial style reflected in the gleaming chrome of the audacious hearse.

In spite of the posturing, they create an atmosphere of genuine reverence. Greeting the mourners, shaking hands, handing out the programmes of service – *Honouring Those Who Served*.

Norman is the first to spot the author from Brighton.

'Frank! Top of the road. It's the author.'

Frank looks up.

'So it is.'

'He's seen us.'

'Holmeson. Bradley Holmeson.'

'What brings him here?'

'Must be Boyd invited him.'

'You know Americans… Keep everyone on side while checking out the clever play.'

'Friendly to your face, paranoid behind your back.'

'Is this going to be difficult?'

'Let's wait and see…'

Brad makes the decision to act normal. He walks towards them, watching them, keeping cool.

'He looks angry about something,' whispers Norman.

'He does look angry, now you mention it.'

'With us, do you think? Or with the world in general?'

'I'm sure we'll find out…'

Brad reaches the church steps. Gets eye contact. Holds his hand out for a programme of service.

'The fuck are you doing here?'

He didn't mean to sound aggressive. Frank hands him a programme.

'We're the undertakers.'

As a statement of fact, it sounds sarcastic. Frank tries not to smile.

'But how…?'

Brad can't summon his thoughts into any coherence. Too much has happened since their last meeting. He tries to let go of his urgent need to ask questions. But does that mean walking away, or confronting it head on? He's confounded by indecision.

Frank says, 'I'll tell you one thing about that girlfriend of yours, Bradley…'

It shakes Brad out of his confusion.

'What do you know about Jane?'

'…great sense of timing.'

Frank is looking over Brad's shoulder, and rushing up the road, wrapped in a black coat, her hair a summer blaze, comes Jane. Brad turns, and her face lights up at seeing him; his heart skips a beat. The way she smiles is sweet relief. He walks to meet her, thankful for this excuse to turn his back on the undertakers. She reaches him, and plants a kiss. He puts an arm round her waist and hugs her to him. They kiss again, and walk hand in hand into the church.

By the door stand two gym-hardened older men in black suits, buzz cuts and subtle communication headpieces. They nod Brad and Jane through, and the two of them pause in the vaulted sombreness of the building to get their bearings. He holds her close. It's going to be a cold-hearted affair: an emotionless function for a fallen ex-serviceman. No friends or family, just press-ganged officials. It's not even the right venue, with Polonski being born Jewish. It isn't a funeral so much as a PR exercise on behalf of the 51st state of America; a photo opportunity for the caring side of Homeland Security.

Boyd is in the background, orchestrating proceedings; walkie-talkie in hand, whispering security messages to his colleagues. He's in his element here, creating the right amount of pomp to suit the circumstances. In the centre of the main aisle, in front of the altar, Polonski's coffin is draped in the Stars and Stripes. The organ pumps out its opening chords, and the gathered shuffle to their feet as the priest makes his entrance...

It all feels oppressive to Brad, this obeisance to God; the expected deference paid to a construct that doesn't exist. But he knows that religion remains meaningful to a lot of people. This church has stood for almost 800 years; in the Middle Ages it was like an independent state, with vast palatial grounds. So the attraction of worship can't just be the manipulation of innocence. We all need to believe something, and to experience belonging.

There's a part of the brain, the medial temporal lobe, which allows us to experience the positive effects of 'spiritual reality'. Commonly known as the God part of the brain, it's an evolutionary development to help us survive. But is it there as a fail-safe to give the *illusion* of immortality, or is it a doorway to an actual spiritual realm? Because, regardless of scientific rationality, millions of people still hold on to God as a talisman, a witness, and an excuse for suffering. It's understandable; this is all we need from philosophy: positive affirmation and someone to blame.

In spite of any positive reasons a person might have to embrace religious faith, Brad finds the reverence a little creepy. The repeated motif of Jesus' suffering; the extravagant architecture; the kaleidoscopic stained glass... It seems designed to express commercial status, rather than devotion. But it isn't just the church atmosphere that makes him uncomfortable. There's a growing suspicion of deceit; that he's been duped somehow, used as a fall guy... This man they're burying, this ex-serviceman Polonski, was killed by Finnigan; and Finnigan's last move was to try to meet the undertakers... And here they are, with their flamboyant posturing, like they're presiding over a secret joke.

Brad whispers an excuse to Jane and slips out of the church. It's a relief to be outside in the fresh air, but he can't relax. He sees Frank and Norman waiting by the hearse, and walks over, not quite sure where to start. They watch him approach, impassive.

Frank calls it, saying, 'You've got questions...'

'As it happens, yes I have.'

'Okay... Before we get into it, let me ask you something.'

Brad is taken aback. Why should he answer anything they have to ask?

Frank says, 'How was Finnigan last time you saw him?'

The question blindsides him. *How do they know about Finnigan?*

Frank continues. 'How did he seem, last time you met him?'

Brad answers automatically.

'He was like… Fired up! You know, illuminated! I mean, I've only known him for a few days, but he seemed changed, like he was on a mission to prove something.'

Frank exchanges a glance with Norman. They fist-bump.

'What…?' screams Brad under his breath. 'What do you know?'

Norman gestures him to calm the fuck down. He says, 'We assume he made it to your book reading…?'

How do they know about the book reading?

Frank continues, 'And how was he then? Any mention of weird science, visions; any thoughts other than his own?'

'Yes…!'

Again Frank and Norman appear pleased with this.

Brad steps back, and tries to piece together the undertaker's involvement. They know Finnigan, and they knew him before Polonski was killed. It makes Brad suspect that…

He suddenly says, 'Did you arrange to have Polonski killed?'

Rather than act defensively, Frank drops his guard: takes Brad by the arm and leads him across the church steps and down the road a short way, nodding at Norman to stand guard by the hearse. They find a quiet corner of the church wall; Frank leans back and lights a cigarette.

'The man we're burying today? Eugene Polonski? He wanted to die…'

'So you had him killed?'

'Listen… He tried to take his own life several times… In the end, he planned this… Paid us to organise it. The whole thing.'

'Polonski paid you to have him killed?'

'His last wish.'

'Why hasn't anyone found out?'

'What is there to find out?'

'That fact that you had him killed!'

'Says who?'

Frank stubs his cigarette out, flicks it over the church wall. He turns back to Brad and speaks with clear assurance. 'He wanted his death to be meaningful.'

Right on cue, as if orchestrated to fit their conversation, the strains of *The Star Spangled Banner* are heard; boomed out majestically on the church organ while the congregation gives voice to the lyrics:

Oh say can you see by the dawn's early light,
What so proudly we hailed at twilight's last gleaming…

Frank stands there, contemplating the pleasure of job satisfaction. 'He wanted a hero's death… That's what we provided.'

'So you hired Finnigan? How did you find Finnigan?'

'We know people.'

'Okay. You know people.'

'We know a barrister. One of our collectors. He asked around…'

'And it's that easy?'

Franks shrugs. 'Like I said, Bradley, we know people.'

'And why are you being so honest with me?'

'We owe you an explanation… And also, you're looking for that last piece of the mystery.'

Brad turns away to think. What is he missing here?

Frank says, 'Eugene Polonski wanted a hero's death.'

'Yes…'

'He wanted to be taken seriously…'

'Yes, I get it, but what am I fucking missing?'

They walk back round the corner to join Norman, who's waiting on the steps. There's some commotion from inside the church as the doors are being opened. Brad can see this opportunity for discussion dwindling away.

Frank says, 'Ask yourself why Polonski planned this.'

'Because he was mad?'

Brad is desperately grasping at straws, being glib.

'And what drove him mad?'

Norman adds his commentary: 'It's a sad story, man; break your fucking heart when you hear it...'

Frank says, 'You ever heard of a Judas Crime?'

Brad shakes his head.

'It's how Polonski described it. You know he used to work with David Bohm? We told you that, first time we met. But he didn't work with him so much as sell him out to the Feds; the fight against the Red Menace. He contributed to Bohm's exile, and he wanted to atone.'

Norman says, 'We assume you found the notebooks?'

'How do you know about the notebooks?'

Frank shakes his head.

'Like I explained, we know *everything*. The notebooks were part of his atonement, to create an intrigue: an assassination and a collection of hidden notebooks. It was his plan to regenerate interest in Bohm's work. To set his mind straight with the man he betrayed all those years ago.'

Coming at him like a slow–motion lightning–bolt revelation, on a percussive wave of samba that stretched way back to West Africa, on the horns, the swinging hips and the swilling tequila of that particular night, Polonski realised he was fighting for the wrong side... He realised that Bohm wasn't the enemy. He was a humanitarian, a visionary, and criminally misjudged.

Norman wraps an arm around Brad's shoulder. Some kind of apology.

'You were the only part of our plan that was random. After we found your book – by fortuitous accident – we decided to involve you; although some would argue that your book was there to be found, thus you included yourself in the equation.'

'So this was my fault?' Brad takes a step back, trying to assimilate this information. Polonski wanted to be killed, out of misguided remorse. They hired Finnigan for the job. But Finnigan was left haunted by Polonski's thoughts. How did that happen? And whose idea was it?

Brad has a memory of Finnigan before he was shot: he looked radiant. Trying to prove the reality of continuation. A test of faith, but where did the power of conviction emanate from? Then it hits him: if it's possible to cross between life and death with your faculties intact, that's like… immortality. We assume immortality means living forever in the same body, but the way Finnigan saw it, immortality is a continuum of consciousness through successive incarnations. Must be what Polonski was trying to express in his notebooks; how he saw the value of Bohm's forgotten theories. But if this were true, there'd be people on earth who possess the knowledge, if not the practical skill, to manipulate…

He looks back at Frank and Norman.

'Bradley doesn't think it's true,' says Frank.

'Just like you said,' says Norman.

They smile again, as if looking at him from all angles.

From the church door, a rustling of feet, as the congregation stand for the final blessing, prior to the coffin being walked out.

Jane appears, sneaking down the steps to meet Brad.

'Sorry… Bad form to race ahead of the coffin, but… Are you okay?'

'I had to get some air.'

'You look pale.'

'Yeah.'

'Shall we get a drink?'

'Please…'

He takes a few steps, but can't get the story out of his mind; and from inside the church, a bugle call. It sounds a little scratchy, like a lo-fi vinyl recording, but the message is clear: *the day is done…*

Then the organ launches into an exit march: something sombre, demanding attention. They turn to face the church, to witness Polonski's final retreat.

Frank and Norman stand by the open rear door of the hearse.

'See the way they're smiling?' Brad asks Jane.

'Who? The undertakers? Yes, they're smiling.'

'Don't you think that's odd? At a funeral?'

'I think they're just being friendly.'

It takes rehearsed concentration for the honour guard to manoeuvre the coffin down the steps and into the hearse. Boyd follows, with the folded Stars and Stripes under his arm. Several pedestrians and a couple of cyclists stop to watch the procession, acknowledging the passing of a stranger; in recognition of our commonality.

Brad watches how the mourners react to Frank and Norman. But no one does react to them. They're the undertakers; they have become invisible; their presence is understood. No one else is aware of the subterfuge. Not even Jane notices anything different. And they're still smiling; occasionally turning around to smile directly at him.

With the coffin locked and loaded, the honour guard stands to attention. There's a moment's silence for another photocall; then the guard troop back inside the church. Frank walks up to Boyd, no doubt concluding some final business. It leaves Brad with the sense that he too deserves some final closure.

He asks Jane to wait, and calls across to Frank. Seeing Bradley approach, Frank remains true to his function, formally shaking hands. All hint of their former complicity has disappeared.

'It's been a pleasure meeting you again, Bradley.'

He's being given the brush-off. His mind is spinning with the notion of conspiracy, fully aware of having been used as a bit player in some freakish occult experiment. Manipulated. And now dismissed! It's indefensible. He has no idea how to proceed, or even how to process this experience.

'I don't know what to do. How do I deal with this?'

Franks puts a hand on Brad's shoulder, to calm him down.

'Hold on, Bradley…'

He then looks up to Boyd, and they exchange a nod.

Boyd makes the gesture for *I'll call you* and disappears into the church.

Frank turns back to Brad.

'I don't know how to advise you. We all have personality considerations which blind us to the bigger picture. It's probably a good thing. We can't all express the inexpressible…'

Brad is reminded of the Polonski notebook under his arm. It's what the man died for, and clear evidence of staring into the void for too long. He doesn't want to end up like that.

'That's why our job is so difficult.'

'What job?'

'Everything we do. Our chosen function is to leave clues. A secret isn't a secret unless it's allowed to be discovered, right?'

'I suppose...'

'But rest assured, when everything turns to dust, we all have a chance to be saved.'

'So what can I do?'

'I can only suggest you look for the signs.'

Brad walks hand-in-hand with Jane. They're both silent, considering issues of personal need. It's what we do. The bigger picture is out there, but it's rarely our main concern.

Further down the road, about 20 metres away, an old man starts shouting. 'Oi, you... I know you. You two!'

Brad and Jane think he's shouting at them. But he stumbles past, waving his hands at the hearse. The undertakers are back in the car and about to drive away, but Frank spots the old man in the wing mirror. He waits for him to catch up, winds down his window.

The angry man starts shouting at Frank. He seems to know him. He wears the same expression that has witnessed a lifetime of murder, accidental death, torture, rape, mindless violence, and a fair share of fucking idiotic behaviour.

'I know you! I know what you did! And you're going to take responsibility, you hear me?'

Norman and Frank are sitting in the hearse, in conference. They clearly refuse to understand what they're being accused of.

Walsh produces a badge and warrant card. He flashes it at the undertakers. Suddenly this confrontation takes on a judicial proportion. Brad assumes they're about to be arrested. He can't believe it's going to end like this, because in spite of everything, he feels oddly protective towards them.

Walsh is now walking around the hearse, looking for signs. Brad runs up to him.

'Mate, what are you doing?'

Walsh isn't listening. He hasn't noticed Brad trailing him.

'You're interrupting a funeral! Do you know these people? What do you think they've done?'

Walsh looks up. Says nothing. Goes back to his investigation.

Brad stands in front of him.

'Mate! What the fuck are you doing?'

He knows it's wrong to use this approach with the law, but his judgement is impaired.

'You talking to me, son?'

'I was, yes.'

'Want to know what I'm doing? I'll tell you. I'm looking for the bastards responsible for smashing up my motor.'

'You think these undertakers smashed up your car?'

'That's right.'

Brad has had a glimpse into the quest for immortality. One day he plans to write it as a scientific equation that will end world suffering. It will blow everyone's mind. And here's this cantankerous old fucker investigating a contravention of the Highway Code as if his life depended on it.

'They wrote off your car?'

'Someone did.'

'What do you drive?'

Walsh is tired and emotional. 'Jaguar, XK8.'

Brad is genuinely taken aback. It's more serious than he anticipated.

'I can understand why you're so upset.'

'You should have seen it. 4.2-litre. V8. Clean. Less than 30,000 on the clock...' Walsh's eyes mist over.

Brad pulls a sorry face: the man's distress is completely understandable.

Walsh shakes his head.

'That's all it was about, son. That's all it was ever about. My beautiful car.'

Postscript...

During the days that followed the funeral, Brad felt a burden of responsibility towards the notebook in his possession. He read it diligently, cover to cover, trying to unravel its convoluted meanings because this is what Polonski had chosen to die for. His elaborate suicide plot built around one assumption: that the hidden notebooks would somehow inspire a reappraisal of Bohm's work. But try as he might, Brad can't come close to deciphering the content. And he already has his own version of a Bohmian-inspired vision; he has *Death and Physics*. So in the end, Brad takes the selfish option, and bails on the dead man's last wish.

If this initial foray into self-published provocation has taught him anything, it's that personal wonder can easily become confused with absolute truth. He doesn't attempt another public distribution of his work. Instead, he publishes it on a blog site where he expects no one will ever read it.

Hidden in plain sight, available to anyone, drowning in the noise of digital humanity.

See what happens next.

Hopefully nothing.

Death and Physics

This Existential Mystery

Bradley Holmeson
Second Edition, Brighton, 2016

Death and Physics contains information for modern living.
For the post-hip and currently disenchanted.
Nihilists welcome.

Introduction

This book is an attempt to resolve the conflicts between science and religion, with the suggestion of a new paradigm.[1]

It's an ambitious proposal but, according to William Blake, *If we don't create our own system, we'll be forced to live by someone else's.*

William Blake was considered insane by his contemporaries and now he's revered as a visionary genius; how fortunes change with the zeitgeist.

The spirit of our age might be the insurmountable disparity between scientific rationalism and religious fervour, yet there is always a third choice – for even as rationality undermines religious belief, quantum science reveals surprising parallels with Eastern mysticism.

The aim of this book is to tread a desire line between religion and science; to create an optimistic perspective on the human condition.

1. A paradigm is a series of random ideas that collectively imply a new world view. In the (Concise Oxford) dictionary, the word *paradigm* appears between *paradiddle* and *paradise*. Alphabetically speaking, a new vision of the world is preceded by a drumroll, and followed by a state of perfect happiness.

Part One

Reason, enlightenment and revolution

There was a time when the pursuit of knowledge for the sake of knowledge was celebrated as a cool ambition. It was called the Age of Enlightenment.

The philosopher Immanuel Kant describes the Enlightenment with poetic simplicity: *Enlightenment is the freedom to use one's intelligence.*

Previously, our understanding of the world had been based on tradition, superstition and religious folklore. During the Enlightenment we claimed an intellectual right to knowledge.

We discovered how things really worked and created heroic advances in mechanical science.

The Enlightenment was a global movement leading to political and scientific revolution, and the discovery of new worlds.

SO WHERE DID IT GO WRONG?

The strength of the Enlightenment became its weakness. By developing a reductionist attitude, we championed the belief that *every thing* in the universe could be understood by reduction to its smallest component parts. This is a fundamental remit of science: to deconstruct, to experiment, and gain empirical evidence.

The Industrial Revolution generated a new materialism. In turn, this led to rapid population growth followed by squalid urbanisation and a workforce that became slaves to the burgeoning industry. Our reductionist attitude created a sense of duality; as, for example, with the separation of man from nature, and the separation of society from its workforce.

Duality separates the world into distinct, unconnected units, as an endless resource of materials and labour.

Duality undermines any sense or need for unity, resulting in fragmentation and a loss of meaning of the whole.

OPPOSITION TO THE ENLIGHTENMENT arrived in the form of The Romantic Movement – a backlash against the overtly rational; a movement in which artists, writers and philosophers became inspired by the raw power of untamed nature.

The Romantics responded to emotion rather than reason; they were excited by *the mystery* rather than scientific deconstruction, contending that not everything could be understood and defined by a sum of its parts.

The Romantic Movement might sound like a retrograde step in our search for clarity but, as explained by Renée Weber in her book *Dialogues with Scientists and Sages:*

> *The mystic can contribute something to science, namely the sense that nature is not a mere collection of data but a single reality of grandeur and beauty... The one word repeatedly used by mystics to describe their experience is unity.*

THE POST-ENLIGHTENMENT RETURN TO MYSTICISM was primarily concerned with the *reunification* of mankind and nature – a search for the single principle: the source that underlies the universe.

SCIENTIFIC BREAKTHROUGHS have a habit of underscoring new philosophical movements. Advances in scientific knowledge will always lead to new ideas about the human condition. Science creates the bones of empirical truth, and philosophy follows with a moral commentary and ethical concerns.

As described by Alain Badiou in his book *Philosophy for Militants*:

> ... *a new philosophy is called for to clarify and help with the birth of a new science.*

We are living in a quantum revolution. We have defined the secular evolution of the universe, and the evolution of life. We need fresh philosophy to contextualise this new wealth of knowledge.

> *For most scientists the search for coherent laws ends in equations. However, for the greatest scientists, equations alone are not enough to satisfy the scientists' wonder.* (Renée Weber)

Part Two

In search of wonder

THE RATIONAL WORLD HAS ACCEPTED EVOLUTION AS FACT: life on earth is the product of biochemistry, and natural selection. We can no longer cite God as the reason for human existence, and without God as our creator, we must accept that life has no inherent meaning.

This stark truth is the source of much existential angst, causing us to feel empty and pointless.

It's ironic: we can accept evolution as a fact, but being at the pinnacle of evolutionary development, we find it difficult to accept that our ascent has no purpose.

WE ARE MADE OF STARDUST, and demand our right to sparkle. There are 7 billion people currently living. Our solar system is one of 400 billion in the Milky Way galaxy, which is just one of several billion galaxies in the known universe. In spite of this, we claim the right to be unique, and expect our lives to be significant.

THIS IS THE EXISTENTIALIST DILEMMA: God does not exist, our lives have no inherent meaning, and yet we seek meaning.

It's our evolutionary birthright.

Due to a cruel twist of irony, the human brain has evolved a predisposition towards pattern recognition. We are genetically programmed to seek meaningful patterns of behaviour within our apparently random existence.

WE NEED A SYSTEM TO LIVE BY, but which system can we trust?

Science has a monopoly on empirical truth, but science will never have all the answers.

This fact is brilliantly summed up by physicist and mathematician John D. Barrow in his paradox: *The Groucho Marx Effect – A universe simple enough to be understood is too simple to produce a mind capable of understanding it.*

WE MUST ACCEPT THERE IS NO ULTIMATE TRUTH regarding the nature of existence: how can any definition be both simple enough to remain universal and complex enough to stay relevant?

THERE IS NO MEANING TO LIFE except the *continuation* of life. Most of us find value in the simple adventure of existing.

Some of us remain in constant doubt: a state of dreadful introspection provoked by the indifference of life, the absurdity of existence and the fear we should be doing more to resolve these issues.

Something must be done.

The philosopher Marshall McLuhan famously said, *The medium is the message.*

The implication is that deep understanding might best be found in the medium rather than the content of the problem. This argument works with our current existential crisis: the medium of consciousness reveals a deeper clue than its content.

Part Three

Consciousness is not an object

THERE ARE MANY THEORIES OF CONSCIOUSNESS, but it is generally accepted to be a dynamic process, operating at sub-atomic level.

This is where the brain-ache begins, because there are various inter-pretations of quantum theory, and each one reads like science fiction. As once declared by Nobel Laureate physicist Niels Bohr, *Anyone who is not shocked by quantum theory has not understood it.*

WHAT WE ARE AGREED UPON is that the entire universe is an ocean of sub-atomic energy.

This is important.

All atoms receive and transmit energy in the form of photons. A photon is the force carrier for sub-atomic energy, which is also known as *electromagnetic radiation.*

Energy exchanges are constantly taking place within every atom in the universe, releasing electromagnetic waves of varying frequency and wavelength that infuse and immerse all matter.

THE MOST STARTLING FACT is that electromagnetic waves carry not only energy, but *information.*

This is typified by man-made electromagnetic waves, such as television and mobile phone signals, in which complex information is transmitted across space.

Less obvious is the information carried by visible light waves: our surroundings are revealed to us via information carried on the *visible* part of the electromagnetic spectrum.

This is fundamental to our understanding of the world: we are constantly submerged in all manner of visible and invisible light.

THE WORLD IS SOLID AND REAL, but from a sub-atomic perspective, *nothing* is solid or real.

Sub-atomically, everything exists as waves of energy-information known as spectral information.

WE PERCEIVE THE WORLD AS SOLID AND REAL because, from our larger-than-atoms perspective, the world *is* solid and real.

BUT the brain receives this information as *spectral* information.

THE BRAIN IS A LENS THAT FOCUSES THE WORLD. It is this process of translating spectral information into perception that creates conscious awareness.

IT WAS ALWAYS ASSUMED that memory would be organised in the brain like a filing cabinet of facts. This isn't true. The memory is spread across the brain in a matrix. This discovery formed the basis of neuroscientist Karl Pribram's Holonomic Brain Theory.

We could discuss this in detail, but as Pribram himself says, *There are lots of mathematics, but they all fit together… These [concerns] are not relevant to the ordinary person…*

The basis of Karl Pribram's Holonomic Brain Theory asserts that:

> 1. the cells in our body communicate in the form of light waves;
> 2. the images we perceive in our mind's eye exist as a type of hologram.

The third important aspect of this brain theory is informed by David Bohm's deterministic interpretation of the sub-atomic world.

In order to resolve problems within quantum mechanics, Bohm has proposed the existence of a generative energy field that gives rise to all matter: a realm of unbroken wholeness, from which all atomic structure emerges and returns to, called the Implicate Order.

Bohm claims the Implicate Order is the more fundamental order, and that our everyday world of things, the Explicate Order, is a temporary manifestation.

He also proposes that consciousness exists in this implicate order, meaning that consciousness exists in a plane of energy which is not bound by the physical restraints of time, space or matter.

Bohm's Holonomic Universe Theory is supported by experimental evidence and rigorous mathematics.

It also validates Eastern mystical beliefs of a primordial essence: the fundamental nature of the universe – an energy from which all matter is manifest.

REMEMBER: all quantum theory reads like science fiction.

BE AWARE: there are many unscientific ideas discussed under the banner of quantum effects, creating a sub-culture of pseudo-science.

BUT: if we reject every idea that sounds weird purely because *it sounds weird*, we fall into the trap of pseudo-scepticism.

NONE OF US CAN EVER BE TRULY OPEN-MINDED: we all seek confirmation bias to support our prior beliefs. But we shouldn't reject genuine new ideas because they fall outside our weirdness parameter.

A SIMPLE INVESTIGATION INTO THE NATURE OF CONSCIOUSNESS will always cause ideological problems. Most of us assume the mind-stuff is nothing but an intriguing side effect of mechanical brain activity.

And yet consciousness is being revealed as a fundamental principle, deep-rooted in the structure of existence.

KNOW THIS: the brain is a device that allows the universe to experience itself; and our consciousness is a small, personal expression of a vast collective process.

Part Four

The Death and Physics Paradigm

THERE ARE MANY WAYS that science can describe the world.

Paraphrasing Newton's second law of thermodynamics: *everything will ruin and die.*

(And if we're discussing the world of material things, this is completely true.)

Buddhism mirrors this bleak attitude by declaring that, *All life is suffering*.

In the Buddhist vision of the world, suffering is caused by our attachment to transient things; a brutal pronouncement because every material thing in life is transient.

Buddhism doesn't invoke God as our salvation, it just has advice: learn to overcome attachment.

Learn to let go of the transient world.

It is a practised skill.

In the West, we overcome suffering by attaching ourselves to as many material things as possible; then compare our success with the less fortunate.

It makes us feel better for a while.

This is the legacy of Newtonian Physics; an attitude that feeds the grip of Capitalism, implying that commercial success is a virtue, and that wealth will protect us from depression and death.

BUT THERE ARE OTHER WAYS that science can define the world. The Newtonian model is reductive: dividing things down to their smallest components, which are then studied separately. However, not all physical systems can be understood from a discussion of their constituent parts.

In an Emergent System, the whole is radically different from its constituent parts. In fact, the simple components create something entirely new that could never be deduced from an examination of the parts alone.

Examples of these systems are: the economy, ecosystems, developing embryos, ant colonies and the stock exchange.

These are also called Complex Adaptive Systems, because they continually adapt to fit the changing circumstances.

Example: Ants have few choices in life: they forage, they build nests, they fight their enemies; they reproduce, nurture their young and keep the nest clean. As they undertake each of these tasks they secrete a pheromone, a signal pertinent to each particular activity. Every ant automatically responds to another's signal, and they adapt their behaviour to reinforce the strongest signal. Slowly, patterns of behaviour emerge within the group.

The individual ants don't plan to form a social infrastructure. None of them are told what to do. They are merely guided by each other's signal.

Without any perception of the grand scheme, they participate in building a social structure that will greatly outlast their individual lives. By responding to each other in the completion of simple tasks, an adaptive and self-governing structure emerges.

Most man-made systems are dictatorial, so we assume other social systems will mirror ours by responding to the plans of a governing intelligence.

But (for example) the ant colony is an intelligent, self-organising system without a leader. And this behaviour, called swarm logic or hive brain, is created from micro-decisions that lead to macro results.

IT IS THE CONTENTION OF *DEATH AND PHYSICS* that each individual human consciousness is a participant in a complex adaptive system.

By being consciously alive, we contribute to the emergence of a new level of order and intelligence; something that could never be surmised from an examination of individual lives.

There is no meaning to life, except the continuation of life.

Yet through the process of living we absorb information from our surroundings.

This information is experienced as consciousness.

Consciousness exists as a form of electromagnetic energy-information.

This energy-information (the individual mind-stuff) exists as a construct in the sub-atomic world, within an interconnected, universal energy field.

Therefore, as a *by-product* of being alive, we unwittingly contribute to an emergent realm of spectral information: an adaptive, self-governing structure that will greatly outlast the lives of the individual participants.

HUMAN BEINGS ARE DNA-BASED MACHINES which, through the normal process of living, participate in the emergence of an Evolving Collective Consciousness.

As in any adaptive emergent system, there will be a feedback of information from the whole to the individual constituent parts.

IT IS THE CONTENTION OF THIS BOOK that the active feedback from the larger collective consciousness is the transcendent experience some people refer to as 'God'.

If God can be said to exist, it is not as a wilful creator, but a *by-product of human sentience.*

HUMAN BEINGS ARE DNA-BASED MACHINES THAT TRANSFORM ENERGY INTO GOD.[2]

---

2. In which god is a by-product of human evolution and exists not as a 'creator' but as an emergent intelligence encoded into an evolving dimension of sub-quantum energy.

That was the Death and Physics Paradigm, and you're welcome to it

I have no idea what anyone is expected to do with this information. People will say it sounds like religion, even though it describes the only possibility of god as a *by-product* of sentience, and not a top-down dictatorship.

People will say it's unscientific, even though science has described consciousness as a fundamental force that underwrites all of matter.

We affect the world by attitude.

We create the future by consciously creating the present.

We are all occultists by design.

Heaven and Hell exist as an extension of our attitude.

This is the Mystery.

Faith exists beyond proof, so by definition faith is blind.

Cynics are naturally cynical about faith.

Yet at the heart of cynicism there exists a spark of idealism, a glimpse of *something else* that would exist, if only…

It's this glimmer of idealism that ignites the fires of our contempt; it's why we gather on street corners to bark at people; it's the spark that drives our certainty.

And where can you find certainty without constructing it yourself? As Socrates said, *The unexamined life is not worth living*. We can't leave these things to chance and listen to the voices. They might start telling us that life is empty and pointless, which is specifically what we're fighting against.

There will be signs.

The author hopes this information is useful.

brad@selfhelpforcynics.co.uk

If you have any negative comments, keep them to yourself.

DISCLAIMER:

Death and Physics has been created from ideas.
Ideas, being the radiance of the mind, are not to be avoided.

Tibetan Yoga and Secret Doctrines

I'm not mad, I've just read different books.

Ken Campbell

Author's Note

The facts of David Bohm's life and work have been represented as accurately as possible, within the confines of this novel.

It's true that due to his political beliefs he was unable to work in America; that he moved to Brazil and relinquished his American passport. He was followed to Brazil by FBI agents, but to my best knowledge he didn't befriend any of them.

It is also true that William Burroughs sought a cure for his heroin addiction in the Ecuadorian Rainforest, around the time that Bohm was in Brazil; but there is no evidence they ever met.

All other characters might sound similar to people I know, but are obviously fictions.

And the science… The research was extensive, difficult, rewarding and non-conclusive. The mystery still exists; however, I have tried to deconstruct and represent the various concepts as accurately as possible.

Permissions

Frontispiece

Deep down the consciousness of mankind is one. This is a virtual certainty because even in the vacuum, matter is one; and if we don't see this, it's because we are blinding ourselves to it.

David Bohm, in conversation with Renee Weber 1986, in *Dialogues With Scientists and Sages: The Search for Unity* (Routledge & Kegan Paul, 1986), 41.

(All efforts have been made to establish copyright holder, c/o Adele Parker, Rights Manager, Taylor and Francis Group).

We have drunk the soma, and have become immortal.
We have gone to the light, and have found the gods.
What can the hatred and malice of a mortal do to us now,
Oh Immortal One?

Rig Veda

Public domain translation from www.sacred-texts.com.

Chapter 3

Handcuffed to a fence in Mississippi – reference to a song by Jim White, from the album, *No Such Place*.

As Vladimir Bukovsky the notorious Russian Activist once explained, *We create it, publish it, distribute it and get thrown in jail for it…*

Paraphrase of a longer quotation by Vladimir Bukovsky, from 'My Life As A Dissenter'.

Chapter 6

He mis-remembers a quote from Marilyn Monroe: *All we want is our chance to sparkle.*

The actual quote, as found in *Give Us A Kiss*, by Daniel Woodrell, is: *All we demanded was our right to twinkle.*

Chapter 7

If we rise above the animal emotions, we're set free... if we become like the clear and cloudless sky, we will have risen above the beast.
Paraphrase from *The Tibetan Book of The Dead*.
Guttenberg free domain translation.

Each of the special agents of the FBI must be ready and capable to meet any challenge. The security of our nation and the life of a loved one may depend upon him...
America has no place for those timid souls who urge appeasement at any price; nor those who chant the 'better red than dead' slogan. We need men and women with a capacity for moral indignation, men and women of faith, men and women of conviction, men and women with the God-given strength and determination to uphold the cause of democracy.
J Edgar Hoover, 'The Courage of Free Men', 2/22/62.

Chapter 9

Communists have surrendered their rights as persons made in the image of God... They make loyalty to one's country a despicable thing; treason is their accepted code of conduct. They are unfit to teach in schools or universities, for they are part of an international conspiracy...
Harry W. Dodds, speech from F. David Peat, *Infinite Potential: The Life and Times of David Bohm* (Basic Books, 1997).
Reprinted by permission of Basic Books, a member of the Perseus Books Group.

Einstein famously said, *God does not play dice with the world...*
He also said, referring to the need for a new quantum interpretation, *If anyone can do it, then it will be Bohm.*
Albert Einstein in conversation, taken from F. David Peat, *Infinite Potential: The Life and Times of David Bohm* (Basic Books, 1997).
Reprinted by permission of Basic Books, a member of the Perseus Books Group.

Chapter 10

Not my place to make reply, not my place to reason why, I'm just here to do or die, into the valley of death I ride...
Mis-quote from Alfred Lord Tennyson's 'Charge of The Light Brigade'.

Chapter 12

Matter, as it were, is condensed or frozen light.
David Bohm, in conversation with Renee Weber 1986, in *Dialogues With Scientists and Sages: The Search for Unity* (Routledge & Kegan Paul, 1986), 45-6.
(All efforts have been made to establish copyright holder, c/o Adele Parker, Rights Manager, Taylor and Francis Group).

Deep down the consciousness of mankind is one. This is a virtual certainty because even in the vacuum, matter is one; and if we don't see this, it's because we are blinding ourselves to it.
David Bohm, in conversation with Renee Weber 1986, in *Dialogues With Scientists and Sages: The Search for Unity* (Routledge & Kegan Paul, 1986), 41.
(All efforts have been made to establish copyright holder, c/o Adele Parker, Rights Manager, Taylor and Francis Group).

Light is the potential of everything; the ocean of energy is an ocean of light.
David Bohm, in conversation with Renee Weber 1986, in *Dialogues With Scientists and Sages: The Search for Unity* (Routledge & Kegan Paul, 1986), 45-6.
(All efforts have been made to establish copyright holder, c/o Adele Parker, Rights Manager, Taylor and Francis Group).

Chapter 15

Each man must create his own system or be forced to live by another man's...
William Blake

Chapter 16

A universe simple enough to be understood, is too simple to produce a mind capable of understanding it...

Reproduced with permission from the author, John D Barrow. (Created for the Edge Annual Questions Announcement, 2004, originally referred to as the Groucho Marx Effect, and published online at www.edge.org/response-detail/11659).

Chapter 22

Gysin said the experience made him feel he was *high above the earth in a blaze of glory...*

Ian Sommerville, in a letter to Brion Gysin, Feb 15, 1959, describing his use of the Gysin invention The Dreamachine.

http://www.noah.org/science/dreamachine/

Chapter 24

... much of our personal memory may be stored in an ambient, collective quantum holographic memory field delocalised from the individual... in the universal holographic medium of the quantum vacuum... memories are accessed by the individual from the ambient field. This is fully consistent with the romantic idea, increasingly validated by the foundations of quantum theory, that all nature is interconnected, and that the separateness and discreteness of things in the commonsensible world are illusory.'

Mae-Wan Ho, *The Rainbow and the Worm: The Physics Of Organisms* (WSPC, 2008), 243.

Copyright @ 2008 World Scientific Publishing Co.

Reproduced with permission.

Chapter 24

...the truth that can be spoken is not the eternal truth.

Tao Te Ching

Chapter 25

... look on my works, ye mighty and despair! Nothing beside remains. Round the decay of that colossal wreck, boundless and bare the lone and level sands stretch far away...
'Ozymandias', by Percy Bysshe Shelley.

Chapter 26

We have to absorb what is useful, and reject what is useless...
Attributed to Bruce Lee.

Chapter 26

We're not humans having a spiritual experience; we are spiritual beings having a human experience.
Pierre Teilhard de Chardin

Chapter 27

The Lord of Death will lick up thy brain, drink thy blood, eat thy flesh, and gnaw thy bones; but thou will be incapable of dying...
Although thy body be hacked to pieces, it will revive... and the repeated hacking will cause intense pain and torture.
From *The Tibetan Book of the Dead*.

Chapter 29

New Philosophy is called for to clarify and help with the birth of a New Science...
Alain Badiou, *Philosophy For Militants* (Verso, 2012), 1.
Reproduced with permission.

The Medium is The Message.
Marshall McLuhan

...anyone who is not shocked by quantum theory has not understood it.
Niels Bohr, *The Philosophical Writings of Niels Bohr* (Ox Bow Press, 1987).

There are lots of mathematics, but they all fit together… These [concerns] are not relevant to the ordinary person…
Paraphrased from Karl Pribram and U.G. Krishnamurti, 'on Mind/Brain', in *Thinking Allowed: Conversations on the Leading Edge of Knowledge and Discovery* (Council Oak Books, 1995).

Enlightenment is the freedom to use one's intelligence.
Emmanuel Kant

An unexamined life is not worth living.
Socrates

… ideas, being the radiance of the mind, are not to be avoided.
The Tibetan Secret Doctrines, The Ten Things Not To Be Avoided.

I'm not mad, I've just read different books.
Ken Campbell, *The Bald Trilogy* (Bloomsbury, 1995), 235.

Acknowledgements

It is a pleasure to acknowledge the band of generous people who helped this novel towards publication:

My old friend John Lenahan for introducing me to Scott Pack, who forwarded my manuscript to Xander Cansell.

Xander, who by accepting the manuscript, changed my life.

The great editing team at Unbound, presided over by the tirelessly helpful Annabel Wright; plus the brilliant and incisive input of structural editor Jamie Groves, and the stunningly meticulous copy editor Alex Newby.

Amanda for her kind help with procedural details.

And finally, love and gratitude to those who read early drafts and gave such positive and essential feedback, providing me with the confidence to see the book through to the end, especially Tessa, Rollo and Carey.

Patrons List

Bennett Arron
Jason Ballinger
Steve Best
Simon Bligh
Alex Boardman
Eddy Brimson
Penny Bryant
Ali Burns
Gemma Coles
Barnstormers Comedy
Al Cowie
Tiernan Douieb
Keith Dover
John Dowie
Nick Dunn
George Egg
Michael Fabbri
Dominic Frisby
Dave Griffiths
Sally-Anne Hayward
Andrew Hearse
Penny Hennessey
Sue Hollins
Kate Howard
Joshua Howie
Charmian Hughes
Wendy and John
Joss Jones
Tim Kerr
Mit Lahiri
Mark Laing
John Lynn
John Mann
Simon Mason

Stephen McGowan
Erinna Mettler
Garrett Millerick
James Moakes
Edward Moloney
Roger Monkhouse
Ian Moore
Richard Morton
Simon Munnery
Susan Murray
Ben Norris
Jeremy O'Donnell
Scott Pack
Stefano Paolini
Toby Philpott
Lisa Pitch
Matt Price
Mary Purchase
Robert Ramsay
Simon Randall
Marilyn Raynes (Hollins)
Andrew Robinson
Colin Simpson
Michael Smiley
JoJo Smith
Judi Stafford
Henriette Stavis
Huw Thomas
Dave Thompson
Mike Scott Thomson
Phil Walker
Matt Welcome
Jason Whitehead
William "Woody" Wilding
Richard Wren
Imran Yusuf
Chaz

Teaser Chapter, from The Karma Farmers Return, book two of The Karma Farmers Trilogy.

Chapter One: Rex D. Boyd

Boyd was now rolling in the mud, naked. It had been a slow process before the drugs took hold of his mind. After ingestion, there was the obligatory four hours of nausea and vomiting. Followed by the quiescence of the external world. But now he was really into it; howling, and imploring some god of his tortured imagination to release him and show mercy for the sins he presumes to have committed.

Frank and May have kept watch. It's been a long day. Ibogaine is a complex and unforgiving narcotic; presenting like a form of mental torment when used by westerners with their protracted first world guilt. It's late in the afternoon, and a low ceiling of grey cloud spills a constant but gentle rain.

May leans into Frank's side, resting her head on his shoulder. He pulls her in close. Her style-changes are frequent but always this side of artful punk. Today she's rocking something of a Tank Girl look from the eponymous graphic novel: spikey pink quiff, and black beanie; tattoos hidden under a baggy jumper and dungarees. And Frank in his black suit; always with the white shirt, black suit. Standing together under the roof of the South porch, sheltering from summer rain with the garden a muted blaze of wilderness blooms.

'What's he done anyway?'

'Boyd? Killed a man,' says Frank.

'Just the one?'

'Just the one that troubles him. The rest were legitimate combat situations. This one was close up. A man in custody… It's the personal nature of it that's causing him grief.'

'You're saying he tortured someone to death?'

'How it looks to me.'

'He was in Afghanistan, right?'

'His first tour took him to Afghanistan. He loved it out there,

Kabul and Kandahar, full of vinegar and righteousness... Then he gets sent to Iraq, stationed near Fallujah. Gets himself involved with interrogation.'

'So he was working for Military Intelligence?'

'Not exactly. But it appears the regular soldiers were encouraged to soften the detainees up.'

'Meaning what exactly?'

'Ha! Well, that's the question no one wants to answer. Iraq was cast as part of the War of Terror, so they were working outside of the Geneva Convention. Human rights went out the window.'

'Just like that?'

'Of course! The way Boyd tells it, there was a complicit under-standing. They'd get to *smoke* the detainees or *fuck* them. Meaning the degree to which they'd hand out the torture. Sometimes they'd be instructed to do it, sometimes they were just letting off steam.'

May shakes her head at the abuse we're so ready to hand out to each other.

Frank shrugs.

'Difficult to remain impartial when you're hell-bent on Imperial-ist Vengeance. Must be difficult to find the compassion. The mistake Boyd made was taking pictures of the torture scenes. You remember that? The Polaroids? Was in the papers for months, back when. Not just the fact they seemed to be enjoying it, they were relishing it.'

'I remember that. Abu Ghraib, right?'

'Not sure if Boyd was at Abu Ghraib, but yeah, same story... Posting torture porn on Facebook like he was sharing holiday snaps.'

'Is he going to be okay?'

They both turn to look. A country graveyard in the summer rain; forgotten gravestones rising up through the sea of meadow grass half turned the colour of straw, and speckled with poppies, cow slip, Michaelmas daises. Broken angels and Celtic crosses coloured with yellow and orange lichen; tall cedars and poplars feeding on nutrients of the long deceased. And far away from the gravel track that leads to the church, hidden from any passing observer, Boyd remains mud-spattered and lost. There is a pallor to his flesh that catches in the late afternoon light, muscles hard and tense, twitching with anxiety, shiv-ering with the cold.

Boyd is immune to his physical discomfort, as past events replay before his eyes; such is the power of the Ibogaine. It's hallucinogenic; a compound derived from the roots of the West African shrub Tabernathe Iboga. The authority of the drug lies in its ability to return the user to situations of previous emotional turmoil. To revisit the consequences of past actions, allowing the initiate to... Let's say, to acknowledge the hurt they have caused others, to adjust their karmic debt.

Boyd is standing, and shaking with the fever. His inner reality describes a makeshift prison cell: timber frame and wire mesh partitions bolted into the rough stone walls. The floor is concrete and sand. In his immediate vision a man is dangling by handcuffed wrists to a hook in the ceiling. The man's feet barely reach the floor. He's all but naked, just wearing a pair of grubby trunks. Dark skinned, underfed, and bearded; his eyes flash around the room unable to focus. His chest, arms and legs are covered in blood and bruises. Boyd can see the reality he failed to accept at the time. The man is pleading to be released. Praying to be understood.

Malik was caught driving on the wrong side of town without papers. His taxi was searched and impounded. He ended up here in Forward Operating Base Mercury, near Fallujah. Anyone who can't account for themselves is considered a suspect. This is the fallout from liberation. Malik needs to get with the programme. He needs to learn some manners and respect the situation.

There's always pressure to get results. As a soldier, Boyd knows this. But right from the get-go he knew the interrogators were strictly adhering to Standard Operating Procedures: no waterboarding, and no electrical currents were used. So Boyd was making their job easier by working the suspects into a state of compliance.

The detainees are referred to as *Persons Under Control,* and identified by a number; they're considered less than human. Smoking a PUC is just another day in the office. Weaken them. Strip them naked. Humiliate them. Chain them up, and break them down. Put the dog's teeth near their balls. You can always find soldiers with sadistic tendencies; soldiers who have suffered personal loss, and now looking for retribution.

Thanks to the Ibogaine, Boyd is re-living this life. He's exhausted. Combat weary. He's seen the mutilated bodies of local villagers killed by enemies of the coalition; innocent people tortured with electric drills and decapitated. He's seen his brothers die by random IED attack. He doesn't question the politics or the morality. People in crazy situations do crazy things. And this is a crazy situation: it's 45 degrees in the shade, it's a foreign planet made from rock and sand; it's near impossible to distinguish between insurgent and ally, because it seems every last motherfucking Iraqi is trying to fucking kill him. And war isn't the place where we look for our death. War is about the protection of the tribe; it's the place where you discover how to keep living.

For the first two days, with the canvas bag over his head, Malik's voice had been muffled; but even with the bag removed he remains incomprehensible. He speaks Kurdish, occasionally lapsing into an ancient dialect of Eastern Aramaic, the only two languages he knows. But yelling these words that no one understands can only result in more punishment.

He's no longer Malik Rassam, taxi driver from Sharafiya in the Nineveh Plains region. He's *Person Under Control, number 408*. And all Boyd is doing is de-stressing; letting off a little steam. But this screaming-for-mercy act is wearing thin, and he strikes Malik again and again. Hitting a dark-stained bruise at the top of the man's thigh. Hitting him where it won't do any lasting damage. There's no remorse. It's not meant to hurt. Boyd strikes him with a wooden baton to shut him up, because the noise of the man's torment is fraying his nerves. It's ironic: most of them won't talk, yet Boyd is beating Malik senseless because he won't keep quiet.

Frank and May watch as Boyd waltzes with the demons. He's standing under a branch of the tallest cedar, a branch that reaches across the entire graveyard. It's supported by an iron framework, rusted and embedded deep into the heart of the tree. In his mind's landscape this corroded metal is manifesting as the bedframe onto which Malik was later tied with baling wire. Another standard stress position, Government approved; but due to the beatings, Malik is slowly bleeding to death from internal injury.

Through the drug-induced vision, Boyd is discovering his culpability. Malik stares into Boyd's eyes; the men whispering to each other, looking for common ground. Boyd's in for a long night; searching for the means to live with the fact he once beat an innocent Christian man to death, believing him to be a random Muslim terrorist.

'Will he be okay for a while?' asks May. 'I should get some supper on.'

'What are we having?'

'We cooking for Boyd too?'

'He'll be wrestling with this till the early hours. He'll need something…'

'How about soup, so it's there whenever you need it? I bought some lovely bread from Waitrose.'

'Yeah? I love that Waitrose bread.'

'One of those huge French boules…'

'You think they use genuine French flour? It tastes so different to the Tesco's bread.'

'I know!'

'Soup would be perfect, May. Could you bring it in a flask, and maybe a blanket or two?'

'Of course…'

He smiles.

'I love you, May Osman.'

'Thanks, baby… I know you do.'

She turns to go indoors.

He holds her hand until the last moment.

Silence of soft rain.

Boyd howling among the tombstones; paying top dollar for this particular form of therapy, and determined to get his money's worth. Frank knows he should be out there, talking him through it. Not just for Boyd's sake. Not yet sure he can trust this naked man in his graveyard: ex-active service, recently transferred to some manner of psy-op research. So although the given aim here is to resolve Boyd's personal issues, Frank has a feeling this experience will be feeding into professional objectives, whatever they are. Shadow Operations. That's what he talks about. Deep counter intelligence, men who stare at goats, psychic warriors and such.

Boyd is entrenched in military zeal, but he's taking to occult adventure like a kid in a hall of mirrors. Must be the same fervour he brought to his interrogation work; why he was considered a success, not counting the accidental murder: he has an appetite for the intensity.

May returns with the blankets. Frank appreciates her help. But there's something else on his mind.

'What's up, Frank?'

'Could you check something…? Did Boyd bring a laptop with him, and a mobile?'

'I can have a look. Why do you ask?'

'Just thinking, we could clone his devices…?'

'Really?'

'I don't know how much work-information he'd keep on a personal laptop. But hacking into his phone could reveal something useful. Something compromising.'

May thinks about it.

Considers the morality of it.

Then she says, 'That's more Norman's skill set. I could give him a call…?'

'Good idea. Let's get Norman over. We might need some help if Boyd flips out.'

They look at Boyd again: wild-eyed, tear-stained, speaking in tongues.

May says, 'Backup is good. If he runs amok, you'd have to kill him to slow him down.'

Frank laughs.

'That's what I'm afraid of.'